SCENTS OF WOOD AND SILENCE:
SHORT STORIES BY
LATIN AMERICAN WOMEN WRITERS

SCENTS OF WOOD AND SILENCE: SHORT STORIES BY LATIN AMERICAN WOMEN WRITERS

Edited by
Kathleen Ross and Yvette E. Miller

Introduction by
Kathleen Ross

LATIN AMERICAN LITERARY REVIEW PRESS
SERIES: DISCOVERIES
PITTSBURGH, PENNSYLVANIA

YVETTE E. MILLER, EDITOR

1991

The Latin American Literary Review Press publishes Latin American creative writing under the series title *Discoveries*, and critical works under the series title *Explorations*.

Translation © 1991 Latin American Literary Review Press

Library of Congress Cataloging-in-Publication Data

Scents of wood and silence : short stories by Latin American women writers / edited by Kathleen Ross and Yvette E. Miller ; introduction by Kathleen Ross.
　　　　　p.　　cm.
　　　　Translation from the Portuguese and Spanish of twenty-three stories published since 1980, with critical commentary.
　　　　Includes bibliographical references.
ISBN 0-935480-55-2
1. Short stories, Latin American--Women authors--Translations into English.
2. Latin American fiction--20th century--Translations into English. 3. Latin American fiction--Women authors--Bio-bibliography.　I. Ross, Kathleen. II. Miller, Yvette E.
PQ7087.E5S36 1991
863'.01089287--dc20

91-30002
CIP

Scents of Wood and Silence: Short Stories by Latin American Women Writers may be ordered directly from the publisher:

Latin American Literary Review Press
2300 Palmer Street, Pittsburgh, PA 15218
Tel (412) 351-1477 Fax (412) 351-6831

ACKNOWLEDGEMENTS

This project is supported in part by a grant from the National Endowment for the Arts in Washington, D.C., a federal agency.

The editors wish to warmly thank all the authors and translators who participated in this collaborative effort, contributing their time and talent to a project that could not have come together without their cooperation. We are especially grateful to Claribel Alegría, Ana María del Río and Luisa Valenzuela for sending us new and unpublished material, and to Sylvia Molloy for the translation of her own work. All responsibility for the final volume, of course, is our own.

We would like to recognize the superior research skills of María de los Angeles Nevárez, who assisted with the compilation of the Bibliography in a thorough and creative manner. The staff of Latin American Literary Review Press has worked diligently and competently. José Piedra suggested the choice of Ana Mendieta as our cover artist, thus expanding the volume and its themes into a powerful visual representation.

We acknowledge the following:

Clarice Lispector, 1979 and Heirs of Clarice Lispector.

"Tosca" from *Stories of Eva Luna*, translated by Margaret Sayers Peden. Reprinted by arrangement with Atheneum Publisher, an imprint of Macmillan Publishing Company from THE STORIES OF EVA LUNA by Isabel Allende. Copyright © 1990 by Macmillan Publishing Company, a division of Macmillan, Inc.

Cover Photo: Courtesy Galerie Lelong, New York.

"La oveja roja" from *La oveja roja* (Buenos Aires: Editorial Sudamericana, 1974).

"The Awakening" from Claribel Alegría.

"Por la vereda tropical" from *¡O Gloria Inmarcesible!* (Bogotá: Instituto Colombiano de Cultura, 1979).

"Olor a madera y a silencio" from *A horcajadas* (Santiago de Chile: Mosquito Editores, 1990).

"Susundamba no se muestra de día" from *Por qué...cuentos negros de Cuba* (La Habana: Ediciones C.R., 1948).

"La casa" from *Celina o los gatos* (México: Siglo XXI Editores, 1968).

"Lavaza" from Ana María del Río.

"A estrutura da bolha de sabão" from *Filhos pródigos* (Sao Paulo: Livraria Cultura Editora, 1978).

"Camera Obscura" from Diana L. Vélez for the International Writing Program, University of Iowa.

"A Eduardito no le gusta la policía" from *Vos también lloraste* (Buenos Aires: Libros de Tierra Firme, 1986).

"A bela e a fera ou A ferida grande demais" from *A bela e a fera* (Rio de Janeiro: Editora Nova Fronteira, 1979).

"Otoño" from *Dicen que me case yo* (México: Cal y Arena, 1989).

"Sometimes in Illyria" from Sylvia Molloy.

"Una mujer al amanecer" from *Otro rumbo para la rumba* (Costa Rica: Editorial Universitaria Centroamericana, 1989)

"Un corazón tierno" from *Porque nos queremos tanto* (Buenos Aires: Ediciones de la Flor, 1989).

"Creation" from *La Furia y otros cuentos* (Madrid: Alianza Editorial, 1982).

"El arte de la pérdida" from *Una pasión prohibida* (Barcelona: Seix Barral, 1986).

"O calor das coisas" from *O calor das coisas* (Rio de Janeiro: Editora Nova Frontiera, 1980).

"Recuerdos oblicuos" from *Intentos* (México: Grijalbo, 1987).

"Desde el exilio" from *Desde el exilio* (Lima: Ediciones Muñeca Rota, 1984).

"Tango" from Luisa Valenzuela.

"Despojo" from *Encancaranublado y otros cuentos de naufragio* (Río Piedras, P.R.: Antillana, 1983).

TABLE OF CONTENTS

Introduction: Translating the Scents of Wood and Silence

I.   Scents of wood and silence: the surprising juxtaposition of senses in Pía
Barros' synesthetic phrase is an appropriate title for this collection of stories by
Latin American women writers in English translation. The twenty-three stories
included here have been grouped together for their diversity as well as their
common themes, for the ways in which they may challenge received notions
and open windows of understanding for the reader. No essential archetype of
gender holds across all boundaries of time, place and experience, but the
development of an extensive literature written by women in Latin America
during the last fifty years demands that the limits of those boundaries be
considered in a regional context by readers of English. By asking where these
stories converge or part ways, the reader poses fundamental questions of difference that contemporary Latin American women are themselves asking.[1]

Women have been writing in Latin America since the colonial period of
the sixteenth, seventeenth and eighteenth centuries, when the continent was
called the Western Indies by the conquering Spanish and Portuguese col-
onizers. The Europeans brought with them forms of writing and literature that
quickly dominated the pictorial and oral traditions practiced by native Indians
and imported African slaves, although those traditions have never disappeared.
Writing, of course, demanded a level of education reserved for the few. Then,
as now, literacy was a privilege more men than women enjoyed.

While writing has always been reserved for those with education, time
and space to practice their art,[2] historically such freedoms have been gained
for women in Latin America—as in other parts of the world—thanks to the
labor of other women, who reared children or kept houses in order. But in this
century, writing has also become a way of life for women who have chosen
lives far different from those of previous generations. Sometimes these
changes have been imposed by outside forces that make a break with the past
necessary through exile or emigration. Many of these writers are employed as
journalists, educators, academics, editors or civil servants, again either by
choice, economic necessity or a combination of both. Today's women writers
represent a broad range of experience: living in the country called "home" or
living elsewhere, with or without men, with or without children, but always
with the obsession of language, words, and images to be committed to paper.
It is the varied expression of that fascination with words that Yvette Miller and
I have wished to present in this volume.

The translator too is obsessed with words, the words of two languages.
The experience of thinking through both brings me back to the trope of synes-
thesia, the perception of one sense through another. Translation can be very
much like that, an multi-layered practice in which correspondences are usually
far from neat or even occuring in the same realm of sensation. A word in
either one language or the other may evoke for the translator a sound, smell or
sight that will suggest something entirely different in the "equivalent" terms of
the other language. The translator, like a trained psychoanalyst, comes to

recognize the baggage that she or he brings to the process, and to set it aside if necessary.

Translations are neither originals nor copies, but separate creations. This is such a simple fact that I almost hesitate before writing it, but as any translator knows, it needs to be stated. The illusion of a "true" or "correct" translation is still an idea too commonly held. In this collection of translated stories, the diversity of narrative voices employed by the authors is matched by that of the translators. Each brings a different approach to the work, an individual idea of what it means to be "faithful" to the text; several have theorized elegantly on their practice.[3]

Some of these translations have been carried out in close collaboration with the author, or by a translator who knows the author's work intimately; indeed, sometimes the translator is the author herself. In other cases the English version has been written at a far remove from any personal contact or knowledge. The reader who confronts these stories should consider them interpretations, the ultimate kind of close reading that can be performed on a text. As such the translations are critical works in their own right, to be evaluated seriously as the inconclusive readings that they are, and approached with a broad criteria of evaluation.

Like a translation, an anthology is never definitive, but always indicates a multitude of contributing factors. The selection is finally a personal one, dictated by the tastes, contacts and interests of the editors. *Scents of Wood and Silence* is no different in that respect. Yvette Miller and I have brought some conscious goals to this project: to achieve a representation of authors from different regions of the continent, to see several writers translated into English for the first time, to include new or recent work by established writers, and to gather the work of some excellent translators of Spanish and Portuguese.

A good measure of chance enters into the making of an anthology involving so many people as contributors. We brought stories to translators, and translators gave stories to us; we suggested authors, translators suggested authors, authors themselves gave us work. Translators suggested other translators. Authors' biographical entries were written by the translators, or by one of the editors; in each instance the initials following indicate the writer responsible. Translators contributed their own biographical statements. The book thus reflects a true collaboration of many talents.

Scents of Wood and Silence joins a burgeoning group of anthologies that collect short fiction by Latin American women writers in Spanish, Portuguese and English translations. The trajectory of these collections over the last decade would make an interesting topic of study in and of itself.[4] At the time I write this, I am also aware of several other books presently in preparation. Each has its own special characteristics and contributions, and we acknowledge all.[5]

We believe that the particular strength of our own collection rests in its currentness and diversity. Along with the stories, we have included an extensive bibliography covering work on women writers in general, feminist literary criticism, and the writings of each individual author both in the original language and in translation. We have emphasized books and articles written in English, although important works in Spanish and Portuguese are included. This is meant to be a resource for further study of the wealth of literature written by Latin American women, including those not represented in our selection.

II.   Although this volume stresses stories published during the decade of the 1980's, we have included some important fictions from the forty preceding years as well. This part of my Introduction will serve as a brief overview of all twenty-three stories, considered in rough chronological order.

Lydia Cabrera and Silvina Ocampo, both born at the beginning of the twentieth century, were engaged from the 1920s onward in the vanguard of intellectual work in Latin America. Each was influenced by time spent in Paris during that decade, and each began her career as a painter. For Cabrera, the European passion for "primitive" art spawned a life-long dedication to the study of the presence of African culture in her own country, Cuba. Ocampo became a literary innovator and promoter of new writing in Argentina. Her continued experimentation with the avant-garde aesthetic has resulted in a prolific output of poetry and stories, produced over a span of more than five decades.

Cabrera's "Susundamba Does Not Show Herself By Day", published in Havana in 1948 as part of the author's second volume of stories, demonstrates the legacy of anthropological research done on Afro-Cuban culture by Fernando Ortiz, Cabrera and others during the earlier decades of the century. The story combines Cabrera's extensive knowledge of that culture along with a scathing indictment of the opression of traditional gender roles. The form of the African tale, with its archetypal animal protagonists, is brilliantly exploited on thematic and linguistic levels by Cabrera to present a feminist argument published a year before Simone de Beauvoir's *The Second Sex* (1949) made such discussion widespread among intellectuals in Paris and elsewhere.

"Creation" was published by Silvina Ocampo in her important 1959 collection *La furia y otros cuentos*. The involvement of her literary circle (which included Jorge Luis Borges) with a literature that rejected the *criollista*—local or regional—tendencies of the early decades of this century in favor of a more "universal" culture is evident in this story. At the same time, the dreamlike description, the confusion of perceptions, and the first-person narrative voice identified with autobiography combine in an intensely personal tone of lyricism very like that of a prose poem. This is indicative of the work Ocampo was publishing just prior to the period when the "Boom" of the 1960's made Borges, García Márquez, Vargas Llosa and other male writers known to an international audience.

Julieta Campos's "The House", published in Mexico in 1968, reflects another aspect of that decade: the influence of French literature and theory in Latin American intellectual circles. The inwardness of the French new novel, its self-referential, Heideggerian obsession with time, existence and writing, is clear in Campos's story. This intellectual detachment is paired with a personal evocation of memory, the recollection of a space rather than sounds as in Ocampo's "Creation", although both stories describe memories of a city (Buenos Aires or Havana) in poetic terms. In Campos's story the lives of generations of women inhabiting the house, their moments of reverie or anguish, are mixed with the metaphysical inquiry produced by the act of writing.

The social upheaval of the 1960's and 1970's, following the wake of the Cuban Revolution and worldwide movements for change, are evident in "The Black Sheep" by Margarita Aguirre, Albalucía Angel's "Down the Tropical Path" and Clarice Lispector's "Beauty and the Beast, or, the Wound Too Great". The three stories are entirely different in style, but all share female protagonists who leave safe, private worlds of privilege based on class, wealth or race to enter a potentially dangerous public sphere where they confront the realities of poverty, disease, and hardship. Aguirre's confessional, first-person voice, Angel's flowing images of the freedom of a traveller, and Lispector's ironic, grotesque humor are all employed to critique the status quo of societies that accept bad human conditions as normal. The oppression, and collusion, of upper-class women within those societies is targeted as well.

The stories of the two other Brazilian writers included here, Lygia Fagundes Telles and Nélida Piñón, were published in collections that appeared in 1978 and 1980, respectively. "The Structure of the Soap Bubble" was actually written by Fagundes Telles at an earlier date—sometime between 1958-1977—and first published in a newspaper.[6] This rather mysterious story is narrated by the voice of a woman living somewhat outside social convention, whose mordant commentary lends a witty, black humor to the tale. It is a story that hints at the destructiveness of human emotion, and the tangled relationships brought on by sexual jealousy, in an oblique fashion.

Piñón's "The Heat of Things" also centers on interpersonal relations, here the oppressive attachment between mother and son. The strange sensuality of the narration, with its images of grease and meat, flesh and sweat, create an enclosed world that becomes progressively more surreal. Piñón here achieves a highly disturbing juxtaposition of pleasure and pain, shocking in its humdrum details.

In the stories published since 1980, certain themes repeat from one story to the next, echoing some of the writing from earlier decades. But many changes are evident also. While this past decade has been one in which women writers have emerged from the shadows of the figures of the Boom to become recognized in their own right, it has also been an economically disastrous period for most of Latin America. While some stories look back on the past to consider the lives of women of previous generations, others look to the very recent legacy of torture and disappearances under authoritarian governments. Still others portray the fragmented reality of people struggling to survive, and of relationships wearing under the strain. The changes in women's roles both in the family and the larger society, the impact of those changes on sexuality and perception of self, ring clearly through these narrations.

The interior space of Campos's house is present also in Mariella Sala's "From Exile", a double interiority of a mother at home with her child and a writer wrestling with blocks to creativity. The story portrays the conflicts of a woman unable to take full responsibility for her own actions, yet nostalgic for a room of her own to write in, perched on a flat roof where she can be alone. This same image of a room on the roof—the *azotea*, where traditionally servants have lived—appears in María Luisa Puga's "Memories on the Oblique." Here another woman struggles with issues of creativity and love, and the questioning of her Mexican identity while living abroad, alone.

Memories of immigration or emigration are evoked in Olga Nolla's "A Tender Heart," Angélica Gorodischer's "Camera Obscura," and Sylvia Molloy's "Sometimes in Illyria." Nolla's working-class Puerto Rican couple are presented in a prose that blends neo-realism with the pathos of shattered dreams. The story strips away any romantic notions of hard times. The humorous feminism of "Camera Obscura," which portrays the moment of truth when a woman recognizes the oppression of her life and rebels against it, also captures the language and culture of Eastern European immigrants and their Argentine descendents. In Molloy's evocation of a woman's memory of another house—a former mansion converted into an English-run boarding school for girls—other Argentine immigrant groups appear. The ethnic, linguistic and erotic tensions of the story surface through a veil of words left unspoken.

Mythical, magical language, or "magical realism" combining the commonplace with the supernatural, is a vehicle that has been identified with Latin American writing for the better part of this century. It is represented here in different ways in the work of Claribel Alegría ("The Awakening"), Carmen Naranjo ("A Woman at Dawn"), and Ana Lydia Vega ("Death's Pure Fire"). Alegría comments on class differences through her fantastic story, producing a barbed humor in the process. The tone of Naranjo's story is reminiscent of folklore and myth, transposed to the bleak surroundings of poverty in the countryside. Here sexual violence is presented bluntly, in all its cruelty. In Vega's polyphonic narration, the voices of different women play off one another, or from inside each other, in a strong statement condemning the exploitation of one human being by another.

"Tosca" by Isabel Allende and "Autumn" by Silvia Molina also examine relationships between men and women, and the ways in which illusions of romantic fantasy are destructive to real human life. In "Tosca" it is an aging woman who must face the poverty of a life spent in the pursuit of romantic drama, in a story set in the past in Venezuela's hinterlands. "Autumn" is a snapshot taken from the life of an intellectual woman in today's Mexico City, accepting her own maturity and sexuality with the bittersweet strength of experience.

Other myths of gender and sexuality are put into question in the work of Cristina Peri Rossi and Luisa Valenzuela. The former's "The Art of Loss" centers on a man victimized and hollowed by the present economic situation, grasping for something to be his alone that will fill the lack and restore his identity. Whether or not that special something is gender-specific is an underlying query of the story. Valenzuela's "Tango" deconstructs an Argentine national myth against the background of the economic crisis, portraying alienation in the midst of the dancers' passion. Here again the meaning of that crisis for traditional gender roles is questioned, through the dance-floor rules that never change.

The violence of military dictatorships and torture, realities for Chile and Argentina through the 1970's and 80's, are seen in the works of Matilde Herrera, Ana María del Río and Pía Barros. Herrera's "Eduardito Doesn't Like the Police", which is really her re-creation of a real-life anecdote, depicts the experience of grandmothers left to care for grandchildren when their sons and daughters were put in prison, or disappeared. It also presents the strength of human spirit under the most hopeless of situations. "Washwater", by del Río, takes a different but equally strong direction, using the shock of pre-adolescent sexuality and pleasure to put into doubt any simple measurements of good and evil. And Barros' "Scents of Wood and Silence," which gives this collection its title, creates a dreamworld where the sexual torture inflicted on women can be only briefly transformed by romance, before its banal cruelty reappears.

III.   In the art of Ana Mendieta that graces our cover, wood is a metaphor of nature, of women's power and sexuality. It is the "Tree of Life" that creates art, as well as children. The silence of the absent body next to the wood is a magical trace, more powerful for its unseen presence. Yet it also calls to mind Mendieta's own life, and the violence of the death that silenced her creative powers.

The silences of women may be vehicles of creation, if they reflect an inner space of thought or feeling. But as is evident in this collection of fine stories, silences for Latin American women have usually implied otherwise: the silence imposed from without, through exile, torture, and oppressive social restrictions and gender roles. The transformation of that silencing into the power of words is what these stories represent. And even more: the silencing of the original texts and their reappearance in another language, carved out and given new voice by English translations.

Kathleen Ross, Associate Editor
Duke University

NOTES

1 See especially the article "Un diálogo entre feministas hispanoamericanas" by Gabriela Mora in the volume *Cultural and Historical Grounding* edited by

Hernán Vidal (1989). Other books that reflect this dialogue are *La sartén por el mango*, eds. Patricia González and Eliana Ortega (1984) and *Latin American Women Writers: Yesterday and Today*, eds. Yvette Miller and Charles Tatum (1977). All these volumes are included in section II of the Bibliography.

2 Sara Sefcovich's introduction of her anthology *Mujeres en espejo*, volumes 1 and 2, eloquently speaks to this privileged position.

3 See Suzanne Jill Levine's forthcoming *The Subversive Scribe* (Greywolf Press); Margaret Sayers Peden's Introduction to her translation of *Sor Juana Inés de la Cruz: Poems* (Binghamton, 1985); Diana Vélez's Introduction to her volume *Reclaiming the Medusa* (1988). Also in this regard, Carol Maier has recently published two very suggestive articles on translation and Latin American literature: "Notes After Words: Looking Forward Retrospectively at Translation and (Hispanic and Luso-Brazilian) Feminist Criticism" from the volume *Cultural and Historical Grounding*, and "Reviewing Latin American Literature in Translation: Time to 'Proceed to the Larger Question' " in *Translation Review* 34-35 (1990): 18-24.

4 See Naomi Lindstrom's "Feminist Criticism of Hispanic and Lusophone Literatures: Bibliographic Notes and Considerations", included in Vidal's *Cultural and Historical Grounding*, for an analysis of some of this literature.

5 See section III of the Bibliography for a list of these anthologies and others including both male and female writers.

6 As stated by the author in a note to her collection *Filhos pródigos*, where the story was reprinted. She does not identify a specific date for this story, although she does do so for others in this gathering of "prodigal children."

MARGARITA AGUIRRE was born in Chile and attended school in Argentina and Chile. She graduated from the Instituto Pedagógico at the Universidad de Chile. Her first book, *Cuaderno de una muchacha muda*, was published in 1951. Since then she has written extensively; among her best known works are her novels, *El huésped* (1958), *La culpa* (1964), and *La oveja roja*, a collection of short stories (1972). (YEM)

PAMELA CARMELL received her Master of Fine Arts in translation from the University of Arkansas. She has translated the novel, *The Last Portrait of the Duchess of Alba*, by Antonio Larreta, as well as the poetry of Belkis Cuza Malé and Gloria Fuertes. She is currently translating contemporary short stories from Spain and the novel, *Este era un gato*, by Mexican writer Luis Arturo Ramos.

THE BLACK SHEEP

By Margarita Aguirre

My name is Marta Figueroa Rosales. I'm nearly 30 years old and at this moment I'm at my Aunt Melania's wake. Like all the Rosales Madriaga women, she was very beautiful and proud. Right now her beauty shines like a flower on the white satin framing her face. Her hair is gray, almost silver; her features, accentuated—her mouth, with its full lips, and her large dark eyes, closed in her deep and blue-rimmed sockets. Through her slightly wrinkled eyelids and despite her death, something of her gaze seems to hover still; I'm sure that that gaze was always clear, luminous, serene, warm. Until a few hours ago, her sick woman's eyes always regarded me with extraordinary sweetness, without surprise, trusting. I would have come to adore that look in her eyes, just as the women surrounding me, praying and crying, adored it.

They say that many years ago my grandparents locked her up in a convent because she was pregnant. And they never heard another word about her. She must have been raped by some tenant farmer. This story is told with great secrecy in my family. They say it was invented by the servants at the El Recuerdo estate, where my family used to live. My family takes every opportunity to deny the story, claiming it's idle gossip circulated by country riffraff and they ask us not to repeat it. That always makes you suspect the story was true.

At one of my first dances, my Uncle Ramón was looking for my cousin Charito—his daughter—and me. I hated my Uncle Ramón. A worldly, frivolous man, with no redeeming qualities. Besides, that night I wanted to stay and dance "until the stars stop shining." I really liked to dance!

"I'll leave later, with the Ortuzar girls," I told him. "They live near our house."

He insisted on taking me home, doubting my intention to return with my friends. Firmly, he said to me:

"Let's go. Don't hang around like a tramp."

I got indignant. I always get indignant when someone doubts me. And then I remembered the story of my Aunt Melania.

"Who says I'm going to act like a tramp?" I answered defiantly. "Has there been some loose woman in the family, by chance?"

"What do you mean?" he interrupted me, paling. And I broke out laughing.

"Oh, you all wouldn't think twice about locking me up in a convent, would you? It's a family tradition."

He took me by the arm.

"You've been drinking," he said to me. "I can't leave you here in this condition. And I'm doing this for my sister, your sick mother, who can't deal with you anymore. You are an insufferable little girl."

Livid, in a blind rage, he guided me firmly by the arm toward the exit.

"I'm going to start shouting and make a big scene," I announced.

Leonor Vial came up to us.

"What a great looking guy!" she said.

"You can have him," I answered furiously, twisting loose of him.

But I couldn't make myself scream. Because, unfortunately, I too had the Rosales upbringing, the Rosales good taste, the Rosales sense of dignity or sense of the ridiculous, the Rosales bull-shit which has filled every year of my life and which even now I try to shake off.

And on my wedding day, this same uncle—I have no choice but to put up with him at family parties (funerals, weddings, baptisms)—came up to me with his worldly smile and a glass of champagne:

"A toast to the happiness of my prettiest and smartest niece," he said.

"I had to get married to get a compliment from you." I had to say something to him.

"I've always thought you were intelligent. Your mother is my smartest sister."

"That must be why you've helped her," I said, this time sarcastically.

"It's not easy helping out sisters."

"You're referring to Melania, right?"

"I'm referring to her, although sometimes I ask myself if she really existed."

"You never did anything to find out."

"I didn't have time."

"...because you know she existed. You weren't so little when they locked her up."

"I had nothing to do with that. It was her own fault."

"Fault? What fault?"

"They said she went down the wrong path."

"The wrong path! It wasn't so easy then. I assure you even now it is rather complicated. Here's proof, look at me in this white dress. I need lace to sin."

"Quiet down! You're obscene. I can't tolerate the girls of today. Tramp!"

"That's the same thing you called me years ago. I swear I've done everything I could to deserve your opinion of me. Now about my Aunt Melania..."

"When will you realize all of that is a fairy tale? I've gone along with you to laugh at you."

"You've gone along with me to find out what I figured out about this story. I know. I have the same lack of decency as you, what I call the Rosales Madariaga bull-shit. Don't go. Listen to me. You're afraid that Melania exists and she'll claim the inheritance you stole from her. Yes, what you stole from her. I know all about it."

His champagne glass fell to the ground. The waiters came running.

"Good luck! Good luck!" cried some girls and hugged me just for show. And my Uncle Ramón, a bit pale, his elegance accentuated, got lost in the crowd.

When I returned from my honeymoon, my mother, crying, said to me, "What did you say to Ramón on your wedding day?"

I didn't recall right away and I stood there thinking. She went on.

"He sent you a gift, a case filled with silverware. You know very well he helped me pay for your party."

"I didn't want a party, Mama, and as for the silverware..."

I stopped talking. My mother was crying silently, lying back on her pillows. I have always hated to make her suffer. Her deep-set, intense, soft eyes, eyes that looked at me in horror, begged for my pity and finally lodged in my soul. If only I had known my father! I would have fought on equal footing with him. With her, I couldn't. When I was young, I ridiculed her victim's airs, but I learned to respect her the day she told me her life story. And she understood that, in my own way, I was fighting not to be a failure like she was. Since then, my mother is my daughter in some ways.

My mother is the youngest of the Rosales Madariaga sisters. She was in diapers when the incident with my Aunt Melania happened. They never knew each other. For years my mother believed the Melania's story "was invented by the servants." I had to tell it to her and I don't know if she believes it even now. My mother is an invalid and nearly blind. I haven't told her that my Aunt Melania has just died. What's the use?

Tonight there is no other blood relation but me keeping watch over her. The poor women look at me with surprise and a while ago one of them brought me some herb tea. How they love her! They come up to the coffin, arrange the flowers, kiss the glass, cry and pray. Those poor women! How like the Rosales women to say something like that. I wonder what my Aunt Melania called them. In my presence once she called them by name, but not the way you'd talk to an equal. Other women in the family would have done the same thing, of course. Even my mother. It's the smallest way for them to demonstrate the class distinction they feel. Because all the Rosales women, in a matter-of-fact, reasoned way, are convinced of their superiority. Not one of them thought to question this superiority, as I did, in the company of the maid who brings us breakfast in the morning: what makes us different? And to go on reflecting: she is the same age as I am, as smart as I am, made the same way. Only upbringing separates us; only having been born in a humble family or a society family. And while the maid opens the Venetian blinds and says, "It's cold out, Miss, you need to bundle up," you ask yourself: why? Why are we different? If she'd had the same opportunities I have, would we be this way? Is this fair? These ideas of mine have always shocked my family. "The black sheep," they call me. My aunts pray for me. One of them—my Aunt Lucrecia—sends me encyclicals from the Pope about Communism and, in the handwriting she learned from the English nuns, on one of her elegant communion cards, she writes: Wanting with all my heart to help you. My family! I could write long novels about my family and everyone would say I had a wild imagination. My Uncle Ramón died not long ago, leaving a large inheritance to his already millionaress wife, my Aunt Amelita Larrazabal. A lot of tongue rolling, a very vinous last name—over the years I've said the only thing her name was good for was the ink, she's so stiff and rigid with torticollis. Since I am a poor niece, she has always honored me with her scorn. On the street, she doesn't acknowledge me, even when I'm dressed in my cousin Charito's (her daughter) old dresses. Charito is the mother of seven. Her husband is skinny and transparent. He plays polo, she plays canasta. So, what more could you say about them? Nearly all my cousins are like that. One likes the theatre, another music. And they all like the good life, "to live it up!" to make money. When they get involved in politics, they are conservatives, liberals, one progressive cousin is a Christian Democrat. When they go to Europe, they come back and say: We had a super time, a wonderful time. Call me and I'll show you what I bought.

My Aunt Carolina died, too, years ago, of tuberculosis. I think she was pretty nuts or "odd", as they used to say in those days when it wasn't important to be sane. One of the odd things she did was fix her own food—just mashed potatoes cooked on a filthy stove—locked up in her room, surrounded by cats. An old maid, it goes without saying. She was so debilitated when she died that just dressing her for her funeral broke her little bones.

My Aunt Palmira, who is still living, is locked up and crazy. And my Uncle Carlos Alberto is a likely candidate to go mad. A bachelor, he lives in low-rent boarding houses, closed up in his room and, when he goes out, he dresses in turn-of-the-century clothes.

My Aunt Lucrecia—the one with the good-hearted cards—is married to a diplomat and suffers from mental fatigue. She travels through her world dragged down by a refined and elegant nervous prostration.

José Ignacio is the shame of the family. A drunkard and a gambler, he has swindled people and has been put in prison. Once I went to see him in jail. What I can't stand, he told me, is being with these pieces of shit who believe in the right to treat a guy as if he were their equal. And really, he's worse than the rest: he has embezzled money invested in a large company for earthquake victims. In one night, he gambled away the livelihood of hundreds of disaster victims.

My Uncle Pedro Luis lives in the United States. We know very little about him. When he got his medical degree, he left to become a specialist and never came back. He married a gringa and had a baby whom they educated according to all the modern theories. When she grew up, she threw herself from the 20th floor on Fifth Avenue. I was fifteen then and felt very proud of having a cousin commit suicide. I shocked my family proclaiming this admiration.

Perhaps I am unfair to my mother's side of the family. Perhaps everything I say is nothing but an absurd caricature. Here, before my Aunt Melania's corpse, I ask myself once again: Can anyone judge a human life? Are we to blame for what we inherit? Was she to blame? All those years my grandparents kept her locked up in a convent. And Melania was always sweet and good. She asked to return to the outside world to do charity work. She came to this house and was surrounded by abandoned girls whom she taught to work and be honest. It's these women who are crying now disconsolately. It's as if Melania had accepted the blame and had wanted to redeem her sin. But I know for sure she wasn't to blame. My Aunt Lucrecia told me the story clear-eyed. It was one summer afternoon. She was just getting home from Cairo and wanted to put my Aunt Palmira in a private clinic. She asked me to go with her in her car. They took my Aunt Palmira out in a straightjacket, all disheveled, dirty, hoarse, and fetid. She was such a sad sight the doctor offered to go with us.

"Don't be afraid," he said. "She's calm now. The idea of change brought on this crisis. It has passed now, but I'll go with you anyway. I know how painful this is for family members. We're used to it by now."

He talked on and on to make us forget. We got her out at the new clinic. My Aunt Palmira stayed asleep, foamy drool still trickling down. They carried her to her room on a stretcher and put her to bed. We were telling the doctor good-bye and were returning to the car, when they called to us. The nurse wanted to see us. My Aunt Lucrecia tried to refuse, but I confronted her: we should go, I told her. Aunt Palmira was sitting on a chamber pot, seemingly calm, when we entered.

"Is that you, Lucrecia?" she said. "Why are you locking me up?"

"We aren't locking you up, Auntie," I said.

"You, be quiet," she ordered me. "I don't know you. But her, I know her," she shouted. "I know her." The nurses came running. They stood her up. The chamber pot splattered on the ground. They tried to get her into bed. "It's your fault they locked her up, because the two of you, Melania and you, hear me well, you were the shameless ones. Lost girls. Whores. Whores."

They pushed her onto the bed and put on the straightjacket. They threw cold water on her. She went on shouting and they asked us to leave. A nun came to see us out. "The nurses will take care of her," she said. "Calm down."

In the car, just the two of us, crying black mascara tears, my Aunt Lucrecia confessed to me:

"Melania followed me around. We were less than a year apart. We had run down to the river together when that incident happened. I have come to understand many things years later, when it was too late. Poor Melania, she didn't understand a thing either. We were so innocent! Just kids. She didn't understand a thing."

"And you? Couldn't you help her? What happened?"

"Oh, child, let's don't talk about that."

We got quiet. Over the years, I've continued to piece together her story. She was thirteen when "that incident" happened. Last century, at thirteen, one wasn't responsible. Believe me. A man came and got on top of me and poked me, Melania says in her diary without adding anything more. When I went to bed with someone for the first time, I was the one who decided to do it, clear-eyed. What's more, I decided to do it out of hate, because I thought that that way I would offend my family, my good name, destroy the prejudice of virginity—a series of things I was already fed up with. I just chose some guy, a guy who would cause me the fewest complications. Get it over with, I told him. I felt the pain of a blow, a physical blow to my body, that burns still. And while I was washing the blood off the sheets in the bathroom, I thought: I have wounded myself. I could have also said: A man came and got on top of me and poked me. I wouldn't have been to blame either, I am sure of that, but rather innocent. The other extreme of innocence. The type of innocence that knows too much. That believes ingenuously that an act of rebellion is enough to break taboos, to a woman, to be free. And thinking that way, you end up with the second-rate, false, dimwitted upbringing that we "little ladies of the family," "the nice little girls" receive.

Tonight, with absolute clarity, I see what this death, my aunt and I all have in common. Perhaps for that reason I never doubted her existence, I always looked for her, I went along little by little following her footsteps, unraveling the tangle of her story, making the most of every word that those who had known her let slip, but they abandoned her, left her alone, buried her. After a while, it wasn't just a question of honor or shame, as it was for my grandparents. For her brothers and sisters, it was mostly a question of money, of property. She wasn't mentioned in my grandparents' will. She was dead. And if the dead were resuscitated she would have had to inherit something. They weren't willing to share the riches. My Uncle Ramón would tremble indignantly when my mother would tell him my theories. "That can't be," he would say. "My father would have known it." And that meant: she would have inherited something. But "she doesn't figure in the will." That was always the most important thing. It didn't matter that her death certificate didn't exist, that Doña Carmela López de Orrego helped out some mysterious lady who had a laundry. It was a tale the servants had invented. Things that are attributed to an honorable family out of envy. Because, naturally, my family is considered very honorable, despite my Uncle Carlos Alberto's scandalous homosexuality, another uncle's swindles and drunken sprees, Palmira's craziness and my cousins' life in Zapallar.

Zapallar! I adore Zapallar. I don't belong to that branch of the family, of course, but I should acknowledge that it is one of the most beautiful places in the world. The mountains, overrun with flowers, fall into the sea. And in very comfortable and elegant houses, the married couples swap around to amuse themselves, they chase Jews on the beach or stab a "middle class doctor" walking along, who dares to invade the aristocracy's Sundays. Some of my cousins have gotten married to people from Zapallar. I've been in their homes and I've listened to them, watched them and gotten to know them. The terrible thing is I also like them. But, at this level of sophistication, can such a redout as Zapallar be allowed to go on existing? There the isolated aristocracy amuses itself alone. They haven't allowed a railroad to be built. They travel by car. There's misery in Chile? But, I do help the poor a lot. Tomorrow I have a canasta game to collect funds for the parish. And in the end, my dear girl, the government is to blame. Since these lowlife radicals came to power, everything has gone to the dogs. "Let's drink and drink, let's gamble and gamble. With our girlfriend, not our wife, we'll live a happy life."

This is what my class of people call honor. You can do anything, just do it with dignity, my Aunt Lucrecia would advise me, reproaching me for my cocky behavior. To hell with acting like a lady was my answer. That was my position over the years. I was pretty; perhaps that always gave me the self-assurance to do what suited me. Besides, my Uncle Carlos Alberto, who is an aficionado of the theatre, says I always had histrionic tendencies. I don't doubt it. I was playing a part then. When you don't have very much depth, when the only thing you've been given in life is baggage full of useless things, you design a role and play it heroically, even though you go against your own way of life. When I was young, I played the part of "enfante terrible." Mostly, because I liked to be different from the rest. And on another level, because I sensed that it wasn't only my game, but also the game of an entire society in decay and that it was more honest to put my cards on the table. I boasted of having the guts to realize our decadence. When Uncle Ramón died, I said at his wake: how distinguished we seem for a family that's so rotten. Maybe the social revolution has an aesthetic weakness and will spare our heads. I have been tremendously snobbish and callous. I offended them a lot more than they deserve and, admittedly, in a totally stupid way. I'm not sorry, because I had to do it. And they've benefitted from having a relative who points out such things. My nieces tremble when I warn them they'll have to work in a factory as laborers. Because the new order isn't going to spare them on account of their last name nor pretty face.

The women who surround me have suggested, more with vague gestures than with words, that I go with them to pray. I pretend not to notice. I can't pray anymore, at least not in a conventional way and in public. I would like to have talked with Melania about God. Not about the God of the convent and the nuns, the rosary and the masses. What do I know about God? I don't even know if I have really thought much about Him. Over the years I have received the religion that was before me, the same as the clothes on my back or the food at lunch time. When I became a teenager, I asked myself: Why aren't I a Muslim or Buddhist? Why do I accept this religion they have thrust upon me since I was a little girl? It was so easy to quit going to mass and, as for praying, I realized I hadn't done it since I left the nuns. That was that. When I learned about social injustice and pointed it out, they countered me with religion, with what Christ also used to say. If that's what he says, what have you done in nearly two thousand years of civilization? I reply. They blame my studies at the Experimental Theatre. It's a stronghold of Communists, my mother would assert. So did my Uncle Carlos Alberto and mothers of other rich girls like me, who had found in the Experimental Theatre a marvelous world in the midst of our empty lives. As always, they were wrong. At least in my case. In the theatre they called us "jetsetters," the women hated us and the men, despite their scorn, tried to get us to go to bed with us. The director censured our "high society" way of expressing our feelings. But it didn't take me long to realize—humiliated—that that censure also encompassed envy and an ass backwards form of flattery. I can't forget the night long ago when, with such anxiety to learn, I asked one of them: why, why are you a Communist? What do you expect me to be? I never got the chance to wear a tux, was his answer. I felt like crying. That was the only explanation for why he was a Communist. No. I didn't learn anything from the Experimental Theatre nor the thousand stupid things I did in those days. Communists because they didn't have the chance to wear a tux! Communists who would say to us: Let's go to the party at the ritzy El Siglo, just wear street clothes and dab on a bit of French perfume. A clever phrase that nauseated me for its frivolity, bad taste and cynicism. I should have scorned them with the same intensity I scorned my own social class.

Melania, Melania dead in your commoner's pine box, you would have understood me. You who loved God up to the last instant of your life. You who surrounded yourself with these women of the masses, of the noble, suffering Chilean masses. Almost everything I am now—and that's very little, I assure you sadly—I owe to the people of my country. When I can't take it any more, when I'm fed up with everything, I'm going to eat sopapillas in some very poor household where I have friends who give me a warm welcome. They're the ones who have taught me the truth. I have poor people, too, Melania, only I call them comrades, and I don't teach them to pray and I don't give them money. I don't give them anything, they give to me. We should have talked about all of this, Melania, but I found you too late, you were sick and old and would have been too sad to say to me: What you do is hardly a drop of water in the sea of Chilean misery. What the world needs now isn't Christian charity, discredited Christian charity. It is unbelievable that, if only from instinct to preserve the status quo, more people don't understand that. They're afraid and in vain cover up what is so clear, they win battles on paper, talking about democracy or freedom. They rail against the dictatorship of the proletariat, but after all, it's been carried out with the same rights they themselves always have had.

It is completely absurd to think these things while I watch over my Aunt Melania. For a few moments I have felt very sure of myself and my love for my new role: the social redeemer. No. I'm not that either. I'm a Rosales, too.

That is to say, the character my family was missing, along with the homosexual, the swindler, the suicide victim, the worldly man, a "black sheep" as they say. We're all descendents of our country's founding fathers. My ancestors fought for independence. They were old criollos, valiant and generous, with cunning wisdom and lofty rhetoric. But we, their descendents, are poor specimens: burned-out, mediocre, superficial. I regret that we aren't good for anything; nothing good could ever be done with us. Oh, I wish the social revolution would come and cut our heads off. A psychoanalyst would say I'm self-destructive out of a guilt complex and a lot more crap like that. I hate psychoanalysts. Years ago my mother took me to one. I was in the middle of a crisis. I had come back ill from a trip abroad. I had the dangerous tendency to withdraw like my aunts and uncles. I fainted, felt pains and wanted to be alone. Alone. My kin's old mania. I get it from both sides of the family. My father died alone in Paris when I was little. After an appendicitis attack that turned out to be nothing, the family doctor diagnosed "acute psychosomatic neurosis accompanied by anxiety." Only an analyst could cure me. So we went to an analyst. I can see him now, a dark little man with glasses, white dustcoat and calm speech. He listened to my mother. Then he tried to talk with me alone. We went to a little room. I burst out crying.

"Why are you crying?"

"I'm sick."

"What's wrong with you?"

"Appendicitis, or something like that."

"I think your illness is something else."

"OK, acute psychoneurosis, so?"

"You believe in psychoanalysis?"

"I also believe in myself. I can cure myself if they leave me in peace. If they leave me alone, I'll get my thoughts straight and cure myself."

"There will always be a scar. It's like when you have a wound and they don't take stitches to sew it up."

"I prefer that."

"What problems do you have?"

"Sexual ones. That's what you want to hear."

"What have you got against me?"

"Oh, what do I care about you? Go to hell."

I burst into tears. I had stuttered throughout the conversation. He asked my mother if I was a stutterer. She said no. They asked me to wait in the car and I left with the tremendous urge to stick my tongue out at him.

The psychoanalyst told my mother that my condition was very grave and that she should put me in a clinic. My mother didn't tell me that at the time. When we got home, my cousin Teresa decided to take me to Zapallar. Sea air, solitude, why not? And I cured myself. Every time I see that analyst, fatter and darker each time, he's driving down Santa Lucía Avenue in a dark luxury car. I feel like shouting at him: Come see my scar. And from then on I have hated analysts. But the truth is, scar or no scar, for better or for worse, I'm alive. But if I end up crazy, it will be because there's craziness in my blood. I suppose that's because we're the end of a line or caste, that we have gone on degenerating by dint of pleasures or vices of those relatives who gambled their life away long ago in Chacabuco or Maipu. When I say these things to Teresa, for example, she replies: Forget those foolish things! She goes on living as if we were perfect and nothing were happening in the world. Getting ready in the afternoon to go out with her husband. Spending the weekends on the coast, taking the dog to the hairdresser (what a shame there aren't any here like the ones in Switzerland), sipping cocktails at the country club, reading best-sellers, attending concerts. Teresa is charming and she has been very nice to me. You're so unusual, that's what she says to excuse me. I worry about how these people will be educated when the social revolution comes. Because they aren't bad. They can't see beyond their noses. They're closed up. But they're not to blame. The system is so many years behind. Blame? Where does the blame lie?

Where does blame lie? Sometimes I've thought that we have no choice but to accept our own destiny. Melania, once again I understand why your role always appealed me. You accepted your destiny, meekly. The pages of your diary attest to that. You never showed a hint of rebellion. Not a shadow of a doubt. And, in your own way, you lived happily, doing good deeds. But I can't. Understand? You would have understood, I'm sure. I have delved into terrible social problems. I would have liked to tell you some things. How I feel safe and happy at times and so I set off down a road that I believe to be the only good road. Let me go on crying like this, sobbing. And make these women leave me alone—they bring me water, and I want to shout at them, "You don't understand anything!" They think I'm crying for you, but you know I'm crying for myself. For the absolutely alone and disgraced way I feel. Because I don't understand anything. Because I'm nothing but a poor, superficial, frivolous woman. Because I can't leave this black tunnel that is my life, although I see shining clarity on the other end. For you that clarity was heaven but it can't be for me. I have seen too many injustices committed in the name of your heaven. I still am horrified recalling that, when I was little and with the nuns, I used to buy the souls of Chinese children. I had god-children in millenarian China, did you know that? Godchildren who probably lived dragging Mandarins or English soldiers along in their rickshaws. God-children who are probably now building and fighting to get, in this life, that happiness which the religious communities promise them in the next: life everlasting.

Perhaps for you, it would be a sin to have the audacity to seek happiness now, in what you would call "this valley of tears." Happiness. What is that? A state of equilibrium, I would say. Feeling you're alive. Faith in what you do. In the end, I don't know. It would be fairer to say that it is something you hopelessly run after. *Something*, nebulous word, defective. Something, which exists and we don't know what it is. Something, life. Life that we love crazily, hopelessly. With nearly thirty years on my shoulders, this is all I'm sure of: I love life with all my strength. Beyond the good and the bad, the ugly and the beautiful, culpable or innocent, something essential beats inside me, inevitably: life.

And you, Melania, you are dead.

Translated by Pamela Carmell

CLARIBEL ALEGRIA was born in Nicaragua in 1924. Her family moved to El Salvador while she was still an infant, and she counts herself among the ranks of Salvadoran writers. She lived in El Salvador until the late 1940's, and since then has resided in many places throughout the Americas and Europe. Presently she lives in Nicaragua and Mallorca, Spain. Alegría is known best for her poetry, especially the volume *Sobrevivo* which was awarded the Casa de las Américas prize in 1978 (many of the poems from this book are translated by Carolyn Forché in *Flowers from the Volcano*, 1982), but she has published many other notable works of prose fiction and testimony as well. Some of these, such as the 1966 novel *Cenizas de Izalco* (*Ashes of Izalco*) or the 1983 testimony *No me agarran viva* (*They Won't Take Me Alive)* have been written in collaboration with her husband, Darwin J. Flakoll. Together Alegría and Flakoll compiled an early, important anthology of Hispanic American writing in translation, *New Voices of Hispanic America* (1962). They also collaborate on translations of their joint and separate work, such as he unpublished story "The Awakening" included here. Claribel Alegría is an active and eloquent spokeswoman for the causes of human rights and social justice in Central America, travelling frequently to speak on the historical and political issues that inform her written work. (KR)

THE AWAKENING

By Claribel Alegría

It was mid-May. Laura and Juan Carlos, seated at an outdoor table, contemplated the seascape as they sipped their Extra Secos. They were spending the weekend at Montelimar in one of its many bungalows: Number 233.

"Why don't we go for a swim and finish our drinks when we come back," Laura suggested. "The sun is setting and I want to see the green spark. You've never seen it, have you."

"No," Juan Carlos said, "I think it's something you invented."

"Let's go." Laura stood up.

"Don't take our drinks away," Juan Carlos told the waiter. "We'll be back in ten minutes."

"That's fine, but you should pay for them now."

Juan Carlos handed him two bills.

"Keep the change," he said.

Laura ran down to the beach in her flowered bikini, while Juan Carlos followed her at a leisurely pace.

Hurry up," Laura called to him, "or you won't see a thing."

Holding hands, the two waded into the surf until they were waist deep. The sun, an enormous red disk, was sinking below the horizon.

"Don't take your eyes off it and try not to blink," Laura chanted in her siren voice. "When you see the green flash, make three wishes, and you'll see how they come true."

"Superstitious!" Juan Carlos squeezed her hand, and they both stared into the setting sun.

"There, it's about to go under," she said, when an enormous wave flattened them against the bottom, separating them, tumbling them helplessly and sucking them seaward in the undertow. Laura threshed to the surface, tried to scream, but couldn't. Her mouth and throat clogged with sea water, and she was crazed with terror. Another gigantic wave swept her under, shook her in its jaws like a rag doll, pressed her flat, and then she did scream, the sea entering her mouth and nostrils to muffle her howl. The seconds stretched out, became hours, while her arms and legs jerked convulsively. After an eternity, one foot touched the sand, and she oriented herself in a world of up and down, of distinct planes of air and water.

She struggled blindly to reach the beach and flung herself flat, digging her fingers into the sand in the wake of a receding wave. She raised her head groggily. Juan Carlos was some yards away from her, trying to get up, and she pushed herself erect and stumbled toward him.

They kissed each other desperately and sank down on the sand, bruised and aching.

"What a fright!" Laura gasped. "I was sure I was dying."

"Me too. It couldn't have lasted more than a minute, but it felt like centuries. And something strange happened: suddenly I lost all fear and thought, what a stupid way to die, and I saw my whole life unreeling before my eyes."

"It's a shame we didn't see the green spark."

Juan Carlos smiled and said nothing.

"The incredible thing," she changed the subject, "is that I must have swallowed tons of water, but I don't feel anything in my lungs."

"Neither do I. We must have vomited it up without realizing it."

"We might have died," Laura's eyes widened. "I swear I'll never go surfing again."

"After a scare like that," Juan Carlos grimaced and shuddered, "what I need most in this world is a shot of something strong to toast life. How about going back to the bar?"

They got up painfully, trudged back slowly. Their drinks were still awaiting them on the table.

"This tastes fantastic," Juan Carlos said. "Much better than it did a few minutes ago."

"You're right. The flavor is finer."

"On the other hand," Juan Carlos twisted around, "that music hurts my ears. I'll ask the bartender to turn it down."

He got up, went to the bar and made his request. The bartender ignored him; Julio Iglesias kept singing at full blast.

"I was looking at this lemon slice," Laura said when he returned. "I'd never before noticed this green, iridescent color lemons have. It's strange I've just discovered it."

"It's as if everything has intensified," Juan Carlos agreed. "Just look at the waiter's face. Have you ever seen such enormous sadness."

Laura raised her eyes from the slice of lemon and looked at the waiter, who was serving the other two customers at the adjoining table.

"Incredible," she said. "He makes me want to cry."

"Do you want another rum?"

"No, love. I'm terribly tired, and I can't stand this music."

As they left, Laura raised her eyes to the heavens. The stars were enormous, larger than she'd ever seen them. They shone strangely, and for a moment she felt dizzy.

"You know," she said, "I feel just like that time we took LSD. Remember?"

"That's right. I feel the same. It was the only other time I've felt everything so intensely. We almost drowned. Could that be it?"

"It was horrible," Laura squeezed his hand. "Let's try to forget it."

The bungalows all looked the same. They walked two blocks in silence and then turned left.

"I think it's around here," said Juan Carlos, "but I'm confused."

"This is a labyrinth."

"No, it's not here. I think we should have turned right."

"I'm worn out. And not a soul to ask. Did you notice that, apart from that couple we left in the bar, we haven't seen any other tourists?"

"That's true. The crisis is terrible, but it's nice to have the beach to ourselves, isn't it?"

They kept walking, losing themselves in the twisting streets until, nearly an hour later when both of them were exhausted, Juan Carlos discovered No. 233.

Laura entered first and went straight to the bathroom. When she returned, Juan Carlos had already fallen asleep without even removing his bathing trunks. She stretched out beside him, nude, clicked off the light on the night table and fell asleep.

She dreamt: the morning light streamed through the window, filtered through the curtains to illuminate the room. Two girls dressed in blue uniforms with white aprons entered the room chatting. Laura tried to sit up, but couldn't. Her body was torpid. She tried to remonstrate with them but was unable to. No sound issued from her mouth; it was as though it were stuffed with cotton. She tried vainly to awaken Juan Carlos. More than fear, she felt indignation. She realized she was trapped in a dream, felt the familiar nightmare sensation of being unable to alter her circumstances.

The two girls went to the wardrobe closet.

"Let's start here," one said.

Laura gazed at them, astonished, mute, as they began to remove clothing and stuff it into the suitcase that reposed on a bench. When they finished, they went into the bathroom.

" 'Opium' by St. Laurent!" one of them exclaimed. "I'll keep that as a tip."

"Fine," the other laughed. "I'm going to take that yellow bikini I found in the closet."

They returned to the bedroom and, between the two of them, lifted the suitcase onto the foot of the bed to close it.

It was only then, when they lowered it over her legs without her feeling anything—absolutely anything—that Laura understood.

Translated by Darwin J. Flakoll

ISABEL ALLENDE is one of the most widely-read Latin American authors writing today. She was born in Lima, Peru in 1942 to Chilean parents who soon returned to their native country. In Chile she began, at an early age, her successful career as a newspaper, magazine and television journalist. After her country's 1973 military coup, she worked in various capacities with resistance organizations, but ultimately left with her family for Venezuela in 1975. There she wrote novels that have become best-sellers in many countries and languages, the first of which was the 1982 *La casa de los espíritus (The House of the Spirits)*. Her books weave detailed sagas of families and individual lives caught up in the political turmoil of present-day Latin America, and all have strong female protagonists or narrators. "Tosca" is one of the stories included in Allende's most recent book, the 1990 *Cuentos de Eva Luna (The Stories of Eva Luna)*. Isabel Allende currently lives in California. (KR)

MARGARET SAYERS PEDEN is a Professor Emerita of the University of Missouri, Columbia. Among her most recent books are translations of Isabel Allende's *The Stories of Eva Luna* and Pablo Neruda's *Selected Odes*. A book of interview-essays entitled *Out of the Volcano*, on contemporary Mexican authors, with photographic portraits by Carol Patterson, will be out in November 1991 (Smithsonian Institution Press).

TOSCA

By Isabel Allende

Her father first sat her down at the piano when she was five years old and, when she was ten, Maurizia Rugieri, dressed in pink organza and patent leather shoes, gave her first recital in the Club Garibaldi before a benevolent public composed principally of members of the Italian colony. At the end of the presentation they placed bouquets of flowers at her feet, and the president of the club gave her a commemorative plaque and a porcelain doll bedecked with ribbons and lace.

"We salute you, Maurizia Rugieri, as a precocious genius, a new Mozart. The great stages of the world await you," he declaimed.

The girl waited for the applause to die down and then, making her voice heard above the sound of her mother's proud sobs, she spoke with unexpected hauteur:

"This is the last time I ever play the piano," she announced. "I want to be a singer." And she left the room, dragging the doll by one foot.

When he recovered from his embarrassment, her father enrolled her in voice classes with a severe maestro; for every false note he bestowed a rap on the knuckles but he did not succeed in killing the child's enthusiasm for the opera. As she emerged from adolescence it became clear that she had a small, birdlike voice barely strong enough to lull an infant in the cradle; despite all her efforts, she was forced to exchange her dreams of being an operatic soprano for a more banal fate. When she was nineteen, she married Ezio Longo, a first-generation immigrant, an architect without a degree and builder by trade who had proposed for himself the goal of founding an empire on cement and steel and, at thirty-five, had nearly achieved it.

Ezio Longo fell in love with Maurizia Rugieri with the same dedication that had made it possible for him to strew the capital with his buildings. He was short in stature, heavy-boned, with the neck of a draft animal and an expressive if somewhat brutal face with thick lips and black eyes. His work forced him to dress in rough clothing, and from being so much in the sun his skin was dark and crisscrossed with wrinkles, like tanned leather. He was good-natured and generous, he laughed easily, and he loved popular music and abundant, simple food. Under this rather common exterior hid a refined soul and a delicacy he did not know how to translate into deeds or words. When he gazed at Maurizia his eyes sometimes filled with tears and his chest contracted with a tenderness that shame caused him to disguise with a cuff or a smack. It was impossible for him to express his feelings for Maurizia, and he thought that by showering her with gifts and bearing with stoic patience her excessive mood swings and her imaginary ailments he would compensate for his failings as a lover. She provoked in him an urgent desire renewed each day with the ardor of their first encounters; frustrated, he would embrace her, hoping to bridge the abyss between them, but his passion dissipated on contact with the affections of his wife, whose imagination was eternally fired by romantic novels and recordings of Verdi and Puccini. Ezio would fall asleep, conquered by the fatigue of the day, exhausted by nightmares of twisting walls and spiral staircases, but he awakened at dawn to sit on the edge of the bed and observe his sleeping wife with such attention that he learned to divine her dreams. He would have given his life to have her return his affection with equal intensity. He built for her a mammoth mansion supported by columns, in which the confusion of styles and profusion of adornment disoriented the senses, and where four servants worked constantly merely to burnish the bronzes, polish the floors, clean the crystal teardrops of the chandeliers, and beat the dust from the gold-footed furniture and imitation Persian rugs imported from Spain. The house had a small amphitheater in the garden with loudspeakers and stage lights where Maurizia Rugieri liked to sing for their guests. Ezio would never have admitted under threat of death that he was unable to appreciate those birdlike twitterings, not only to conceal his lack of culture but, especially, because of his respect for his wife's artistic inclinations. He was an optimistic man, and extremely self-confident, but when a weeping Maurizia announced that she was pregnant, he was overwhelmed by an ungovernable apprehension; he felt his heart would burst open like a watermelon, and that there was no place for such joy in this vale of tears. He feared that some violent catastrophe might wreak havoc on his precarious paradise, and he prepared to defend it against any attack.

The catastrophe came in the guise of a medical student Maurizia met on a streetcar. The child had been born by that time—an infant as vital as his father, who seemed immune to all harm, even the evil eye—and his mother had recovered her girlish waistline. The student sat down beside Maurizia en route to the city center, a slender, pale youth with the profile of a Roman statue. He was reading the score of *Tosca* and quietly whistling an aria from the third act. Maurizia felt that all the day's sunlight was captured on his cheekbones, and her bodice grew moist with sweet anticipation. Unable to restrain herself, she sang the words of the unfortunate Mario as he greeted the dawn before being led to the firing wall. And thus between two lines of the score, the romance began. The young man's name was Leonardo Gómez, and he was as mad about bel canto as Maurizia.

In the following months the student received his medical degree and Maurizia relived, one by one, all the tragedies from the operatic repertoire, and no few from romantic literature. She was killed successively by Don José, tuberculosis, an Egyptian tomb, a dagger, and poison; she was in love in Italian, French, and German; she was Aïda, Carmen, and Lucia di Lammermoor and, in every instance Leonardo Gómez was the object of her immortal passion. In real life they shared a chaste love, which she longed to consummate but did not dare initiate, and which he fought in his heart to preserve out of respect for Maurizia's married state. They met in public places, occasionally holding hands in a dark corner of some park. They exchanged notes signed Tosca and Mario; naturally, Scarpia was Ezio Longo, who was so grateful for his son, for his beautiful wife and all the blessings heaven had bestowed, and so busy working to provide for his family's security that, had a neighbor not come to repeat him the gossip that his wife was riding the streetcar too often, he would never have learned what was going on behind his back.

Ezio Longo had prepared for the contingency of a business failure, and for any illness or accident that in his worst moments of superstitious terror he had imagined might befall his son, but it had never occurred to him that a honey-voiced student could steal his wife from beneath his nose. When he heard the story, he nearly laughed aloud, because of all misfortunes this seemed easiest to resolve. After his first reaction, however, his bile flowed with blind rage. He followed Maurizia to a discreet tearoom where he surprised her drinking chocolate with her beloved. He did not ask for explanations. He seized his rival by his lapels, lifted him off his feet, and threw him against the wall amid the crashing of broken china and shrieks of the clientele. Then he took his wife by the arm and led her to his car, one of the last of the Mercedes imported into the country before the Second World War had interrupted commercial relations with Germany. He locked Maurizia in the house and posted two of his bricklayers at the doors. Maurizia lay two days in bed, weeping, without speaking or eating. During her silence, Ezio Longo had time to think things over, and his rage was transformed into a mute frustration that recalled the neglect of his infancy, the poverty of his youth, the loneliness of his existence—all that bottomless hunger for affection he had suffered before he met Maurizia Rugieri and had believed was resolved through love. On the third day he could bear no more, and he went into his wife's room.

"For our son's sake, Maurizia, you must get these fantasies out of your head. I know I am not very romantic, but if you help me, I can change. I'm not a man to wear the horns, and I love you too much to let you go. But if you give me the chance, I will make you happy, I promise."

Her only answer was to turn to the wall and prolong her fast for another two days, at the end of which her husband returned.

"Dammit, I would like to know what it is you don't have in this world; tell me, and I'll try to get it for you," he said, defeated.

"I don't have Leonardo. Without him, I will die."

"Very well. You can go off with that clown if you want, but you will never see our son again."

Maurizia packed her suitcases, put on a muslin dress and large veiled hat, and called a rented car. Before she left, she kissed the boy, sobbing, and whispered into his ear that very soon she would come back for him. Ezio Longo, who in a week's time had lost a dozen pounds and half his hair, tore the child from her arms.

Maurizia Rugieri arrived at her beloved's boardinghouse to find that two days earlier he had left to work as a doctor in an oil field, in one of those hot provinces whose name evokes Indians and snakes. She could not believe that he had left without saying goodbye, but she attributed it to the drubbing he had received in the tearoom; she concluded that Leonardo was a poet, and that her husband's brutality had disrupted his behavior. She moved into a hotel, and for days sent telegrams to every conceivable palace Leonardo Gómez might be. Finally she located him, and telegraphed him that for his sake she had given up her only son, defied her husband, society, and God Himself, and that her decision to follow him until death should them part was irrevocable.

The journey was a wearing expedition by train, bus, and, in some places, riverboat. Maurizia had never been alone outside a radius of some thirty blocks surrounding her home, but neither the grandeur of the landscape nor the incalculable distances held any terror for her. Along the way she lost two suitcases, and her muslin dress became limp and yellow with dust, but finally she reached the river landing where Leonardo was to meet her. When she decended from her conveyance she saw a pirogue at the dock and ran toward it with tattered veil and escaping curls flying. Instead of Mario, however, she found a black man in a pith helmet, and two melancholy Indian oarsmen. It was too late to turn back. She accepted the explanation that Doctor Gómez had been detained by an emergency, and climbed into the boat with the remnants of her battered luggage, praying that these men were neither bandits nor cannibals. Fortunately they were not, and they bore her safely through a huge expanse of precipitous, savage territory to the place where her lover awaited her. There were two small settlements, one of large dormitories where the workers lived, and another for staff consisting of the company offices, twenty-five prefabricated houses brought by airplane from the United States, an absurd golf course, and a stagnant green swimming pool filled each morning with gigantic frogs, all enclosed within a metal fence with a gate guarded by two sentinels. It was an encampment of transient men; life turned around that dark ooze that poured from the bowels of the earth like inexhaustible dragon vomit. In these solitudes there were no women but a few suffering companions of the workers; the gringos and bosses all journeyed to the city every three months to visit their families. The arrival of Doctor Gómez's wife, as they called her, upset the routine for a few days, until everyone grew used to seeing her pass by with her veils, her parasol, and her dancing slippers, like a character escaped from some tale.

Maurizia Rugieri did not allow the roughness of the men or the unrelenting heat to vanquish her; she intended to live out her destiny with grandeur, and she very nearly succeeded. She had converted Leonardo Gómez into the hero of her personal opera, investing him with utopian virtues, and exalting to the point of mania the quality of his love, never pausing to measure her lover's response, or gauge whether he was keeping pace with her in their grand passion. If Leonardo Gómez showed signs of lagging behind, she attributed it to his timid character and the poor health made worse by the accursed climate. In truth, he seemed so fragile that she cured herself once and for all of her imagined ills and devoted herself to caring for him. She accompanied him to his primitive hospital, and learned the duties of a nurse in order to assist him. Attending victims of malaria and treating the terrible accidents from the wells seemed better to her than lying in the house beneath a ceiling fan reading for the hundredth time the same old magazines and romantic novels.

Among the syringes and bandages she could imagine herself as Florence Nightingale, one of those brave heroines she sometimes saw in the films shown in the camp clubhouse. She refused with suicidal determination to acknowledge any diminution of her reality; she insisted on embellishing every moment with words, though in fact she now had no other alternative. She spoke of Leonardo Gómez—whom she continued to call Mario—as a saint dedicated to the service of mankind, and set herself the task of demonstrating to the world that they were the protagonists of an exceptional love—which served at least to discourage any company employee who might have been stirred by the only white woman around. Maurizia called the rusticity of the camp "contact with nature," ignoring mosquitos, poisonous insects, iguanas, the hellish heat of the day, the breathless nights, and the fact that she could not venture alone beyond the gate. She referred to her loneliness, her boredom, her natural love of the city, her desire to dress in the latest fashions, to visit her friends and attend the theater, as a vague "nostalgia." The only thing she could not give a different name to was the animal pain that sank its claws in her every time she thought of her son—so she chose never to mention his name.

Leonardo Gómez worked as a camp doctor for more than ten years, until tropical fevers and climate destroyed his health. He had lived so long within the protective fence of the National Petroleum Company that he lacked the spirit to make a new beginning in a more competitive atmosphere; in addition, he had never forgotten Ezio Longo's fury as he threw him against the wall, and thus never considered the possibility of returning to the capital. He sought a post in an out-of-the-way corner where he could continue his low-key existence, and in this way one day found himself in Agua Santa with his wife, his medical instruments, and his opera recordings. It was the decade of the fifties, and Maurizia Rugieri descended from the bus dressed in the latest style, a tight polka-dotted dress and enormous black straw hat she had ordered from a catalogue in New York, a vision like none ever seen in Agua Santa. They were, at any rate, welcomed with typical small-town hospitality, and in less than twenty-four hours everyone knew the legend of the exceptional love between the new arrivals. They called them Tosca and Mario, without the least idea of who those people were, though Maurizia soon made it her business to instruct them. She gave up her nursing duties at Leonardo's side, formed a parish choir, and offered the first voice recitals held in that village. Mute with amazement, the citizens of Agua Santa saw Maurizia on an improvised stage in the schoolhouse, transformed into Madame Butterfly, decked out in an outlandish bathrobe, with knitting needles in her hair, two plastic flowers over her ears, and her face painted plaster white, trilling away in her little bird voice. No one understood a single word of the song, but when she knelt and pulled out a kitchen knife, threatening to plunge it into her stomach, the audience cried out with horror and a spectator rushed to the stage to dissuade her, grabbing the weapon from her hands and pulling her to her feet. Immediately following the performance there was a long discussion about the reasons for the Japanese lady's tragic decision, and everyone agreed that the North American sailor who had abandoned her was a soulless brute, and that he was not worth dying for since life goes on and there are many men in the world. The evening ended with general merrymaking when an improvised band played *cumbias* and everyone began to dance. That memorable night was followed by others: song, death, explication of the opera's plot by the soprano, public discussion, and closing party.

Doctor Mario and señora Tosca were select members of the community; he was in charge of everyone's health, and she was responsible for their cultural life and news of changes in fashion. The couple lived in a cool, pleasant house, half of which was occupied by his consulting room. In their patio they kept a blue and yellow macaw that flew overhead when they went out for a stroll in the plaza. You could always tell where the doctor or his wife were, because the bird accompanied them, gliding silently some two meters above their heads on large brightly colored wings. The couple lived in Agua Santa many years, well respected by the citizenry, who pointed to them as exemplars of perfect love.

During one of his attacks, the doctor lost his way among the byways of fever, and did not return. The town was moved by his death. They feared that his wife might do herself harm, as she had in the roles she played, and they arranged to keep her company day and night in the following weeks. Maurizia Rugieri dressed in mourning from head to toe, painted all her furniture black, and carried her sorrow around like a tenacious shadow that incised two deep furrows at the corners of her mouth. She did not, nevertheless, attempt to put an end to her life. Perhaps in the privacy of her room, when she lay alone in her bed, she felt a profound relief; now she would not have to bear the heavy load of her dreams; it was no longer necessary to keep alive the character she had invented to represent herself, nor constantly juggle facts to mask the weakness of a lover who had never lived up to her illusions. But the habit of theater was too deeply ingrained. With the same infinite patience with which she had created for herself an image of the romantic heroine, in her widowhood she constructed the legend of her despair. She remained in Agua Santa, always in black—although mourning had been out of mode for many years—and refused to sing again, despite the pleas of her friends who believed that the opera would be a consolation. The town closed about her in a circle, like a strong embrace, to make her life bearable and help her retain her dreams. With the town's complicity, Doctor Gómez's memory grew in popular imagination. After two years, people took up a collection and commissioned a bronze bust to be installed on a column in the plaza facing the stone statue of the Liberator.

That was the year the main highway came through Agua Santa, which altered forever the look and spirit of the town. At first, people had opposed the project; they believed it would mean that the inmates of Santa María Prison would be brought in shackles to cut down trees and crush stone; that was how their grandfathers said the road had been built during the time of El Bene-factor's dictatorship. Soon, however, engineers arrived from the city with the news that modern machines, not prisoners, would do the work. Behind the engineers came surveyors, followed by crews of workers in orange helmets and jackets that glowed in the dark. The machines turned out to be enormous steel beasts that the schoolteacher calculated to be roughly the size of di-nosaurs; on their flanks they bore the name of their owners, Ezio Longo and Son. That very Friday, the father and son came to Agua Santa to inspect the work and pay the workmen.

When Maurizia Rugieri saw the signs and machines bearing the name of her former husband, she hid in her house with doors and shutters locked, in the unrealistic hope that she could somehow escape the past. But for twenty-eight years the recollection of her son had been a pain buried deep in her heart, and when she heard that the owners of the construction company were in Agua Santa having lunch in the tavern, she could not help yielding to her instinct. She examined herself in the mirror. She was fifty-one years old, aged by the tropical sun and the effort of feigning a chimerical happiness, but her features still bore the nobility of pride. She brushed her hair and combed it into a high bun, not attempting to hide the gray; she put on her best black dress and her wedding pearls, saved through her many adventures, and with a gesture of timid coquetry drew a line of black on her eyelids and touched crimson to cheeks and lips. She left her house under the protection of Leonardo Gómez's umbrella. Sweat ran down her back, but she did not tremble.

At that hour the tavern shutters were closed against the midday heat, so Maurizia had to stand a moment while her eyes adjusted to the darkness before she recognized Ezio Longo and the young man who must be her son at one of the rear tables. Her husband had changed much less than she, probably because he had always seemed ageless. The same leonine neck and shoulders, the same solid build, the same rather coarse features and deep-set eyes—softened now by a fan of good-humored laugh lines. Bent over his plate, he chewed enthusiastically, listening to his son's conversation. Maurizia observed them from a distance. Her son must be nearly thirty. Although he had her long bones and delicate skin, his gestures were those of his father; he ate with the same pleasure, pounded the table to emphasize his words, and laughed heartily. He was a vital and energetic man with an uncompromising sense of his own worth, a man ready for any struggle. Maurizia looked at Ezio Longo through new eyes, and for the first time appreciated his solid masculine virtues. She stepped forward, touched, breathless, seeing herself from a new dimension, as if she were on a stage playing out the most dramatic moment of the long theater of her life, with the names of her husband and her son on her lips, and with warm hopes of being forgiven for all her years of neglect. But in those few instants, too, she saw the minute gears of the trap in which she had enmeshed herself for thirty hallucinatory years. She realized that the true hero of the drama was Ezio Longo, and she wanted to believe that he had continued to desire her and wait for her during all that time, with the persistent and impassioned love that Leonardo Gómez could never give because it was not in his nature.

At that moment, when she was only inches from stepping from the shadow and being exposed, the young man leaned forward, grasped his father's wrist, and said something with a sympathetic wink. Both burst out laughing, clapped each other on the shoulder, and ruffled each other's hair with a virile tenderness and staunch complicity that excluded Maurizia Rugieri and the rest of the world. She hesitated for an infinite moment on the borderline between reality and dream, then stepped back, left the tavern, opened her black umbrella, and walked home with the macaw flying above her head like a bizarre archangel from a book of days.

Translated by Margaret Sayers Peden

ALBALUCIA ANGEL, Colombian novelist, short story writer, poet and essayist, studied art history at the University of the Andes, in Bogotá, and continued her studies at the Sorbonne, and in Rome and London. She began her career as an art critic and has worked as a journalist. Her books include: *Los girasoles en invierno* (1966); *Dos veces Alicia* (1972), *Estaba la pájara pinta sentada en el verde limón* (1975), which was awarded the "Vivencias" Prize by the Segundo Concurso Bienal de Novela; *¡Oh Gloria Inmarcesible!* (1979); *Misia señora* (1982); and *Las andariegas* (1984). (PC)

DOWN THE TROPICAL PATH

By Albalucía Angel

The night is as black as the inside of a wolf's mouth but she decides to go for a walk. Ever since this morning when she arrived at the airport, the gale has bent palm trees and bushes in two, rattled zinc roofs, threatening to pull them off by the roots, gray and rainy, what a welcome! A tropical paradise, the poster said, or so she thought, by now she doesn't know for sure, with all the commotion caused by the people waiting by the gate where she had to sign a card declaring her purchases for customs. I don't plan to buy anything, I came to look around, she explained to the guy who looked her over, pressed a stamp on the page and looked at her again this time more relaxed, handing her passport over to her finally. Now a taxi. But right away she thought of Gloria and her advice: for the best deal, go down by the beach. Around the airport, taxis overcharge.

She walks very slowly down the street, trying to sidestep the puddles that had formed during the day and she notices the shacks. The lights muted by Japanese or Chinese lanterns, people in doorways or in narrow little walkways, talking or silent, each of them fanning the air with every kind of fan, indifferent they watch her pass by, and she feels damp, the wind sticky, the music from many transistors happy, lively.

The shadow of Morgan and all the pirates. The legends. The story of people on the coast versus the story of the islanders. The black man's lament echoed over and over, his song, the black rhythm you couldn't hear right now over the noise of the transistors but which had hatched here, in the palms' roots, in the hostile starless sky and in the quiet expressions of its race, she thinks.

She goes into a bar and orders a beer but doesn't finish it because the chachachas make her head spin better to get out in the fresh air, where there is a faint smell of cracklings and cooked beans, from the Antioquena Restaurant directly in front of her. She sits down on the curb alongside the Casino and begins to look around her, to listen to the hub-bub, to watch the boys and girls walk by, exchanging flirtatious looks, to watch the dark-skinned natives dressed in bright satin shirts, so this is paradise, she says out loud again, or maybe she just thinks it, she doesn't know which, hearing the silly patter of the hawkers of the *boite-de-nuit* where the light is black and you can get American beer, German beer, Dutch beer, Scotch beer, Danish beer, Finnish beer, any brand of whiskey, cigarettes, etc. and so she sighs, resigned, I'm going some place quieter.

She walks along the streets where there are shops that display figurines perfumes bikinis eyeglasses make-up toys stereos cassettes camera equipment things for the home refrigerators washing machines clothes for men women and children shoes wallets suitcases handicrafts liquor stores, and finally dizzy she refuses to look at one more shop window. If it's all like this I'm going back, but she remembers that planes leave just once a week from the island, and really it isn't fair to judge a book by its cover, this is the first night, let's not jump to conclusions.

The smell of niter, of damp wood is overpowering. She tries to imagine a sea the color of agapanthus she always saw in pictures, until a red truck or something with a red paint job that once was a truck makes its way down the palm-lined avenue and stops in front of her. A rotund guy of indeterminable age climbs down and walks toward her, not in any particular hurry, Are you sad? he smiles, sitting down beside her not letting introductions get in the way, and what does this guy want, what's he up to now, but he offers her a cigarette, smiling at her again with very strong, very even teeth. She—I'm not sad, I'm just fine, I'm looking at the scenery, and he—ahhhh....! and not another word, and for a while they sit in silence listening to the rattle of the wind in the palm trees and that pounding of the sea.

My name is Lau-Chau, he says after taking a deep breath, and she doesn't know whether to say well my name is such and such or dismiss him once and for all since he must have mistaken her for someone else, but she comes face to face with his straightforward look, with those huge, very tired eyes arrested gently in their surprise. She smiles shyly, to ease slightly the tension that had sprung up a while before and he tells story after story, as if they were really sitting on one of those wood frame porches, fanning themselves, drinking coconut milk, very close friends. He'd had thirty-one children and been to Vietnam as a cook on an American ship, the Liberty. He had gone to Africa and Japan, I saw the Second World War and I went half way around the world. Just because I'm black, don't think I didn't get an education, he assures her, all the while speaking a mix of English and Spanish, and pointing to the red truck: I sell copper over in Medellin. Anyone who comes here to buy won't pay the price. Want a coconut? And he gets up as he's offering, hunts for a good one, one with lots of milk.

This has all changed he says with a bitter tone and a wave of his hands. Now everything smells bad, even the rocks. Even the people don't last as long. Look around at the trash on the beaches, the oil slicks, and that tar residue they leave behind, tourists with no respect who don't realize how they damage the landscape, trash it with plastic bags, litter from picnics, damn, fuck it! They don't care a damn, fuck damn of nothing! blending English and Spanish curses. And he sadly shakes his head, Come to San Luis, he invites her. There it's different, and he gets up suddenly, sticking out his hand, flashing his dazzling white rows of teeth again, bye bye...testing the air the way sailors do. This morning the wind will die down, it's going to be a nice day, and with one last wave, come back tomorrow, I have another story to tell you.

Translated by Pamela Carmell

PIA BARROS was born in Chile in 1956. She began writing during the military dictatorship, participating with other young writers in the publication of alternative literary magazines. Since 1976, she has directed her own literary workshops, dedicated principally to women, in which her students explore gender issues through writing short stories. As director of the Ergo Sum press, she has edited more than twenty collections, including the narrative of her students. She also participates on the editorial boards of the magazines *Obsidiana*, *La castaña*, and *El organillo*. Her many literary honors include the Gabriela Mistral Prize, awarded in 1977. "Scents of Wood and Silence" is included in her second collection of short stories, the 1990 *A horcajadas*. Pía Barros is presently preparing her first novel, provisionally entitled *El tono menor del deseo* to be published in 1991. (AN)

ALICE A. NELSON is a doctoral candidate in Spanish at Duke University with interests in gender issues, Latin American feminist thought, and cultural theory. She is preparing a dissertation examining the relationships of gender, culture and the construction of the body in Chilean literature published during the military dictatorship.

SCENTS OF WOOD
AND SILENCE

By Pía Barros

To Cecé

"You seem different this morning."

"It's just that I dreamt about sea gulls," she said, jumping out of bed to toast and eggs, steaming coffee and the daily ritual of shared breakfasts. She didn't hear him when he said:

"That's strange, you've got green grass between your fingers."

It had been a game so doing the laundry wouldn't be so dull. She began dreaming about hands that reached out of the sheets searching for her breasts, they should be large, coarse hands, bony and neglected, with long fingers, that would touch her painlessly, vigorous hands, rising and falling over her nipples, tracing her bristling skin, roaming all over her.

She smiled when she saw that the washer had quit running long ago and shook off her lethargy, plunging into the sheets and pillowcases that she would hang up, still perturbed by that caress.

For a time, she closed her eyes and in the shadows, while Ismael slept, she let herself be carried away by those hands, she took them, in turn, to show them the secret trace of her pores and her trembling pleasure.

Ismael was eating his breakfast as always, immersed in the news, and he found her beautiful and transparent. Life was secure and he felt fulfilled.

One afternoon in which the heat flushed her and made her dream of lakes in winter, she wanted him to have narrow hips, a small tight buttocks to dig her fingernails into, dark down outlining his genitals.

He found her asleep on the rug, with rumpled clothes and slightly open, moist lips. He put down his briefcase on the table and wanted to make love to her right there, but he controlled himself, because that image seemed virginal to him, and she was so delicate that he didn't want to attack her, and he sat down for a long while smiling, watching her sleep, so abandoned, sweet, with a face made childlike by her dreams.

But she was licking hips, kissing buttocks, clawing.

He didn't worry about her paleness until much later, when he noticed how obsessively she was sleeping. She seemed to seek out every possible moment to close her eyes, and when the house began to show neglect, he asked her to see a doctor, because he had heard that excessive drowsiness was a symptom of anemia. The tests came back normal and he didn't mention it again.

Autumn arrived when she wanted him tall, though not too tall, just enough so that embracing him would bury her face in a chest that made her feel vulnerable. She spent long hours roaming over him with her naked body, her nipples rising and falling as if sketching out his flat stomach. She adored the extreme thinness with which she had dreamt him and she liked imagining how her bones left traces on his stomach. Sleeping was gradually transformed into an art of not being caught and she liked using differently colored sheets to cover herself up and go away, far away, where intimacy offered a refuge where she could give voice to her fantasies.

Once, the vertical rain over the darkening city seduced her, and the window widened for her until she could imagine the countryside and wet horses in the distance. Winter kept her drowsy and rain splintered the landscapes. It was then that she gave him a face, and she thought with a shudder that from that moment on, she was being unfaithful. She brushed aside that idea because he didn't exist, he was only multiple pieces of many somebodies, fragments of attraction that made her guilty of nothing but her dreams. She smiled, relieved and anxious, and she desired him with a green horizontal gaze, thick dark eyebrows, and she felt safe, because she understood that he was far away, on the other side of the threshold, where it was possible to invent his salty skin to lick bit by bit, unhurriedly, until taking it, making it hers, reshaping it.

Ismael began to monitor her sleep, to see the thin darkhaired man smiling in her slightly open eyes. He knew that she was going toward him, that he was waiting for her...but then she closed the tunnel of her eyelids all the way and left him on this side, defenseless, aching, and laughing at himself, while she, far-away and other, tossed in the sheets and smiled.

'Why did you take so long,' he said, tall and enigmatic, just as she dreamed him.

It was hard to fall asleep, she responded, hugging the body that smelled of wood and silence.

She knew that on this side everything was her own, that he would love her, aching and torn, his soul full of horses. On the other side remained pressing tasks, guilt, schedules.

Morning surprised them as she wanted it to, their skin intertwined, and he said Don't go yet, and he began kissing her, looking for answers in her nipples, questions in her buttocks, and she was dressing and walking toward the door of the cabin and he was following her, all grinning and boyish, and he was throwing her on the grass and he was loving her with a delightful penetration, where the sea gulls of time exploded in their fingers, and orgasm came with all the sky in her eyes and she grabbed onto a blade of grass so that she wouldn't feel as if she were dying, in the midst of the commotion of a bird flying overhead and the hoarse, deep laugh that flowed free, full, vibrant.

Ismael's hand on her shoulder had broken through the threshold and he was saying

"You seem different this morning."

"It's just that I dreamt about sea gulls."

Ismael watched her. He waited until she fell asleep and then tried to see through the intermingled space of her drowsy eyes to where they were making love, toward where she was looking. The cabin, the lake and the sea, those were her refuges, the islands anchoring the dreams that left him injured, defenseless. Ismael discovered small objects that she had brought back from the threshold and left around, forgotten: some grains of sand, weeds, a small paper boat, the remains of winter in the middle of summer, or the blades of turf tangled through her hair when she awoke. He had grown accustomed to inspecting the sheets, painfully searching for the traces, humiliated by the mist that he didn't know how to fight, hiding the proof of her faraway dreams.

She slept, reared up or transparent, spending almost all her time on the other side of the threshold. In the house, dust accumulated under the furniture and dirty plates spilled their contents around different spots in the kitchen.

The rain made her close her eyes again. 'Come here,' she had heard in the distance. He began nipping her, licking her, bending her, making her submit. She wanted to dream about sea gulls again, but each bite hurled her toward strange images, a mouth crying out in the darkness, a half smile slightly parted by a cigarette, a man's shoes on the grass..., his tongue and teeth clawing her nipples launched her directly toward an angry sea and the urgency of her desiring skin, toward a flaming inferno that dried out her mouth and blurred her own voyeur's silhouette spying on the game...the hand and the green gaze crawled over her skin and she opened her thighs calling him, with an ancestral scent that she didn't recognize in herself and the cabin became a fissure in the rock that was scraping her shoulder and the sea was there, bellowing, licking the calves that she raised to keep astride the vertical man who the sea seemed to be trying to topple with its waves, and the foam roaring over her buttocks and her legs crossed over the back into which she dug her nails trying to mark, to leave a trace, and the man attacked her until her eyes clouded, leaving a small thread in the juncture of her lips...

This time, she wouldn't be able to hide her scarred back, the teeth marks on her hips. Ismael stopped smiling, but he didn't ask questions. He was afraid he wouldn't be able to stand the answers. There was no one to blame.

Bit by bit she became thinner and by then she didn't even attempt the parody of getting out of bed. It was useless for Ismael to raise her head to make her open her eyes and swallow a couple of spoonfuls of soup. She was over there, in the delirium, offering fingers and possessions, 'because I exist in you, it's my flesh that's heating you up, come on, lick me, let your green eyes glide over the water...' Fever arrived slowly one day when the sheet became damp, leaving the trace of two sweats. Her bony, translucent fingers barely rose to gesture for a little water. The fever gradually impregnated her hands, her forehead, and began taking her dreams far away.

"Ismael," she called out in the darkness, I can't dream, help me.

Ismael feared the anguish that hoarsened her voice. But later, a long while afterwards, he smiled and quit giving her the medicine.

In her delirium, she was asking him to help her remember, to reconstruct the lake and his eyes, and how I made his chest, Ismael, the size of his hands grasping my hips to push inside of me, help me Ismael, this afternoon there would be swings and we would go up, up, we would be kites and laughter and our skins would call each other by name up there, Ismael, up there, where guilt has no place and no bird will ever go astray...

But Ismael only put water to her lips and smiled.

"Everything will be all right, I promise you, everything will be fine again."

She struggled desperately, trying to grasp his hands, his hair, something that would take her back over the threshold, while fever was erasing the contours of the cabin, the man's smile, the coarse hands that scratched as they caressed, the scents of wood and silence.

Help me Ismael.

Everything will be fine.

She was crying, while in the distance, the anguished voice faded as it called 'Sleep, dream me again,' but it was no longer a voice, it was the memory of having heard some voice and the horror and emptiness and hips and shoulders and the green gaze diluting until it disappeared.

Afterwards, there was only a long silence and the end of winter, while her fever dropped and a taciturn paleness began to take hold of her body.

Sleep found her empty and too weak to dream him again.

Ismael opened the window to change the thin air of those months, and she felt that air take away with it the last vestiges of memory.

The window was only a wide frame, displaying buildings and streets and cement.

She gave up the fight, it was no use. In her forlornness, the sheets became dull stains once again. It would be impossible for her to restore in them the scents of wood and silence.

Translated by Alice A. Nelson

LYDIA CABRERA, born in Havana, Cuba, has had a rebellious and exemplary, if politically convoluted, life that has managed to combine the island's richest salons with its poorest black ghettoes, her own furniture factory and homespun antique dealership with a frustrated career in painting and pioneering studies of anthropology in Paris. Her intellectual work led her to a crusade against racial and cultural prejudices, a subtle patronage of feminism, and an even more subtle claim of sexual difference. At the height of her career, she published *El Monte* (*The Sacred Wild*), her best known work, which is a most unusual "novel" on Afro-Cuban anthropology. The short story, "Susundamba Does Not Show Herself By Day," belongs to her collection *Por qué...Cuentos negros de Cuba* (*Because...Afro-Cuban stories*). (JP)

JOSE PIEDRA is Associate Professor of Romance Studies and Director of the Hispanic American Studies Program at Cornell University. An avowed post-colonialist, he studies the anti-colonialist voices within the lingering colonial cultures of Latin America. He has previously translated works by Alejo Carpentier.

SUSUNDAMBA DOES NOT SHOW HERSELF BY DAY

By Lydia Cabrera

"Cha-cha... Chazz!"

The Owls, deep in a valley encircled by frowning mountains, swarmed around in a populous tribe shunning the sun. (The sun shunned them too.)

By virtue of the same shriek of bad luck, they were related to all of those damn birds that, from the time the first stars shone, have made men's hearts tremble at night with sudden and indescribable terror; but, until the fiasco that I am about to narrate took place, no one knew about them. Not even the kestrel, a bird that had traveled the skies high and wide, had a precise idea of the owls' existence.

Ignorant of, and ignored by, the rest of the creatures who peopled the earth, the Owls lived many a century meditating, perhaps happily, in the most total isolation of the very same night hole. This was so until Owlito, a young male owl with the inquiring spirit of "look-hard-and-look-over-and-look-again" —because of having fortuitously shifted away from his place on the branch upon which he meditated year after year in stereotypic fashion—, unexpectedly raised his head to survey the skies that stretched from zenith to zenith and viewed an exceedingly clean, freshly ironed cloud, which gracefully picked up its own tail and crossed the double barrier clinched with furrowed brows. And this sleepless Owlito, while all the others slept late into the morning, became curious and bent his head over backwards to spy upon the sky traffic, in a way that no other macho owl had ever imagined could be done. He began to suspect that the sky and the earth extended somewhat beyond the other side of the mountains. He then became talkative and inquisitive. No longer capable of fitting into the old lot of relentless solitude and silence, this macho owl began to question the situation with a secret anxiety that would not become apparent on his fixed expression. He experienced, without realizing it, the inner tortures of the soul preceding the simplest of revelations. The situation merited it.

"Where do the clouds come from, where do they go?"

Actually no one knew and no one cared, the eyes would not see beyond the obvious, would not transcend the profile of the wilderness of mountains burnished on the sky. One could still count on the eyes of the wisest owl, a relentless gaze that could pierce mountain peaks. But the other wise members of the tribe—to keep seeming wise—wisely kept their silence. Their facial masks hardened and widened ever more, as if chiseled in stone, obstinate in their reticent silence. Only the oldest of the thinkers, the wisest, Okbó-Alase, keeper of the words and secrets of the tribe, who from time to time would absentmindedly announce a death which was imprinted deep within each pupil, consented to address and clarify the mystery.

He was as old as the valley and the night combined. His tongue was the sum total of every truth.

Owlito opened up his eyes even more, not to lose one word drenched in light, as the old one, who readied himself to talk, extended a wing paternally over him in a solemn gesture of confidence. But the tongue moved without a word and the mouth exhaled a heavy mist... The explanation became a thick, indolent fog, spreading to cover and mystify the valley, fading and confusing it all. To his great surprise, as the imprecise forms lost themselves in a world without edges where indefinable trees, mountains, and fuzzy macho owls dissolved into a wandering fog—including the biggest of the big wise owls, and with it the whole tribe and the rest diffused and confused—everything remained suspended probably as long as the nebulous speech of the Great Father was supposed to have lasted. Owlito was eminently dissatisfied, and freeing himself from the misty mess in which he was tangled up, and sensing heat and vigor surging from the site of his heart, he bit himself awake. He then enthusiastically endorsed a decision that he spread among his kind, who did not pay the slightest attention.

"I will fly high, as high as I can, and flow with the wind."

In the whole sullen circle of the wild horizon, the brows of eternity furrowed. Owlito did not overlook the mute and awesome reproach of the ancient mountains dressed in grieving black, solemnly lifting and joining their peaks at the first nocturnal sign of light, in order to make him feel insignificant and hermetically closing off the valley in their sleep.

Owlito seemed to hear, above and behind the immense dark expanse of silence and stone, the sound of livelier skies. In the imprecise and distant rumble he seemed to distinguish a name. A call... Below, the sobbing wind from the valley trailed one shadow and then another. The owl reached the mountain. Above, Afén, the free sweeping wind from the heights, carried him far, throughout the skies of his intuition; far away, on the unknown cushion of a moon-filled sky.

Thus he arrived in Henland.

"Hunkee-hunkee-doree-Zap!"

As soon as the adventurer had hit the ground, he felt surrounded by solicitous hens who welcomed him. The whole population of the cornfields suddenly awoke, and the news that a stranger had landed—from the moon—spread like wildfire.

"Praise the Lord! A man, a man!"

"Is he a man?"

"Did you get a good look at him?" wondered the blind hens reaching out into the empty space.

"He is even good-looking!"

"White and pretty like the moon!"

Having said this, night in Henland festooned itself with heartfelt thrills: it was a happy crackling event of the highest caliber. The cornfields themselves reached out with welcoming arms; a metallic rustle ran over the earth, the tatters and locks of golden straw bristled and bumped into each other. The tender husks grinned their tiny grainy teeth and tore through the veils laughing away without knowing why, with the sort of unbridled happiness with which crazy child brides burst into whimpers—just like the laughter of Mama Panchita's wild wind, like the song of Titundia's beckoning at sea, and like the knocks of Juan Perillán's boy dolls playing in the closet.

The enthusiasm peaked in disorder: as soon as they knew all the hens came over, even the broody and the old, even the dying and the condemned, ready to dip their beaks into the matter.

With little concern for appearances, they overdid themselves in showing signs of hospitality and friendliness. So much so that the cocks became alarmed and, naturally, reprimanded them.

"Doodoo-doodoo-doodoo-don't!"

However, they were flirting with so much excitement that they paid no attention.

"Lay-low-lay-low!"

Owlito had happily spent half the night in Henland a-praising. His show of love was repaid with sighs, flaming glances, burning promises. Then he began to fear the light of dawn—because in the darkest regions of his memory light brought forth the old quarrel between the sun and his kind—enough to ask:

"What time is it, miladies?" a punctual cock then announced three o'clock.

"Cock-a-doodle-doo-cock-a-doodle-doo-cock-a-doodle-doo!"

"Bye bye, my pretty ones, bye bye, my shining lights!" sighed Owlito. And leaving them all smitten with love, he fled:

"Cha-hunk-zap!"

Upon his return home, he told of his incredible adventure in the town square by the pathetic guasima trees (from whose branches hung, like nightshirts, the souls of so many victims of boredom).

Who would suspect anything just by looking into the eyes of the hens?

He spoke about happiness, sweetness, and grace, unprovable notions that sprang up in lands where thinking was kept to a minimum. He referred to the hip and saucy things that they said over there.

"What hens, brothers! How sweet and pretty these ladies are!" Owlito, moved by emotion, assured his audience. "To see them is to want them. They are so loving, grateful, and generous. They are all happy-go-lucky and pretty. So happy! So good... Hens are so good!"

Owlito's happiness was contagious. It was a feeling deep within his body, that seemed to lighten him up, to render him more mobile, while perched on the guasima branch, enthralled in his own overwhelming enthusiasm and in the pleasure emanating from his own confession. The pursuit of happiness struck every listener; it unified them. At the same time the turgid heart of the owls harbored the old sadness, the secret and chronic pain that pushed against their eyes to produce a single tear. The anxiety of happiness made the owls cry.

"It's raining!" pronounced the indifferent bystanders who promenaded under the trees.

So it was that every owl bore a tear from which flowed centuries of the most repressed, obstinate, and muzzled suffering. This lightened the load of their hearts and made them burst into an exclamation that was as sinister as it was decisive:

"We want to be happy! We want hens!"

That evening at eight o'clock, half the tribe of owls fluttered their wings of starry whiteness on their flight to Henland.

> Cha
>> Cha
>>> Cha
>>>> Zap!

"More men, holy Jesus, more men!"

"So many, holy Mary—one for each—praise Her!"

While shaking with joy upon the owls' arrival in droves, the hens made the sign of the cross thanking the God in the heavens. They had refused to go home after the sunset prayers. With the rush and the high, they now trampled their own nests, squashed their eggs and creamed their yolks. From the earliest sign of dusk, they had waited, doubts burning their insides, their gaze fixed on the sky as the limit, imploring every single star that timidly showed up in the firmament.

"Kn'ck, kn'ck, nooo-no!" protested the nervous cocks, in their fumbling riot.

"Wow, Wo', Wo', What?"

(Watch out, you cocky cock, don't butt in. Beat it!)

Now was the time for greetings, parties, social graces. At the beginning the owls—awkward and ceremonious—could not believe that they were escorting the hens arm in arm around the park. While the thrumming of crickets echoed across a night perfumed with a fresh and lovely scent, ladies and gentlemen went around and around, until they were dizzy. Finally the hens gave in to their sentimental inclinations, losing their heads. That very night in the park they did it passionately under the gaze of a shut-eye moon. They did it without guilt and without regret...

Henceforth the loving Hens met often with their suitors; and there were so many suitors and so many maidens losing their honor in this way, so many married ladies succumbing to adultery while taking a walk in the park—even the Hen Queen cockled away at the foot of the Bishop's orange tree—, that the disowned Cocks, put on hold, scorned, incapable of putting a stop to the infamous conduct of their women, secretly convened a meeting.

Thus spoke Maratobo, Gent-Mayor-and-Alderman, with an irate flap of his wing:

"Could you have ever imagined a heavenly shower of hunks! We cocks are all...!"

Necks cocked up and shoulders shuddered. Headcrests shook. Convulsive looks were exchanged, panting beaks opened among all the cocks of the world; and Captain Quirito Cock could no longer shy away from what he had to do, ruffling his feathers was not enough. The same was true for the haughty Giro Cock and the ballsy and hardheaded Girolí Cock.

Maratobo the Top Cock withdrew into silence, perhaps because he was suffering the collective pain of the infamous line he had felt short of completing, but that every one had heard and felt like a sharp spur in their flesh.

"We're in bad shape. What should we do? This will be the end of us all. This situation is turning us into... Who is going to continue my line? Cocks will disappear... and Maratobo Top Cock will die within me—no more Maratobos on the face of the earth! This is intolerable!"

The hens in love, letting it all out, without trying—not even out of politeness—to do things on the sly, had declared a rebellion and didn't bother even to maintain appearances. They would not follow the old paths in good or in bad faith. They remained deaf to the Grumpy Logic of the Cock, the one that sermonized them in vain. They did not fear marital authority after landing with a vengeance on their own two feet. They despised them, insulted them, dealt with them on equal footing, pecking away at them. No more eggs. As early as the first dusk they adorned themselves with wreaths of marigolds, in shameless anticipation of their lovers.

The Cocks argued among themselves without finding a solution. In the end they could only invoke the good old times, without evil and without oddities, a time when every Hen was honest. As some Cock would begin to speak and fumble in his speech, another would interrupt to complicate the problem even more. The most intelligent Cocks slept on in order to forget a threatening situation. The honor of a whole society had been wounded where it hurts the most. Even after so much yakking they couldn't find a way to solve the problem. Finally, someone had a fortuitous idea.

"Peter the Animal," someone proposed, "let's ask the advice of Peter the Animal; let his opinion be our guide."

Ah! Good Old Gent, Peter the Animal, dreadlocks and all, crawling with lice, good Crocodile front teeth and bad filed-down canines in Calabar style, iron arms and fists, Break-a-Hammer ribs, stone chest as hard as Saint

Michael's shield. Good Old Gent, Peter the Animal, was as brave as Tiger, as shrewd and distrustful as Turtle who carries its home safely on its back.

In the forest, a Silk-Cotton Tree; in the air, a Hawk; a Shark in the sea. Who would dare win a victory against Good Old Gent, Peter the Animal's failproof will?

The entire animal kingdom respected him, for he was an animal with the words and intelligence of a human, and since he knew everything animals know he knew more than any human. (May God continue to be on his side.)

Well, a commission made up of the most self-respecting and wounded Cocks was named to confer with Peter the Animal about the domestic conflict that made life impossible for everyone in Henland. By mid-afternoon, the commission found him taking a siesta in a grotto. They confided in him that "the Hens were going to lay Owls' eggs," something that they could not put up with. Furthermore, given the fact that Cock's country had been paying Peter the Animal a tribute of many thousand baskets of the freshest eggs, the cocky eminences were counting on this fellow Peter to launch a revenge against their women's relentless lover boys.

Half asleep, Peter the Animal thought that the cocky emissary had come to tell him the tall tale of "Do You Really Want Me To Tell You 'The Tall Tale of The Bald Cock'?" and paid little attention, assuming that if he half-heartedly consented to their telling him the tale, the follow-up would be: "This is a tale of a Cock with tattered feet and a turned-around head. Do you really want me to tell you the tall tale of the Bald Cock?" But this non sequitur was not to be. As he awoke, after the Head Cock insisted on unloading his sorrows, he made sense of the matter of the eggs, which Peter the Animal considered a delicacy. Alarmed, he struck himself on his own ample chest, hard as Saint Michael's tombstone and crawling with good dead souls, and emerged from his slumber ready to assume the loose reins of that unbridled business, one that without a doubt had become a personal threat. And this is what he said:

"Night is a Witch who lies and hides. She is the Owls' whore madam and godmother. This is a very old legend, convoluted and long... Never mind, make the Hens see the Owls as they are, not as they imagine them in their dreams. Let the sun shine on the truth, the sun that does not lie or hide, that sweeps away all illusions!"

The Cocks agreed: "Aahe yeah! yeaah!"

Peter the Animal then said: "In order to fool and fulfill the visitors and with the pretext of repaying their visits to the Hens, invite all the animals, from the Elephant to the Termite, to a dance in honor of the Owls. Let no Cock sing away the time, so that the sun surprises them and the animal kingdom bears witness to the event."

And so it was. An invitation full of curlicues, like a tray of puff pastries delicately baked by the hens themselves, was sent to Queen Susundamba. The Queen of the Owls wanted to know them but not out of jealousy for, in spite of the whole array of things that she imagined were happening to her subjects in this beautiful faraway land, if the whole truth be told, she was neither male nor female: just Queen and Owl.

The fact that the males from Owlland thrust themselves into foreign and forbidden skies in search of love did not have the slightest effect on the females. The females—like the males before them—had no other concern than thinking away the time for no apparent reason. They existed so buried within themselves that they could not surface from their own depths, like a stone lying at the bottom of a well. When a macho Owl's body mechanically covered theirs, they remained as seriously unperturbed as one would with the most remote and faint of stars. This did not affect their own self-immersion while their kind, pensive and taciturn, multiplied itself... It was a routine matter. Besides, many of the female Owls were Iyalocha priestesses consecrated to Yewá, the gloomy virgin goddess of death, who rules with her two sisters the subterranean and secret life of cemeteries. And these Iyalocha priestesses must be as chaste as Yewá: the heart clean, the eyes clean, the hand and tongue clean. Their sleep is chaste.

Deep in the valley of the night all the Iyalocha priestesses served the cause of Yewá and none of them sinned, even in their thoughts. They had aged as virgins and, thus, all the she-owls in the shadowy valley appeared to be old.

The night of the dance, Queen Susundamba materialized from thin air playing the drum followed by an entourage all in silver:

"My foot-foot-ehhh, one, two, chacha-chazzz!"

So solemn, so pensive, with her wide searching eyes and her silvery hair in a bun, the queen played the drum to a mysterious rhythm that brought happiness to all animals known to gather around her, dancing away.

And yet all was not well. The Cocks followed the vow of silence offered to Old Gent, Peter the Animal, and went on panting around. "Kockle, kockle, kockle, doo..." such was the tune to which they thrust their bodies on those of the scandalized Hens.

Queen Owl—they say she was so very lovely—, danced a slushy, one-leg rumba, checking on the sky every once in a while with an eye on uncertainty while advising her subjects:

"Please tell me when the day has come,
With the drum-drum sound, Ma' Bella!
Please tell me when the day has come,
With the drum-drum sound, Ma' Bella!"

Suddenly Sijú, the Banana-eating bird, who was among the guests and who had come to the dance because the godson of the cousin of a stepson of his godfather the Drover had mentioned to him that everyone had begun to believe that these Hens were whores—whores without decorum—fearing that things could get out of hand, tried to get a hold of his nerves and called out:

"Sijú, See Who, Sijú!"

And his screams were heard for a second above the surrounding noise. Hearing this, the Cocks—first living clocks in the world—could not keep from thinking that an impostor had taken away their traditional job:

"Tchlá, tchlá!" they flipped their wings and marked the hour, "Cock-a-doodle-doo!."

The He-Owls sensed the day was near, not knowing whether it was the song or the sun or the song of the Cocks in the golden voice of Maratobo.

"Cha-chaa... Chazz... "

They fled the party, with the Queen at the head of the crowd, playing the drum.

Queen Owl, a lady who usually shunned happiness, had had a very good time. She returned the next night with her people. And there was another party, in which she took the drum and danced an even slushier rumba.

"My foot, my move, eh, one-two, one-two, chachachazzz!"

It was late when she said:

"Please tell me when the day has come,

With the drum-drum sound, Ma' Bella! "

Sijú, who had left the dance out of breath and was drinking from a pond, suddenly discovered his own image at his very feet, reflected in an upside-down sky of trembling pale moon and stars—one star especially vibrant twinkling at the tip of Siju's beak. He congratulated himself enthusiastically until he cried out to himself in a trance-like frenzy:

"Sijú, See Who, Sijú."

Again the startled Cocks began to malign the intruder, stung by his accuracy, and rushed to silence his voice with the official singing of the correct time, which was to cover the entire width and depth of the night:

"Cock-a-doodle-doo! Cock-a-doodle-doo! Cock-a-doodle-doo!"

The shadows held back. The fields fluttered their lashes.

"Cha-ch... Chazz..."

And the Owls fled, their Queen leading the way with the drum and a Love-me-love-me-not flower dripping with moon juice.

It was necessary for the Cocks to take their case once more to the cave of Peter the Animal, this time to declare their failure.

Peter the Animal's cupboard was out of fresh eggs. He offered no explanation; drumming instead on a little drum to summon the Chief of the Fireants along with millions of subjects.

Then Peter blew on a seashell. A long blue voice emerged from the shell, to summon the Chief of the Crabs, along with millions of subjects, overcoming imaginary obstacles, some carrying bags of sand, others stones in their claws.

Peter then released seven types of herb (where two pinches of Kimbinchi pepper would have sufficed).

Peter sang: "Hunkee-hunkee-hunk, hunkee-hunkee-hunk"... The song echoed in the Wild. The trees obeyed, marching on from within the thicket, crossing the savannah, until they reached their goal. They all crawled like octopuses on their roots—mimosas, jocumas, acanas, cedars, and mahoganies.

Peter the Animal did his two-finger whistle and the Chief of the Woodpeckers took flight, followed by every other Woodpecker perched on the surrounding branches.

Self-satisfied, Peter the Animal looked around him. He began to reflect... Freshness was missing; no, no, there was not enough water in that neck of the woods. All he had to do was to stretch his arm, stretch it and reach with his hand far enough to loosen a crystalline river caught between his index finger and thumb; he brought it over and made it run nearby, exactly where it suited him.

In a short time, the Fireants, the Crabs, and the Woodpeckers—knock-bang-knock—built a masonry mansion.

By now everyone was only thinking of dancing and for this purpose Good Old Gent Peter the Animal invited to his home all the world's animals, big and small. In order to improve the quality of the party and make it joyful he also invited black people. He forgot no one... Not even the Gnat, who put on a new pair of mittens, the sweet and sad Tick, Little Green Roach, and poor old Chichí, the blind lightning bug. (The Chigger swore it would not bite.)

Thus, with the fresh wind, the dreamy trees, and the enchantment of the night, everyone began to arrive from the four corners of the world; the poor on foot, the rich on horse or by carriage. Assured that every single guest had arrived—even the slowest Slug—, Peter the Animal shut the doors and windows down tight. The Cocks were left outside, fuming on the balconies and ledges with their beaks muzzled by canvas straps, clueless about the true reason for the party. (That's a Cock's memory for you.)

An irresistible drum summoned from the inside:

"Bongo-in, Bongo-out."

The tone deepened and increased. The dance fired away the hips and burned away with fiery music the beasts of creation locked up inside. The drum never stopped, red and magnificent like a tempest screwing away in ever-tightening ecstasy.

"Tookoo-tootootoom-tookoo-tootootoom!"

The Queen Owl asked early in the night, either as a precaution or out of habit, but she could not stop shaking her body or shaking her body away from the controlling power emanating from the drum:

"Please tell me when the day has come,

With the drum-drum sound, Ma' Bella! "

while looking at the dark wooden ceiling she took for the sky.

That night the Hens felt particularly proud of their beaus as they watched them enter the dance party preening around Peter the Animal's salon with their gorgeous footwear shiny and squeaky, sounding something like:

"Squeekee, squeekease..."

This was a mark of supreme elegance. And they, in turn, were so self-satisfied and happy with their shoes that they could hardly imagine anything but continuing good luck.

Force of habit would make the Owls greet each other with a half-hearted:
"Is it day yet?"
"Not day yet."
"Well bámbara, fotuto wasasa, ekitiyá," and they would continue dancing without a care.

Around three o'clock in the morning, Queen Susundamba had lost her bearings. She no longer asked the time. Time for her ceased to exist. She found herself in the eye of the vortex of a cyclone of rumba. The more the Queen Owl felt the gushes of wind lashing her body, and the rolling drum beating down on her a rainpour of sound, the more she felt like joining the black mob panting and possessed in their dance.

The animals and the blacks drank sugarcane firewater until they were all drunk. Including the Owls... even the Lice.

At three o'clock sharp, stinking-drunk Sijú, after having whistled to everyone without success, without even anyone's turning their head, had a momentary flash of intuition of more or less delirious proportions, about whether he was a sijú or not. Feeling scattered and giddy from the drumming, trapped as it were in his own extravagant web of terror, he cried out:
"Sijú!, Sijú? See Who? See meeee...!"

Staggering through the silver-tipped blue grass, the party house, its rooftops, balconies, and walls danced to the rhythm of the "Kaínke-Kinché-Kinchéke-Kecheke-Keché" while the moon trailed behind, frightened, disheveled, with a raving mad face, dragging the morning star tied to a string of light.

It must have been about five o'clock when the Turtle turned belly-side up and the Millipede stood on its last two feet; the mustached roaches belly-flopped around on broken wings; and Sweet Roach Martínez fainted in Rat Pérez's arms.

The Horses shoeless, the Bulls hornless, the matronly Cows with loosened bras, the Rams, the Goats, the Dogs; the honorable Pigs, the Deer, the Cats, the Rabbits, the Agoutis, everyone in short with four legs, tree-climbing or slithering being, such as Sir Snake of Santa María; the Birds, and all of the air-dwellers including the Osprey, the gooey-eyed and bare-necked bird (who, perched on his master rafter, tapped a tune and vomited, self-contentedly, on the dancers' heads), even the Hummingbird frail and fleeting as an instant, and the translucent Dragonfly were out of breath and staggered with exhaustion, yet holding onto the powerful magic of the drums, as they danced on and on alongside the entranced panting black mob.

When the sun came up in the sky clutching the hairy locks of the palm trees, and there was not a single lagging shadow and the morning was in full swing, Peter the Animal suddenly opened up some windows.

An avalanche of unwanted light poured in, strangling the interior voice of the house with a momentary silence, followed by the trapped night swiftly undoing itself. At the same time the Cocks, now unmuzzled, emerged from the forgotten hours to sing their hymn to the sun while, in the midst of the clamor of the blinding lights, the Owls confronted the cruelty of a time resurrected. The old enemy pricked their bubbles with a shower of burning arrows fired point-blank. So full of poisonous hate were these that the late-to-arise Owls knew then and there that there was no way out, that they were beaten, irrevocably discredited for the rest of their lives, and as far as their loving was concerned...

"Praise God!" interjected from her corner behind the door the Black Widow Spider, another creature of the dark, astonished after her double take.

"Yansa, jekua jei!" chanted loudly the chorus of blacks, who had regained consciousness.

Queen Owl, who hours earlier had shone, appeared now to be the most hideously ugly of birds. The sight would freeze anyone in horror. Her distended pupils paralyzed the members of the audience as if a dreadful and unavoidable mystery had been suddenly revealed to them. They were lugubrious birds like scarecrows devised in the bowels of death itself. The white gentlemen from the Moon, the stylish dandies who manhandled with tongue and hands every Hen in sight, beckoning them to sleep on their chests, the very same sharp dressers whose shining shoes squeaked to please—Squeekee, Squeekease—, became suddenly so horribly sickening, so lugubriously sinister in their new guise as frightened stumpy weirdos manufactured by the Devil and the Hidden Evil Eye—heralds and ushers of bad luck—, that the Hens deafened the world with their cries, while the Lady Turkeys ran around frightened that they too could have succumbed:

"Spare me! Spare me!"

"Chill off!" screamed the mob upon coming in contact with the Evil Eye and the very accomplices and emissaries of death.

In the havoc of the world's species, the Owls, riddled with screams, bellows, howls, brays, barks, roars, neighs, buzzes, struggled to escape, bumping against the bright walls and losing feathers while swimming against the current in a sea of curses and threats. Blinded by the elements while being pursued by a wave of solid terror, their flapping wings tangled up in a web of light, they barely managed to stumble across the rivers of morning gold to scatter in every direction until their shrieks of ill omen were muted by the distance.

The Hens, shamed in public, cried and cried inconsolably, paying no heed to public opinion.

"Ay," they said, "if only we hadn't seen them with our very eyes!"

Resigned to their fate, they began again the endless task of laying eggs and raising chickens, submissive to the Cock and the destiny they had intended to trick.

Oh, but on moonlit nights! In the thrust of that great melancholy that sleeps with us at night, and of the land that moves and dreams around us, nothing exists but emotions, nostalgia, and insistence about the way it once was... The Moon awakens the Hens and they can be heard stirring about nervously in the henhouses. All was forgotten, all should be forgotten, but at times—always—the Moon drags in ghosts of inconclusive love. The He-Owls who would never return do return, while the Hens suffer from heartache—an unforgettable ache...

Translated by José Piedra

JULIETA CAMPOS is a writer of fiction, literary criticism and translation whose many works are well known throughout Latin America and Europe. Born in Havana, Cuba in 1932, since 1955 she has made her home in Mexico, where she is an active participant in literary, intellectual and academic life. She has collaborated on the journals *Plural*, *Vuelta* and *Revista de la Universidad de México* (of which she was editor), taught at the National Autonomous University (UNAM), and served as president of the P.E.N. Club of Mexico. She has translated many books from English and French into Spanish for the publishing houses Fondo de Cultura Económica and Siglo XXI. Both her fiction and essays of literary criticism demonstrate a concern with self-referentiality in the writing process, and its relationship to the passing of time inside and outside the narrative. Among her best-known works is the 1974 novel *Tiene los cabellos rojizos y se llama Sabina*, for which she won the prestigious Xavier Villaurrutia Prize that year. Her most recent (1982) book of essays examines the storytelling of the indigenous Nahuas in the Mexican state of Veracruz. The story "The House" ("La casa") forms part of the 1968 volume *Celina o los gatos*, made up of five stories and an introductory essay. (KR)

KATHLEEN ROSS teaches Latin American literature at Duke University, where she specializes in the fields of colonial Spanish America, translation, and women writers. She has translated (with Richard Schaaf) *The Black Heralds* by César Vallejo (Latin American Literary Review Press, 1990), as well as works by Roque Dalton, Alejo Carpentier, Nicolás Guillén and others, and has published scholarly essays of literary criticism. She is an Associate Editor of the *Latin American Literary Review*.

THE HOUSE

By Julieta Campos

They've just put the cradle in the same corner as always. The cradle made of white iron, lined with lace, with a tulle mosquito netting. They walk from one side of the room to the other. I don't move. They are talking about the new baby.

"Have you noticed the resemblance...? He's the spitting image. If it had been a girl..."

Everyone comes closer. It's the women who carefully part the net. Prince, who then is an Irish setter, approaches too. He puts up his two front paws and sticks his nose in. They push him away, tell him to leave. But there he stays, beneath the cradle, stretched out, with one of his front paws sweetly tucked under the other and his nose completely flat on the floor. He remains there, stretched out beneath the cradle. How many years has Prince been lying under the cradle, guarding the new baby? I, who have been watching all this time, can't remember.

Now Prince is sitting on the wicker sofa, between Consuelo on one side, and a young American who could be called Jim. Consuelo is dressed in black and has on an enormous hat with long ostrich feathers. She barely smiles. She has on her glasses, lightly sitting on the bridge of her nose: oval-shaped glasses, the lenses surrounded by a fine band of gold. Consuelo smiles like a Leonardo archangel, with a vague, faraway ambiguity. On Prince's other side, Jim calmly looks straight ahead from behind his myopic's lenses, expressionless. His wavy hair has been parted in the middle. On his lap, a straw hat. Neither Consuelo nor Jim needs to speak.

At a certain point, Prince has lunged from his place on the yellow sofa. Then he has taken off at a run, leaving between Consuelo and Jim a void that could only be filled with words. And neither one is willing to say them.

At the back of the room, the folding screen situated precisely in a place where the sun shines in with excessive intensity. So much so, that the screen floats surrounded by a halo, levitating in the somewhat heavy air of three in the afternoon. This screen is fairly new. Consuelo's father has had it placed there recently. And already it seems definitive, rooted there forever. Albertina, twelve years old, places herself near the screen holding a fan she begins to move too slowly, with an absent gesture. When she stops fanning herself, she is eighteen, and no longer looks distractedly at the oversized Majolica vase, but fixes her gaze on an imprecise point situated—perhaps one could say—in infinite space. Prince is not, at that moment or any other, anywhere at all.

Prince sits at the feet of the elder Consuelo, who sits in turn in a rocking chair by the balcony. Consuelo rocks unhurriedly, sure that she may continue doing so for as long as she wants; that she may, if she so wishes, never stop, because there is nothing more important to do in the world—nor, perhaps, will there be from then on. Then with a sudden decisiveness she leans down to pick up Prince, who is a small Pomeranian, and rock him interminably on her lap. Next she begins to speak to him in a low voice, as if she needed to tell him a secret.

Everything around me is new. The breeze reaches us day and night, because the windows are never shut. I settled in here two days ago, when the last workman left. I am this place. I am this place, and I am located here, I am both at the same time. I constantly look out from the windows, the balconies, the terrace, to get a glimpse of the sea. We are just a few steps from the sea. Between us and the sea stretches only the street, the *malecón**, and the raised wall where children sometimes walk, parents holding them by the hand. The upstairs terrace has many columns. That's where I like to be. It's the area of the house I most prefer. The terrace has a roof, but no windows. Only columns, and between them, unceasingly, the sea air.

When will I see you? You haven't even walked by on the *malecón* like you have at other times. I've stopped counting the days since I last saw you. Why, sometimes, do you stop loving me like this? Every day I position myself behind the louvered balcony doors. I love you so much! I spend whole hours remembering the color of your skin, and your eyes, and your hair. I can't go on living without having you. One of these days perhaps I'll die. Will you come this afternoon? Yes, I mustn't doubt it. That way, at least I'll have all day long to hope and wait. I will wait for you, then I'll go on waiting through the afternoon, from behind the louvers. Don't fail me. Don't leave me waiting yet another time, until night falls and there's no longer any doubt that you won't be coming. Love, my love...!

Translator's note: *malecón*: Havana's seawall boulevard, initially constructed in 1901 and lined with large houses built in the grand style. During winter months when strong winds blow from the North and waves crash over the embankment, parts of the *malecón* are closed to traffic.

Meanwhile, she busies herself arranging flowers. She doesn't know how to do anything else. Not even sew. Or embroider. Or play the piano. How could she not have learned all that in school, when her sister...? She keeps an eye on the flowers, changing them as soon as they begin to wilt; it is a mania, she cannot stand them to wilt. Or perhaps she keeps changing the flowers simply because she doesn't know how to do anything else.

It is her uncle, or her father, who reads on the terrace, seated in a woven rocker. The breeze is too strong and it blows the pages of his book. So then he secures them with a small marker made of gold metal, worked precisely in enamel with leaves and flowers. While he reads, he absentmindedly caresses the enameled details with the ball of his thumb. Albertina comes up without making a sound and reads over his shoulder. "... I am totally convinced that the common opinion of naturalists is correct, that is, that they are all related to the wild dove (*Columba livia*...) ..." The breeze is too strong and it blows Albertina's dress and her hair.

Prince jumps up with a leap onto the chair, woven into patterns of spirals and circles. Since then he has not come down again. But he is not the same Prince that lay down underneath the cradle. He is the other one. And there is yet another. This one, the third one—or perhaps the first—is on top of the golden cage, trying to catch a little bird as if he, Prince, were a cat. Actually he is a diminutive black Pekinese. Julio, Albertina's father, Consuelo's father, husband of the elder Consuelo—long before any of those three relationships exists—attacks Prince with a small stick, a flexible little rod they have just given him as a present. Then he inserts the rod into the cage and moves it from side to side, until he drives the bird crazy, as it keeps flying around trying to find somewhere to perch. This scene lasts only for about two minutes because the bird collapses, exhausted, before the boy or the dog get tired. All of this happens here, in this room, the same one with the cradle and with Prince, the Irish setter, keeping guard.

"What could have been those memories that were torturing you eleven years ago, on an October afternoon?" The hand writing at this moment, my hand, only repeats something that another hand is writing at a moment exactly the same as this one, prolonged until now, on a gray and melancholy afternoon of Sunday, October 16, 1927. Another hand, holding not a fountain pen, but a long-handled pen that has to be dipped constantly into a white, yellow and blue porcelain inkwell, a very large inkwell with a tiny round receptacle on top filled to the brim with sepia-colored ink. The two hands, the two dates, August 28, 1967, October 16, 1927, blur into a present that, from now on, will not disappear again.

Everything around me—and I myself, who form part of this second-floor window of polished glass from where almost the entire house can be made out—is slightly less new. Sometimes dust settles for many long days on one of us, and no one bothers to remove it. I've heard it said that the house has deteriorated a little. Perhaps that's true, if they say so.

The sofa where the younger Consuelo, Jim and Prince or Prince, Jim and Consuelo are sitting—because the order can be reversed if desired—suddenly disappears, without my having noticed when this happened, has happened or is happening. In its place is a large chair upholstered in flowered linen, empty, and then (it is difficult to say then, or to think it, because everything occurs at the same time) the same large chair is occupied by the elder Consuelo, dressed in a long white robe with too much starch that covers her down to her feet. A ray of sun, entering through one of the balconies facing the *malecón*, illuminates only Consuelo's forehead, her not yet completely gray hair parted down the middle, and the legs of the marble statue of an Italian peasant girl placed atop a column. The statue is behind Consuelo, a bit to her left. I couldn't say if this happened before, or after, the moment when Jim, Prince and the younger Consuelo were together on the sofa, in the same place in the living room. It's the first time my memory fails me.

Albertina, pregnant, reclines amid the pillows of the chaise longue, wrapped in a warm bathrobe of velvety white plush. It is cold. No one knows —she doesn't know—why in the middle of winter they leave the windows open. They should think about the sea being so close, and that at that hour of the day it is windy, it is always windy. But she cannot get up to go shut them. Now she is very tired. This is normal. Prince, the Pomeranian, comes over and licks her bare feet. Then she realizes why she was cold.

"Has he called you again on the telephone? I told you already I don't like him. If your father were alive...or your brothers... You should be more careful. He's a stranger."
"Someday I'm going to marry him."

She is no longer there in that window, watching the sea; she is looking out another window where you can also contemplate the Atlantic, but now from her house in New York. Behind her, in the bed, her father lies dead. Her father has died of pneumonia in New York. She accompanies the body in a cargo and passenger ship that slowly heads down toward the Gulf. The ship makes calls at almost all the Atlantic Coast ports. From the deck, she (who could be Albertina or Consuelo, because in this circumstance they are interchangeable) spends hours looking toward land, just as before—here in this window and back there in the house in New York—she looked toward the sea. While she rests on the deck, covered up to her shoulders with a Scottish blanket the first officer has brought especially for her, she remembers things that happened when she was a little girl and was never apart from her father.

But she remembers gradually, both she and her memories wrapped in a gelatinous, dense substance, like that of dreams.

Julio, his two sons and his two daughters come every day to see the house, now that it is almost finished. He is glad to have decided it was worth making a slight effort to buy such a well-situated lot by the sea. Every day his children will see the ships come in and go out. That way, they will want to know other lands, to travel, not to stay anchored forever like him in Havana. Until now he has spent his life dreaming of the trip he will make to New York. Meanwhile, he has satisfied himself looking through the catalogues of import houses (he is a Customs supervisor) and twice a year ordering the most beautiful objects offered by representatives of the most prestigious companies of Paris and New York.

My fear of losing you is infinite. I'm jealous. Fierce feelings of jealousy eat me up inside. Jealous of all the desires you may have had. Jealous of those you might still have. When will we definitely be together? Today you mentioned something a woman once said to you, and it implied an intimacy of the kind you and I still haven't been able to have. I would like to penetrate into the deepest part of your being, to convince myself that there, inside, I'm the only one who matters in your life. And that you are mine, and mine alone.

We've never had a garden. Only a few flowers up on the flat roof. She was the one who wanted to make an arbor out of vines, thinking how much he would like it, but perhaps the sea air affected it badly. It never took well, and later on her mother came and planted jasmine. With the jasmine, what happened was that the breeze almost always blew away its perfume. But no one dared take it away. A plant like that, so fragile, so intimate, can't be touched again once it has been planted. She, who spends so much time arranging flowers inside the house, has never again thought about the small garden on the roof.

Consuelo has just sat down at the piano for the first time in so long. Music cannot be played while in mourning. "I never would have thought he would leave us so soon." "I want you to convey to your mother, to Albertina, to your brothers, the pain I feel along with you." "My old world is so far away! I have received a hard blow with this news." "Please believe I share the grief that has stunned all of you, from the bottom of my soul." Czerny exercises, after all, are not music. It's the same thing as practicing a lesson; no one could criticize her for it. But first she caresses the piano and remembers the day there was a cyclone, when the windows opened tumultuously from the force of the wind, the rain came in, and the piano, full of water and covered with leaves carted in by the storm, ended up in a corner of the hall, crushing the marble statue of a young Italian peasant girl as it rammed into her. The scales, with no transition, slide into a more complex harmony, and suddenly the house is inundated with the sonorous melodies of Beethoven.

Prince, up on the lap of the elder Consuelo; sitting on the sofa between Jim and the younger Consuelo; licking the bare feet of Albertina, five months pregnant and reclining on the chaise longue in the hall, is a black Pomeranian, so black that it is difficult to make out his eyes in the middle of all the hair around them. Prince, on guard beneath the cradle, being petted by the younger Albertina who is also pregnant, supporting her hand on his left front paw while she pets him, is a red setter with a smooth, shiny coat and big eyes the color of dark amber, at the same time tender and far away. When Prince is up on the sofa, he has a kind of cruel look in his eyes. When Prince lets the younger Albertina pet him he has a look that could be called melancholy, if he weren't a dog.

The new baby is several months old now, and she is a girl. The elder Consuelo holds her while she rests, seated with her back to the gold-framed mirror where all the light coming in through the balcony dazzles. For a moment when the movement of the waves is very strong, the mirror captures it, and the living room (situated on the first floor) oscillates briefly in the middle of the sea, at the same level as the ship on the horizon beginning its entry into the bay.

The elder and the younger Consuelos appear for an instant at a second-floor window, looking out at the sea, surrounded by the window frame as if there were someone outside ready to take their photograph. The elder Consuelo, standing forward, is still young, dressed in black and white with a tight bodice, resting a closed fan on the edge of the window; the younger Consuelo, to her left, is slightly behind in such a way that she can put her (right) arm around the elder Consuelo's shoulders while leaning a bit on the left shoulder, with her left hand lightly touching the left arm of the elder Consuelo. The daughter is dressed in white and has her hair tied back with a ribbon of the same color. Both contemplate the sea.

I think about those postcards I waited for so anxiously day after day and that filled me with emotion. You, between bronze lions in a park in New York. You, with your felt hat in your hand, in that same park, but now next to a tree completely bare of leaves. You, leaning on the rail of the ship, waving goodbye to me. You, climbing the three steps of the boarding house where you live (used to live) in Brooklyn. And sometimes the other postcards, with too-delicate colors, postcards with roses, lilies, hydrangeas, spikenards. All of them dated in the same place, between February and November of 1918.

There are empty lapses. Shorter or longer periods during which the living room is empty, and also the dining room, the rooms on the upper two stories, the terrace, and the small garden on the roof. As hard as I try to fill them, or at least to recall some memory, a living image, the anticipation of something not yet taken place, a contact, a desire, someone's dreams, the loose words of an interrupted dialogue, a silhouette behind the polished glass panes; as hard as I try to concentrate on all the traces that must have been left, I can't discover even the slightest sign. Everything stays mute. And then I, who form part of this window from where the entire house can be made out, am incapable of awakening something I imagine must be there, palpitating in the edges of things, as if held inside a hollow tuning fork. Sometimes when this happens, the chair woven into an excess of spirals, into a baroque lace of circles and movement, begins to stand out in solitary splendor apart from everything else. All the other objects disappear and the chair is left, in that place in the living room where Albertina, at twelve years of age, sits fanning herself for a period of time indefinitely prolonged.

But now Albertina is not present. Not present either, there at the back of the living room, almost within the luminosity penetrating inside from the patio, is that tall woman whose name I have forgotten, if I ever knew it (someone who left no memories, someone whom the house has forgotten). Only the chair is there, almost majestic, alive, pulling away from the fragile matter that makes up a serene permanence, an indestructible certainty. Only the chair is left.

The room has grown dark. The nun, seated in a high-back chair that is too stiff and straight, is reading a thick missal, or perhaps the Imitation of Christ. The others have gone to bed. In the room there is an intense smell of medicine, of alcohol, of old things, of concentrated dampness. The nun gets up, goes over to the bed, and sits down again, approximately every fifteen minutes. At that hour of the early morning there are no sounds to be heard, just every now and then the bell of a passing streetcar whirling light into the room as it goes by, after which everything becomes dark again. The nun reads by the light of a small green glass lamp. She gets up and goes over to the bed again, with the same indifferent manner, like someone carrying out a mechanical job with imperturbable precision. This time the elder Consuelo has stopped breathing. The nun takes the intravenous needle out of her bone-thin arm. Then she takes a small mirror from the dresser and holds it over Consuelo's lips, although she knows this is useless. Immediately she puts a white handkerchief pulled from her pocket onto the emaciated face, and lightly presses shut the partially-open eyelids. Only once she has done all this does she take down the crucifix that was hanging over the headboard and put it between Consuelo's hands, which she has first carefully placed one over the other. Then she goes to wake them up.

Albertina, at eighteen, pulls away from the place where she was fanning herself and sits on the marble top of a console table, clutching a scattered bouquet of roses. Then, her back to the mirror, she holds only one rose in her right hand, the one corresponding to the arm she leans on the staircase railing. The mirror duplicates the crystal chandelier and the excessive brilliance coming in from the balcony. She closes her eyes a little to avoid being blinded by the light.

Prince, the Pomeranian, runs around the house as if he didn't know where he was. Changes have been made. They've taken away some pieces of furniture and brought in others. And in addition, because of an extravagant whim of Julio's (opposed in vain by the elder Consuelo who is so austere), a room that will be his is being built on the top floor. A place he can go as a refuge, that will be noticed from the outside as an enclosed gallery jutting out from the façade, and that above all will be noticed because it breaks up the unencumbered harmony the façade had until now—crowned simply by the terrace colonnade—into ripples of carved borders, garlands and edges, into a vegetal profusion invading the upper part of the three gallery windows, extending down to the ironwork of their little balconies and to their glass panes, stained colored and white, decorated with fleurs-de-lys and the leaves of fantastic plants. Julio wanted to add a French detail to the house; once again, he wanted to console himself for not being able to travel to Europe. Now the house has its Art Nouveau gallery. The sunflowered window panes tint a violent light that acquires an orangey glimmer inside when the windows are closed. The objects already have started arriving, milk glass vases in blue, green, red, orange, enameled table lamps, sphinxes inlaid with mother-of-pearl, plates to hang on the walls painted with irises and hydrangeas and with languid-eyed women's faces, framed by long vegetal locks. Prince has found his spot: a chair with dragonfly-shaped arms that seems to have been made for just such a tiny creature. It is likely that this will be his permanent place. The gallery, of course, has been built on the northern façade, facing the sea. Julio likes to stay there for hours, doing nothing, contemplating his treasures, especially when a strong wind is blowing outside and the sea is churning, when the waves leap over the sea wall, wetting the street and even spattering the ground-floor portico. It is then, inside that profuse, somewhat delirious atmosphere where all voids have been filled to the brim, that he imagines himself to be in the stern of a sumptuous ship, heading towards the unknown. It is now 1907.

This morning I woke up feeling anxious. I had just had a very strange dream. A dream in which you, my love, were marrying my sister and then going away alone on a trip, a long trip from which you would never return. I got up tired, as if I'd been walking all night without stopping. This happens to me often. I dream, dream without stopping and wake up fatigued, worn out, empty inside, just as if they'd drawn all the sap from me, as if I were a plant no one bothered to water or take care of, abandoned in the darkest part of the garden. How silly I'm being! That's your fault, it's you who makes me feel this way, and it's because of you, because of your fickleness and the temperamental way you are, that I dream these things. My dear little boy, don't you ever pause to think about the way you're hurting me?

Consuelo takes down books from the shelves one by one, cleans them off and leafs through them lazily with no desire to read, just to take in effortlessly the stimulus of a phrase to savor slowly that afternoon when she goes to the concert, where she can fantasize, imagine, that all the melodies she hears are merely the development into infinity of that small phrase, found at random in a book about Bruges, the gray city, with drawings by a Spanish illustrator.

Once again, another of those lapses where everything stays silent. The lights, the sunlight and the lamplight go out, and the surfaces of things, where memories remain locked up, become opaque. How long will it go on this time? That is difficult to know, because in reality nothing happens within a kind of time where events follow one after another, where there is a past, a present and a future. Everything is happening now, in an unlimited now, where what was the past and what could have been the future vanish. Everything evens out, carries the same weight of existence, happens at the same time and never stops happening. For it has never ceased to be a possibility, and all words and things have found their place again in something called always. But the danger is that suddenly this always (assuming that the possibility of something coming about suddenly exists within the ineludible reality that things happen always) will turn, definitively, into an absolute nonexistence of time. A danger always lying in wait.

The calendars mark, at the same time, the following dates: September 21, 1929; March 25, 1955; December 2, 1964; October 10, 1916; October 31, 1930. A strange phenomenon that probably will not be repeated.

All the outer walls facing the sea now appear to be invaded by a fungus, or a malignant rash. First the paint cracked, and then it fell off in some places along with the plaster, both softened by the humidity. The columns of the portico and the upper terrace, the stone parts of the façade, show small holes opened up by the constant spray of the sea. For although the waves have never come up far enough to bathe the façade, the salt-heavy air ceaselessly deposits drops that pull away from the surf jumping over the retaining wall, the sea wall that separates the street from the rocks and the sea. The peculiar smell of the sea, brought in by the breeze or the wind, has taken possession of the interior of the house, which more and more has the character of an absurd ship careened on the ocean shore. The house is no longer the house, but an enclosure made for the sea, impregnated by its marine smell, taste, consistency. A mossy green peeks out from between the bricks uncovered by its corrosive, penetrating motion.

Albertina and Consuelo, standing by the console table and the mirror, speaking in low voices, go back vertiginously to a similar moment lived twenty years before when they were five and six years old, respectively. Albertina, with her short hair full of curls; Consuelo, with very long hair almost down to her waist, straight and tied back with a white ribbon. They are passing seashells back and forth to each other, seashells which are almost all broken; stones; pieces of rough wood and smooth glass, their cutting edges now removed; snails; coiled and hardened worms, preserved like fossils without decay; pressed leaves that resemble fish skeletons, their veins like bones; a seahorse; pieces of sponge; pebbles. They divide everything up silently, without arguing. Twenty years later in the same place, Consuelo—saying something in a low voice—gives Albertina a sealed envelope that Albertina hides inside the book she is holding, because at that moment the elder Consuelo approaches. During this entire scene, both Albertina and Consuelo have the feeling that they are repeating something they have lived through before.

Albertina sits at the open desk full of little drawers and lockers, and picks out from among several notebooks a black one, an oblong rectangle covered in Russian leather. She opens it to the second page and inscribes there: "Eleven years, how life goes on..." She writes in the elegant, slender, straight hand that is a part of her identity. It pleases her to write with an exaggerated perfectionism, as if that way she were leaving an eternal, inerasable trace. "The monotonous sound of the rain, hitting the tiles of the passageway, keeps reaching my ears. There is a sticky humidity in the air and only the night permits ... " All the rest is ellipsis.

The good thing is that now time has ceased to pass, and from now on (which will never cease being now) everything will be identical to itself. The instant when she held the pen for the first time to write in the album covered in black leather has remained suspended, latent and at the same time fulfilled; filled up with all that is in itself, with all that might have been, with an infinity of possibilities that will never be realized, and for that same reason will be present forever while memory exists and even afterwards, although this is not so evident. And just as that gesture has remained suspended in a deferral that only waits for the beginning of another identical gesture to be redeemed, reproduced and set, all other planned and completed gestures, projected and accomplished movements, spoken and pondered words, dialogues, goals, desires and dreams also have remained in a latent state.

Julio has ordered everything repaired: painters, bricklayers, carpenters and blacksmiths have returned. The house is looking like new. In this window one of the panes was broken, and they have replaced it. It's the one just next to me, and an intense cold has been coming in through that hole since the first days of January, when the North wind started. Now that the little girl is living in the house, sometimes she used to come over, pull up a stool and stick her hand through the hole in the glass. Then she would start to shout that it was raining, or cold, or that the waves were spattering up there. She liked to leave her hand outside for a long time, until it was totally wet. Now she can't do it anymore because they've put the glass back. Ever since they started repairing the house, they all walk around confused, from one end of it to the other, as if they didn't understand what was going on. Only Julio seems to walk with a sure step: he gives orders, stands up on chairs to point out details, takes down paintings to get them new frames, changes the placement of the furniture, the decorations, the family photographs. However, he doesn't allow them to touch a thing in the enclosed gallery, nor has he wanted to rearrange things there. What will they do now with everything that's been stirred up, that used to be silent, tranquil, peaceful? With everything that had been sleeping, and now is agitated and restless, as if someone had profaned the place where the remains of long-dead relatives were being kept? I don't know if they realize it, but I can feel it, I perceive around me a disquieting itchiness of buried life that has suddenly been brought up to the surface, violently demanding a release, a way out. As if the souls of people and things had been waiting for this moment in a prolonged purgatory, now impulsively and imprudently opened up, to be flung to the four winds. Why has Julio done it? Perhaps because he has always lived like this, as if he were floating above everything, with a kind of irresponsibility, with excessive gaiety, forgetting that the world is full of sadness and serious matters. I only know that if this goes on, if no one comes to put a limit on this avalanche of unbound emotions, something sinister is going to happen, something like a slaughter: the feelings stored away in the corners, the lethargic words, will throw themselves at the walls, will open up cracks in the floor and in the ceiling, will bring on an explosion like when a covered pot is put under enormous pressure, and the house will collapse on us and on them, alive and dead.

This month is as gray and rainy as that other one was thirteen years ago when we met... The water has a fatal effect on me: it makes me succumb to sleepiness. Thirteen years ago you gave me the bracelet I still wear around my ankle. And nevertheless...I'm growing sick from nostalgia, from desire. That infinite vertigo I feel seeing myself in your eyes! How long will the torment of living apart from you go on? Everything would be so different if you wanted it to be, if you decided to put an end to this waiting that is so sad, so cruel. You know that you are my only reason for living and even despite that... Today, since it was the anniversary of the day we met, just to celebrate, I don't know why, maybe so I could leave you the memory before getting too old, I went to the photographer's studio and had several pictures taken of myself. I'm so afraid! Afraid that all of what I'm feeling now could be extinguished, that my body will lose its flexibility, that my eyes won't overflow with passion, that my gaze will be extinguished... The photographer had me pose several times, always with roses in my hands; standing up, slightly in profile, with one rose in my right hand; facing straight forward, holding two roses this time in my left hand; sitting on a marble-topped table, clutching a scattered bouquet of roses in my arms. Other roses, many more, had been placed with studied neglect on top of the marble. He promised he'd have the pictures ready in three days. You already know they're for you, all for you.

The Italian peasant girl has disappeared from her pedestal, and it is impossible to locate Prince the Pomeranian, Prince the Pekinese or Prince the Irish setter—without forgetting that the three of them are one and the same—in any of the places where they ought to be. The cradle has disappeared too, and the wicker sofa, and the large chair upholstered in flowered linen, and the chaise longue that was placed next to the stairs. Clearly this is why it is impossible to find the dog (the dogs) anywhere. But the chair with the woven spirals hasn't disappeared, and he isn't there either. Could it be possible that they are completely gone, definitively? I don't think so, and will keep searching.

Until when will this summer go on? I long for the North winds, I want the wind to go wild and penetrate everywhere, for it to open up the louvered doors wide and make the chandeliers swing, so that I can hear the noise the crystals make when they bump against each other. Everything becomes so languid when it is sunny for entire days, one after the other without stopping! Now I realize that those lapses when everything is dead and silent, sunken into a profound lethargy, always occur in the summer. The humidity and the wind are necessary for things to go on living. And for them, also.

It is strange that the cradle (which had been lost), the chair woven in spirals now painted white, and the open casket where she lays with a rosary made of seeds from the Mount of Olives twined in her hands, all coincide in the same place. Probably because of that strange coincidence, Prince the Irish setter has come back to lie down beneath, reappearing after such a long time. It's an effort for me to see, because the atmosphere is clouded and visibility is erratic. The interior of the house, and all of them gathered for this reason, vanish or rather dissipate, as if they were only there in a dream. I think I can make out from here that all of them, women and men, are praying. Someone, however, has stayed standing next to the coffin for the entire time and now, an instant before they come to close it, has let a scattered bouquet of intensely red roses fall inside. Then, finally, the scene darkens.

From time to time, small corners light up again, there are flashes that briefly reveal a forgotten gesture, voices, slight shudders. The house has been empty for too long.

Translated by Kathleen Ross

ANA MARIA DEL RIO was born in Chile. She has taught Latin American literature both in Chile and in the United States. She has published two books, *Entreparéntesis* (1985), a collection of short stories, and *Oxido de Cármen*, a short novel which won her the María Luisa Bombal award in Chile in 1986. She also received the prestigious Letras de Oro literary prize in the United States in 1989 for her novel *Tiempo que ladra*, to be published by Editorial Sadat in Miami, Florida. (YEM)

WASH WATER

By Ana María del Río

The Little Girl is covered with starch, a light blue satin ribbon in her hair, combed and combed, even her thoughts coiffed into calligraphy. Walking along, her fresh-scrubbed knees bright, she came to the patio, twirling around on a wing of her dress freshly ironed on the wrong side over a little pillow. With a toe of her shoes, the Little Girl slowly dug in the damp yard next to the large cement tiles, buried on the leafy, black dirt, but from up above the altar of the kitchen window, the voice, covered with age spots, reached her over the hairs on the crown of her head.

"Wait here, quietly, okay? Don't leave the patio. Don't start running around dragging your feet over the gravel. Don't dig with the toe of your shoes. Don't go and get the hem of your dress dirty, I'd have to wash it again and that'd take all the starch out. Think it's easy to iron it? Oh, and don't tug at your socks with one hand. That's so low-class."

The reflecting pool had no gold fish in it, the ones that had big, unblinking eyes in the days when everything was in its place. Now the water swayed to and fro with an empty silence. In the middle of the patio, the apple tree flung a leaf down as a lament. Not even the chickens were moving.

"Wait right here, and don't move a muscle, hear me? We have to leave right away and I have to wash the others. I don't have a moment to breathe. Now remember—don't go and get your shoes dirty. They're patent leather—the best they make. I had to spit on them to get them shiny because right now there's no vaseline, I had no other choice," said the hand with throbbing veins, that moved down to the Little Girl's satin sash and picked at a tiny spot with its nail, pulling up her socks for the last time.

The wait kept on throbbing. Grains of wheat spattered over the tiles on the ground.

*   *   *

The Little Girl looks at herself and her eyes run down her dress, her eyelashes stiff with starch, her ankles rustled framed in bright white socks all the way to the toe of her patent leather shoes, and you heard the sound of wrapping paper where the skirt crisscrossed the blouse with a round apron in front and the velvet ribbon at the neck. The buttons march downward on a long row, decorating the front seam but at the bottom, the dress doesn't button; it's sewn up. The tucks and the gathers of the cloth turn up at her waist, at her chest, all over the body of the Little Girl, well dressed, well turned-out, in a blouse with long cuffs, silently looking at the sun scaling the thick wall of ivy. Her arms covered with tiny buttons and a linen jacket in case the afternoon turns cool.

The Little Girl fidgets then stands quietly. She won't be able even to play ring-a round-the-rosy. Or jump rope, because the bow of the sash at her waist holds in all the gathers and presses tight against her belly button and the elastic in her panties digs into her with every step and leaves a red welt.

The Little Girl struggles to get up, takes little steps like a doll barely wound up, careful, careful. She heads for the apple tree, she squatted down and threw a little rock at its roots:

"That's for not giving us any red apples," she said. From between her fat, mischievous hands the white lace of her dress was sticking out. "I hope they hurry up," the Little Girl thinks. "I hope I can wait and not breathe or move around like those people inside want." And she thought about the statues in the plaza waiting all their life for the second heroic step of a gallop that never came, just the first shot or the lone gallop in the midst of silence.

She has to stay there until they come to look for her, she doesn't know why they put gloves on her nor where they will take her. That's how it always is, but now the not knowing goes on longer than usual. The Little Girl would like to know a short cut for all this. They have taken hours, standing, in a slip, in the sewing room, ironing each ruffle of her dress and you'd better not move a muscle so you don't get dirty, see what a sacrifice it is getting all of you dressed, you all get your clothes dirty, and then if they don't look sparkling clean and white, they take it out on me, if you all only knew how hard I have to work to keep you looking decent.

"If you need to sit down, spread out a newspaper, one of those in the cellar, by the henhouse, a sheet without much ink on it," they told her.

The Little Girl looks at the long, long stairway that leads to the cellar where lingering colds come from and things you can't talk about.

Like the Belgian man's son, who had a bruise that lingered around his eyebrow, who was kind of a friend of hers, if she had gotten up earlier that Sunday she would have seen him leave, with the Belgian man who bought things other people weren't using anymore, and sometimes, young, tender girls, he would say laughing and give her a look.

And from the cellar came the thought embedded in her mind about what happened to the cook's sister-in-law, who threw herself naked over the cliffs at Quintero, a little piece of paper clutched in her hand forever and no one could read it because the ink was smudged.

She would have to go on standing, until they came to look for her and put on her coat. The starch in her dress has started to crack, like all imperious things. It explodes into millions of minuscule laments. The chickens peck rhythmically, their heads all in a row, eating machines shooting corn everywhere. No one would ever know what happened to the son of that Belgian professor who'd been in the Second World War and had eaten potatoes raw, skins and all and he used to beat his son for not knowing the twelve regions of Chile. They walked around in wooden shoes and knapsacks, like they were saying good-bye for good.

The Little Girl thinks that one day she will sit down, just the way she's not supposed to, in the gravel with her legs crossed to eat watermelon, in the middle of the patio, a watermelon all to herself, and no napkin, who cares if she spits the seeds everywhere.

*   *   *

Just then, the handyman shows up at the patio, the guy who also washes windows outside and cleans chimneys inside. He's big-faced man and the Little Girl looks at him and likes his face, his eyes like black bullets, huge, half-laughing and pointed ears, as if nothing were terrible in this life, his two hands as large as his tools.

The Little Girl walks toward him, very slowly down the gravel road, sucking her finger and the handyman, who is also an artistic gardener in lean times and who robs rubber planters to make ends meet, sees her and then looks at her fleshy, dull-colored knees and he touches them with his dirt-covered palm. The Little Girl feels like she has to pee.

The day huffs and puffs and the heat has dissolved into the reflecting pool. From the apple tree fall slow pale green tears, since it's the only tree with time to cry. The Little Girl remembers what she's heard in the kitchen: terrible things from the people who sop up stew with their bread and shake their heads talking about relatives. Terrible things are happening out there to anyone who goes out alone and—they sop up the gravy with more bread—the Nation isn't what it used to be, blood pours from the ground, and be careful what you say on the bus, where does blood pour out, wonders the Little Girl, looking at the ground, scraping it with her patent leather shoe, but nothing comes out, not even the good that was there before, nothing but a little piece of dirt that tumbles around next to the rocks at the edge of the reflecting pool. Even the halos on the statues of saints look flattened by the heat.

The handyman, who also has to act as fireman in the poor neighborhood where he lives because his house sits next to the water tap, and who doesn't go to union meetings anymore, he's a goner if he does, clips the grass with scissors along the edge of the little garden paths, which before, when times were different, had an English lawn, and the Little Girl edges closer and closer to him. The handyman moves closer to her, the Little Girl sees the whites of his eyes, they're yellowish and warm like fried things, the handyman is on his knees cutting the grass, the blood of the earth that has been ours for centuries flows through his veins, and someone shoves dirt in his veins, though the world may be topsy-turvy, falling to pieces, nothing is in its place, say the terrified grown ups, burying their faces in their napkins because they think that out of the dirt those people are going to come kill them. The grown ups miss the way it was before when the owner came first and he was the one who gave order to everything and the two classes of people walked separate paths and no one got confused, but nowadays...

Before everything was easier, but now people come down from the slums, people with thick-veined hands and who thumb their noses at everything, my God, what became of the line to get into heaven stretching from upper to lower class, intelligent to dull-witted, pale-skinned to dark, what became of the hell with pitch forks for the evil ones and the drunks and for those who didn't have any place to lie down and die and for people who got sick when they ate rich food.

*   *   *

The handyman, for whom two pairs of dark glasses are waiting in the street when he returns to his damp house tonight, is crouched very close to the freshly watered dirt and the Little Girl would stay there forever with her nose filled with damp earth if they'd let her, because it's the smell that takes her anywhere she wants. The handyman, who also dances around throwing knives at the show put on for sailors at the port, moves closer and hands her a fistful of black dirt with one hand, up to her nose and while the Little Girl sniffs and sniffs he starts at her ankle, moving very slowly over her his finger, finger, finger, over both her legs, the Little Girl sniffs the damp dirt all the way up to her gullet, her nostrils filled with little pink worms and then she sees the man's face up close, looking at her and his nose breathing her in like the damp earth, those eyes are really black almonds to those who have given him the eye longingly, eyes that have roamed Lord-knows-where, combing garbage dumps filled with rotten cats and rings still on their owners' fingers, he's really gotten around this guy who still can whistle with a nose so thin it looks like someone sewed it up and next comes his mouth that a warm wind pours from, you're right out of a painting and you have ears like triangles, and you don't smell low-class, says the little Girl. "No?" he asks looking at her. "What do I smell like?" "Wet dirt," answers the Little Girl. "But like something else, like a cigar, a lemon, smoke from a fireplace, I've got it!, you smell like vacations," says the Little Girl and the hand with the finger has reached her panties and then, softly, because it's an indecisive finger, it goes in, no, it doesn't want to go in, it pulls out, it goes in, pulls out, it pokes out of the lower edge of her panties, taking refuge in all the folds, sliding along the fat, damp legs, and takes refuge there, just farther than it should, but not too far, right there, says the Little Girl, looking at him, they don't let me scratch myself there. "Not there?" asks the handyman's voice softly, gone hoarse, like a tom cat, that doesn't know what it's getting itself into, is lost, the handyman, who signed, had to sign yesterday refusing to strike forever and ever and receiving his ticket with his thumb, from the company store, "Don't you like it there?"

His voice is so warm that it drips on her and he's no longer the handyman, just what remains of his face, what shows above his shoulders, the Little Girl feels like a roasted potato, but suddenly she's an impulsive Sleeping Beauty, her panties oily and limp, the juice of sleep flows inside her and he is stretching her out like a boiling shoe mold, the Little Girl squeezes her legs together a bit seizing his finger; the handyman, who's been marked since the day he was born, this guy can't pull the wool over our eyes, this guy is tied to the groups, takes his finger away and all that's left is the smell, *qué rico*, the Little Girl begins to moan rolling over her r's over and over she sits down by the reflecting pool and the finger, oh, that's nice, and because it felt like the finger didn't want to and she opened her legs up a bit for it, she opens her hole up wide for him so the finger could stick in deeper and deeper, I like this game a lot, know that?, but I shouldn't sit down here because I'm all starched, my dress, and we're going visiting and the Little Girl is pulling him by the hand, he lets himself be led off slowly, this guy is walking on eggs, but now we've sure got his number this guy is against us and has been playing the fool, got to pin something on him, anything to get him, the handyman's behind her, the two walking, the handyman gets to the garage, the Little Girl drags him behind the closet in the garage, where the cockroaches run out at night but during the day, there's a mat of grass growing inside, pale, sort of white, the handyman breathing in her ear, the Little Girl delicately stretches out, the handyman, who is up to his neck in trouble and just makes it look like he's against the union, moving his finger inside her panties, where something metal that is the Little Girl's motor starts up, the finger grows warm, gets wet, moves around, gropes and touch my thing real fast, murmurs the Little Girl, touch me, murmurs the Little Girl, hoarse, the closet creaks a bit, his mouth is so warm that the Little Girl opens it up, opens his mouth and sees his long tongue, long as his finger but wet, nicer, and pushing her dress behind her, look, I can't sit down on the ground because of the starch, see? and what if they check me over and the patent leather is delicate and they don't have vaseline to put on it, and the Little Girl climbs up on the shelf and the handyman, who still doesn't know what's good for him, he's got no record or mug shot until tonight when he gets back so we can land him and black-list him all in one trip, he's down on his knees at the Little Girl's orders said with her tongue boiling, barely making any progress between words, the handyman's hands sweat, he's a wet handyman, the handyman's tongue goes in, put-it-in-me, like the thrums from a sleepy fish's tail and then the Little Girl with her thighs opening up for him, a nut, holding up with one hand her organdy dress with the sash that's getting away from her, the stupid bows that are getting away from her, the tongue that is pulling out a little, don't take it out, wearing the white linen jacket you just have to look at to get dirty, sits down, straddles the handyman's face, who in his free time is a painter at the Mothers' Center and the tongue navigates a sea of something like rubber that comes from the

Little Girl along with the silent rumbling, like sobs of a temper tantrum, try-ing to keep up the wave of bronze that rises to his thing, sweet little thing, murmurs the handyman, who on his drunken days recites poems in the liquor stores and doesn't mind, the Little Girl twists around not forgetting her dress and the ruffles of its collar, each one has an eyelet at the end.

The finger, the tongue, finger, tongue, something really nice is happen-ing to me, something nice is happening to me, the Little Girl gallops on, not letting up, by now, round and round above him, all the cats and the turtles of the world are upside down, flat on their backs, the face of the handyman, who's really made some bad moves since the day he was born and that's why he's gotten mixed up in all this now, that's what everyone born on the other side of the river is like, this guy sneaks into the meetings after the night patrols are gone, they've got his number now, the handyman's face is half open and he sucks up every last one of the Little Girl's drops the velvet handyman even sucks up the entire Little Girl, slow, inch by inch, again, you want it again?, once more?, again?, yes the Little Girl cries from her stomach that wrinkles the back of her fancy party dress just a bit, mounted on the handyman's huge warm mouth, holding up her cotton-candy petticoat pleated between her sluggish, tangled-up hands, the handyman has been marked for months, tailed by the long arm of the law now his tongue with an urgent, desperate need of its own becomes a furious carrousel anchoring itself in slippery little rings, so nice, the warm finger, the oh-so-slow tongue, the Little Girl thinks her legs have changed into an iron statue, her eyes are rolling back, two iron swallows, the Little Girl turns so hard it's impossible to touch her, she sees with rumbling pupils, they bounce around above the handyman, who is no longer a handy-man and who tonight won't have a tongue long enough to confess the entire list of his crimes against the Law of Internal State Security, he was one of the bastards behind that blackout that went from Pudahuel to San Antonio, he takes the Little Girl in his arms and he starts to take his hand away softly, there, there, my baby doll, how nice, my little baby doll, the Little Girl's curls hang down sleepily and her legs are lifeless in tangles of thin, limp hair, the handyman carefully lays her out over the sacks behind the closet, the Little Girl sleeps hard for just an instant and not even in her ooze does she forget about the pleats in the front of her dress.

"That is so nice," says the Little Girl kissing the handyman, the guy an unmarked van is waiting for, in the prime of his life. "When can you do that to me again?"

"Did you like that?" the handyman asks looking at her as hard as he can amazed at how the Little Girl's eyes shine:

"You are so prett...," he says.

The Little Girl sticks her nose under the handyman's arm. "I like that smell," she says. "But Aunt Celia wouldn't. She'd give you some deodorant as a Christmas present." The handyman licks her, covering her with thick starchy saliva.

"Can you come everyday and do that to me?" says the Little Girl.

"Yes," says the handyman, who has a record of bad school conduct and gnawing hunger.

*   *   *

Then the voice that washes by hand, that scrubs the floor, that washes her face with a wet towel before she goes to sleep, called to the Little Girl from the kitchen door.

The Little Girl sets off dragging her shoes, smoothing down her dress, turns her attention to the thousands of bows, to the rose at the back of the sash, tugging at her socks with one hand.

"Leave you alone for a minute and look what you do," crows the voice. "Look what you've done to your dress. What have you been rolling in?"

The Little Girl is filled with amazement. Her mother is a witch, she thinks, she knows things without seeing them, and she's about to tell her about the nice thing the handyman did to her, when the voice says bitterly, pushing her:

"No! You're impossible. I'm going to have to wash you again. Look at your hair, it looks like an army of ducks slept in it... And that smell? You'd think you'd gotten into the wash water... What am I going to do with this child?"

The Little Girl looks down at her socks. They're soaking wet. She isn't going to tell Father Benedict about this. Suddenly she thinks she's from the underworld and she doesn't want to reach the stars with good acts nor get to the rose at the end of the brave road. She thinks she's never going to be like her cousin who's so grown up and wears convention as if it were perfume behind her ears.

Suddenly, the voice felt her socks and thundered: "Pig! You're disgusting! You wet your pants again. Now I AM going to have to spank you, understand?"

And, the voice pushed her toward the bathroom.

Translated by Pamela Carmell

LYGIA FAGUNDES TELLES is a São Paulo native who published her first collection of short stories while still an adolescent. Although she has a law degree, she practiced that profession only briefly and decided to devote herself fully to literature. She won the "Afonso Arinos" prize granted by the Academia Brasileira de Letras for her second book of short stories, *O Cactus Vermelho*. Other prizes would follow, including an international award for the French translation of her story "Antes do baile verde" ("Le bal vert"), from her collection of the same title. She has published several other collections of short stories, including *Seminário dos Ratos* (1977) and *Mistérios* (1981). Her novels include *As Meninas* (1973) and *As Horas Nuas* (1989), which received the Pedro Nava award for novel of the year, granted by the Secretaria de Cultura do Estado de São Paulo. (DG)

DAVID GEORGE is an Associate Professor of Spanish and Portuguese at Lake Forest College. He has translated a collection of short stories and a novel, both by Edla Van Steen: *A Bag of Stories* (Latin American Literary Review Press, 1991) and *Village of the Ghost Bells* (University of Texas Press, 1991). He has a also translated the novel, *Happy Old Year*, by Marcelo Rubens Paiva (Latin American Literary Review Press, 1991).

THE STRUCTURE OF THE SOAP BUBBLE

By Lygia Fagundes Telles

That's what he was studying. "The structure, I mean, the structure," he repeated as he opened his pale white hand and waved it in a circular motion. I sat staring at his imprecise gesture because a soap bubble really is imprecise, not solid or liquid, reality or dream. Membrane and hollow. "The structure of the soap bubble, understand?" I didn't understand. No matter. What mattered was my childhood garden with its green blowpipes, cut from the tenderest shoots of the papaya tree, which made the biggest and most perfect bubbles. One at a time. Love hastily measured out as my breath unleashed the process and shimmering clusters dripped from the tube and burst against my mouth. The foam streamed down my chin and soaked my chest. After which I'd hurl the tube and the bottle away. Only to begin again the next day, yes, the soap bubbles. But what about the structure? "The structure," he insisted. And his feeble gesture of approach and avoidance seemed to make contact yet keep its distance, take it easy, very easy, hey! Patience. Passion.

In the darkness I felt that passion tightening its slippery coils around my body. I'm turning into a spirit, I said, and he laughed, making his finger-wings tremble, his hand straining like a dragonfly on the surface of the water without clouding the bottom, wandering flush against the skin, yes, ritual love. Bloodless. Screamless. A love of transparencies and membranes, condemned to burst.

I even closed the window to keep it inside, but with its surface that reflected everything it charged blindly against the glass. A thousand eyes and it saw nothing. It left a circle of foam. That's all there was to it, I thought, when he took the woman by the arm and asked: "Were you previously acquainted?" He knew quite well we'd never set eyes on each other but phrases that cushion social situations gave him pleasure. We were in a bar and her Egyptian eyes were squinting. The smoke, I thought. They expanded and contracted until they were reduced to two slits of lapislazuli, and they stayed that way. Her bee-stung lips also tightened nastily. Too much mouth, I thought. Too artificially sensual. So how could a man like him, a physicist who studied the structure of bubbles, love a woman like that? Mysteries, I said, and he smiled; we amused each other by expressing fragments of ideas, scattered and random pieces of a game we played haphazardly.

I accepted their invitation to sit down. Their knees pressed against mine and the small table was littered with their glasses and breath. I took refuge in the ice cubes piled in the bottom of my glass and offered a suggestion: he could study the structure of ice, wouldn't that be easier? But she wanted to ask questions. An old friend? An old friend. Did you work together? No, we met on a beach. Where? Somewhere, on a beach. Oh. Her jealousy slowly took shape and overflowed thickly like a blue-green liqueur, the color of her eye makeup. It ran down our clothes, soaked the table cloth, it trickled, drop by drop. The perfume she wore was cloying. The inevitable headache: "I've got a headache," she repeated who knows how many times. A bright flash of pain that begins at the back of the neck and radiates to the forehead, along the eyebrows. She pushed her glass of whiskey away. "Bright flash." She pushed her chair back and before she had a chance to push the table he asked for the check. See you around sometime, ok? Sure, see you around, of course. Once outside he considered giving me the usual simple kiss but that made him uncomfortable and I came to the rescue. That's ok, dear, everything's fine, I understand. I'm going to get a cab, you go ahead. When I looked back they were turning the corner. What could they be saying to each other as they turned the corner? I stood in front of a shop window displaying luggage and pretended to be interested in a red checked plastic suitcase. I saw my pale reflection in the glass. But how could it be? I'll cry when I get home, I decided. When I got home I telephoned a friend, we went out to dinner, and he concluded that my scientist was perfectly happy.

Perfectly happy, I repeated when early the next day he phoned me to explain. I cut short his explanation at the *perfectly happy* and on the other end of the line I heard him laughing just as a soap bubble would laugh. The only unnerving thing was that jealousy. A perfumed omen—she on the other extension—made me change the subject immediately; she was the type of woman who'd listen in. I tried a more fruitful tack, ah, theatre. Poetry. She hung up then.

We ran into each other the second time at an art exhibit. At first, the same cordiality. The extravagant mouth. He pulled me aside to look at a painting he'd liked very much. We stayed away from her for five minutes. When we got back, her eyes were once again reduced to two slits. She massaged the back of her neck. She furtively rubbed her forehead. I said goodbye before the bright flash of pain started. It's going to turn into sinus trouble, I thought. The sinusitis of jealousy, a good name for a painting or an essay.

"Did you know he was sick? That guy who studied bubbles, isn't he a friend of yours?" Surrounded by a seething mass of people. Music. Heat. Who's sick? I asked. I knew perfectly well who it was but I needed to ask again, you have to ask once, twice, to hear the same answer; that guy, the one who studies that bubble nonsense, wasn't he my friend? Well, he was very ill, the information came straight from the lips of his wife, pretty, sure, but a bit on the coarse side. She'd been married to an industrialist, a fascist type who came over here with a forged passport. Even Interpol had been alerted. During the war he was involved with this fellow who claimed to be a count but was really nothing more than a smuggler. I reached out with my hand and grabbed his arm because he was going off on a tangent, and I could hardly make out my source departing, disappearing among legs, shoes, trampled hors d'oeuvres, tooth picks, descending the stairway in a dizzying escape toward the door to the street, wait! I said. Wait. What's wrong with him? This friend of mine. The tray balanced precariously above our heads, and the whiskey glasses clinked when it listed to the right, to the left, a single, sliding dance on a pitching deck during a storm. What was wrong with him? The man emptied half his glass before he answered: He didn't know the details and he could care less; after all, the only interesting thing was that the guy studied the structure of bubbles, how weird can you get! I took his glass and slowly drank the rest of the whiskey with the ice cube pressed against my lips, burning them. Oh god, not him. Not him, I repeated. Even though my voice was low, it penetrated all the layers of my breast until it touched bottom where all points finally converge, what was the right word? The bottom, I asked and stood smiling at the man in his bewilderment. I explained the game I used to play with him, with the friend, the physicist. My source laughed. "I swear I never thought I'd meet anyone who studied stuff like that," he mumbled as he whirled around to snatch two more glasses from the tray. Man, where's that tray been all this time? "Tell me something, didn't the two of you live together?" The man remembered to ask. I pulled down a glass flying through the squall. I was naked on the beach. Sort of, I answered.

Sort of, I said to the taxi driver who asked me if I knew where that street was. I'd considered trying to find out more via the telephone but that extension was a deterrent. And there she was, pleasantly opening the door. Happy to see me? Me? She complimented me on my purse. My undone hairdo. Not a sign of sinusitis. But it'll start up soon. Bright flash.

"We had quite a scare," she said. "But it's over. He's almost good as new," she added, raising her voice. If he listened he could hear us from his room. I didn't ask anything.

The house. At first glance it hadn't changed, but a closer look revealed fewer books. More smells: lively fragrance of flowers in a pitcher, fragrance of oils on the furniture. And her own fragrance. A clutter of mass-produced knick-knacks replacing rare objects now sitting obscurely on ancient book shelves. I examined her as she showed me a rug she'd woven during his stay in the hospital. And the bright flash? Her eyes remained wide open and her mouth was relaxed. Not yet.

"You could have gotten up, couldn't you, dear? But we've been spoiling you, haven't we?" she said as we went into the bedroom. Pleased with herself, she began to tell the story of a thief who'd broken into the cellar of the house next door, "mamma's house," she added as she rubbed his feet under the woolen blanket. The robber's screams woke them up in the middle of the night. He was crying for help 'cause his hand was caught in a rat trap 'cause there were rats in the cellar and the night before mamma had set a huge trap to catch this giant rat, remember, sweetie?

Sweetie, in a green bathrobe, was sitting up in a bed covered with cushions. His pale white hands were folded on his chest. Beside him, an open book with a title I put off reading so I never found out what it was. The story of the burglar sparked his interest but he was distant from the burglar, from me, from her. Now and then he gave me a questioning look that suggested shared memories but I knew he was being tactful, he was always extremely tactful. Attentive and oblivious. Where? Where could he be in his oversized bathrobe? Was it all those folds of flesh that gave me the impression he'd gotten thinner? Twice he turned pale, almost ashen.

I began to sense something was missing, was it a cigarette? I lit one which failed to dispel the agonizing sensation that something was missing. What was wrong there? When it was time for his pink pill she went to get a glass of water and he looked at me from over there, from his world of structures. Bubbles. For a second I relaxed completely: "Our game?" We laughed together.

"Swallow, dear, swallow." She held his head. And she turned to me: "I have to go next door to mamma's house and the maid is off. Would you mind staying a while longer? I'll be right back, it's the house next door. If you'd like something you'll find what you need in the kitchen, whiskey, ice, make yourself at home. The telephone's ringing, you mind if I...?"

She went out and shut the door. She shut us in. Then I realized what was missing. Oh, lord. Now I knew he was going to die.

Translated by David George

ANGELICA GORODISCHER was born in Buenos Aires, Argentina in 1928, but has lived in the city of Rosario for many years with her family. She began to publish stories in the 1960's, and since then has become one of the best-known writers of science fiction in Latin America, winning many nation al prizes in that genre. Her 1973 collection *Bajo las jubeas en flor* (*Under the Yubayas in Bloom*), with its story "Los embriones del violeta" ("The Violet Embryos") is the work for which she has become most famous. Some of Gorodischer's more recent texts, however, demonstrate another aspect of her writing, one that humorously communicates a clearly feminist perspective. Such is the case of "Camera Obscura", which also highlights the Yiddish culture of Argentina's Eastern European Jewish immigrants. (KR)

DIANA L. VELEZ considers translation an act of love. Sometimes it is unrequited, but nevertheless, it is always worth the effort. She has, to date, concentrated on bringing into English the work of Luis Rafael Sánchez, Rosario Ferré, Ana Lydia Vega and other Puerto Rican writers. Her collection of translations *Reclaiming Medusa: Short Stories by Contemporary Puerto Rican Women Writers* was published by Spinsters/Aunt Lute in 1988.

CAMERA OBSCURA

By Angélica Gorodischer

To Chela Leyba

Now it turns out my grandmother Gertrude is quite a character and you can't say a bad word about her in this house. So, since I've always said nothing but bad things about her all my life and so has the rest of the family, the only thing I could do was shut up altogether, and not even mention her name. Give me a break, who can understand women. But I can't complain on that score either, because my Chaya is as good as they come. Compared to her, I'm no great shakes. I mean, you only have to take one look at her, and believe me, everyone started to look at her as soon as she turned sixteen, so blonde and pretty and with those eyes and that way of hers, the way she holds her head up high. There wasn't a shadchen around who didn't think of the money he could make by marrying her off well, and I mean really well, with maybe one of old Saposnik's son's, Saposnik the motor parts dealer, and by the time she was seventeen, they were driving my mother-in-law nuts with marriage proposals and this, that and other, that she should aim high and what not. And that very Chaya who married me and not one of those rich boys, although, to tell the truth, I'm not doing too badly, she who at thirty is even prettier than she was at sixteen, and, who would even think she has two children to look at her—Duvedl and Batia they are and just like her they look but with my dark eyes—yes, that very Chaya who's always so sweet and so tender, went into a sudden rage when I said there was no reason for us to have grandmother's portrait with the gold-leaf oak frame hanging over our mantelpiece. A pretty penny it must have cost, that frame. And of all photographs, that one.

"Let's just drop the subject right now," Chaya said to me when I suggested we take it down. "I put that photograph up there and that's where it stays, period."

"Well, all right," I said, "but at least not that particular picture."

"And what other one would you suggest, if I may ask?" she said. "It was the only one she ever had taken in her entire life."

"Thank God for little things," I said. "Zi is gevein tzi miss!"

I don't even want to remember what she responded to that.

But it was a fact that my grandmother Gertrude was ugly. Ugly with a vengeance. Small, squat, dark, cross-eyed and walked with a limp. She wore these round wire-rimmed glasses that had a broken frame that had been fixed with a length of chicken wire tied in a knot. She always dressed all in black from the kerchief she wrapped around her head to the tips of her house slippers. My grandfather, on the other hand, what a tall, handsome man, with that full moustache of his, dressed like a country squire, filling the whole picture with his figure and those piercing eyes of his. You can hardly see my grandmother next to him; a good thing, too, I tell you. To top the whole thing off, all the children are in the picture, full grown and good-looking, all of them: six men and two girls. My uncles Aaron, James, Abraham, Sol and Isadore and Samuel, my father, the youngest of the men. Then there were my aunts Sarah and Rachel, seated on the floor near my grandfather. In the back you can see trees and part of the house.

It's a large photograph, mounted on heavy cardboard, tinted in that wine color they used in the old days, so you know the frame must have cost her plenty, especially with those curlicues and all. Not that I pay attention to such matters, I mean, Chaya can go and spend whatever she wants and I can say in all honesty that I've never let her or any of my children want for anything at all. As long as I'm able, they're not going to be lower than anyone else, no sir.

That's why this business with the photograph in the gold-leaf frame hanging over the mantelpiece hurts me so but I can't complain because it's my own fault for talking so much. But why shouldn't a man tell his wife things about his own family, huh? I would almost say it's her duty to know everything he knows about his own family. And yet when I told Chaya what my grandmother Gertrude had done, half jokingly and half seriously, I mean I made light of it a little to play the tragedy down a bit, but also with a little indignation because, after all, I wanted to let her know what's right and wrong and I didn't pick up any of those bad traits from my grandmother, when I told her about it one hot summer night when we had just come back from an air-conditioned movie and were sitting in the kitchen eating the ice cream we had bought since the kids were asleep, she stopped eating and, when I finished talking, she slammed the spoon down on the table and told me she couldn't believe it.

"But, it's true," I said, "of course it's true. It happened exactly as I've told you."

"I know," said Chaya as she got up and stood next to me with her arms crossed and an angry look on her face. "I know it happened just as you've told me, I can't imagine you would make it up. What I can't believe is that you'd be so unfeeling as to laugh at her and say she was a bad woman."

"But Chaya," I objected.

"Don't but Chaya me," she yelled. "It's a good thing I didn't know about this before we were married. A good thing for you, because as far as I'm concerned, it's a shame I'm only finding out now that all this time I've been married to an insensitive boor."

I didn't know what she was talking about and she walked out, slamming the door behind her. I sat there, alone in the kitchen, wondering what I had said to bring that on. I walked to the door but changed my mind. We've been married for ten years now and I know her pretty well, though I'd never seen her so angry before. Better let her calm down. I finished eating my ice-cream, put the rest in the freezer for the kids to eat later, wiped off the table and put the dishes in the sink. I checked the doors and windows to make sure they were locked, turned off the light and went up to bed. Chaya was asleep or making believe she was. I went to bed and lay back staring at the ceiling with its gray light filtering in from the open window. I touched her gently:

"Chaya, mein taier meidale," just like when we were courting.

Nothing. She didn't budge or respond, her breathing didn't change. "Fine," I thought, "If she doesn't want to, fine. She'll get over it soon enough." I pulled my arm back and closed my eyes. I was already half-asleep when I looked up at the gray light on the ceiling again because I thought I heard her crying. But I must have been mistaken, because, really, it wasn't that big a deal. I fell asleep for good and the next morning it was as though nothing ever happened.

But that evening, when I get home from work tired and hungry, what do I see but that picture of my grandmother Gertrude in the heavy gold-leaf frame hanging over the mantelpiece.

"Where'd you get that thing?" I asked, pointing to the picture.

"It was up on the top shelf of the closet with all the pictures of you as a child that your mother gave me," she said with a big grin on her face.

"No way," I said, reaching up to take it down.

"I'm going to tell you this just once, Isaac Rosenberg," she said very slowly. And I knew it was very serious because she always calls me Chaqui like everyone else does and when she calls me Isaac it's because she's none too pleased and she's never but once called me by my full name, "I warn you that if you take it down, I will leave this house and never return and I'll take the children with me."

She was dead serious. I know her. I know she meant it because the other time she called me by my full name she had also threatened to leave, that was a long time ago before we had the kids, and, honest, things were not at all like she thought they'd been but maybe it's better not to talk about that now. I dropped my arms and put my hands in my pockets and thought this was probably a whim of hers and, o.k. let her do as she pleases and maybe I could bring her around slowly. But I never could convince her and the photograph is still there hanging over the mantelpiece. Chaya got over her anger and said, let's go eat, I made rice kugel.

She makes it following my mother-in-law's recipe and she knows how much I like it, enough to have three servings without fail, and I know she knows and she knows I know that she made it that night for a reason. So I had the three servings but in any case I couldn't stop wondering about why Chaya had gotten so mad and why she'd put the photograph over the mantelpiece and anyway what it was with my grandmother that could cause such a ruckus in our house.

Nothing, I mean, she had nothing, not even a good Jewish name, Sara or Tiertze, like other people's grandmothers, no sir: Gertrude. It's just that she never did anything right or on time, not even be born. My great grandparents came over on the boat with their three children and my great grandmother pregnant. From Russia, they were coming, but they had taken off from Germany en route to Buenos Aires on the "Madrid" and, as soon as the boat reached the dock, right then and there my great grandmother's labor pains started up and everyone was thinking my grandmother would be born in the hold amongst the trunks and packages and all and with people coming and going all around, but I mean, they didn't know it was my grandmother coming yet because they didn't know it was a girl yet. But my great grandfather had to disembark because everyone was getting off and my great grandmother stayed up there twisting and writhing and seeing that the rest of her family was on Argentine soil and then she thought maybe it would be better if she, too, came down and gave her baby a chance to be Argentine. So little by little, by little and hanging onto the railing and gripping the sailor's hand who was helping her, she started down. And wouldn't you know it, right on the plank, my grandmother was born. So what happens? Yes, right there on the walkway she's born. My great grandmother let herself fall on the wooden planks amidst the ravings of that German marine whom nobody could understand except the other German sailors and with the help of a woman who ran up to help, right there was my grandmother Gertrude born in the world.

From the first right away, there was trouble with her. I mean my grandmother, was she Argentine or German? I think neither Germany nor Argentina could give a hoot about the issue but the immigration officials were full of regulations that had nothing in them about this particular case and nobody knew what to do. Besides which my great grandmother was pretty sharp and, despite having just given birth, she was hollering about how her daughter was Argentine as if anybody could understand what the heck she was saying and as if she was giving her new country a big gift. Some gift.

In the end she wound up being Argentine. I don't know who resolved it or how, probably some employee who wanted to go to lunch, and they entered her in the book as Argentine, born in Germany, though she had never left here to travel there and then it was another whole deal when they asked my great grandfather what to name her. I mean, they had planned to name it Ichiel if it was a boy but with the travelling and all it had never occurred to them to think what to name the kid if it turned out to be a girl, because a girl, too, needs a name, you know? So my great grandfather looked at my great grandmother, which was what he did whenever there was a decision to be made, but she was exhausted from the pushing and the heaving and the thing on the walkway and the yelling afterwards about her daughter's nationality, her daughter who, throughout this whole thing was on the counter, bleating like a sheep and wrapped in her father's jacket.

"Why don't you call her Gertrude?" says the guy from the immigration. "Gertrude's a nice name."

"What?" asked my great grandfather, of course, he asked it in Russian.

"My girlfriend's name is Gertrude," said the guy.

It wasn't until later, when they were leaving the port area with the family, that my great grandfather understood what the man had said, and that was only because Naum Weisman translated it for him after going to get the carriage. By then, my grandmother's name was already Gertrude.

"Yeah, yeah," said my great grandfather, a little confused by it all.

"Gertrude, understand?" said the employee. "It's a pretty name."

"Gertrude," said my great grandfather, as best he could and mispronouncing the r's, and that's what she was called, because that's what they named her right there.

I could tell you about the other problems that came later, with registering her as a citizen and with her birth certificate, but let's not even start on that. Things settled down after that and there were no problems for a while, I mean, there were problems but my grandmother had nothing to do with them.

So they stayed at Naum's place about a month until they got their feet on the ground, then they moved out to the country. My great grandfather worked as a farmhand for a while, but then he bought a bit of land and farmed it well, working from dawn until dusk at first along with the rest of the family. Later it got easier and they hired some peons. Things went along all right and little by little he got more land until he had quite a nice spread there.

By this time my grandmother Gertrude was sixteen and she was already horrible. Cross-eyed she'd been since the day she was born on the walkway from the German ship, but now she was thin as a rail, she walked with a limp and anybody would have thought she was a deaf-mute because she hardly ever spoke. My great grandfather had dozens of friends in the surrounding farms. They knew people in town, too, because every Friday night they'd stay overnight visiting a cousin of my great grandmother's. But neither he nor my great grandmother had much hope of marrying off that ugly and obnoxious daughter. Then my grandfather Leon appeared like a gift from heaven.

My grandfather Leon wasn't born on the walkway of a German or any other kind of ship. He was born the way you're supposed to be born, at home, or rather, at his parents' home, and from that moment on he did things right and on time, that's why he was so well loved and respected and nobody laughed at him or thought he was disgracing the whole family.

He was a widower without children when he showed up the first time at my great grandfather's place. He'd been married to Ruth Buchman, who'd died a year back. Somebody must have tipped off my great grandmother because she bathed and combed and perfumed her daughter and she warned her not to talk, though that wasn't really necessary, and told her to look down at the floor at all times so he wouldn't notice her crossed eyes, and also so she would look like the shy and wholesome girl she was.

And that's how my grandfather married Gertrude, not despite her being ugly but precisely because of it. They say Ruth Buchman was the prettiest girl around, the prettiest girl not just around those parts but for miles around, maybe even in the whole country. They say she was a redhead with hazel, almond-shaped eyes and a pouty mouth and peaches and cream complexion and long, delicate hands. They say she and my grandfather made such a handsome couple that people would turn around and stare at them on the street. But they also say she had such a temper on her that she made life hell for her parents, her brothers and sisters, her in-laws, her neighbors and the rest of the town, too. And she did the same for my grandfather Leon while she was married to him.

To top it all off, she never bore him any children: not even one was she able to give him, probably did it just to make him look bad, because it seems that that woman's poison would go even that far. When she died, my grandfather heaved a big sigh of relief, slept for two days straight, and, when he woke up, decided to let himself relax, wax his moustache every day and go into town on his horse in order to visit those friends of his which Ruth had managed to offend with her yelling and her bad manners.

But that couldn't go on for long; my grandfather Leon was a real man and couldn't remain single, besides which his house was starting to show signs of needing a woman's touch. His land was starting to look ragged, tthe point where some people had started figuring on buying it at a pretty low price eventually, thinking my grandfather would have to sell it dirt cheap. That's why one year after his wife's funeral he decided to marry again, and since he remembered the living hell he'd had with Ruth, he decided to marry the ugliest one he could find this time. He married my grandmother Gertrude.

The wedding party at my great grandfather's farm lasted three days and three nights. The musicians took turns playing out in the large shed while the women tried to keep up with the cooking in the kitchen, on the stoves out in the peon's quarters and in the three huge charcoal pits set up for the day out back. It's a fact that my great grandparents pulled out all the stops for the occasion. But to tell the truth, it was to be expected. I mean, they killed two birds with one stone that day; they got that weight off their backs and hooked her up with the best catch in the country no less.

My grandfather didn't spend the three days celebrating. Right away the next day she set to work straightening out her husband's place and nine months later my uncle Aaron was born and a year later my uncle James and eleven months later my uncle Abraham and so forth. But she never stopped working. You should hear the things my aunt Rachel would tell about how she would get up before dawn and prepare food for the whole day, clean the house and go out to work in the fields; and about how she'd sew at night while everyone else was sleeping to make shirts and pants and dresses and even underwear for all of them as well as table linen and bedsheets and everything else that was used around the house; and then the candy and preserves she'd put up for winter and she could handle horses and wrap, pack and carry a load as well as any man. And all this she would do with out saying a word, always quiet, always with her eyes downcast so nobody would notice her crossed eyes. There's no denying she lightened my grandfather Leon's load in the world, small and thin as she was, because she could take as much as two men put together. By late afternoon my grandfather would be done with his chores and he'd get all spiffed up and go off to town on his best horse with the fancy saddle which my grandmother had already prepared for him, and, since she didn't like being around people all that much, she'd stay at home and work on and on. And things went on that way and they had eight children and my aunts say that even when she'd just given birth, she'd get up and go on working. Never stayed in bed for even one day.

That's why what happened was so awful. Sure, my grandfather was no angel and he liked women as much as the next guy and they liked him, too, and one day some mean-spirited neighbor woman came to her carrying tales, but my grandmother never said a word nor did she cry or carry on or complain even though my grandfather suddenly remembered Ruth Buchman and went around for a while with his tail between his legs expecting the worst. I'm not excusing him, but these things happen and women know they have to look the other way sometimes and frankly, that was no cause to do that to my grandfather, she who should have been grateful to my grandfather for marrying her in the first place. And the irony of the thing was that my grandfather had wanted it to be a surprise gift for his children. And for my grandmother Gertrude, too, of course.

So one day, while all eight of his children were sitting around having dinner and my grandmother was bringing in the serving dishes and the pots, my grandfather started telling them about the travelling photographer who had come to town and they all wanted to know how he did it and how the pictures turned out and who had had their pictures taken and had he seen them. And my aunts begged my grandfather to take them into town so each one could have hers taken. Then my grandfather laughed and said he'd already spoken to the photographer and that he'd be coming out to the farm with his cameras and his equipment the next day to take pictures of all of them. My aunts laughed and carried on and kissed my grandfather and right away started trying to decide on what they'd wear and my uncles pooh poohed the whole thing, saying it was women's business and city slicker stuff but every once in a while you could see them straightening out the creases on their pants and looking at themselves sideways in the mirror.

And the photographer went out to the country and took that maroon picture of all of them that's now hanging over the mantelpiece, the one with the gold-leaf frame that Chaya won't let me take down.

The photographer was thin and medium aged with blond, curly hair. He had a pretty bad limp. He arranged the family members outside the house with their best clothes on and made up to look their best. All of them except my grandmother, who was dressed in black as usual and who hadn't even bothered to make sure she had on a decent dress. She didn't want to be in the picture and refused so many times that my grandfather had given up and stopped insisting. But then the photographer went up to my grandmother and told her that if anybody had to be in the picture, it was her; and she told him something that I'm not sure now if they told me what it was and I've forgotten, or if nobody heard what it was and nobody told me. And he told her that he knew very well what it felt like not to want to be in a photograph or something like that. I've heard this story dozens of times but I don't remember the exact words. So anyway, my grandmother got next to my grandfather Leon, among her children and they stood there like that, still and smiling for a good long while and that tall, skinny photographer with the limp took their picture.

My grandfather Leon told the photographer he should stay there that night so he could print the photograph and so the next day he could take some more. So that evening my grandmother fixed his meal too. And he told them all about his work and about the towns he'd been through and the people he'd met and about how people treated him and about odd things that had happened to him or or that he'd seen. And my uncle Aaron says he was looking at my grandmother the whole time as if he were talking only to her but who knows if that's true because he wouldn't have been the only one to notice it. What is true is that my grandmother Gertrude sat at the table with all of them that night and that was something new because she was always busy with getting the food on the table and serving them and going in and out of the kitchen while the others ate. When they were done eating, the photographer went outside to have a smoke because there was no smoking in that house and my grandmother brought him a bit of sweet liquor and I think, though nobody's ever told me, that they might have talked a little out there.

The next day, the photographer took pictures all morning: first my grandfather Leon by himself, then him with his sons, then him with his daughters, then him with all his children, then just my aunts all dressed up in their Sunday best; but my grandmother Gertrude didn't show up at all, she was busy with the housework. But isn't it strange that I, who never met her—I mean, my father was still a kid and hadn't even met my mother—I can picture her hiding, watching the whole thing from behind a housebeam while the food was burning on the stove. It's probably just something I made up because according to what they say, my grandmother never once burned a meal nor did she ever let any of the housework or the fieldwork slide even one bit.

The photographer printed the photographs and had lunch and in the afternoon he mounted them with an engraved border and dated them and my grandfather paid him. When they finished having dinner, it was late already, he took his leave and left the house. He had already packed his belongings in a worn carry-all he'd had ever since he showed up in town and he called out his goodbyes to them in the dark. My grandfather Leon was real happy because the photographer had taken some really good pictures but he didn't walk him beyond the door because he had already paid him for his work and he'd paid him better than anyone else in the area or even in town. Then they all came back inside and you could hear the horse galloping away and then silence.

When someone asked after my grandmother Gertrude, which to this day they argue about because each one claims he was the first to ask, my grandfather Leon said she was probably out there busy doing some chore and after a while they all went off to bed.

But in the morning when they woke up they found the lamps had never been blown out and the doors had not been locked. There was no fire going nor was there food ready and the cows hadn't been milked and there was no drinking water nor water to wash with nor bread in the oven. Nothing. My grandmother Gertrude had run away with the photographer.

And now I ask you: Am I right or what in not wanting that picture hanging there over the mantelpiece in my own house? What if the kids should ask about it? I said that to Chaya once. We'll see, she said. Well, of course they asked about it, I was right there when they did. Luckily Chaya had the sense not to go into too much detail.

"It's your father's family," she said "many years ago when they lived in the country and your grandparents were still living. See? Zeyde and Bubbe, uncle Aaron, uncle Isidore, uncle Sol."

And she named them all, pointing to each one without making a remark of any kind. The kids got used to the picture and didn't ask any more questions.

Even I started getting used to it. Not that I approve, mind you, what I mean is that I don't even notice it now, it just doesn't attract my attention unless I happen to be looking for something and have to move that heavy gold-leaf frame. One of those times I asked Chaya who happened to be in the room moving things around on the bookshelves:

"Are you ever going to tell me just what it was that made you put that picture up there?"

She turned around and looked at me right in the eye.

"No."

I wasn't expecting that. I was expecting maybe a chuckle and for her to say, sure, she'd tell me about it some day, or maybe for her to just tell me right then and there.

"'What do you mean, no?"

"Just no," she said without smiling. "If you need to have it explained, it means you don't deserve to have me explain it."

And that's where it stood. We found whatever it was we had been looking for; or maybe we didn't, I don't recall, but Chaya and I never again spoke about that picture with the heavy gold-leaf frame. But I still can't help thinking it's an offense for a family such as mine to have hanging, in such a prominent place, the photograph of someone who appeared to be such a good, hard-.working woman, a homemaker, who one day just up and ran off with another man, leaving behind her husband and children out of sheer spitefulness, without any good reason.

Translated by Diana L. Vélez

MATILDE HERRERA (1931-1990) was born in Buenos Aires, where she was a journalist and poet. Her three children—two sons and a daughter—and their three spouses all disappeared during 1976-77, the first year of Argentina's last military dictatorship. Her daughter and one daughter-in-law were pregnant at the time of their kidnapping; their unborn children were never found. Herrera was able to recover two other grandchildren who had been kidnapped with their parents. She went into political exile in Europe and became an outspoken leader of the resistance movement against the dictatorship. Subsequently she was a founder of the association *Grandmothers of the Plaza de Mayo*. Herrera's poetry was included in an anthology of Argentine poets published in Madrid, and later translated and published in Warsaw and Rome. After the end of dictatorship (1983) she returned to Buenos Aires, where she died in 1990 of cancer. "Eduardito Doesn't Like the Police" forms part of the volume of stories *Vos también lloraste*, written in 1982 and published in 1986. Each story is based on an anecdote told to the author by others or present in her own memory. Matilde Herrera also published *José*, a long testimonial biography of her older son narrated through his letters, in 1987. (KR)

RICHARD SCHAAF is known for his translations of Latin American writers and poets including Roque Dalton, Leonel Rugama and César Vallejo. His translation of Pablo Neruda's Spanish Civil War poem *Spain in the Heart* will be published in the fall of 1991 (Floricanto Press, Encino, CA). Currently he is translating a book of poems by Chilean poet Marjorie Agosín. He lives in Washington, D.C.

EDUARDITO DOESN'T LIKE
THE POLICE

By Matilde Herrera

You could feel the tension through the streets of the city. As the sun went down, passersby, commuters on the public transit, avoided looking at one another. Little by little fear and mistrust had taken hold of everyone. The best thing was not to offer a direct, disarming look at anyone. For on this day demonstrations had been called for just before dark in different parts of the capital.

Ana had nearly run from the bus stop. She arrived at the huge portal-entrance to the school and hurried in. The students were forming in the court-yard. She asked where the rally was being held. On the first floor, they told her, and you better hurry because it's about to begin. She climbed the stairs and ran into a lawyer friend of hers:

"If they don't hear us today, on this second anniversary of the massacre, they will forget forever. We have to force them to remember. If we let them get away with these sixteen murders, if we don't get justice about this now, who knows what they'll do later on... Today a new generation is taking to the streets to demand justice."

A new generation. Ana had decided to participate in this demonstration so as to accompany her younger son, just fifteen, who was going to his first political action.

When she entered the lecture hall, she joined the few adults present at the rally before leaving for the march. The young students were all very serious and tense. Some were only twelve, thirteen years old. Many of them were holding up a banner with the portrait of one of the victims. A few of the demonstrators were nearly the same height as their placards. Ana tried to pick out her son. There he was, in front, with his big placard, his blue eyes, his freckles. She didn't do anything to make him see her. He knew that she would be there. In any case, her presence was much more important to her than to the boy. She she saw a friend's son, watching her out of the corner of his eye. He avoided greeting her. Ana smiled to herself, inside; she felt a deep tenderness for the boy, he looked kind of like a dwarf, so serious, so small, sticking out in his blue jacket and tie. She wanted to go up front and kiss him and hug him. But she couldn't. That apparent hardness of the demonstrators that seemed to verge on solemnity was for a good reason. For the first time these kids had gotten together to demand something very serious: that justice be done about a mass execution. And of course for the first time they felt a bit weak in the knees.

The widow of one of the victims spoke at the rally. She was young, very young. It was possible to confuse her with any of the students present. "I won't ask for a minute of silence, in honor of our beloved dead," she concluded. "But I will ask for a minute of applause: that silence or forgetfulness will never be their fate."

The column formed. In front, the boys and girls with their placards, followed by the rest of the students. Behind, the adults closed off the ranks of the demonstration. Ana stood up on her toes, she jumped up, but she couldn't see her son any longer.

Just as they were leaving the school a fine drizzle started to come down. An older woman, with a small boy, had to work harder, limping, to keep up with the pace of the march.

"Allow me, señora? The cobblestones are slippery and you're liable to stumble."

She held the señora by the arm. The boy was half-running on the other side of his grandmother, trying to keep up. It was a very dark night. The older woman was stepping very cautiously, and little by little they were falling behind until they were the last ones in the column.

"We're falling back, it's the dampness that makes my leg go bad. You go on, señora, the boy and I will be fine."

Ana wanted to accept the offer. She was nervous and they were moving so slow, and the feeling that they were becoming separated from the others made her feel worse. She had no time to think over what she might do. The streetlamps were casting but a very faint light; then suddenly the wet cobblestones were lit up brightly by a light from behind. Even before turning around, Ana had sensed that the beam of light was sending a cold chill down her spine. And when she did finally turn around to look, the cause of her uneasiness was confirmed. A police car, moving slowly and steadily, was following right behind the demonstration. Only fifteen or twenty feet from the strange trio comprised of Ana, the older woman and the small boy.

"Grandmother, grandmother, grandmother!"

Clutching his grandmother's arm, clinging close to her body, the boy called out to her in an anguished whisper.

She kept walking forward, dragging her leg, as though nothing were happening.

The boy kept trying to catch a glimpse behind him, being very careful not to totally turn his head around. He started tugging rhythmically on his grandmother's sleeve.

"Grandmother, I'm scared!"

Ana didn't know what to do. She was supporting the older woman by the arm, and she too was glancing over her shoulder every so often in the hope that the car had left. And with her free hand she was now holding an umbrella, since the rain had intensified. The light beams from the police car were a bit defracted and dimmed because of the rain; but still they were there.

The grandmother was undaunted.

Ana decided to intervene.

"Señora, I think your grandson is very nervous, he says he's frightened..."

"Yes, I heard him. Eduardito doesn't like the police."

It was like a nightmare. Ana, who at this point also felt afraid, tried to calm the boy down.

"Don't worry. That car is only to make sure that nothing happens during the demonstration. This march is legal. Do you understand? The police have issued a permit. They're not going to bother anyone. Now there's no reason to be afraid."

And she felt really stupid. She was certain that her feigned calm wouldn't convince anyone.

"What is your name?"

"Eduardito."

"Eduardito. And your family name?"

"My name is Eduardito."

The older woman raised her head and stared at the woman. Then looking straight ahead, she spoke:

"Eduardito's parents are in prison. When they detained them they also took the boy. Before putting them all in the car they tore apart the entire house. The neighbors told me that the noise and screams could be heard from far off. In the police station they tortured his parents in front of him. They do that sometimes to see if the prisoners talk faster. After two days in there, they let Eduardito go. This is why he doesn't like the police. He can't even look at them. His papa and mama were transferred to the prison."

Ana thought she was going to faint. Meanwhile, they continued walking, it continued raining, Eduardito continued yanking on his grandmother's sleeve, and the car's headlights continued shining on them from behind.

"Let's go, grandmother, let's get out of here."

Ana wasn't sure if she was sweating or if it was the rain dripping down her face. And for the first time the older woman, still limping, addressed her grandson:

"I know you are afraid, Eduardito. I'm afraid too. But we're not going to leave this demonstration."

They hadn't stopped, but Ana had the sensation that the march was moving much slower. The older woman's words came out one by one. They were inundating her, as well as Eduardito, who now seemed less anxious. It wasn't that the fear had disappeared; no, it was here, oppressive, piercing. But as happened more than once to her and would be repeated in other circumstances, the stomach was in knots, the shortness of breath, the legs that only wanted to go the other way, gradually were transformed into a steady breathing, into a sensation of the ground being under their feet as they continued marching. No, the fear persisted, but the slightest reason that might justify it, at that very moment, served to check it. Ana realized that she was beginning to recover—even if only for a few minutes—her ability to think. As she continued marching, supporting the older woman by the arm, she was listening to her words:

"And I'm going to tell you why we are not going to leave. All those marching in front of us are young boys and girls. Some almost children. They are also afraid. But they're not stopping or leaving. Do you know why, Eduardito? Because they have understood that injustice is more intolerable than fear. You know that today marks two years since they murdered the compañeros at Trelew. Nothing about that has ever been cleared up. You know that your papa and your mama are prisoners, that they have harmed them badly and that they have suffered a lot. And still they haven't the decency to accuse them of one single thing. All these things, child, are terrible injustices. And because of all this and so that worse things don't come to pass, is why these kids have come out into the streets today. We too want justice and we're not going to abandon them. Don't look behind you, Eduardito. Let's keep marching. Forward. If papa and mama were free, I'm sure they'd have brought you here by the hand to be with the other boys and girls. Sing something, Eduardito, let's teach this woman a song. When you sing you feel better."

Ana didn't know if she wanted to sing along or start crying. She did know, however, that once again she was losing her strength. And the older woman, who she was trying to support, also realized it. She unhooked her arm and took Ana's hand. She then offered her other hand to her grandson, who seemed calmer keeping up alongside her and singing softly. It had stopped raining and when the demonstration stopped for a moment, they could move up some into the ranks. Being freed from the two light beams that were stabbing them in the back helped them to calm down.

Eduardito let go of his grandmother's hand and was now jumping up and down to the rhythm of the chanting: "They will see, they will see, when we avenge the dead at Trelew." "Never forget, never forgive, never forget, never forgive." Ana couldn't keep from watching the boy. What was passing through his little head, so full of brown curls? Was he listening to the words that kept beat to his jumping up and down? When would the fear return? Would he always be afraid? What would Eduardito remember in the future? What would his memory select in order to sustain him?

Her thoughts were interrupted by the older woman's voice:

"Eduardito always visits his parents in prison. I take him every week. One Sunday to the prison where his mama is, the next to visit his papa. Fortunately they are both close to the capital and we are able to see them. There are children who can hardly ever visit their parents because they have transferred them very far away. To the south, or to the north... It's awfully expensive to travel there. Tell her, Eduardito, tell the señora how happy you are when we visit mama and papa. They look well, at peace. For New Year's, they allowed the boy to go in and embrace his mama. It was something very special. They call it a 'contact' visit. All of us were crying. It was so moving. The difficult thing was separating them when the allotted ten minutes were over. But all the same it was beautiful to be able to embrace his mama. Isn't that right, Eduardito?"

Eduardito nodded his head amidst his jumping up and down, totally caught up in the different rhythms of the chanting.

"Because all the other visits always take place through a glass window, with microphones. Some of the boys think their mama is going to appear on television. Others ask why their mama no longer has legs. Others run away from their grandmothers and start pounding on the window; sometimes they get very agitated. So I explained to the child that his mother was sitting down behind there. And that jails are like this because for some reason the cops are the ones who are afraid. What power do we have against all these police armed with submachine guns? We, grandmothers and children. The boy understood me. At first, he couldn't get the hang of using the microphone but now he does just fine: he waits for them to talk from the other side, and then he holds the button down and he talks. Eduardito is very bright."

It had been a while already since the demonstration had turned down the avenue. Ana felt sick. She was looking at Eduardito like he was a Martian. At the same time she was trying to fight off the feeling of horror that was besieging her more and more. The placards had stopped moving up there, at the head of the column. There was no more chanting. For a few seconds there was a strange silence. Ana instinctively looked at the boy. He was totally rigid as though he sensed danger in every part of his body. The first gas bomb exploded. People started running back. The grandmother grabbed Eduardito by the hand and they both slipped through, over to the side. The confusion was terrible.

Ana took off, walking, and sat down in a bar in order to pass some time. She managed to calm down and persuade herself that her son would be all right. There hadn't been any ambulance sirens, or any police cars filled with young demonstrators. It had only been a police provocation. People would become more and more fearful, prudence will give way little by little to order. And so on.

She went back to the site of the demonstration. Only a few isolated groups remained. Surrounding them, the imposing empty city, the night, the silence, and rage.

She decided to return home. Suddenly she heard a voice calling her.

"Señora! Hey señora, we're over here!"

It was Eduardito's voice. They were okay. But she didn't want to turn around. She was afraid of facing the grandmother and the boy. She was afraid of prisons, of the screams of torture, of children in despair. She was afraid that her memory would remain marked forever. She hurried off.

Translated by Richard Schaaf

CLARICE LISPECTOR (1925-1977) was born in a tiny village in the Ukraine. She emigrated with her family to Recife, Brazil, when she was still an infant. Later, the family moved to Rio de Janeiro, where Clarice would graduate from law school in addition to making a living as a journalist and beginning to cultivate a career as a creative writer. Indeed, her first novel, *Perto do Coração Selvagem* (*Near to the Wild Heart*), was published in 1944, the year she took her law degree. Although Lispector had occasion to live in various parts of the world (including Washington, D.C.) during the years that followed, she returned in 1959 to Brazil, where in 1977 she died of cancer at age fifty-two. At the time of her death, Lispector was widely hailed not only as Brazil's premier writer, but as one of Latin America's most important narrativists as well. *Near to the Wild Heart*, for example, can easily be read as Latin America's first complete "New Novel." Later works would also gain international recognition, with *The Passion According to G. H.* (1964) ranking as one of the most powerful narratives of the 1960's and *The Stream of Life* (1973) gaining eminence as the prototype of the kind of writing that the French critic, Hélène Cixous, conceptualizes in the term "L'écriture Féminine." By the 1990's, Clarice Lispector had earned a well-deserved reputation as one of Western Literature's most compelling and unique authors. "Beauty and the Beast, or, the Wound Too Great" (1977) is a complex and fittingly enigmatic conclusion to the career of a brilliant writer. (EEF)

EARL E. FITZ is a professor of Portuguese, Spanish, and Comparative Literature at The Pennsylvania State University. He is the author of *Clarice Lispector*, *Machado de Assis*, *Rediscovering the New World* and numerous articles on Brazilian and Spanish American literatures. Currently, he is at work on a book-length study of post-structuralism in the narratives of Clarice Lispector.

BEAUTY AND THE BEAST,
OR,
THE WOUND TOO GREAT

By Clarice Lispector

It begins:

Well, then she left the beauty salon by means of the Copacabana Palace hotel elevator. The chauffeur wasn't there. She looked at her watch; it was four o'clock in the afternoon. And suddenly she remembered; she'd told "her" José to come pick her up at five, not figuring that she wouldn't do her toe and fingernails, that she would just have a massage. What should she do? Take a taxi? But all she had with her was a five-hundred cruzeiro bill and the taxi driver wouldn't have change. She'd brought money along because her husband had told her that a person should never be out and about without money. It occurred to her that she could go back to the beauty salon and ask for her money in smaller notes. But...but it was a May afternoon and with its perfume the fresh air was an open flower. So she thought it was marvelous and strange to be walking the streets—with the wind ruffling her hair. She couldn't remember when she'd last been alone, with just herself. Maybe never. She was always with other people, and it was in these other people that she saw herself reflected at the same time that it was they who were reflected in her. Nothing was...was pure, she thought without understanding. When she saw herself in the mirror—her skin tanned by the sunbathing that made the golden flowers close to her face in her black hair stand out—she had to contain herself in order not to exclaim, "ah!," since she was fifty million units of beautiful people. There had never been—in the entire history of the world—anyone like her. And even later, in three trillion, trillion years—there would still never be a woman exactly like her.

"I'm a living flame! And I light up this darkness again and again!"

This moment was unique—and during her lifetime she would have thousands of unique moments. Until, because of all that had been given to her and by her avidly taken, a cold sweat broke out on her forehead.

"Beauty can lead to the kind of madness we call passion," she thought. Then she added, "I'm married, I have three children, I'm secure."

She had a name to preserve; she was Carla de Sousa e Santos. The "de" and "e" were important, they marked her class and four-hundred years of being a Carioca*. She lived among the herds of women and men who, yes, who were simply "able." Able to do what? Well, simply "able." And yet above all viscous, since their being "able" was well oiled from the machines that sped around without the clamor of rusting metal. She, who was a potency. A generation of electric energy. She, who in order to rest used the vineyards of her country estate. She possessed rotting traditions, but now she was on foot. And since there was no new criterion to sustain her vague and great hopes, those same heavy traditions still strengthened her. Traditions of what? Of nothing, if she were wanting to purify herself. She had in her favor perhaps only the fact that their inhabitants had a long lineage behind them, one that despite being a plebeian lineage was still sufficient to give them a certain appearance of dignity.

Then, completely entangled, even while she thought about being a woman, which seemed to her a funny thing to be or not be, she also knew that if she were a man she would naturally be a banker, this being the normal thing that happens with "their kind" of people, that is, to people of their social class, to which her husband, however, had gained entry by dint of hard work and which therefore classified him as a "self-made man" while she was not a "self-made woman." At the conclusion of her long thought, it seemed to her that...that she hadn't thought about anything.

A one-legged man, dragging himself along on a crutch, stopped in front of her and said:

"Will you give me some money so I can eat?"

"Help!!!," she shrieked to herself when she saw the enormous wound on the man's leg. "God help me," she whispered.

She was exposed to that man. She was completely exposed. If she'd kept her appointment with "her" José at the Avenida Atlântica exit, the hotel where the hairdresser's shop was located would not have permitted someone "like that" to come around. But out on the Avenida Copacabana everything was possible; there were all kinds of people. At least different than hers. "Hers?" "What kind of people did she know that were 'hers'?"

She...the others. But, but death doesn't separate us, she thought, suddenly, and her face took on the beauty of a mask and not the beauty of a human being; for a moment her face hardened.

The beggar's thought: "that woman with the little golden stars painted on her forehead will only give a little if she gives me anything at all." Then, a little tired, it occurred to him, "She'll give me almost nothing."

She was terrified. Since she was almost never out on the street—she always went from place to place in a car—she came to wonder, is he going to kill me? She was confused and so she asked:

---

*A native or longtime resident of Rio de Janeiro.

"How much does one normally give?"

"Whatever you're able to give and wish to give," responded the beggar, utterly astonished.

She, who never herself paid at the beauty salon, the manager of the place sending a monthly bill to her husband's secretary. "Husband," she thought. What would he do about the beggar? She knew what—nothing. His kind don't do anything. And she...she was "his kind," too. Could everything be given to him? Could she give him her husband's bank, their apartment, their house in the country, their jewelry...?

But something that was the touch of avarice everyone has then asked:

"Is five-hundred cruzeiros enough? It's all I have."

The beggar looked at her, still astonished.

"Are you laughing at me, lady?"

"I?? No, I'm not. I've got the money right here in my purse..."

She opened it, took out the bill, and, almost seeking his forgiveness, humbly handed it to the man.

The bewildered man.

And after laughing and exposing his almost vacant gums, he said, "Look, either you're a really good person or you're not right in the head. I'll accept it, but don't go telling later on that I robbed you...no one's going to believe me. It would be better if you'd give me some change."

"I don't have any change, all I've got is this bill."

The man seemed startled. He said something that was almost incomprehensible because, having so few teeth, his diction was bad.

While all this was transpiring, his head was thinking, food, food, good food money, money.

Her head was full of celebrations, celebrations, celebrations. Celebrating what? Celebrating the strange wound? One thing united them: they both had vocations involving money. The beggar spent everything he had, while Carla's husband, the banker, collected money. His daily bread came from the Stock Exchange, and inflation, and profit. The beggar's daily bread came from his round, open wound. And more than anything else he must have feared being cured, she guessed, because if he got well he wouldn't have anything to eat, Carla knew that, and she thought, "after a certain age, if you don't have a good job..." If he were a boy, he could be a wall painter. Since he wasn't, he was investing in his big wound, in living and purulent flesh. No, life was not a pretty thing.

She leaned up against the wall and deliberately resolved to think. It was different because she wasn't in the habit of doing so and she didn't know that thought was vision and comprehension and that no one could simply order themselves to think, like this: think! Ok. But it happens that to resolve something was an obstacle. She began, then, to look into herself and things really began to happen. She had only the silliest thoughts. Like this: that beggar, does he know English? Had that beggar ever eaten caviar while drinking champagne? They were silly thoughts because she knew clearly that the beggar didn't know English and that he'd experimented with neither caviar nor champagne. But she couldn't stop herself from seeing born in her one more absurd thought: did he do his winter sports in Switzerland?

Then she became desperate. She became so desperate that there came to her a thought made up of only two words: "Social Justice."

Death to all rich people! That would be the solution, she thought happily. But...who would give money to the poor?

Suddenly...suddenly everything stopped. The busses stopped, cars stopped, watches stopped, people in the streets were immobilized...only her heart was beating, and for what?

She saw that she didn't know how to run the world. She was an incompetent, with her black hair and long, red fingernails. That's how she was, like in an out of focus color photo. Everyday she made her lists of things that needed doing or that she wanted to do the next day...that was how she'd become so tied to idle time. She simply had nothing to do. Other people did everything for her. Even the two boys...for it had been her husband who'd determined they would have two children...

"You've got to make an effort if you want to win in life," her dead grandfather had told her. Would she, perhaps, be a "winner?" If to win meant to be down on the street in the middle of the afternoon, with one's face smeared with make-up and spangles...was that what winning was? What patience you had to have with yourself. What patience you had to have in order to save your own little life. Save it from what? From judgement? But who would judge? She felt her mouth go completely dry and her throat on fire—exactly like when she'd had to submit to her school exams. And there was no water! Do you know what that's like—not having water?

She tried to think of something else and forget the difficult present moment. Then she remembered some lines out of one of Eça de Quierós' posthumous books that she had studied in school: "Lake Tiberíade glittered transparently, covered in silence, bluer than the sky, hemmed in by flower-filled meadows, by dense orchards, by porphyry rocks and by open stretches of earth between the palm trees and beneath the swooping of the turtle doves."

She knew this line by heart because when she was an adolescent she'd been very sensitive to words and because she desired for herself the same glittering destiny as Lake Tiberíade.

Unexpectedly, she had a murderous impulse to kill all the beggars in the world! Just so that, after the killing, she could enjoy the usufruct of her extraordinary sense of well-being.

No. The world was not whispering.

The world was SHOUTING!!! through that man's distended mouth.

The young banker's wife thought she wasn't going to put up with the lack of softness that they'd given to her so well made-up face.

And the celebration? What would she say at the celebration when she was dancing, what would she say to her partner who would be holding her in his arms...? The following: look, the beggar has sex, too, he said he had eleven children. He doesn't attend social engagements, he doesn't get into Ibrahim's columns or Zózimo's, he's hungry for bread, not for cake, he should, in fact, eat only gruel since he doesn't have any teeth to chew meat with.... "Meat?" She vaguely remembered that the cook had said that "filet mignon" had gone up in price. Yes. How could she dance? Only if it were a crazy and macabre beggar's dance.

No, she wasn't a woman given to swooning and fastidiousness and feeling faint or ill. Like some of her high society "colleagues." She smiled a little when she thought in terms of "colleagues." Colleagues in what? In dressing well? In giving dinners for thirty or forty people?

She herself, taking advantage of the garden in the summer that was extinguishing itself, had given a reception for how many guests? No, she didn't want to think about this, she remembered (why without the same pleasure?) the tables spread out over the lawn, candlelight..."candlelight?" she thought, am I crazy? Did I fall into some kind of game? A rich person's game?

"Before getting married, you were middle-class, the secretary of a banker with whom you got married and now...now, candlelight. I'm just playing at life, she thought, life really isn't like this."

"Beauty can be a great threat." Her extreme grace became confused with bewilderment and a deep melancholy. "Beauty frightens." "If I weren't so pretty, I would have had some other destiny," she thought, adjusting the golden flowers in her jet black hair.

Once she'd seen a friend become entirely undone by a broken heart and driven crazy, crazy from a powerful passion. After than, she'd never wanted to experiment. She'd always been afraid of things that were too beautiful or too horrible...she just didn't know deep down how to respond to such things or, if she did respond, whether she'd become equally beautiful or equally ugly.

She was frightened, like when she'd seen the Mona Lisa's smile that time in the Louvre. Like when she'd become frightened at the man with the wound, or at the wound of the man.

She felt like shouting out to the world, "I'm not a terrible person! I'm a product of I don't even know what...how am I going to understand this misery I feel in my soul?"

To change how she was feeling—since she didn't want to endure those sentiments any more and, out of her desperation, since she felt like violently kicking the man's wound—to change how she was feeling, she thought: this is my second marriage, that is, the previous husband was alive.

Now she understood why she'd gotten married in the first place and why it was an auction: who'll raise the bid? Who'll raise the bid? Then, you're sold. Yes, she'd married herself off the first time to the man who had "raised the bid," she'd accepted it because he was rich and because he was also a little above her in terms of social class. She sold herself. And the second husband? Their marriage was coming to an end, he with his two lovers...and she putting up with it all because a divorce would be a scandal: their name was, after all, often cited in the social columns. And would she go back to using the name she'd had when she was single? Until she could become accustomed again to her single name, she was going to delay things a lot. Besides, she thought, laughing to herself, besides, she'd accepted the second one because he'd given her considerable prestige. Had she sold herself to the social columns? Yes. She realized that now. If there were a third marriage for her—she was, after all, rich and beautiful—if there were, with whom would she marry? She began to laugh a little hysterically because she thought: the third husband was the beggar.

Suddenly she asked the beggar, "Do you speak English?"

The man didn't even know what she'd asked him. But, obliged to respond since the woman had just bought him with so much money, he did so evasively.

'Yes, I do. Aren't I talking with you right now? Why? Are you deaf? Then I'll shout: I DO."

Frightened by the man's enormous shout, she broke out in a cold sweat. She was fully aware that until now she'd pretended that there really weren't people who were worse than hungry, who spoke no language, and who were anonymous multitudes begging just to survive. She had discovered this, yes, but she had also turned her head and covered her eyes. Everyone, yes, everyone...they know and they pretend they don't know. And even if they didn't pretend, they were still going to have a bad time. How couldn't they have? No, they wouldn't, not even this.

She was...after all was said and done who was she? Without commentary, especially because the question had lasted only an instant of a second: the question and its answer hadn't been thoughts of the head, they were of the body.

I'm the Devil, she thought, remembering what she'd learned as a child. And the beggar is Jesus. But...what he wants isn't money, it's love, that man got lost from the rest of humanity, just like I got lost.

She tried to force herself to understand the world and she succeeded only in remembering fragments of phrases said by her husband's friends: "Those plants will not be sufficient." My God, what plants? Minister Galhardo's? Would he have plants? "Electrical energy...hydroelectric?"

And the essential magic of life...where was it now? In what corner of the world? In the man sitting on the corner?

Is money the mainspring of the world? The question became her. But she tried to pretend it wasn't. She felt herself so, so rich that she became ill at ease.

The beggar's thought: "Either that woman's crazy or she stole her money, because a millionaire she can't be," millionaire for him being only a word and even if in that woman he'd wanted to see a millionaire incarnate: hey, man, where have you ever seen a millionaire get stopped on the street? Then he thought: is she one of those tramps who charge their clients dearly and who are always keeping some promise?

Later.

Later.

Silence.

But suddenly that shouted thought:

"How is that I've never realized that I'm a beggar, too? I've never begged for spare change but I've begged for love of my husband, who's got his two lovers, I beg for the love of God that people find me pretty, happy, and acceptable, and the clothes of my soul are ragged..."

"There are things that equalize us," she thought, searching desperately for another point of equality. Suddenly, the answer came: they were alike because they had been born and they would die. They were, therefore, sister and brother.

She felt like saying, look, man, I'm pathetic, too; the only difference is that I'm rich. I...she thought ferociously, I'm close to discrediting the money, threatening my husband's standing in the market. I'm about ready, any moment now, to sit down on that strand of sidewalk. My worst disgrace was to have been born. Having paid for that damned event, I feel like I've got a right to everything.

She was afraid. But suddenly she took the great step of her life; courageously, she sat down on the ground.

"You see, she's a communist!" thought the beggar, half-clearly. "And as a communist, she would have a right to her jewels, her apartment, her wealth, even her perfumes."

She would never again be the same person. Not that she'd never seen a beggar. But she'd seen this one at the wrong time, as if she'd been shoved and gotten red wine spilled on her white lace dress. Suddenly she knew; that beggar was made of the same material she was. Simply that. The "why" of it was what was different. On the physical plane, they were equal. For her part, she had a median culture, and he didn't appear to know about anything, not even who the president of Brazil was. She, however, had a keen capacity for understanding. Was it possible that she'd lived up to now with a kind of built-in intelligence? But what if she'd done so only recently, since she'd come into contact with a wound that was asking for money to get something to eat...had she only now come to think about money? Money that had always been evident and visible to her. And the wound, she'd never seen it from so close up...

"Are you feeling ill?"

"I'm not ill...but I'm not well, either. I don't know...."

She thought: the body's a thing that gets sick and that people carry around. The beggar carries himself.

"At the dance this evening madame will feel better and everything will have returned to normal," José said.

In truth, at the dance she would be regenerated by the things that were attractive to her and everything would return to normal.

She sat back in the seat of the refrigerated car casting, before departing, a final glance at that companion of an hour and a half. It seemed to her difficult to say good-bye to him, for he was now her alterego "I," he would be a part of her life forever. Good-bye. She was feeling dreamy, distracted, her lips half-open as if there were some words about to come out of them. For a reason she didn't know how to explain...he was really her. And so, when the driver turned on the radio, she heard that the codfish produced nine million eggs per year. She didn't know how to deduce anything from that phrase, she who was in need of a destiny. She remembered that as an adolescent she'd sought a destiny and had selected singing. As part of her education, they had easily arranged a good teacher for her. But she sang poorly, she knew it herself and her father, a lover of operas, had pretended not to notice that she sang poorly. But there was one moment when she began to cry. The teacher, perplexed, had asked her what was wrong.

"It's that, it's that I'm afraid of, of, of, of singing well..."

"But you sing very poorly," the teacher had told her.

"I'm also afraid of singing even, even, even worse. Really, realllly badly!" She was crying and never had another singing lesson. That story about seeking understanding through art had happened to her only once; later, she dove into a kind of oblivion so profound that only now, at age thirty-five, because of that wound, and because she knew she had to sing either very badly or very well, only now was she disoriented. For a long time she hadn't listened to what they call classical music because to do so would awaken her from the automatic slumber in which she was living. I...I'm just playing at life. In the upcoming month she was going to New York, and she discovered that that trip was like a new lie, like a bewilderment. To have a wound in your leg—that's reality. And everything in her life, from the moment she'd been born, everything in her life had been soft and smooth, like the leap of a cat, like a charade.

(riding in the car)

Suddenly she thought: I didn't even remember to ask his name.

Translated by Earl E. Fitz

SILVIA MOLINA was born in Mexico City in 1946. There she writes works of prose fiction, does editorial work and teaches at the National University, where she studied Hispanic literature; she has also studied social anthropology. Molina has published three novels and two collections of stories. Her first novel, *La mañana debe seguir gris*, won the important Xavier Villaurrutia Prize in 1977. Silvia Molina's prose draws upon her keen observation of life in her native capital city—often focusing on the middle and upper-middle classes—as well as her knowledge of indigenous and provincial cultures. "Autumn" is included in her most recent collection of stories, the 1989 *Dicen que me case yo.* (KR)

AUTUMN

By Silvia Molina

For Juan Manuel de la Rosa

Remember the eyes that looked upon you,
the voices that trembled for you.
Body, remember.
—Cavafis

Evening was falling as for the last time I imitated the steps of a defeated woman.

I was ready to put an end to misunderstandings. I was returning to the same, familiar hotel room, remembering his arm lifted to wave goodbye, his grimace of pride. I did not forget for a minute that he was suffering more than I.

I rode up in the elevator like a person who is to give the jury the evidence that will condemn an innocent man. In my heart, I hoped no one would be in the room, but I would ring the bell and wait, breathing in the indefinable smell of the corridor. I felt I wanted to abandon myself to the anguish postponed for so many months.

He will be there, I thought, pacing back and forth, wearing only his pajama trousers, repeating over and over that we can change the past. All that suggested to me the unpleasantness to come, a pitiless way to deflect the recriminations of an immutable outcome I would not have changed anyway, for any price.

Before the door of the elevator opened I had reconstructed his trip, the whole complex of absurd and familiar explanations he used to rationalize a foolish past. I saw him landing in Mexico City, only this morning—a large man, hearty, unruffled—saw him taking a taxi to this hotel on Insurgentes. I imagined him unpacking, bathing, and then sitting a long while in that armchair, not knowing what to do. From time to time he must have got up to look out the window, hoping to catch a glimpse of the Parque Hundido, but he would only have succeeded in inhaling the sickening odor from the food stands below. He would have felt it was silly to be nervous, and that he would let me talk, and reason...and then make me see where I was wrong. He would, nonetheless, be afraid I might change my mind. Maybe, he would think, if he hadn't rushed this trip, if he hadn't come so suddenly, if he had just asked me to write him a line....

I remember the moment when after he left Mexico City the last time I thought I would never see him again.

I could sense him calculating, making plans that turned into different plans, mulling over our meeting, what he was prepared to propose. I could see him yawn and smile as he waited for me.

When I first met Julio he was still not twenty, and I had a six-year old son. He had fallen in love with my fits of assurance, with the fact I found everything simple and entertaining, that I had introduced him to our endless conversations in cafes, to afternoons with Bergman and Allen, to nights with Gurrola and Ibáñez, to books by Cortázar and Onetti, to the music of Mozart and Debussy. I had teased him, seduced him, with my slenderness, with my bewildered expression, with the sexy gaze I hid behind my eyeglasses. I knew he could not contain himself when he looked at my breasts and that he lost his head over my abrupt shifts of mood.

Strangely, Julio had begun to recognize himself in me, as if suddenly in me he was finding himself. Watching me, he began to grow and expand.

As for me, during that time when I had just been divorced, I loved him deeply. I sought his company to avoid sinking into loneliness and the vacuum of failure. I submersed myself in him, until he was overwhelmed by a feeling of death.

At first we wrote to each other. He came to Mexico City as often as money permitted, but with time we began to be lovers by mail, and I surrendered to other arms.

Julio tried to reclaim me; he persisted in not growing up, in living an idealized past, a romantic novel.

Now when he saw me he would have to understand that prolonging our relationship would be grotesque, that it was incapable of nourishing memories any longer. To do so would be a heartless game that would end in my humiliation. He would also have to accept that he still is not thirty, and that I have a sixteen-year old son.

When I saw the door to his room at the end of the hallway, I knew that the years had settled comfortably on my shoulders; I felt sorry for him and, in memory, I loved him. I was no longer frightened by the possibility of his becoming one of those ghosts we cannot free ourselves from, one of those spectres that dominate and tyrannize us.

I discovered I was free of the past and of responsibility for the present. I was ready for Julio to understand that he would not have my body because it had been possessed by time.

Like the bougainvillea past its flowering leaves a smooth carpet of blossoms beside it, so years ago I had fallen, dewily moist with pleasure, at Julio's side.

Translated by Margaret Sayers Peden

SYLVIA MOLLOY, a literary critic and writer of fiction, was born in Argentina. She currently holds the Albert Schweitzer Chair in the Humanities at New York University where she teaches Latin American and comparative literatures. She previously taught at Yale University, Princeton University and Vassar College. Molloy is the author of a novel, *En breve cárcel* (1981), translated into English by Daniel Balderston as *Certificate of Absence* (1989), and of numerous short stories. Her critical work includes *La Diffusion de la littérature hispanoaméricaine en France* (1972), *Las letras de Borges* (1979) and *At Face Value: Autobiographical Writing in Spanish America* (1991). Considering fiction and criticism as two complementary aspects of the same exercise, Molloy is usually happiest when she can work simultaneously on both. She is currently writing a new novel, as yet untitled, and preparing a study on dandyism, decadence and the notion of national health in turn-of-the-century Latin America.

SOMETIMES IN ILLYRIA

By Sylvia Molloy

When she first saw the girl she knew that something different lay in store for her. She knew—in a manner of speaking. One, among the thirty faces that greeted her that first day, held her attention. She quickly took in the quizzical eyes, the unruly black mane above them, the very white skin. The schoolroom was small, not as long as it was wide. There were four horizontal rows of green desks facing her and Maria (when she took attendance, trying to match faces and surnames, she found out her name) sat in the back row, next to the aisle that divided the class in two. Lifting her eyes from the roll-book that the fussy headmistress wanted checked off always in the same blue ink, she once more met that gaze, those eyes half-open yet intent, scrutinizing her. Then she realized that the surname she had called out, mispronouncing it perhaps, was unmistakably Irish.

She set about building up enthusiasm, as she always did when meeting a class for the first time, presenting her subject as if it were a privileged topic in an otherwise humdrum curriculum. Year after year this enthusiasm was rewarded (this was surely why she kept it up) by the admiration, even the fear of successive groups of teenagers. She would often hear them speak of her as she crossed the courtyard during recess. They used an article before her name, as they did with the names of other, much older teachers, to mock them. In her case, she was sure, the intention was different: they wanted to set her apart from the others, as a diva is set apart from lesser singers. That knowledge and the flattering image she so laboriously worked on to fend off the treachery of insomnia, allowed her to keep up, in her teaching, something akin to fervor. And, if her enthusiasm occasionally struck her as forced, she would quickly tell herself that at least it helped someone learn something, in that foreign school whose standards were certainly not her own. She was aware that this line of thought was barely rewarding but, once she had persuaded herself of its reason, she was usually able to go back to sleep.

The school was old (and surely has not changed), sprawling over two city blocks that in her grandparents' time were probably open fields dotted with turn-of-the-century summer estates. It was easy to imagine the dirt roads, easy to ignore the new, gaudy California-style houses with red roofs and decorative rubber trees that had invaded the neighborhood, easy to replace them, mentally, with old mansions and *paraíso* trees. Due to the vagaries of zoning laws, two of those mansions, belonging now to the school, were left together on the same block. Deprived of their original gardens and trees, of their very own limits, sharing space and forced to mingle with their neighbor, they felt like society belles in decline, of whom one whispers that they must make do with the little they still have. In what was doubtlessly once the main parlor of the more lavish house, the one with the marble staircase leading up to it from the garden, was the school library. Its holdings were limited, not for lack of funds but because very little reading got done in that school. The rest of the building had been gutted. Flimsy dividers had been set up to create new spaces, with the exception of two rooms left intact: a study, perhaps, and the dining room. There the Englishwoman who had left London for Buenos Aires as a governess and had ended up founding a school for girls, either slept or kept guard. In another part of that house—in the basement, she believes—the boarders took their meals. The other old house, relegated to a corner of the same city block, was even more melancholy. It bore a name for which all clues seemed lost: Villa Barga. While she was never inside, she knows that boarders slept there, girls she barely knew, ruddy English girls, faintly smelling of damp underwear, whom she rarely saw in her classes since they usually dropped Spanish the moment it stopped being a requirement. She imagined them immersed in nostalgia or dreaming of unending sports. One of the few she ever had as a student surprised her one day by admitting (she can't remember how the confession came about, perhaps on a last day of class when she allowed them to chat) that what she most missed from home was the *mate* she sipped everyday at daybreak in the kitchen. The girl lived in the provinces, in the *camp*, as the English called the Argentine countryside, near Venado Tuerto. She spoke Spanish with an accent, had eyes not quite as blue as Maria's, and that lackluster, ashen hair the English insist on calling blond.

The classrooms where she taught were on the same block as the old houses. Of more recent construction, they were shoddily built, and their damp walls, for some reason, attracted huge, probably harmless spiders. They would slither down the curtains, disturbing the students who exaggerated their terror. Since she herself was bothered by spiders, she opted for a quick solution: she had the desks moved away from the window and when a spider fell, when she saw it beginning to fall, she would come up to wait and would squash it underfoot. Leading to these classrooms—more like sheds, really, senselessly (perhaps angrily) put up against the walls of one of the old mansions—was a long tiled walk overhung with wisteria that, in the spring, seemed like a fragrant, endless, blue tunnel. Years ago, when she had arrived at the school as a substitute on her first teaching assignment, the length of that tunnel was for her a source of comfort: she was young and afraid. She taught her first class in a low voice, well aware that the eyes that had greeted her as she entered, to appraise her and gauge her authority, were rapidly abandoning her as the clock ticked on. Each desktop raised was a defection. She knew that there was a book or a magazine on nearly every lap, while she continued to speak into the void. As she left that first class, she vowed, once and for all, to look her students straight in the eye. And now someone, from the back of the classroom, was staring back.

This had happened before. Throughout the years she had learned to defeat adolescent stares and disarm their insolence. Face-offs, mute challenges, were difficult in the beginning: she had to do two things at once, teach and, at the same time, save herself by keeping up a presence that would overcome the wandering eyes and the raised desktops. To her surprise she was able to do these two, apparently very different things simultaneously, in one gesture. She cultivated this modest theatricality that nearly was (but really wasn't) an imposture. It was no better than what that English school deserved, with its contempt for Spanish, with its annual school plays (Shakespeare plays, always the same ones, directed by the Englishwoman and performed on the lawn) so fastidiously planned that they seriously jeopardized the course of study. The school year would end with that performance, on the lawn at the foot of the marble staircase leading to the more important house, a lawn transformed into the forest of Arden (or sometimes into Illyria) where more or less Argentine girls recovered (or learned the hard way) an intonation that the headmistress deemed ancestral, invariable and unique. The lawn was bordered by symmetrical flowerbeds and had, in its center, a French-looking fountain having less to do with the passionate fantasies of England than with the very concrete desires of the rich Argentine burgher who had built the house. In that school, however, everything—except Spanish—could be rescued, adapted. A student of Italian descent whose English was shaky was asked, on one occasion, to play Malvolio. The girl did it admirably well.

She herself taught math, in Spanish. Maybe that was the reason she could hold the girls' eyes so well: they came to her exhausted, needing something to hold on to as they emerged, at two o'clock, from their morning immersion in things of the Empire followed by compulsory gym. Morning hours, when students were fresh, were devoted to English. The girls that came to her were of different origins, usually immune to British fervor, even when an odd drop of two of English blood ran in their veins. They were girls that remembered in amazement how the headmistress had gathered the whole school in the assembly hall one morning to listen to a crackling, barely audible radio coverage of the future queen of England's wedding. That very same year, the English flag was lowered one last time in India, but no one at school spoke of that, or no one remembered. Besides these students in her class, there was the occasional English girl, like Howard who sipped *mate* in Venado Tuerto. And then there were the Irish, like Maria.

Maria did not dive under the desktop; Maria was not a bully, as she had feared; Maria just stared. She grew used to that face in the middle of the back row, even began to seek those motionless, impassive, half-closed eyes. Maria's features were neither coarse nor prominent. Two or three generations settled in the country before her (as was her own case, though her national origins were different from those of Maria) had successfully muted the Celtic brutishness, leaving but traces. One day, as she was explaining the lesson, she saw that Maria's cheeks were very lightly freckled. But no, coming to think of it, she could not have seen those freckles from her desk. It must have been some other time, as she was walking up and down the aisle while someone, perhaps Howard in her faltering Spanish, recited a theorem so slowly that she turned it into a story of suspense. Another afternoon, as she was leaning against the back wall waiting for students to take down dictation, she saw Maria bite a thumbnail till it bled. And she also saw, as she looked at the injured hand on the copybook, that Maria took very little, practically nothing, down. Instead she saw, in the margins, drawings totally unrelated to the course, unexpected illuminations that she would never have dared dream of herself, either as a child or as an adult, the detail of which distressed her. When she left the classroom she couldn't stop thinking of Maria. As she walked along the wisteria-covered walk—only there were no flowers now, just bare stalks rolled around flaking posts—she reached a spot where the pattern in the tiles broke, a spot that as a child she would have recognized as magical, and she trembled, remembering the drawings.

That was when she began to seek out Maria, not only watching her but spying on her. She caught herself in acts she would have found unthinkable, ridiculous, and that now tempted her like a slight, pleasurable vertigo. For example: she would cross the courtyard during recess and deliberately walk past Maria's group, knowing that they would leave off talking while she was near—their silence was quite obvious—but feeling strong and, in an odd way, part of the group by the very act of interrupting them. As if her world were, for a moment, that circle of awkward girls, with their legs and arms grown too long and their tummies still round, figures at once anxious and arrogant, with that strange assurance one adopts in stages of transition and that she, for a second, would live through again. Maria was the center of the group, of that she is sure, although the girl gave not the slightest sign of authority. Maria stood in the group like the others, lowered her eyes like the others, was silent like the others. If she ruled, she did so underhandedly.

Often, she would see some of her students on the train she took back to the city. She found those encounters outside school (but still feeling like school, what with uniforms, books carried under arms or in satchels) quite pleasant since they prolonged an atmosphere that, as the train drew closer to Retiro station, seemed less and less real. Sometimes a girl would sit next to her, shyly, wanting to chat. Even now she remembers one, eyeing the cigarette she had just lit up. The girl's name escapes her but she can still remember the hat on her head. According to the Englishwoman's strict rules, any student seen without a hat on the way home from school would be severely punished. But then, who would have reported the culprit? Rules or not, many heads were uncovered as soon as the train (like a ship, leaving territorial waters) reached the first station. That soft, black velvet hat wasn't at all bad, she thought, it gave even the most rebellious girl a vague, orphaned air.

She has forgotten the name of the shy student who sat down beside her but not the names of the others, the Irish girls. Maria is not the only one she remembers. Haughty and rebellious, these girls bore names that in nineteenth-century Britain had designated scoundrels and adventurers; now, in twentieth-century Argentina, they had become the names of the genteel and the well-to-do. In their defiance, the Irish girls unwittingly imitated their oppressed forebears: they spoke English as little as possible, even in the morning period when, if caught, they risked being expelled. This resistance faltered half way through the school year, not because the Irish girls had discovered the sweet pleasures of obedience but because they all considered themselves (some quite accurately) born actresses, and were eager to be chosen for the play. They were often quite pretty, healthy, tall for their ages. If they came from mixed national backgrounds—their mothers were frequently of solid Argentine stock—the results were harmonious, combining the best traits on either side so as to compound them instead of opposing them. On the train back to Retiro, the Irish girls unfailingly removed their hats.

The last thing she would have expected, on that train, was for Maria to come up to her, as she did one day. Her hat, pushed all the way back, was about to fall off: the train was close to Vicente López station. Shapeless, with the stitching on the brim long gone, it looked as if it had belonged to others before her. Not at all unlikely, she thinks, since several of Maria's sisters had preceded her in school. Besides, it was far too small. (A moment later, when the train started to pull into the station, she saw that Maria was the first to take off her hat. But then she also noted, half an hour later when they reached the city, that Maria was the only one to put it back on.) Standing in the aisle next to her, looking down at her so that she, in turn, was forced to raise her eyes, Maria was saying that she needed to speak to her. It would be better to speak at school, she answered, there would be more time then, wouldn't there, during recess or at the end of the class, perhaps. Cornered, she could think of no other way out: what could Maria want to speak about? Maria accepted this, smiled at her for the first time, and she felt uncomfortably happy.

It took some time for her to realize what Maria wanted. Rather, it took some time for her to realize that the meeting Maria had asked for would not take place immediately, and that, of the two, she would be the one to wait. In her mind she cursed Maria, because she felt, welling inside, a social resentment she had stifled so successfully she never thought it would still be there. And she cursed Maria because she knew, full well, that she would have to keep on waiting. It was around that time—it was spring and unseasonably warm—that she began to look at students in a different way when she taught. She would let her eyes wander over them as if they had only one blurry face, and would then look out the window (all the while teaching her lesson), out at the wisteria's blue tunnel, by then in full bloom. Rehearsals had begun on the lawn: it was *Twelfth Night* that year. Also around that time, she devised another ritual: instead of leaving the classroom as soon as the bell rang, she fell into the habit of lingering. She very nearly went back to her old awkwardness, to the shyness that had paralyzed her long ago, when she first started teaching. The smell of the wisteria became intolerable, as did the break in the tile pattern on the walk, as did the wait. She took it upon herself to approach Maria.

And she did. On one of those sweltering afternoons (it really was unseasonably warm), at the end of the period, she stopped Maria on her way out and said she needed to speak to her. The other girls, sleepy from too much heat and geometry, spilled into the white-hot courtyard while Maria, waiting by her desk, amiably looked at them filing by. She, in the meantime, busied herself gathering up books and papers. At some point (this is a difficult afternoon to remember), Maria leaned back on the blackboard covering herself with chalk, a blurry theorem on a blue serge tunic. Then, when she told Maria to sit, Maria surprised her by installing herself at her own desk, leaving her to stand against it. With a voice she barely recognized as hers, she finally asked, "Some time ago you asked to speak to me. What about?"

Still sitting, Maria does not answer. How old can she be? Fourteen, fifteen at the most. Suddenly she feels lonely, daunted by the silence that this child, frowningly absorbed in drawing with her finger on the chalky surface of the teacher's desk, is imposing on them. "Yes," Maria finally says. "Yes, I really did want to speak to you." Spurred by the immediacy of something she knows is there, nearly within her reach, something she does not want to lose, she hears herself say, "Perhaps we should talk about those drawings in the margins, don't you think?" Unintentionally, she has given the phrase a mocking turn. Maria makes a face and, as she stands up, erases her drawing with a sweep of the arm. Maria never spoke to her again. As the two of them left the classroom and went into the courtyard, she felt exhausted, as one who has held her breath for very long, for a lifetime perhaps.

She has two more memories of Maria, from that year which turned out to be her last at that school. The day after the encounter, at recess, although she was at a good distance from Maria's circle, she overheard shrill words, a phrase purposefully loud so that it would reach her: "I won, because she came to me and I didn't tell her beans." The other memory is more pleasant. That year Maria, in her unfamiliar English, played Curio. One night at the beginning of summer, on the lawn with the French fountain, she heard Maria say, "Will you go hunt, my lord?" And then, when the Duke asked what there was to hunt and Maria answered, "The hart," she, who was lost amidst the spectators, was touched to tears when she heard the pun in the answer, a pun she doubted Maria was aware of. For a moment, it was a comfort to think that the words had been addressed, perhaps, to her.

Translated by the author

CARMEN NARANJO is an acclaimed novelist, poet, and short story writer from Costa Rica. "A Women at Dawn" is from her most recent collection of short fiction, *Otro rumbo para la rumba* (1990). Previous collections include *Ondina* (1983) and *Nunca hubo alguna vez* (1984). Naranjo has served as Minister of Culture and as an ambassador for her country, and now heads EDUCA, the Central American University Press. (LB)

LINDA BRITT is assistant professor of Spanish at the University of Maine at Farmington. Her translation of Naranjo's *There Never Was A Once Upon A Time* (published by Latin American Literary Review Press) appeared in 1989. She has also published essays on Naranjo, Josefina Plá, Federico García Lorca and Miguel Cervantes.

A WOMAN AT DAWN

By Carmen Naranjo

I didn't want to open my eyes and find the clothing, my clothes, the ones I wore yesterday, heaped haphazardly on the chair; verify that those wet and dirty shoes are mine, too. I never want to wake up, come out of my stupor, and realize that I am insignificant down to my bones. No matter how I search my memory I can't recall a single happy or crazy moment, one that's capable of making me reach towards hope, and I can't remember ever feeling that I'm on firm ground but yet flying. It's that capacity to fly that offers another perspective and allows one to see across times in a clear and inspiring synthesis. I am lacking in everything that exalts, inflames, idealizes; I am in reality constantly grounded at a small airport to which no airplane arrives and from which none takes off. On dry land, isolated, confined in the everyday, without even a window that might show me a different view.

Of course you don't want to get up, or even open your eyes and achieve something in life. You are laziness personified, inertia is liquidating you. Infantile, you are an aged child who believes that things, good things are going to fall out of the sky for you, through the effort and the grace of the Holy Spirit. You are out of step, in these times one cannot walk with a rhythm other than that of the fast lane. Acts are summoned, sought, planned for personal benefit. Now there's not even a crack to let generosity in, we are in the kingdom of egoism in which the only valid sum is that of profits. One wins if one plays the game with the firm strategy of achieving the goal. You are behind, way, way behind, I would say out of bounds, out of the game, out of the world, without even the desire to live and triumph. You spent your best years within yourself, in front of the mirror trying to figure out who you are or else immersed in that false dream of escaping. Yes, now you don't want to open your eyes and wake up, although you neither sleep nor stay watchfully awake. Ingenuously you believe that you are winning against time but time, your time, has run out and it has begun to claw away at you with its cruel hand that knows how to let ruins decay of their own will.

Why have they never let me enjoy the slowness that intoxicates me? Why don't they know that I don't belong to the world of light, of speed, of exhibitionism and of loud voices? I have been "making" myself in silence, everyone else will read "unmaking." I have to think a lot before I say something, since I have no facility for words and others see me as so clumsy in matters of speech that they avoid me. At any gathering I am surrounded by empty chairs because it's really not pleasant to sit beside someone who has nothing to say, no comment to make. I understand them and I even identify with them because I am quite sure that I would never sit next to a person like myself. I would love to relate something really interesting, to create an image that would make them remember me as vivacious, entertaining and even ambitiously agreeable. I imagine another person telling some stranger what I said, what I opined, what comment I made as if it had an exemplary value worthy of quoting and mentioning. But I am not that way, nor can I ever be so. The truth is that it doesn't interest me, nor does it seem important. I prefer to dream and in my dream, walk wherever I want with incredible agility and pronounce an address or a speech worthy of the most distinguished professor. Also in my dreams, I love and am loved with an intensity that would not be understood in this age of convenience. My beloved doesn't have a face or a name, but I see him as a very generous human being, noble even, capable of giving himself to me completely and exclusively. He is mine only and I am only his. Why don't they understand why I like so much to dream?

When you finally open your eyes, you don't say anything, not even hello, as if you've never heard of "good morning." You get up for a cup of coffee and you look tired, alien to your surroundings, it would seem that nothing interests you, perhaps that's the case. However, there's something that betrays you, something strange that constantly declares your sadness, your silent pain, the strange and meaningless battle that you take pleasure in hiding. There are many false things that I have been discovering in your common postures. For example, the stammer that you seem to suffer and your difficulty of responding to questions, your silence protesting the effort of continuing. I have deciphered it; you have a keen desire for calling attention to your strangeness, your eccentricity, but you're mistaken because you only give the impression of being mentally retarded and in this day and age that doesn't attract anyone. Can you imagine how everybody sees that caricature of a person? A burden that they are not inclined to hoist on their backs, a tepid being, helpless, who perhaps takes care of her necessities away from the appropriate site and whenever she wants, bored, sickly, stunned, expressionless, the kind people call useless and try to keep at a distance, thousands of kilometers away from them. In reality, you are an insufferable romantic, you believed in good faith that pity still exists and so you dedicated yourself to cultivating it. Pity, because you are ugly, foolish, slow, stupidly mute, not remotely sympathetic, lacking even the slightest trace of charm or of intrigue, showing not even the most minimal hint of conformity. Do you really believe that in this age knights in shining armor still exist, ready to right distant wrongs? Neither are there princes who, with their kisses, restore miserable beings who have been reduced almost to animal states. We lack friends who can transform ugliness into beauty, poets who can make pedestals for those who have fallen from them due to their own clumsiness. Today there could be no Dr. Faustus because even without receiving an offer, almost everyone is inclined to sell themselves, no matter if the buyer is the devil himself.

Children are given mirrors very early in life so that they can learn to identify themselves. They are shown where to find their eyes, their nose, mouth, ears, hair, forehead, chin, jaws, teeth, eyebrows, tongue. In front of the mirror I discovered my ugliness, everything is big, too big, all out of proportion and with a sickly accent, yellowish, highlighted in certain parts with red while others had a greenish hue. But that was nothing. The main thing showed up in the clumsy gestures, uncoordinated, too slow, incommunicative, that kind of girl, insecure, lacking in grace and communication, and one mustn't desire or love her because she'll be a problem, an impediment, a step backwards in the family pedigree. I was already classified in the card-catalog under "sub" and I accepted my fate, I did nothing, I didn't make the slightest effort to be otherwise, I let myself be carried toward my destiny by fixed and unchangeable forces. I submerged myself in the nos, no to any other opportunity, no to the perhaps if you persisted, if you put a little effort into it, if you were committed to distinguishing yourself in something. I ignored all the advice, you can take advantage of your limitations, maybe if you tried to write poems you could win a prize, if you threw paint on some canvasses perhaps you would achieve something because now everyone's a hit as an artist, or if you thought about the theater there are many idiots who succeed easily and even make one laugh. I ignored every effort, it was enough that I persisted in abandoning my sleepy state, and I contented myself with that walk between the bed and the kitchen, which after all is everyone's road and includes a stop in the bathroom.

I don't think there's any hope because, stammering, she keeps saying that next year things are going to be different. There have been many new years without any change, without any variation in her not doing anything, not wanting to wake up, trying to sleep in order not to face her total failure, her sad and self-imposed reality as an invalid, in spite of the fact that we tried to make things different, if only she had been capable of taking some sort of advantage of her limitations. We brought don Roberto to her, an old widower full of tricks and schemes, but she didn't even let him touch her breast, although he was offering marriage and security as long as she was accommodating. And I know she was capable of passion because, watching her sleep, I've seen her writhe with pleasure from her own caresses, but she rejects him with a violence worthy of a better cause. Now at almost fifty the old man is a bargain, he's the last chance for an eccentric, for want of calling her something else. The old man likes her because she is strange, and the strange ones are ready to offer such unimagined pleasures that they can resuscitate even the most motionless and (because of disuse) useless parts of his shrunken body. They say that mongoloids have such sexual attraction that their careful protection seems a waste to those people who covet the strange and the forbidden. But she reacts to don Roberto with unexpected violence, she pinches him, she spits at him and sticks out her tongue, which doesn't discourage him but on the contrary excites him even more. I only want to be able to situate her somewhere because she really is a burden for me, and for Miguel who also has become senile with time, because now, after so many years of complaints and protests, he somehow finds that his stupid daughter is a beautiful woman who learned happily to live, or rather to dream.

I really fly in your arms, my love, for you are love translated into being. I like your unshaven face, aged, bleary. I love your smell of tobacco, of whiskey, of last night's sleep. You have an interior light that burns me and arouses me. The heat rises with your steps toward me, that's why I wait for you from dawn until nightfall so I can open the door for you. Who is that repugnant character looking at me with his lust-filled eyes? Whose dirty hands are seeking my intimate, damp corners? Whose old, obscene voice speaks to me of raving desires and pleasures? Why doesn't he understand that I belong to another, that I have always loved another and I always will?

I have let him into her bed, some day she has to learn and to assume her responsibilities. Don Roberto offers great advantages for everyone: economic relief, security; he's an old man who soon will be senile and then I will manage his affairs, I am skillful at making profits. I must think about her, she has woven herself a bad future, I have to create hope and security for her. Miguel has always left everything serious and weighty in my hands, and now he can't even handle trivial, everyday matters; he has always been useless, but now he is as heavy a burden as she is.

I am confusing the other man with this one who is tireless in his harassment, who comes at me from every corner, who turns out the lights, fills me with darkness and doesn't let me find the one who is truly mine.

He proposed that I let him bathe her and I told him yes and thank you because it frees me of a tiresome chore, accomplished with some difficulty once a week. What's bad is that he's washing her twice a day and I think they're going to become ill from all that dampness. He coughs a lot and she sneezes for quite a while every morning. Where is this crazy passion of don Roberto's going to stop? I see that she lets him do it and she even smiles strangely. What can she be thinking about? Does she like the old man? In any case she doesn't protest and she goes along with his pampering.

The night has become dark and dense; when I wake up I can't see any light. Have I gone blind? The voice speaks to me of going in search of the sun but I know I will never find it. I was born forbidden to know the meanings of the words sea, forest, river, mountains, friends, parents.

I don't like what's going on now at all. I have to do something but I'm afraid it's too late. I hate morbid, dark, different things. She was, even with her laziness and her insistence on not living, uncomplicated, and her defects were as visible as they were undeniable. Don Roberto is a weird animal, with bizarre habits, but I took him in here absolutely confident that his degree of abnormality was slight, a simple deviation of old age. Old men become dirty to a more or less acceptable degree, but this one is refined and dangerous. I am afraid of him and he takes advantage of my fears, he has taken charge of everything, of my space (I feel that now I don't have a house or any privacy), of the little will she has, and he manages Miguel's imbecility at his whim. How can we get rid of this degenerate?

He has offered me so much that I see him as very generous, capable of creating a kingdom for me, who never had anything. He has given me rings, bracelets, necklaces, perfumes, dreams and projects. He tells me beautiful stories, then I sleep and I forget them, but he tells me again, and sometimes I can repeat them and feel like I'm a character in them. He has bestowed words and masks on me. He thinks I'm beautiful and perhaps for him I am, that's the only important thing. Tomorrow we will go to a house by the sea; finally it will be more than a sound with no image.

Today when we woke up they weren't here. I know I've lost them forever. I spoke with Miguel of my suspicions and he only answered that I should be patient, time would clear up everything. I felt that his head was in the clouds, without the least flicker of worry.

He began to bite me with a voracity that frightened me. The sea is splendorously beautiful and it illuminates me, it reminds me of the other man, lovely, good and gentle. Now he doesn't give me bracelets or perfumes. He showers me with aromas that remind me of the marinades Mama always used when she prepared meat. His bites hurt me.

I received a letter from don Roberto in which he tells me that she went away with the other one. I know he's lying.

I am covered with scars and with fresh wounds. The sea hurts me, it takes away my new skin, it opens my scars, it is cruel as it wounds me, it takes away and gives me sores. It returns me wrapped in appetizing salts. He licks and licks, then nibbles softly until I scream for the piece that he swallows without more preamble than to saturate it with his saliva and with his rapid gnawing.

Yesterday don Roberto came back with an air of desolation. He told me that he couldn't forget her and that she—ungrateful and heartless—had gone away with the other one. There was no other one, except in her feverish imagination. From his empty prattle and his sad and disconsolately narrated tale, I learned that she was now a news item from the police log, the half-eaten woman who had appeared on a river bank, disfigured and eaten by some wild beast and strangely washed with a painstakingly cleansing detergent. I didn't want to tell him what I knew with absolute certainty, because in the end she always was a real dish, one of those exquisite ones, preserved in her own sauce, for me, for Miguel, for don Roberto and for the other one and all the rest. How could we not eat a piece of her, first a little piece, then a bigger piece and almost all of her? I'm sure that she herself was thinking, on being bathed in the river, now almost more of the other world than of this one, that a woman at dawn was a dream-like delicacy.

Translated by Linda Britt

OLGA NOLLA was born in Puerto Rico, where she still resides. She co-founded, along with Rosario Ferré, the literary journal *Zona de carga y descarga* and has also directed the journal of the Federación de Mujeres Puertorriqueñas, *Palabra de Mujer*. Nolla has worked as a journalist for a local newspaper, *El Nuevo Día*, and *Prensa Libre*, and is currently the editor of *Cupey*, the literary journal of the Universidad Metropolitana de Río Piedras. She has published three poetry collections. "A Tender Heart" forms part of the volume *Porque nos queremos tanto* (1989). (MN)

MARIA DE LOS ANGELES NEVAREZ was born in Hato Rey, P.R. in 1964. She currently resides in Durham, N.C., where she is working towards her Ph.D. in Latin American literature at Duke University. Ms. Nevárez has authored several volumes of poetry. Her latest, *Naturaleza salvaje y femenina que inventamos*, awaits publication.

A TENDER HEART

By Olga Nolla

For a number of years, the neighbors of the barrio Cristí envied the happy marriage of Juana and Arcadio Sánchez. Juana was a seamstress at the workshop belonging to Marialuisa Arcelay, and Arcadio worked in construction of buildings and roads. Even though they lived in a rented house, the rose bushes that Juana had planted in the narrow strip of land between the house and the road were a pleasure to behold. During the early decades of the century, in the city of Mayagüez, it was customary to build wooden houses a few feet above ground level. A concrete balcony embellished the facade. These balconies used to be built in different styles, and the house where our characters lived sported one of the most popular types. The balusters were shaped like vases, and three lone flowers sculpted in relief decorated the side that faced the road. Every afternoon, coming back home from the workshop, Juana climbed the five steps that led to the balcony. She would arrive exhausted, her eyes shining and her forehead beaded with sweat. María, Juan, she would start calling the minute she crossed the threshold to the small living room. Pedrito! she kept on calling as she parted the curtains that hung at the entrance to the bedrooms. From the dusty backyard, mixed in with the cackling of the hens and the cheeping of the chicks, rose the rambunctious little voices of the children.

Some time later, Arcadio would arrive, and at night they would both attend meetings. Juana was a well known activist at her work place; her speeches in favor of the improvement of working conditions for women in the needle industry had earned her great prestige. She respected the law and was cautious, and during her leadership there were no strikes worth recording in that space of memory allotted to transcendental events. People concurred in praising her good judgement. Arcadio admired her. He would have liked her to join the party to which he belonged in Mayagüez, but Juana possessed an eminently practical instinct and didn't want to get involved in party politics. If both of them lost their jobs, she thought, what would become of their children? And, sure enough, it was true that Arcadio was often unemployed because membership in the Nationalist Party was not well thought of by employers. There were times when they survived thanks only to Juana's salary.

By the end of the 1930's their situation reached a critical point. Arcadio was jailed in thirty-seven, and when he came out it was impossible for him to find anybody who would hire him; but even so, they managed to survive for a few more years on Juana's salary.

When the war ended they decided to emigrate. They packed their belongings, and left behind their little home in barrio Cristí. Juana cried. Her three children had been born there. She loved those light yellow wooden boards, she loved the green mouldings on the doors and the windows, she loved the balcony with the vase-shaped balusters, the sound of the rain falling on the tin roof, and the far-away murmur of the sea that kept her company during the stifling tropical nights of her insomnia. They had been told that there were good opportunities in New York, that there they could really move up in the world, that the salaries were higher and the children would learn to speak English. Juana suggested the idea first. It was not for her own sake, no, it was the sight of Arcadio lying on the cot staring at the ceiling for hours on end that was splitting her soul. His country's situation, political persecution, and his inability to decently support his family were a heavy load on Arcadio Sánchez's heart. He was a man with arms like steel cables. Tall and wiry, standing on the speaker's platform he presented an imposing figure, and the clarity of his patriotic dream illuminated his words and his eyes.

Arcadio Sánchez cried too when they left behind the little house in Mayagüez. For him exile was a mutilation; he felt as though a part of his own body was being pried apart. Terribly saddened, he embraced his wife and children; and together they turned their backs on years of happiness. They left for New York on the tenth of September of 1945, and were welcomed at the docks by Juana's relatives. They appeared fat and contented and spoke glowingly of life in the city. Arcadio observed with bewilderment the skyscrapers and the throngs of people moving along the wide avenues. It seemed to him that he was crossing through a tunnel, the whole city seemed to be a cement and steel tunnel. This is like living under ground, he thought, people walk forward without looking around them, like sleepwalkers. He felt a great weight in the center of his chest, and looked at his wife. Juana was scared and amazed, but she didn't want to miss a single detail. Look at that, she exclaimed, and that, and all that, she repeated with wonder. The children echoed her.

Juana had no difficulty finding a job. A week after her arrival she was hired by a Jew who owned a fancy female undergarments factory. She earned three times as much as she did in Mayagüez, and couldn't believe it. She had to get up at five in the morning in that terrible cold that very soon started to gnaw at their skin, but it didn't matter, she was earning a lot of money and felt as though she was accomplishing something important. Now, they were really going to move up in the world, she would tell Arcadio. He would sigh, "I hope what you say is true," and would leave every night for his 8 to 4 a.m. shift as a dishwasher in a Broadway restaurant. From that job he moved to a luxury hotel on Park Avenue, and after two years was promoted to waiter. In the meantime, Juana was made a supervisor. They had found an apartment on 105th Street, a fourth floor that you had to enter through the kitchen. It was long and narrow like a train car and had only one window, the one facing the street. The room with the window was Juana and Arcadio's bedroom; the three children slept in the other bedroom and the third room combined the kitchen, the bathroom, and the dining room. This place looks like a junk store, Arcadio would growl under his breath.

The man was not happy. He would speak to his children in Spanish, and they would reply in English; he would ask Juana for his dinner and she would answer that he could get it himself; he would arrive home expecting them to welcome him happily and celebrate his triumphant entrance, and no one paid him any attention; they were all busy with their own things to do. My children will be professionals, Juana insisted, and she would make them hit the books the minute they walked into the house.

Arcadio would look at her in astonishment. Juana paid the rent, did the groceries, cooked, washed and ironed, and made decisions without consulting him.

Some Saturdays she would take the children to the movies and he wouldn't even know about it. During the first few years, Arcadio often visited the Party headquarters in New York. He felt good there. There he understood, if only for a brief moment, some of what was going on around him. But after the events of 1954, Juana forbade him to go back to the headquarters. Far away from those who could understand him, Arcadio became taciturn. His expansive personality pulled inward, and he stopped talking. When he hugged his children he felt like crying. When he embraced Juana he felt afraid.

One day he noticed Juana getting dressed in a hurry without even telling him whether his dinner was in the oven. Sitting up in bed and tasting every word, he murmured with bitterness:

"And just where is Her Majesty off to?"

An ironic smile foreign to his generous personality trembled on his lips. Juana continued to adjust her belt. She seemed not to have heard the question. Arcadio then stood up and asked again, almost yelling.

"Where the hell are you going?"

Juana stared at him coldly, over her shoulder:

"I'm going to the Union dinner."

Then she added:

"Go get something to eat somewhere, or fix yourself a sandwich. The children are spending the night at Aunt Angela's."

Arcadio would have liked to have found the strength within his soul to grab her by the hair and give her a good beating. That's what she needed! He would show her who wore the pants in this house. He would have liked to hit her until she bled, until she screamed and screamed, and even if the neighbors heard, it wouldn't matter, to him nothing mattered anymore. But the respect he felt for her was so great that he controlled himself. He only said:

"OK."

And walked towards the kitchen.

Juana received the letter three days later.

Dear Juana:

I have returned to our homeland. Here, I will work for the future of our children, and so you can have everything that you deserve and not have to work for a living. I did not tell you about my decision because it was so painful for me to leave all of you. We did not have the money to all return together, and here, I don't know for sure if I will find a job, but being alone I'll manage. Don't worry about me. I dream of building you a house on top of a hill. I will paint it white, and plant a rose bush in front of the balcony. You'll see how pretty it's going to be. There we will be truly happy. A man away from his land is like a plant without water. Take good care of yourself. As soon as I have the house I will send for all of you. God bless you. Every day I pray for you.

Your husband,
Arcadio

She read the letter several times. Then she buried her face in her hands and stayed in that position, without moving and without shedding a single tear, until dawn started to break. The light that was coming in through the sole window forced her to raise her head just a bit. Her hands lay on top of the letter. Shriveled up as dried twigs, they pressed the paper against the glass of the table. With the warmth of the light, little by little the fingers stretched out; the hands opened slowly until they were naked, offered up, asleep with their back to the paper, on top of the cold glass. Then they closed again; atrophied as though affected by a lack of oxygen, gasping for air, terrified, cornered. Juana didn't hear the children, already awake, calling to her. She didn't feel their small hands pulling on her skirt. María, the eldest, got scared and called a neighbor.

The letters that never arrived from New York did not discourage Arcadio Sánchez. Week after week, year after year, he worked without rest. He was a bricklayer for a construction company during the day, and after hours he did odd jobs like flooring, fixing roofs, and enlarging kitchens. In barrio Cristí, where he had returned, the neighbors all loved him, and every time there was a job to be done he was the one they called. He was available whenever and however they needed him, no matter if it was a holiday or a Sunday, day or night. He slept in a small, dingy room that a cousin lent him as an act of charity. Poor Arcadio, poor, poor Arcadio, the neighbors would say seeing him retire early for the night stooped with fatigue. He would go hungry. Sometimes his cousin had to force him to eat a plate of rice and beans that she herself would take to the little room. He had no more clothes than those that were given to him, old clothes already used by uncles and cousins and other relatives. Depending on the season he would go to work in Aguadilla, where he stayed with other relatives, and in that fashion almost ten years passed. He would deposit every penny he earned into a savings account. Arcadio Sánchez grew old saving the money to build the house of his dreams, high on top of a hill and white as the foam of the sea. During all this time he was not known to keep women or to have any vices. Finally the house was ready. He designed it himself and and his neighbors helped him build it. He made with his own hands the molds for the balusters, shaped like vases with three flowers sculpted in relief. He planted a rose bush in front of the balcony. A white wall surrounded the little plot of almost half an acre. At the gate, just to the left of anybody who entered, he placed a plaque that read: JUANA Y ARCADIO SANCHEZ. When the roses bloomed, Arcadio thought that the world was identical to his dream. Then he sent for her.

Juana listened to the cousin's appeal while she held the unopened letter. She looked at him, without really seeing him, and stared at the stains on the upholstery of the chairs and the cracks in the walls. She heard the description of Arcadio Sánchez's toils and tribulations. She listened to the description of the house. When he finished Juana looked at him without blinking:

"Are you done?"

The cousin nodded. Then Juana took the letter, still unopened, and holding it with the thumb and index fingers of both hands, ripped both envelope and letter into four pieces. "This is my answer," she said. She looked at the cousin, and with a firm yet dulled voice she added:

"Arcadio left me when I needed him the most. I had to bring up the children by myself, support them alone. I sent for him and he never came to help me. The children are already grown. Tell him it's too late."

Juana walked the cousin to the kitchen door. Her hair had gone completely grey. Her eyes reflected no pain. Life's injustices and twenty years of living in New York City had hardened that tender heart from Mayagüez.

Cousins and relatives took care of Arcadio Sánchez until death took pity on him. He never lived in the house of his dreams. He kept on waiting for Juana to come back to Puerto Rico, and would send her messages every time he knew somebody who was traveling to New York. Sickened with solitude, he would sit on the steps of the cement balcony talking with his memories, and calling his children to come play on his lap.

Translated by María de los Angeles Nevárez

SILVINA OCAMPO, born in 1903 in Buenos Aires, Argentina, began her career as a painter, studying in Paris with Léger and de Chirico. Eventually she turned from painting to literature and published her first volume, a collection of short stories, in 1937. Since then she has been a prolific writer of both stories and poetry, producing some two dozen titles, the most recent of which appeared in 1988. Ocampo's name is frequently linked with that of her sister Victoria Ocampo, founder of the distinguished literary journal *Sur*, on which Silvina collaborated along with Jorge Luis Borges and her husband, Adolfo Bioy Casares. Silvina Ocampo's poems and stories (most less than five pages in length) have been anthologized often, but the volumes themselves are less well-known, despite the fact that she has been awarded prestigious national prizes on several occasions. The stories are marked by her own cosmopolitan background in art and literature; a combination of fantastic, grotesque and mundane elements that results in a sometimes cruel or irrational ironic humor; and the use of eccentric first-person narrators, many of them children. "Creation" is included in one of Ocampo's major collections, the 1959 *La furia y otros cuentos*. (KR)

SUZANNE JILL LEVINE is a professor at the University of California in Santa Barbara and chairperson of the Latin American and Iberian Studies program. Her latest book, *The Subversive Scribe: Translating Latin American Fiction*, on the art of literary translation, will be published by Graywolf Press in the Fall of 1991. Her translations of Latin American fiction include the works of Adolfo Bioy Casares, G. Cabrera Infante, Julio Cortázar, José Donoso, Manuel Puig, and Severo Sarduy. She has twice received the National Endowment for the Arts Fellowship Grant for literary translation, and was awarded the first PEN West translation prize in 1989 for Bioy Casares' most recent novel, *Adventures of a Photographer in La Palta*, coming out in paperback by Viking Penguin (Summer 1991). Recent projects include her collaboration on Julián Ríos' post-Joycean *Larva* for Dalkey Archive Press, and her translation of Manuel Puig's latest novel, *Tropical Night Falling*, for Simon & Schuster (Fall 1991). She has just received an National Endowment for the Humanities Research Grant to translate *The Selected Stories of Aldofo Bioy Casares*.

CREATION
(AN AUTOBIOGRAPHICAL STORY)

By Silvina Ocampo

No musical instrument, not the Roman bagpipe, the Japanese *fuya*, the Hebrew *nebel*, the Chinese transverse flute, the Rumanian *fluira*, the Greek *floyera*, nor all of them together had ever resonated in such a bizarre way. They came from the river, amid drumbeats, emitting light and persistent whistles, and headed toward the dark square dampened by the rain that made the statues and stones in the fountain glisten. Beneath the benches the usual papers or peelings or excrement were missing. Dogs sniffed after some buried bone. Sheltered by the dark, deaf-mute little girls had lingered on the swings, swaying frenetically, their aprons flying in the wind. Since you couldn't see their faces or hands they looked like ghosts, or chalk white furies. Orange-scented women in mourning carried torches.

Gradually lights came on over the square. The little girls stopped swinging; the girls and dogs joined the procession. The cold and the rain influenced the repercussion of the sounds, resounding as if inside a grotto that multiplied and split into infinite parts.

I heard the first whistles as if in a dream, beginning to grow louder, to acquire rhythm and intensity, when the procession gathered in the square. This music, which lasted till morning, could now be heard from all the houses in Buenos Aires. But the person beside me did not hear it.

Was this music—at first indistinguishable from the whistle of a train or factory, or of the trolley along its cable—a requiem? It went on longer than eternity. Only heroic musicians could prolong such a concert under the rain for so long, without fainting in the night. The delirium grew. At some moment I thought I could make out voices, but I soon noticed that the instruments were human and that no voice could be so heartrending. As in the liturgies on Good Friday, might they not be a chant of curses? Those drums beat like a heart. In its humanity the music became brutal and cold-blooded.

The women put out their torches on the wet grass but light continued to illuminate trees and statues.

What were those people doing in the garden? What were the deaf-mute girls doing? What were the dogs doing, reclining in the shape of a monument?

They all scattered slowly and perhaps the music no longer came from the instruments but rather from records that had been distributed throughout the city, which people who stayed up late were listening to on their phonographs.

If that music was so familiar, how come I hadn't heard it before? Perhaps in my befuddlement I was confusing *jazz*, which I find so appealing, with a requiem. How was it possible that such an excellent work had been written by folks like that, dedicated only to politics, to exalting and deceiving people?

Dawn penetrated the rooms of the city. Vapor rose from the tiles of the damp patios. Buenos Aires had never been so clean. One could no longer hear the phonographs but only the whistling of a solitary man on the roof of a house. The man didn't have a good ear and didn't remember the melody well; and he got the rhythm wrong, cutting short or prolonging in an unsettling way the most important notes. He began the same beat again, with effort: the whistling ended in almost inaudible, wavering, pitifully repetitive sounds. The notes, the modulations suggested the pale pink color that adorns the early morning sky. I thought one could glimpse in those musical stutterings the beauty of the work. But not only the solitary man whistled the melody. Other people, further away, darker, sexless, appearing on a balcony or on the sidewalk, already sweeping the street, tried to intone it. Now a popular song like *Mambru se fue a la guerra* or the *National Hymn* or *Mi noche triste*, it was rehearsed by the deaf-mute girls whose voices and whistling sounded like the croaking of the toads, and by policemen persistently whistling on the corners. The music began to fade, crossing the train tracks and the bridges until returning to the river where it died.

That work had not been composed or written by anyone, I found out the next day. No orchestra played it nor had it been recorded on any record, nor whistled by anyone. I wouldn't be surprised, however, to meet up with it tomorrow at any moment, in any place. Perhaps (this idea now obfuscates me) the most important work in life is produced during our hours of unconsciousness (it exists, though only its creator knows so). I suspect that mine must be wandering the world aimlessly looking for a handhold, with a will and life of its own. How else could one explain that I can't forget this music I composed on the verge of death, as I wouldn't be able to forget—as tired as I might be of them—Brahms' Trio in A minor, Vivaldi's Concerto for Four Pianos or Schumann's Sonata in D minor.

Translated by Suzanne Jill Levine

CRISTINA PERI ROSSI was born in Montevideo, Uruguay in 1941. She obtained a degree in literature, and for ten years worked as a journalist and teacher in Uruguay, publishing in the magazine *Marcha* among others. In 1963 she published her first book of stories. This early effort was followed by other collections of short stories, a volume of poetry, and a novel; two of these books were awarded prestigious literary prizes. Peri Rossi, active in the left-wing resistance to military oppression in Uruguay, was forced to flee increasing persecution in her native country and in 1972 moved to Barcelona, where she continues to live today. In that city she has published the majority of her work of the past two decades, including her most recent novel, *Solitario de amor*, 1990 and collection of stories, *Una pasión prohibida*, 1986. Peri Rossi's work combines personal and political themes through an indictment of powerful institutions—the military, patriarchy, capitalism—that efface individual freedom and identity. She frequently evokes scenes of eroticism and lesbian love, employs a child's perspective on the adult world, and experiments with new forms of narration and genre. "The Art of Loss" has been taken from *Una pasión prohibida*. (KR)

GREGORY RABASSA is Distinguished Professor of Romance Languages and Comparative Literature at Queens College and the Graduate School of the City University of New York. He has translated extensively from Spanish and Portuguese, including Cortázar, García Márquez, Valenzuela, Lispector, and Amado. At present he is preparing a biography of Padre Antônio Vieira from research under a Guggenheim Fellowship.

THE ART OF LOSS

By Cristina Peri Rossi

While he was awaiting his turn at the dentist's office, the man read a two-page article entitled "The Secret of Personal Identity" in an illustrated magazine.

He wasn't a heavy reader. He only read when he had some time to kill, in the waiting room of a railroad station or at the dentist's. Every so often he would read a sports sheet or a news magazine, but in general he preferred television. On the other hand, it seemed perfectly fine to read in the waiting room of a doctor's office or in the barber's chair so as to avoid the temptation of staring at other people's faces and reducing the anxiety of the wait.

He read the article carefully. In it, a psychologist at Anneversie Hospital in a small town in South Dakota stated in clear and absolute fashion that all men possessed a secret: the secret of their personal identity.

That revelation overwhelmed the patient as he awaited his turn, sitting in the rather shabby cretonne armchair (the dentist was a neighborhood practitioner who had to struggle against his growing competition) and it brought on an excitement that was difficult to control. He went back over the sharp black letters (the magazine was printed on glossy paper) that ran off like ants toward the edge of the page. Indeed, Mr. Irving Peele of Anneversie Hospital claimed that all men (he, too, therefore) possessed a secret, the secret of their identity, something they could never reveal completely even if they wanted to and which they carried with them to the grave, unable to pass it on even to their wives or children because it was something essentially inexpressible.

"I've got a secret and nobody knows it," the little man murmured, all excited. He closed the magazine and looked for the date of publication on the cover. He found that it was a very old issue, from two years before. At that time he'd been forty-eight and had been half-smitten by a girl he'd met in a park one afternoon when he didn't have much to do because of a work stoppage that had left his days free. If he could have told her he had a secret, that he possessed an untransmittable but real identity, if he had known it himself, maybe she would have shown more interest in him. At that time his second right upper molar had been aching too, but he wasn't in any shape for extra expenses and, besides, going to the dentist wasn't the most pleasant way to pass the time. He preferred stopping in bars with television sets and watching shots of Julie Andrews or Frank Sinatra, who sang like an angel for all generations, a bit obscene, perhaps, but immortal. How long had the magazine been sitting there on the glass table in the dentist's office with its revelation inside? Why hadn't that news of general interest appeared on television? He would have liked to have seen Dr. Irving Peele on the screen explaining in great detail that every man possessed a secret (maybe women, too, in spite of the fact that he didn't mention them specifically), even if he didn't know it, and the girl might have been stimulated to get to know him and look for his secret, the one he possessed and didn't know it.

For the moment he closed the magazine and hid it under the others because he was jealous of his discovery and he thought it would be best if only a few people knew it. Possessing a secret—even if he didn't know exactly what it was: hadn't the psychologist said it was a question of something inexplicable?—gave him some obscure power in spite of the fact that he still wouldn't know how to use it.

He thought of tearing out the two pages so he could read them in the solitude of his home (he lived with his wife and two daughters, but that didn't lessen his feeling of solitude), but he had a sacred respect for private property, and for property that was a magazine in the waiting room of a dentist's office. He placed it even deeper under the ones that talked about movie stars, the love affairs of princesses and dukes, the latest technical advances in stereo equipment and computers. He felt like hiding it behind a chair so nobody could get his hands on it, but he would have had to make motions that the other people might have noticed. Everybody would then have pounced on the magazine and when they thumbed through the pages they would have discovered the article by Mr. Irving Peele, psychologist at Anneversie Hospital in South Dakota.

He felt a bit nervous when one of the patients (the one who'd come in last) reached out his hand toward the glass table, pushed aside the first magazines, which didn't interest him, and searched under the ones beneath them with a certain hesitation until deciding upon one about cars with large colored pictures.

As a precaution, he let the other patients go first in an unusually courteous action. When the waiting room was empty he breathed freely, calmer now, convinced more than ever that the secret was his.

He strode firmly into the dentist's inner office and looked calmly at the worrisome drill that was still spinning like an angry bee. He exchanged a few pleasantries with the dentist, who was glad to find him in a good humor and less apprehensive than at other times. "It's because I've got a secret," he told him, smiling, and the dentist asked him what it was. "I can't tell you," the patient replied. The dentist adjusted the metal plate to keep his mouth open and went to work with the drill, but he didn't pursue the subject further. He went through the dentist's work without any banter and when he left he made some offhand remark about the soccer game the next Sunday.

He went out onto the street renewed, as if the filling of molar had repaired some other part of his person. The streets were crowded, but the swarm of people didn't oppress him now, didn't make him seem small as had always happened. "They've got a secret but they don't know it," he thought, looking at them with a feeling of pity mingled with one of satisfaction. It was good that Mr. Irving Peele hadn't appeared on television to communicate his discovery: this way it established a difference between him and everybody else.

He stopped in front of a show window with men's clothing and a group of elegant, well-dressed dummies. He examined the beige jackets and genuine leather shoes.

"I've got something you people haven't got," he murmured in a low voice.

At other times the suits and accessories would have tempted him, made him feel inferior because it was impossible for him to buy them. He looked at them without any envy now, as passing fancies, nothing but frivolity.

He strolled along the long avenue, in no hurry, stopping here and there, feeling pleasure because he was looking at things from a different level now. He regretted that the air was filthy with pollution, because otherwise he would have liked to have taken a deep breath. He saw the posters of a travel agency and he stopped, drawn especially to one with a picture of Hong Kong, which he thought was the most exciting and distant place a person could visit. He couldn't accept the fact that Hong Kong existed independent of a traveler: it was the kind of place that existed only if you visited it. Nor could he be sure that Mr. Irving Peele's article obtained in that far off place.

He went into a bar and ordered a cognac. He did it naturally and easily, without the uneasiness he used to feel before, thinking it an excessive expense during a time of recession. He was a man with a secret and the secret was of such a nature that it prevented him from revealing it, it was reserved for just him.

A woman at the bar came over and, instead of feeling intimidated as usually happened (unsure of himself, of his appearance, his future, his past), he invited her to join him in a drink and offered her a cigarette.

The woman told him that he looked like an interesting man and he replied that he possessed something other people didn't have, or didn't know they had. She laughed, thinking it was some kind of dirty joke. He didn't seem to notice. But, surprisingly he was afraid: maybe that woman, of a rather loose sort, would try to take away what he had since he'd been imprudent enough to open up. Possessing something—even if it were a secret—had changed him into a vain man who was giving himself away. He paid and left, regretting his frankness.

Having an identity and being aware of it was changing him into somebody more powerful than everybody else, but he shouldn't go around showing off his secret: he might arouse jealousy and envy, somebody might get the idea to steal it from him.

He thought about calling up the girl from the park. He hadn't seen her in a long time because he'd had nothing to offer her: what could she expect from a mature man that the recession had left without a job and who had no attractions to make him stand out from everybody else? "I've got something now," he intended telling her, but when he got to the telephone booth he stopped, because if she asked him what it was all about, the words describing might not come. If he'd torn out the two pages from the magazine and put them in his pocket, he would have been able to consult Dr. Peele. There surely must have been a sufficient explanation in the text, but he couldn't remember.

He went on his way humming softly: "I've got a secret and nobody knows it." It was the right moment to have something nobody could take away from him. Time had managed to take away his youth as he fulfilled the duties expected of a man: military service, marriage, a job, daughters. The recession had taken care of the rest: it had taken away his job, his car, weekends in the country. He'd slowly been despoiled of everything. ("Dust thou art and to dust willst thou return." He remembered the biblical phrase.), and now, suddenly, he was going to possess something again, but that something was of a secret nature, something that was no good for paying off his bank loan, or paying for his daughters' clothes or his wife's false teeth, nor could he display it like a hunting trophy, but, on the other hand, it had one virtue that nothing before it had had: according to Dr. Irving Peele it was something that couldn't be transferred, something completely his own and something he could carry with him beyond the grave. He laughed. It was nice possessing something at last that, even if it couldn't be noticed (and maybe for that very reason) couldn't be lost.

On the way home he ran into a former employee of the company who'd been let go the same time as he. They weren't friends, but when they met the solidarity of their misfortune brought them to share a few drinks. The loss of his job had embittered his character, he was more aggressive than before, and he never smiled. They had a couple of glasses of wine together and he couldn't resist the temptation of telling the other man, who, head down, was staring at the wooden floor:

"I've got a treasure."

The man raised his head slowly, somewhat incredulous, and he seemed to be examining him carefully.

"Yes. It's true," he repeated with assurance. "I've got a treasure."

Could he have won the lottery? Or could it be a very valuable stamp? Somebody had told him that some of those little pieces of paper were worth a lot: the problem was in recognizing them. How was he going to know, for example, when a stamp was worth anything? Just like coins: but where were guys like them going to inherit a coin from the Roman Empire?

"It's not true," the man answered cautiously. "Nobody who has a treasure loses his job. If you had a treasure you'd still be working, because they only take things away from people who haven't got one."

"My treasure is a secret," he said, ordering another glass of wine, putting on airs.

"A secret?" his companion asked as if weighing the words. People with a lot of money had bank accounts abroad. So nobody would know what they really had, not even members of their family. That was a secret, too. Could he have come into an inheritance? He dismissed the idea at once: only rich people came into inheritances, poor people had no one to inherit from. That's what history's all about.

"I can't explain it to anybody," he added as an excuse, but with a certain satisfaction.

The other man stared at him as if looking to discover in his face what kind of secret it was. Then he drew back a little, reclined in his chair, and said with absolute certainty:

"They'll take it away from you."

Those words made him shudder:

"Impossible," he answered.

"They'll take it away from you," the other man insisted. "Haven't they already taken away everything you had? A poor man only has something so he can lose it," he proclaimed. "Didn't they take your job away? Didn't they take your car away? If you've got a treasure now, they'll take that away from you too."

"They can't," he assured him. "Not if I don't want them to. And it's the last thing I've got."

Did he still have anything to lose? The other man was surprised.

"Be that as it may, take good care of it," he told him in a show of spontaneous generosity.

"Yes, I'll take good care of it," he answered and made a motion to pay.

He found his wife watching television. It was an old set because they didn't have the money to exchange it, but it was turned on every day. And it could still be watched. For whatever there was to see: police serials, old movies replayed year after year, and a few musical shows that shattered your eardrums. She said it kept her company. Something to counter the loneliness that hit her in the midst of dishes to be washed, that hid behind the furniture and the shouting of neighbors. Life had taken everything away: youth, job, weekends in the country, and had even carried off love. Could she also have a secret she didn't know anything about? The article didn't say anything specific about women. Had Mr. Irving Peele forgotten them? Was it taken for granted that they were included? In any case, if she was also the possessor of a secret just like him, she didn't know it, and that's where the difference lay. "We're not the same," he thought and that gave him satisfaction.

"Where've you been?" his wife asked grumpily.

"Walking," was his brief reply.

Life had also carried off the desire to make love along with all the other junk.

"You seem to be happy," his wife murmured without taking her eyes off the set.

"I've got a treasure and nobody knows it," he thought secretly. Something they finally couldn't steal from him. Something inalienable, the article had said, and he remembered the word because he didn't know exactly what it meant. Something that doesn't disappear with time, something that doesn't get carried off with age, with a writ, or with unpaid notes. Something entirely his and which, furthermore, his daughters couldn't inherit. Only rich people leave inheritances, but his treasure wasn't transferable.

"I've got something that nobody knows and that's worth a lot," he announced to his wife because it seemed to him that possessing a treasure and not announcing it was like not having it.

She looked him up and down in disbelief.

"It's true," he stated. "I just found out about it."

Her husband had never hit in the lottery, not even in little neighborhood raffles. What tale was he making up now?

"Then you ought to buy yourself a suit," his wife said, having her doubts. "And the water heater needs fixing."

He hesitated.

"That's not what it's for," he answered then.

She looked at him suspiciously.

"I thought so," she said. "What's it good for, then?"

He reflected. The article said that identity was inexpressible.

"I can't say," he answered.

"He's had too much to drink," she thought, and went back to the television set.

He lay down in the bed across from the open window through which the sounds from all over the building were coming in, and he looked at the whitewashed ceiling. Suddenly it seemed to him that the secret wasn't all that important. If he couldn't tell it, if it couldn't be used to buy a suit or have the hot water heater fixed, if it wasn't good for bringing back the desire to make love, what was it good for? Only so they could take it away from him, certainly. And anybody could take it away because he wasn't going to defend anything that he didn't know, something he didn't even know where it was.

He didn't even have the pages from the magazine with Mr. Peele's article. Maybe if he read it he would get his secret back, the treasure that seemed to be melting away now with the sound of dishes being washed in the next apartment, the mingled voices on the television set, and the barking of a dog on the roof. It must have been a foggy secret that could disappear like cigarette smoke. Had the treasure gone up in smoke without his realizing it when he came into the apartment? Was it that delicate? And what if Dr. Peele had been wrong? If identity was something that only a few men possessed, like fortunes in Switzerland, big land holdings, bank stocks, and sports cars? Maybe his former fellow worker was right and they'd taken his treasure away somewhere. Inadvertently, the way he'd lost the other things, but unavoidably, as unavoidable as his other losses. Maybe he'd only possessed that treasure for a few minutes, just long enough to have a drink with a strange woman in a bar, to hum in front of a shop window, to bear up under a dentist's drill.

He rolled over on the bed and tried to sleep. He could hear the water dripping in the sink and the monotonous sobbing of a child. His identity had also drained off like the water and the sleep that was coming over him was an anonymous, shapeless sleep, the sleep of someone who possessed no secrets.

Translated by Gregory Rabassa

NELIDA PINON is one of the most outstanding writers of fiction in Brazil at this time. She was born in Rio de Janeiro in 1937 and still lives there. Since the publication of her first novel, *Guia-Mapa de Gabriel Arcanjo* in 1961, she has published six novels and three collections of short stories. She has taught at universities in Brazil and in the United States, at Columbia, John Hopkins, and Miami. Her work has been translated into Spanish, French, and Polish, and some of her stories have appeared in American anthologies. Her seventh novel, *The Republic of Dreams* (Knopf) is her first to appear in English. Her latest, *A Doce Canção de Caetana*, will appear soon in a translation also by Helen Lane. Piñón is a member of the Brazilian Academy. (GR)

THE HEAT OF THINGS

By Nélida Piñón

The neighbors called him Meat Pie. And his mother, touched, would repeat my darling Meat Pie. The nickname came from the fat that Oscar could never get rid of, not even with rigorous diets. He lived on water for five days once, but his body didn't react to his sacrifice. After that he accepted his exploding appetite and forgot his real name.

At a rather early stage he got used to measuring his age by the inches around his waist as it grew faster and faster, blotting out the years by celebrating with cakes, bean stews, and platters of macaroni. For that reason he soon felt himself to be an old person among the young. Especially because no clothing could disguise his bulges. If he only could have worn a loose gown at least, it would have hidden those parts of his body that gave him the shape of a piece of pastry.

He constantly rebelled against a fate that had imposed on him a body that was in flagrant contrast to his delicate and fragile soul. Especially when friends admitted unceremoniously how much they craved him along with a glass of cold beer. And the only reason they didn't devour Oscar right there at the table in the bar was because they feared the consequences. But they would pinch him on the belly, trying to force a black olive out of his navel.

The house grew dark on birthdays. His mother would turn off half the lights. Only the candles on the cake would light up the presents on the sideboard. Always the same things, long-handled brushes because his belly wouldn't let him reach his feet in the bath and great expanses of cloth. After blowing out the candles he would make the mirror show him his own face, composed of a lot of wrinkles about the eyes, droopy cheeks, a double chin. He saw the limbs of his body as if they had been pulled together by a kitchen fork so the leftover ground meat wouldn't escape from the masses for flour, butter, salt, and milk out of which he was formed.

In spite of his visible heartache over meat tarts, he would eat dozens of them every day. And when he couldn't find them on every corner, he'd stuff his knapsack with soybean oil, a frying pan, and pastries to be fried. Before frying them on vacant lots over a small flame that his breath fed, he would chase away strangers, who wanted to steal his rations.

His body would always wake up in a different shape. Maybe because certain fats had moved to a different center with greater interest, around the liver, for example, or because he'd gained eight pounds in less than sixteen hours. Physical foolishness that helped lower his pride. The pride of being handsome. On the other hand, it opened in his heart an even greater rancor toward his friends, who still hadn't devoured him that week in spite of the fact that he was looking more and more like the pastries sold on street corners.

At times of greatest sadness he would clutch the medallion around his neck, Our Lady of Fátima, under whose protection his mother had placed him for lack of a saint who watched especially over fat people. At home he would whistle to cover up his displeasure. But the tears from a sobbing attack would come to him so strongly that they wet the floor, which his mother would quickly dry. She pretended not to notice. Only when the puddle looked as though there had been rain, as if the roof had leaked, would his mother go, with some coins in her hand, to close friends and have them take Oscar to the movies at least once a month. Those who accepted one day would resist the next, in spite of the gold piece. And they were already growing scarce when Oscar himself, no longer able to fit into any of the seats, stopped going to the movies and standing up.

The platters steamed on the table on Sundays. Oscar would picture himself in place of the roast, being carved with a fork and silver knife in the midst of family enthusiasm. In order to avoid those punishing visions, he would withdraw to his room on those days.

In the summer his torment would grow stronger because instead of sweat oil, vinegar, and mustard, his mother's favorite condiments, would flow down his chest, and she would be touched by the charm of it. Then she would stroke her son's hair, pull out a few curly strands, and, in her room, contemplate them one by one in the concern of trying to discover how long she would have her son at home, out of harm's way and protected.

Oscar collected that maternal consolation in the box where he stored the leftover fat from his itinerant frying pan. And, wishing to compensate for his mother's sacrifice of drinking the oil and vinegar from his chest, he would smile and she would exclaim in turn, what a beautiful smile you have. It's the smile of happiness, son. Those words would be followed by the ones that wounded his heart and which his mother, weeping, couldn't manage to avoid: oh, my darling Meat Pie!

That expression of affection which his misshapen body couldn't have inspired, would make Oscar drag off to his room, embittered by the bite of the maternal words, which only tried to draw him to the frying pan, burning with zeal, patience, and hunger.

He foresaw a tragic end for himself. His friends, like vultures, ready to peck at his flesh. The picture of his own pain led him to read a detailed account of his possessions on the wall. He doubted the richness of his holdings. The debt column had grown in such a way that he would never be able to get rid of it no matter how long he lived. He owed men his flesh because they were hungry. And even though they owed him a body he could be proud of, there was no way he could collect it.

After his scented bath he would try to imagine what love between living creatures was like, their bodies in bed, free of ungovernable enemy fat. At those moments, deceived by a modest plus balance, he would come to see himself battling his adversaries. A sudden movement was enough, however, for reality to speak to him of an obesity where there was no place for poetry and love. And, immediately, the prospect of being eaten with a knife and fork would become the gloomy subject of his thoughts.

His mother fought against his hazy eyes, his always mournful soul. What terrible thing is there in the world that makes you look at us with that suspicion? Oscar rewarded her with a platinum brooch, for her to plunge into his breast forever. Drops of poison would trickle from his flesh along with the certainty of his own cross. Facing the enigma Oscar proposed to her, the one who had avoided straightforward speech all her life said, oh, my Meat Pie, what a good son!

The more she extolled virtues that they both really despised, Oscar would quickly start worrying about eliminating from the edges of his body remnants that might not fit inside the meat pie he was. He finally gave up the vacant lots where he fried his meat pies. He could no longer stand having people staring at him with a hunger he couldn't take care of. He had nothing to feed the wretches with. They would have to die without any help.

As his consultations with the mirror intensified, the foggy glass barely let him see the body that was pierced every day by the efficient kitchen fork. He would get dressed as a meat pie every morning. As a countermove he set up his easy chair in the kitchen, leaving it only to sleep. He took care of his basic necessities and took on a new habit of sprinkling flour over his body. With the cavities of his nails full of grease, he would receive visitors there, making them smooth his powdered skin.

His mother rebelled against his rudeness. She didn't want her friends exposed to such an ordeal. If he were a prisoner of his fat, let him bear it with dignity. The son returned the affront with his teeth, moving them like an electric saw, almost grinding her arms. And his drive was so convincing that his mother took to protecting her limbs with thick pieces of wool, even in the heat. She left her face showing. And when Oscar had her within reach of his hands, she would slip away behind her jackets and boots.

At the age of thirty Oscar grew weary. Now it was his turn to eat someone he had picked out as a meat pie. Since he'd lent himself to such a role for so long a time, he demanded human flesh for his appetite. He would designate the victim with the greatest of care. He leaned particularly toward people at home, however, fraternal blood. And as part of his scheme he feigned blindness, stumbling against objects in order to distract his enemies. His mother asked for help from the neighbors, who took turns beside her during the first week, leaving her all alone later on. With so much to do, his mother began wearing light clothing, having forgotten about her son's threats.

For his part, Oscar was surprised by the charms of speech. He'd never been seen to discourse with such enthusiasm about objects lost to his sight now. He only recently discovered within his reach the power to combine his hunger with a verbal voracity that had always been in his blood, but to which he had never given any importance, busy defending himself against those who wanted to toss him into the frying pan.

His mother soon got used to his blindness. She treated him like a passenger in an endless tunnel. She would describe the house to him, as if he were a guest there. She wanted him to take part in everyday things and would suddenly blush at her son's sweetness. That was when Oscar opened his eyes, sure that he had won. And there she was, smiling, her arms out, her body exposed. He rapidly reviewed in his memory the times that she, moved by the strength of her love, had called him Meat Pie, almost eating him up. Having suffered for him, his mother immediately caught in his look now a gleam that wasn't coming from a lamp, or from joy, or from the remote truth of a son she barely knew. What his mother was discovering in her son was a flame that was determined to live and the unmistakable manner of an executioner.

She remained beside him, not moving. Oscar would make the necessary arrangements. She was seeing him as a man for the first time. He brought his armchair close to his mother's, which she'd dragged into the kitchen. He asked her to sit down. He sat down, too, first gathering some strands of the woman's hair. And only with his mother's consent did he begin to watch over her.

Translated by Gregory Rabassa

MARIA LUISA PUGA was born in Mexico City and lived in Europe and Africa from 1968-78. Her first novel, *Las posibilidades del odio*, came out in 1978, and since then she has published three other novels and four collections of short fiction; the most recent of these, *Intentos*, came out in 1987. She has worked as an editor for several publishing houses and has taught Creative Writing for the Universidad Autónoma Metropolitana in Mexico City. Puga is currently recognized as one of the most important fiction writers in Mexico. Her second novel, *Pánico o peligro* (1983), received the Villaurrutia Prize in 1984, and her second collection of short stories, *Accidentes* (1981), was also awarded the Villaurrutia Prize in 1983. The publication of *Antonia*, her fourth novel, was noted as the fiction event of the year in the *Encyclopedia Britannica Yearbook* (1989). (LHC)

LELAND H. CHAMBERS is a professor of English and Comparative Literature at the University of Denver, where he was editor of the *Denver Quarterly* for six years. He has published scholarly articles on the *Quijote*, Baltasar Gracián, the English Metaphysical poets Richard Crashaw and Henry Vaughan, André Gide, and Miguel Angel Asturias. His translations of fiction and poetry by Spanish and Latin American writers have appeared in many literary magazines during the last five years. His translation of three novellas and a short story by the Argentine Ezequiel Martínez Estrada, *Holy Saturday and Other Stories*, was published by the Latin American Literary Review Press in 1988. He was given a National Endowment for the Arts Translators Award for 1991 to complete work on a novel by Julieta Campos.

MEMORIES ON THE OBLIQUE

By María Luisa Puga

There is this thing about those grand, stately mansions which have passed down to the people (or to a portion of the people, to those who are able to rent bits and pieces of them after they have been turned into small apartments, which even so still contain a generous amount of space), who in this way share in an always amazing kind of world—luxury. A strange luxury, quite reserved, secure, very calm. It resides in the height of the ceilings, the thickness of the walls, the size of the doors, the dimensions of the windows. An anachronistic luxury in its new urban situation, with a whole city having grown around it.

What I'm trying to say is that something of the sure power of lordly dominion still persisted in the apartment where I loved him and perhaps really fell in love for the first time. What I don't understand is why I'm not with him. Why I don't have a heap of children and a warm, well-used kitchen. Why I'm not growing old beside him, feeling the effect of a sizable habit of knowing him to be there. That's the way it should have been, instead of my trying to define this space which was so unusual, so pleasant, because it allowed room for our presences, gave us the freedom to be. But of course, it was not an ex-seigneurial mansion for nothing. Those lords used to possess the world. They were the world. What was outside it didn't matter. It didn't exist. And now that huge mansion, divided into apartments of various sizes, was true life for people coming from the most remote corners of the world, with all sorts of dreams, ambitions.

One thing only did they have in common: they were able to pay the rent.

I'm avoiding talking about him, I know that, but the reason is that I want to recapture a sensation which only now do I understand: that feeling of well-being within some ample space. It would truly seem that we traipse through the world with shrunken spirits: lame, awkward. And suddenly we run across something, an area, a place, a ceiling lit up by the afternoon, and it's just as if we had come home.

This feeling is one I have often had, although that was the first time and therefore the one I want to tell about, and that's why I dwell on the strange feeling brought on by this discovery. The whole business of our shrunken spirit. Of space. And, in short...of love.

It must have been the servants' quarters in the original villa. It had a tiny bath built into a corner. Kitchen on one side, an ancient, rusty stove, some wooden shelves painted white years and years before. Squalid. On the other side a piece of a mirror, as if this were some shack somewhere, like a piece of a mirror hanging on the trunk of a palm tree, next to the barrel of water.

I am talking about Italy, about a Roman ex-mansion, but what the entryway to the apartment always reminded me of was a room perched on the flat roof, an *azotea*, of a building in the Colonia Hipódromo in Mexico City. The few pieces of furniture there, a table, an old divan with its bottom broken through, the scrap of a mirror, the stove, the frying pans and dishes so faithfully of a piece with the poverty of Mexico that I could spend hours looking at them from different angles, in different lights. Bumping up, every time, against a world that I had previously only experienced from a balcony, from a window. I remember the adobe hut with its corrugated roof. What seemed like hundreds of oil drums for carrying water in, placed around as flower pots, seats; the scraps of things the well-to-do had thrown away. And there they were, the piece of mirror, I repeat, the divan with its bottom out, the man of the house washing his face with a lot of rubbing and splashing, while from the interior of the hut came the a woman's voice scolding him: "You crud, you son-of-a...."

Entering the apartment in Rome used to mean seeing those things. I always stopped for a moment in that first tiny vestibule. It was just as if the sun had abruptly gone in. Everything at pause, even existence itself. I don't know how it changed me, I don't know if it tied me to reality, if it was just a nuisance or a call to attention. I was always tripping over myself there. And after a little while I was able to see everything, but very slowly. First the table. That was where we left notes for each other. Or clues for some game that always referred to our love. To that "us" which was so much our own, so imperious, so once and forever, because before him, and after him, there was nothing.

He had only taken the apartment for three months. Then he was going to leave Rome. His contract with the United Nations had run out and they were sending him back to his own country. He was Austrian, and I think that when he arrived in Rome he was a neatly dressed young bureaucrat and quite meticulous. This is what I assume of course, because of the photos I saw. On the same occasion when I saw those of his wife and two children.

They had gone back earlier, schools and all that, and these three months, he told me, are ours.

My own companion had also left for three months. To his own country. To think, to puzzle things out, to decide if he would return or not and to find out who I was for him. He would know for sure when he returned, he told me. I knew that it would be yes. That's why these three months were a vacation from reality, even though I would have to work every day.

When he first took me to see the apartment I found only a large hall which had an enormous, long window...very high. A table that ran almost the whole way along the breadth of the window, reached the corner, and came on around proudly until it suddenly came to a stop as if someone had given order abruptly: HALT!

And besides, of course, everything was filthy.

"Now you'll see," he said. "When I finish it you'll see."

But I feel a little confused. I loved him so that I think I even feel ashamed. Close to him I wouldn't know how to remember it. It would make us both cry.

He carpeted the whole flat with heavy paper, the kind used to wrap packages. The individual sheets, placed on a diagonal, were held together and stuck to the floor with bands of wrapping tape, a little darker than the paper. It would be nice to give the precise dimensions. Let's say, a surface of 9 x 9, or 81 x 126. Inches. But I haven't a clue. It was simply a huge space.

In the center was the bed. A water bed. That crazy guy. Lamps, cushions. I liked the blankets more than anything. Warm, playful, alive.

Corners that broke up the vast space, suggesting moments of distance. Other states of mind.

It was then that I discovered beauty. I understood it. I began to love it. The beauty of the human essence that creates space, and in creating it transforms it, modifies it, ennobles it.

I am thinking of those cans filled with plants and flowers. Of the red earth swept so smoothly by the woman who, at home in Mazatlan, was the one who used to awaken me every morning. "You son of a bitch, you better not come home today like you did yesterday. I'll take this broom to you. You crud!"

And my parents' voices: Girls, shut that window!

From the houses that surrounded the ex-mansion—homes of working people, traditional Roman families that coexisted with the ex-mansion without any great disturbance because in Rome the people are accustomed to stateliness (I would even say bored with it)—certain complaints reached us: Shut the curtains, please, there are children around here. Bambini.

We always forgot. Everything was such harmony within, so perfect, it all existed so much of the moment (but it's not right to come in with your shoes on, he warned, you have to leave them in the vestibule), even though a progressive deterioration of the decor was inevitable. He was resigned to that, it's just paper.

Time was going by, but I carried my love more deeply inside than I realized. I would awaken at midnight and tremblingly make certain of his presence. Oh yes, he assured me. Yes, he said again calmly, smoking, and with his eyes wide open. The waterbed, with its ample, smiling blankets, loved us. Our movements would set it undulating.

So this is what love is, I thought, gazing at the vestibule when I left in the morning to go to my own room.

The strange thing is that on the way out I always saw it from another angle. It didn't hold me very long. In the mornings we both had to go about our own business. The world forced us to go out. I was waiting until the conference of the FAO began, where I was going to work as a secretary, and which would take place in three months, naturally.

To be a secretary at the "conference," let me explain (and this is why I don't even capitalize that word), meant that I would have to type up the remarks made by the delegates as soon as they came out. The tapes or the shorthand records would be brought to us and dictated. I used to type a million words an hour.

In the meantime I was living in the homes of friends who would rent me a room or for whom I would house sit while they went on vacations. I was waiting for my companion, whom everyone was eager to meet. Also a writer, playing at being the eternal student, rebelling against everything. Like me.

In Rome, the Austrian had learned to de-officialize himself, to act less like a bureaucrat, although he was still within the Institution. When I met him he was the bohemian of the FAO.

So every morning he would very calmly get out his bicycle, unlock it, and, holding up the bike with one hand and throwing his other arm across my shoulder, we would walk to the cafe. There, with my skin burning from so much lovemaking, each of us crammed full of the other's smells, we would have a capuccino and a *cornetto*.

It was cold, right at the end of autumn. Il Messico reached me like a strange fog. I thought how good it was that this is only going to last for three months.

Afterward he would take off on his bicycle and I remained seated on a bench in the square and thought about love and about Mexico.

My body was mine, and I was happy.

I would walk along slowly, in love with Rome, thinking about how to get myself back to Mexico. About wanting to be a writer who would say... about being someone who would be able to get it across that, yes, one could be all right, then.

Then I would begin to feel guilty. And so, to work.

When I crossed the Ponte Sistino and saw below it a river green with filth but made beautiful by life, I thought, Mexico, how can this be done for you? To attempt to say what I was seeing, what I had been seeing for days... weeks, months...years...my whole life: a space where one's spirit is not made uncomfortable by being fainthearted, ashamed, fearful. And I hastened to reach the room I had rented in Trastevere, where I had placed my table right before the window and the din of life in my consciousness (and when life unfolds in Rome, this din is not something which can pass unperceived).

There was no one about at that hour. Everyone worked as office workers at the FAO. I still had money from a previous contract. For me the FAO was my United States. I was a kind of *bracera*. A typist, like countless Italian women. But the Italian women wanted permanency, benefits, security. They were living their real lives and not on the move as I was. I only wanted my money so I could go to my room and write. That's why I was able to get jobs so easily.

Seated in front of my work table I disguised the fact that in reality I was waiting for the time when I would be together with him again. In the meantime I had to make the time at least half real, important, as important as he was because, in order to meet him, it was essential for me to be real...because I loved him.

And so, hugging my existence and my euphoria and my impatience, I would begin to think about Mexico. About this Mexico I had been fleeing from in order to be able to go back to it and never again merely witness it from the window: You crud, I'm gonna smack you good with this broom, and put down that knife now, you sonofabitch!

Not that way. Never again, no: "Shut that window, girls. What are you doing, spying on those people?" The "masses," they called them.

And to anyone who allowed themselves to ask, I would respond, "I'm writing. I write. I'm a Mexican woman who writes."

On one of those writing days, I ran up against the ocean, against my memories of the sea just the way I used to see it from my grandmother's house in Acapulco. The identical, furious, open sea. Sometimes completely wild, absolutely fear-inspiring, while my life was unfolding chained hand and foot to the hope that something would happen.

That's why I would write furiously until the time came to see him again. Except that I run up against the ocean, which up until that moment I thought I hated because of everything it caused to happen during my childhood, with its bombastic, despotic, and unpredictable mien. Double-crossing traitor. With its showy way of making human beings look small, tiny points of light scarcely flickering in the darkness, when because of the heat I used to slip out of my bedroom very late and, taking advantage of the fact that everyone else was sleeping, practice smoking and try to imagine what it would be like to be a fisherman in the middle of all that, so horribly alone.

That ocean appeared to me in Trastevere and made me really feel my body, the air, the light, the water (which was probably on account of the bed, but that was reason enough), a sensual movement that practically caused me to shut my eyes while I was writing about the sea, being the sea itself and understanding it in a completely different way. Feeling it moment by moment. The slow breaking up of the morning, with the certainty that when evening came I would meet him and I would have written something that would produce as much pleasure for me as he did.

I think it was then that I seriously began to observe Mexico and to love it. And to know that I was going to return. And how to understand now that this was how I was gradually pushing him further away from myself and putting obstacles in my way so as not to love him more.

I don't know if he was handsome, intelligent, educated; if he made love well or not; I know that I loved him. That I still love him, and that it will never happen again even though I have fallen in love hundreds of times and it is always different, variations on that first time, embarked on from different angles.

I recall a great deal about walking along any street in Rome and feeling my history and life were fused within me and how odd it was that nothing less than my acceptance of Mexico came out of this. The break with a tone, a language, a way of talking about love and filling it with images.

He was my friend, my very dear friend, and the world was invading us through every pore. And when we made love in the nighttime we did it on the ocean, quite alone and fully given over to the idea that both of us were going to go back to our own separate worlds at the end of the three months. Because we were learning to love better.

How often I thought of Acapulco and felt that it could have been different; that it didn't have any reason to be the lovely, corrupt cosmetic that it was. And how the sea, through my respect for it, could have been something else.

And the phone would ring, we would agree where to meet, and I would close up my machine happily, freshen up, and go out on the street eager to be a child once more.

Tenderly we would cover the world step by step, pausing over every little detail, talking of the future (different for each of us) and how well we would get through it. Because we were strong, and we were equals. And we loved each other.

But, for those three months, equals. Because those three months were the same for us. Because we invented them.

I have always wanted to write about this; I've blamed myself for not being with him ever since I haven't been with him. I always wanted to write about it, and now I see that I will always carry with me the feeling of not being able to tell it well enough.

I was more attached to the rules of the game. Three months, we said, that's it. For me, it was probably because I was going through the world in a scatterbrained sort of way. Everything was equally useful. All the games. And very likely I was playing because it was the first time that I found myself free of Mexico. I was making up the rules. And I am obedient, submissive, respectful of the rules. If the rules are not imposed on me but simply agreed to, I don't see any reason to cheat. And if one accepts the establishing of rules through common agreement, it's because one accepts a "temporal" modification of reality, isn't that right? It's very nice, you discover other angles of reality. But besides, ever since I was a little girl I have taken games seriously. As something real and not something you do while Mama or Grandma is getting dinner ready. A game is a space in which you learn to be, in which you gradually discover the world. You don't just brush it away with a swipe of your hand.

When my companion finally got to Rome, I discovered that my game had been a perilous one: it had simply killed my love for him. Notwithstanding, I was ready to reconstruct it, so I thought, because I had finally learned to love.

I couldn't. That crud, the awful ocean, the burden of those childhood games got in the way. I just couldn't. But I wanted so much to do so in honor of those three months.

Translated by Leland H. Chambers

MARIELLA SALA is a journalist and writer who lives in Lima, Peru, the country where she was born in 1952. She publishes regularly in magazines and newspapers, and is a recognized member of the new generation of Peruvian authors. "From Exile" is the title story from her collection *Desde el exilio*, published in 1984. Sala's work explores the personal and psychological ramifications of social turmoil, especially as it affects women. (KR)

FROM EXILE

By Mariella Sala

To Carmen Olle

I gaze into Gonzalo's watchful eyes and get lost in those two black, unfathomable dots. Ceaselessly he flails his hands about; in him life is pure movement. I lose myself in his eyes and drift off, my mind taking flight, taking leave of my motionless body. At what moment did I lose my freedom, at what moment did I quit ignoring conventions and begin heeding them? The house smells of cauliflower and garlic, but everything is wrapped in silence. A seeming peace. My immobility turns it into an asylum. My indecisive foot-steps prevent strangers from witnessing a normal, everyday scene. When did I lose my rhythm, when did I stop running? Right now I'm filled with so much nostalgia for the garden at my mother's house, the rusty tricycle, the wind whistling against the moth-eaten windows. Sunday I went there to collect myself, to feel that I'd once existed. The house was empty, peopled by ghosts. My mother's ghost was sitting in a chair looking out the window. The ghosts of my brother, my nephews, soulless presences wandering through the cor-ridors of my childhood. My brother came across a bag filled with old letters. Eagerly we set about reading them; here was proof that there had existed a past in common, when we freely went about in search of certain signs that we would never find. We were confused. My brother said that he could set up a store where he would sell the latest-fashion clothing. I looked over at Gonzalo sitting in his baby-carriage, in front of the mirror, and I felt like crying. I didn't though...instead, I lay down on the bed and fell asleep.

On my way back I tried to lift my spirits; when something ceases to be it's because something else is beginning, I told myself. And Gonzalo's life was indeed beginning, but inside I felt as though I were in a dream. When did the day cease? When did I start living a dream? But that night I couldn't sleep. I kept remembering the streets. I was in exile from my very own life. My neighbor, the seamstress, stayed up all night working, and every time I got up for a glass of water I could see the glow from her house filtering in my dining room. She works long and hard, and her life is dreary. It's been a month since

I wrote down a single line and my life is also dreary. Once you lose the lucky charm, your fate is sealed. But that doesn't keep me from feeling an indefinable uneasiness every time I see her light burning in the middle of the night. I too am in the habit of staying up all night, thinking. Motionless, musing, remembering. Now I am unable to construct anything... I can only exorcise the past. I have the key that opens the doors I closed some time ago...but it doesn't open new doors. Once you lose the lucky charm...but I have a son, a creature born of me and who I watch growing hour by hour. Outside, there is the ceaseless struggle; inside, a more relentless and cruel battle is developing.

Yesterday my aunt came to visit me; she brought a kilo of sugar, some peaches and her eternal bundle of worries. "So what are you doing, are you writing? You're not writing? Just take a look at your brothers and sisters; they are doing just fine, they're not lacking for anything. But you, with you there are always problems, don't you see? That's why I have to help you. I feel sorry for you because you don't have the talent necessary to earn a living." And me explaining to her that yes, yes, I have the ability to choose, that I'm not like her or like the people she knows, that I love other things. It's always the same—I was born with the stigma of the defenseless. Everything that happens to me will always move her to pity. Every so often I ask myself: how many times have I betrayed myself just to change the image she has of me? And always I failed, always she won. It's true, no one loved me, everyone stuck a knife in my back.

Always. Until I hid myself away in this little house, in my private asylum. I'm ashamed of a family whose very nature compels it to bemoan its existence at every instant. And money, yes, it's true, this is my big problem. I have to deal with it if I don't want people to pity me. "Look around you," they tell me, "look how everyone is struggling, making sacrifices in order to live a comfortable life." "Money makes the world go round," they explain to me. "When will you understand what life is all about?" Then I become paralyzed with anguish. I can't read, I can't write, I pass the days in bed, sleeping, I worry about my physical appearance, about my house furnished with all the old stuff the family threw away. My feet hurt when I walk, I should have a car. I read a magazine that symbolizes these times, when tinsel and glitter triumph over plainness and simplicity. I think I should be infected with that lustre, going to Hawaiian luaus, wearing fancy, dazzling dresses, being someone who knows how to enjoy life. But sometimes very poor children knock on my door and ask me for a little something to eat. So then I decide to work for a wage, and I begin to feel on the verge of suicide. Forlornness, it is all I feel...a deep forlornness. Yesterday morning, however, when I went for a stroll in the park with Gonzalo and saw the lush, green trees after an all-night rain, the wet grass on a muggy, overcast day, I again felt life's magic. There was that silence of noble endeavors, an atmosphere of destiny that is realized fully, and at that very instant, in the middle of my stroll, in the midst of collecting myself, I understood that I was where I belong. And that everything happening to me ought to be happening to me. Not long afterwards, a seemingly shy young man followed me home and told me that they were going to call him on my telephone. He was so upset that I didn't think anything strange or peculiar about the situation. I had no idea who he was. In a couple of minutes the phone rang and a young woman's voice was asking for him. I went out to get him in the park and he spoke to her on the phone right on front of me as though I wasn't even there. A couple of kids with problems, in flight, an abortion, voices in distress. All this also had to occur on an overcast November morning. The boy left my house and his story is now one of millions of stories that are unfolding nearby there: in the park. "Don't do anything without me," the boy advised the girl, and it is certain that each of them will act according to their nature, will find their own rhythm and perhaps suddenly remember one another without love. Great moments alone constitute the life of each person. A whole life can change with one gesture at the exact right moment. I don't believe in continuity, in routine, in how ants behave: we are not insects but dark beings who are all of a sudden illuminated and just as quickly extinguished, and all of life is like this: a search for light.

I remember those moments very well. At five years old, in my mother's bedroom. My older sister and I looking at one other in the mirror and suddenly that sensation like a ray electrifying my brain. She is not me, she is someone else, I told myself, confused; and then me asking her, who are you, what do you feel not being me, and she looking at me strangely, only to then see herself reflected in the mirror, pointing to it and saying to me, smiling: "I am her." It was loneliness, loneliness, that was my companion . I gazed out across the gray, wintry sea and understood that there was no returning. We are in a great adventure, I told myself, and for the first time I felt afraid. Ever since then I have the same sensation whenever I look at the cold, wintry sea. And yet, the sea in the summer only fills me with nostalgia for my first years, when I was the universe.

But it must be so, they've gone stabbing me in the back. Unlikely enemies have led me by the nose right to the edge of the abyss. And here I am: thirty years old, all my dreams crushed, except for one: the undying dream of being myself. A miracle. And since I decided that literature would be my weapon, I must now get down to the work of writing. I owe money to my neighbor, and the greengrocer. I could write a few literary articles in order to earn some *soles*. But that has its limits. One cannot spend thirty years of one's life pursuing something one has never seen. My books, my non-existent books, will have to appear even if I have to stop eating to do it. In any case, that won't happen, it's not for nothing that Pedro mortgages his life every day. It's not for nothing that we have built a small, shaky canoe that floats on a river full of pirana. And we haven't succumbed to the temptation of going off on our neighbor's yacht, or to falling into the fishes' razor-sharp teeth. Every morning he goes to work with holes in his pants pockets, his shirt mended by himself, but still he is full of vigor and spirit. His image paralyzes me for an hour, and I toss and turn in bed not knowing what to do. All this lost time, and writing, writing sounds like something very abstract when you have a husband who goes out to struggle every morning in order to subsist. In the house the smells of the food are making me feel sick; cilantro, garlic, cauliflower. And yet they are the same smells of my childhood.

I gaze into Gonzalo's unfathomable black eyes and remember someone else's eyes. I am in front of the mirror, I am still an adolescent. I stare at myself, at my thin but long hair, at my very long nose. Frightened and aggressive, I tell myself that after today I will no longer be a virgin, after today I will change. I feel afraid. "A woman's reputation is like a mirror: if you get close to it, it clouds over," my mother would say to me. And I, recalling this, move close to my full-length mirror and my face clouds over. I am prepared: new underwear, perfume. But no, I won't put on any makeup. But none of this keeps me from feeling like a victim. It is an April morning and the sun makes my hair shine when I leave the house. My mother has asked me to run an errand for her at the bank. I kiss her goodbye and I am Judas. I will betray her, I will hurt her by going to bed with a man, I will be a whore. She always told us that sex is disgusting and that proper, upright women—as we ought to be—are frigid. I rebel, I am caught between him and her. He won't put up any longer with a relationship that is nearly two years old without us making love. She will feel her honor has been deeply wounded because, according to what she says, her sole source of pride is her daughters' sense of morality. I walk for a while along the seawall before deciding to go. I am ready for the big moment, and yet something in me resists. I feel coerced. Nothing feels spontaneous. He doesn't love me, but he desires and respects me. But at the same time I can't describe my feelings towards him. I start walking in the direction of his house; he'll be alone now at this hour. Timidly, I knock on his bedroom window. He appears, wrapped in a large white sheet. He resembles a Tibetan monk. When he sees me, he becomes very nervous, he grows excited and runs towards the door, pointing to me to go over to it. I follow him into his room. He is naked under the sheet and when he reclines on the bed, he reveals himself, smiling, watching me. I feel nauseous. I don't want to see that drooping flesh. I turn away and look at the bookshelves and he starts talking, making as if he's calm. Then he entreats me to lie down beside him. I excuse myself and tell him that I only came by in passing, that I really have to get to the bank for my mother. I feel stupid; I can't believe what I'm saying and he begins to grow irritated and lose his patience. The situation then becomes truly comical and this isn't at all what I want. What I want is to disappear, to avoid myself, that everything would be different. I too begin to grow angry with myself. I get up, fully conscious of what I am doing, and start taking off my clothes with a fury equal to my threat: "it's okay, you wanted to do it, then let's do it." It's the first time that I get undressed in front of someone; he just watches me, bewildered. I've surprised him. He's nervous and sweating. I lay down on the narrow bed and our bodies touch. I feel that I'm going to be operated on, that a nurse is going to inject me with a drug. He climbs on top of me and starts pushing, violently. I'm paralyzed. Finally, he says "I'm sorry" and I feel such a relief. I don't know what happened except that I am still a virgin. We take a bath together like you see them do in the movies. As for me, that feigned intimacy repulses me. Then we go out for a walk down the street and he buys me a gift, and when we're about to separate, he asks me not to mention to anyone that we didn't make love. Some days afterwards, so that there's no doubt about his virility, he gets me pregnant. And so our relationship—that was always literary—continued on its course in spite of it.

A woman who becomes a housewife almost always ends up being invisible. It happens slowly, without her even realizing it. She lives in a constant bustle attending to the children, cleaning the house, washing, cooking. That's why her own metamorphosis is nearly imperceptible to her. Until she is forty-five. This age that would be an ideal harvest time is, in a woman, the age of abandonment, of her consecration as an invisible being. She becomes a relic. The children and grandchildren visit her. They watch her attentively, as though thinking she will suddenly disappear. They adore her but they don't listen to her: she is, well, a relic. She has gone camouflaging herself with the furniture in her house and her anonymity is certainly the most outrageous thing of all. Nonetheless, it has been this way ever since she started being a housewife. Protectress of people preoccupied with themselves, she only notices her terrible loneliness when physical presences have gone. I'm thinking about this now that I spend all day in the house with Gonzalo waiting for lunchtime, then for dinnertime, and then bedtime. My mother is alone now in her old house and sometimes I forget that she even exists. I've called her this morning. She says that she feels dizzy, full of anguish. When she climbs the stairs she feels she's going to lose her balance. It's true, a woman accustomed to being surrounded by children tugging at her arms and skirt, always in the midst of people demanding her attention, in the end holds onto them like the pole of a tightrope walker. Once the pole is gone, she loses her balance. My mother is on the verge of falling because she needs a crutch. And now, the same thing is happening to me with Gonzalo, that's why I've decided not to ever leave my little house, my private asylum.

I've asked to borrow some money. At the time I did it I was fantasizing about working at a new job. So I imagined myself a famous journalist, my name on all my writings, living amidst the maelstrom of political events, carried along by the constant comings and goings of the world. I quickly dropped the notion. Surely I want to let the world run its course without me. I want to abstract myself, to live in a parenthesis, until discovering the mystery I carry within me. This is why I write: to unravel meanings. This is my obsession...and it is, well, my longing. And this longing paralyzes me and is therefore what arouses in some people contempt; in others, pity. People often try to shake me out of it. I look at them in confusion, ignore me, I tell them, I am invisible, but inevitably their schemes anguish me. But I understand: we've been programmed to live in an atmosphere filled with tinsel and glitter, and love of appearances is always substituted for true love.

I gaze at Gonzalo's unfathomable black eyes, his dark skin, his features so different from mine. In them I see my hope, my longing to feel I belong to someone. Because that sensation of being a total stranger to everything and everyone around me has always pursued me. I've seen countless persons acting around me, implicating me without being able to participate in my own life. Have I been paralyzed up to today? I've been involved in virtually every scenario without being a participant. I have let myself be pulled along by them, the actors. That's why I am writing a novel in which I am the only character—the rest are ghosts, fleeting apparitions. At times I tried to provide justifications, motives, reasonings, those little traps that ensnare one even more with your fellow man: I failed, failed, in front of them and myself. So I go on being paralyzed; I don't write. To prove myself, I inscribe myself, I describe myself. If it's possible to talk about someone, that someone is real. I am, well, obsessed with being.

During my adolescence, with two beautiful and self-assured sisters, I quickly discovered my ethereal self. While life for others was blossoming outward and into the world, I was almost invisible. I was every character in the books I read, in every book. And while my sisters were looking in mirrors to confirm what the world told them they were, I, furtively, in the silence of the night, looked in the mirror to question myself, to know whether or not I existed. And when reason forced me to accept myself, the world saw to it that I disappeared. But it wasn't my figure that was invisible, but rather the most terrible thing of all: what was missing was my very self. It was my separate presence. And now, only now, do I have the time to think about it and I don't even know if this is worse than not having the time, moving from place to place with this idea that oppresses me, with the fear that this idea will invade me. What are we but a single idea that keeps returning and returning? I'll always be this idea I discovered when I was five years old, when I questioned myself in the mirror. This constant self-doubt that makes me run away from everything and everyone. This indecisiveness that has turned me into an invisible woman, that has trapped me in this asylum of a house.

Gonzalo is sitting in front of me and the typewriter; he interrupts me every minute with his little cries. He reaches for the little spoon from my coffee cup since he has now thrown all his toys far away from him. Bewildered, amazed, he observes it. It is the first time he has held a spoon in his hands, even if clumsily. He discovers it, looks at it, turns it, brings it several times to his mouth in every position. When he has tried it sufficiently, he drops it. For him, only the present exists; for me, only what was and will never come back.

That our image may be a faithful reflection of our being is what wise men have always sought to demonstrate. During my adolescence I sought this perfect composition, constraining myself, reducing my world. I removed myself from all mundane temptations in order not to lie, to be truthful. I inhabited a very dark room on the flat roof of my mother's house, surrounded by novels and poems. Nights, when the house was wrapped in silence, I went out walking, looking at the moon, I wrote very bad poems imitating Bécquer, but I felt whole. I was whole. So much so that I played with death every day. I balanced on the thin rails of the third floor balcony like a tightrope walker. I talked to myself, the future didn't exist. I denied everything except myself and therefore attempted suicide several times. Later on, I was dragged like a tame little dove from my pedantic self-sufficiency. So then I accepted everything and denied myself. As when I was five, I again returned to question the mirror: who am I, who are you? Men always gave me marvelously inconsistent answers, and it was a delight to live those illusions, even though inopportunely. I was a goddess, a muse, a brilliant intellectual in the eyes of others.

Now, at thirty, I am taking on a job for which I still don't feel capable. However, I haven't yet found the clue; the master key I discovered in my childhood. Perhaps I'll reach forty still trying to start over again. Anyhow, lunch is almost ready; I've added some mint to the stew.

Translated by Richard Schaaf

LUISA VALENZUELA is one of the most prolific and widely translated writers of contemporary Latin America. Born in Buenos Aires, Argentina in 1938, she worked as a journalist there beginning in the mid-1950's, writing for well-known newspapers and magazines including *La Nación*. She has lived in Paris, Mexico, and the United States, notably in New York where she was writer-in-residence at Columbia and New York Universities, a teacher of creative writing, and a 1983 Guggenheim Fellow. She currently resides in New York and Buenos Aires. Much of Valenzuela's work, including three of her novels and four collections of stories, has been published in English translation in the United States. She has been personally active in literary and political organizations dedicated to fighting censorship and repression. Luisa Valenzuela's writing throws into question the boundaries between violence and eroticism, or political and personal oppression, through a playful, ironic use of language that exploits puns, colloquial speech and word games. Ultimately this leads to a radical critique of the many hierarchies in society and within language itself. "Tango" is a recent and unpublished story. (KR)

ASA ZATZ began his career in Mexico translating a great variety of texts and most importantly did the bulk of Oscar Lewis' oeuvre. He had gone there to spend a year and when, after 33, he returned to his native Manhattan in 1982 he specialized in literature. Since then his translations have included works by Valle-Inclán, Carpentier, García Márquez, Sábato, Tomás Eloy Martínez, Eduardo Galeano, Jorge Ibargüengoitia, and José Luis González. His latest publication (among a total output of nearly 40 books) was the novel *After the Bombs* by Arturo Arias for Curbstone Press under a New York State Council on the Arts Grant.

TANGO

By Luisa Valenzuela

For Amalia Scheuer

I was told:

In this club the place for you to sit is close to the counter, on the left side, not far from the cash register; have yourself a glass of wine, but don't order anything hard—it's not proper for women, and don't drink beer because beer makes you want to pee and a lady mustn't pee. A fellow in this barrio is supposed to have walked out on his girlfriend the day he saw her coming out of the bathroom. His explanation, it seems, was: "I thought of her as pure spirit, an angel." The girlfriend ended up 'dressing saints,' an expression which in this barrio still carries an echo of unmarried and lonely, something strongly disapproved of. In women, of course. They told me.

I live alone and don't mind it the rest of the week, but on Saturdays I like to have company, to be held tight. Which is the reason I tango.

When I was learning, I gave it all I had, with the high heels and tight skirt slit up the side. Now, I even take the famous rubber bands with me in my handbag all the time which, if I were a tennis player, would be the equivalent of carrying around a racquet wherever I went, only much less bother. I keep them in my handbag and when I'm on a line in the bank or waiting at some office, I'll be absentmindedly rubbing my fingers over them. I don't know, but I guess it may be a consolation to imagine I'm tangoing right then instead of having to wait around till some snotty flunky gets good and ready to attend to me.

I know that no matter what time it is there will always be a club open some place in the city where they're dancing in the darkness, where you can't tell whether it's day or night, in case anybody cared, and the rubber bands are for holding your street shoes, stretched all out of shape from trotting around looking for work, up tight up against the instep.

But on a Saturday night, work is the last thing a girl is looking for. And, sitting at a table neat the counter, as I was told, I wait. The counter is the key spot in this club—it was impressed on me—where the men have a chance to size you up on their way to the john. Having to go is no problem for them. They push open the swinging door, we get a blast of ammonia, and they come out relieved and ready to continue dancing.

Now, I'm able to tell when I'll be getting a partner. And which one it will be. I catch the barely perceptible nod, the signal that I've been picked. I recognize the invitation and if I want to accept I smile the least bit. It's the signal that I accept, but I don't move; he'll come over to me and stretch out his hand. We stop at the edge of the dance floor and stand there facing one another, letting ourselves tense up, letting the concertina swell till we're at the bursting point and, then, on an unexpected chord his arm encircles my waist and we step out.

If it's a *milonga* we skim straight ahead, sailing with the wind, and if it's a tango, we dip. Our feet never tangle because he's so expert at signalling the steps to me, fingering my back. When a new variation with unfamiliar figures comes up, I'll improvise, and click just right, sometimes. I let one foot fly, dip to the left, separating my legs no more than the least bit needed, he steps out with elegance, and I follow. Sometimes, I'll stop and hold when he presses on my spine ever so lightly with his middle finger. 'I put the woman in neutral,' the teacher would say and I'd freeze in the middle of the step to let him go through his arabesque.

I really learned, milked it dry, as the saying goes. It all amounts to a taking of stances on the man's part, suggesting something else. That's the tango. And it's so beautiful you end up accepting.

My name is Sandra, but in these places I prefer being called Sonia, maybe to help me hang in. Actually, not many ask, or give, names, or talk at all. Some men will smile to themselves, though, as they listen to that inner music they dance to which isn't always pure nostalgia. The women will laugh, too, and they'll smile. I laugh when I keep getting picked for dance after dance (and we'll stand in the middle of the floor, not talking, smiling sometimes, as we wait for the next number), laugh because that tango music is sizzling up out of the floor through the soles of our feet, vibrating us and pulling us along.

I love the tango. And so, also the one transmitting the codes for the figures to me through his fingers, dancing me.

I don't care if I have to walk home the thirty blocks or so. Some Saturdays, I'll spend even my bus fare in the club and I don't care. Some Saturdays there's a sound of trumpets, celestial, let's call it, that knifes through the concertinas, and I levitate. I fly. Some Saturdays, my shoes stay on without rubber bands, of their own accord. It's worth it. The rest of the week goes by in the same humdrum way, and I'll hear the usual moronic bouquets a woman gets tossed at her on the street, those head-on compliments that seem so crude in comparison to the sidling of the tango.

And so, in the here and now, almost up against the counter so as to be able to take in the whole picture, I look over the older cavaliers and give one of them a smile. They are the best dancers. Let's see which of them takes me up. I get a reaction from the left side, part way behind a column. Such a slight nod that for a second it seemed almost as though he was going to lean his head over to listen to his shoulder. I like him. I like him. I flash him a real smile and not until then does he stand up and approach. You can't expect him to be forward. None of them here would risk getting turned down to his face and then have to walk back to his place with the shame past the smirks of the others. This one knows he's landed me and loses no time in coming over but, now, close up, I don't fancy him so much anymore, considering his age and that self-satisfied air about him.

It would violate club etiquette for me to ignore him. I stand up, he leads me to a corner of the dance floor off to the side, where he speaks to me! Not like one a while ago, who spoke only to excuse himself for not speaking to me, because 'I come here to dance, not to make talk,' he said and never opened his mouth again. Not this one. He starts out with a general remark and it's almost too much to bear. 'You know, *doña*,' he says, 'it looks like the crisis is getting worse,' and I tell him that yes, I know, I sure as hell do, only not in those words, I'm Sonia and refined, and I say,' Yes, frightening, no?' but he doesn't give me a chance to elaborate because he's already got me in a tight grip all set to step out on the next measure. This one's not going to let me down, I reassure myself, surrendering, mum.

It's a tango, the kind that's pure essence, a oneness with the universe. I can do the same hook steps I watched the woman in the knit dress doing, the chubby one who's having such a good time, flinging her neatly turned calves about so gracefully that one forgets the rest of her overblown anatomy. I dance thinking of that fat woman in the green knitted dress—the color of hope, they say—of the satisfaction dancing gives her, a replica, or maybe a reflection, of the satisfaction she must have gotten out of her knitting; a great big dress for her great body, and the anticipated pleasure of showing it off, dancing. I can't knit like her or even dance as well, but at this moment, by some miracle, I do.

And when the piece is over and he goes back to discussing the crisis, I listen, wide-eyed, not answering, and let him go on to say:

'And have you any idea of the price they're asking for a hotel room these days? I'm a widower and live with my two boys. I used to be able to invite a lady to a restaurant and then take her to the roost. Now, all I can do is ask the lady if she has an apartment, and if it's centrally located. For my part, I can manage the roast chicken and bottle of wine.'

I remember those flying feet—mine—those arabesques. I have in mind the fat woman, so happy with her happy man, to the point where I begin to have a feeling that I could really consider going in for knitting.

'I don't have an apartment,' I let him know, 'but I do have a room in a pension that's clean and near the center. And I have dishes, silverware, and a couple of those tall, green wine glasses.'

'Green? they're for white wine.'

'Yes, white.'

'Sorry, but I don't touch white wine.'

And without anything further, we separated.

Translated by Asa Zatz

ANA LYDIA VEGA is the author of three collections of short stories: *Vírgenes y mártires* (1981), which was co-written with Carmen Lugo Filippi; *Encancaranublado y otros cuentos de naufragio* (1983); and *Pasión de historia y otras historias de pasión* (1987). She has also edited a collection of essays entitled *El tramo ancla: Ensayos puertorriqueños de hoy* (1988) and was co-author of the film *La gran fiesta* (1986). Her work has received many awards including the Casa de las Américas award for *Encancaranublado* in 1982 and the Premio Internacional Juan Rulfo for *Pasión de historia* in 1984, and she received the Guggenheim Fellowship in 1989. She is currently a professor of French and Literature in the Department of Languages and Literature at the Río Piedras campus of the University of Puerto Rico. (CW)

CAROL WALLACE is a Ph.D. student in the Department of Spanish and Portuguese at the University of Iowa. She is currently working on her dissertation on the contemporary Puerto Rican short story, and teaching classes in Spanish language and Latin American literature.

DEATH'S PURE FIRE

By Ana Lydia Vega

I

Even Madama's voice changed whenever The Other took possession of her. It would become honeyed and coy. Her eyes would shine. Her face looked younger. She would run her hand around her waist to touch the ends of the long hair that wasn't there.

The Other was not just any spirit, though Violeta had never taken her very seriously. Spiritualists say so many things, and they always have some unfortunate being around doing its best to drag a person down. But this spirit was a mean one. Madama had already warned her the day she turned twenty, amid the wisps of incense and the tinkling of bells: Walk lightly, child, this woman wants to do you in, don't let her get on you, girl, if you do, no one's gonna be able to get rid of her, 'cause you see, she is one of the evil ones...

Five years later, the dead woman still hadn't given her any trouble. She showed up once in a while during the sessions trying to join the circle around the table. But it never went further than that. Violeta had waited so long now that she was almost looking forward to the encounter. In the meantime, she began going out with Miguel, fell in love, stopped working and got married.

II

Months went by. She stopped comin' around. At first I missed her 'cause she was always so faithful and all. Every Friday at seven, here she'd be, sure as anything. She was a good girl. And such a believer... She never took a step without consultin' me.

One day she shows up here at six in the morning. I'm still half asleep 'cause I'd gone to bed at three, out buryin' a few candles for Saint Martha in Keebler cracker boxes to see if she'd do a little holy number on the Electric Energy Authority for me. But I take her in the best I can. Good works shouldn't be denied a person, whatever the hour.

Her hair's a mess, she's really a sight. Blessed Mother, somebody like her who was so vain and always dressed like one of those models on T.V. I figure it's somethin' to do with her husband. I give her some coffee, I sit her down and ask her how it's goin', if she's gettin' used to it, if the boy's treatin' her all right. And then, Oh my dear Lord, all of a sudden a cold shiver shakes me down to my toes. It's like the yellow fever or somethin', I don't even wanna think about it. She sits there like nothing's goin' on and me there strugglin' with that awful thing that fell on me so sudden. Save me Blessed Virgin, the table's shakin' and the cups are dancin' like crazy. All the strength goes straight outa my hands and legs and I feel limp as a rag doll. I'm prayin' to Saint Jude but that thing won't go away and it won't show itself neither so I can find where it's comin' from. Then Violeta grabs my hand and tells me it's for her, says she's gonna take it, says for a long time they been sittin' in her bed at night and she wants to know who it is. Then, gracious me: All of a sudden I'm feelin' calm, like not a thing happened, so calm I'm just about fallin' asleep.

III

Mama named me Elena after my aunt, the one who was stabbed to death on a sugar plantation because of some jealous quarrel. People should be very careful about what they name a child.

I wasn't very pretty, although I wasn't ugly either, but I had something that drew the men to me. Every man in the neighborhood—bachelor, married, widowed or divorced—was after me. They'd wander up and down my street. They'd serenade me. They'd put my name in songs. Those things didn't impress me much. They amused me a little, maybe, but that's all. None of them managed to get me to leave home. Until Manuel arrived, with his face like an overgrown child and his merchant marine manners.

From the minute he saw me scrubbing Mama's parlor through the cracks in the moth-eaten wood, he began to build us a house. An enormous house up on stilts on a hill that got whipped by the wind. When it was done, he came for me. And I went off with him.

Manuel's turf was the street. I spent my days taking up hems, making pineapple candy, scaring the dust off the chairs, fulfilling my God-given role and polishing the bars of my cage.

One day I opened the door and let a man in. Nothing changed. He just wanted to take me to another cage that was more comfortable, more sunny. That's all.

What had to happen happened. Manuel sharpened his knife and arrived home an hour early.

IV

She got really weird on me. She was always walking around with this smile on her face like she had something up her sleeve. And she was really distracted, out of it.

She didn't fight with me anymore when I got home at all hours of the night. She didn't hide the keys to the door. She didn't give me a dirty look if I brought home the boys from the bar or if I disappeared for two or three days during the saints' day festivals.

It would have been better if she came out fighting. That stupid little smile really pissed me off. I kept trying to do little things that would make her mad, something that would set off her fuse, make her explode. But she never gave me an opening. She just kept smiling with that attitude of hers, like some virgin martyr.

I used any old excuse to get out of there. Sometimes I'd go for a walk by myself in the middle of the night. I wanted to make sure she was asleep when I got back. Laying there beside her in the dark, I took care of myself and enjoyed myself more than I could with any woman.

The house was never clean anymore. The sink was full of dirty dishes, the floor was disgusting, the tub was all stained. I just about died the day Mom came over and saw the state of that house. That woman is a pig, she told me, and she left in a half hour. Violeta hadn't even offered her a cup of coffee.

That's how I got mixed up with another woman. I was always out there in the streets.

V

Violeta had long conversations with Elena. She was a very intelligent and entertaining woman. They no longer needed Madama to be able to talk to each other.

At first, Violeta didn't want to go out. But Elena was so insistent: you have to take to the street, invade their territory, don't stay all shut up, there's air outside, you can breathe. Sometimes they walked around the city or took the bus. They never cared where they were going. Elena led her around to the rhythm of her whims. Violeta got to to know lots of places and lots of men. They all seemed the same to her. She went into lots of bars. She slept in lots of hotel beds. She was always smiling. But none of it really amused her. Once in a while she would disappear for entire days. She hardly ever saw Miguel, who was seldom at home either.

Buying the pistol was Elena's idea. You have to protect yourself. Men are so unpredictable.

VI

I never saw her again after that day The Other got in her head. But I consulted one of my spirit guides—that blessed guide of the island of St. Thomas, a spirit of light that you just can't beat, she never fails me in a pinch—help her out for me if you can, Saint Barbara. She told me all about Elena. I'd already warned her: she better watch out, gotta be careful, oughta take a bath in the sea every Sunday and rub her belly with half an apple to clean off all that bad influence. Violeta wasn't strong. Bless me, I wanted to protect her, like her own mother had asked me on her death bed: Take care of her for me, Madama, they tried to take this one away from me three times when I carried her inside my belly...

But that Elena was bad like only she could be. She wasn't gonna rest till she made that girl her victim. Them spirits that die violent are like that. They always want to drag half the world down with 'em. Now look, right now I gotta rub this red rag over me to keep me safe from that evil spirit.

Since I had to be careful, I fixed up a bath with some eucalyptus, rue, menthol, mint, bicarbonate, bee's honey, mineral salts and flower water, just like my guide told me. Just to give it some body, I threw in a capful of King Pine. That thing was a bomb. And then I sit down to wait for the girl to come. You gotta get her to come on her own, says my spirit guide, she's gotta come, don't go lookin' for her, don't go lookin' for her.

So I waited. But she never come back.

VII

When they opened the door of the room, the two of them were in bed. All cuddled up. Sleeping like babies. The girl's head on Miguel's hairy chest.

Violeta couldn't see anything. She was sweating. Trembling. It was Elena who put the pistol in her hand. She hugged her tenderly. "Go on," she said, "you'll see how easy it is."

Violeta approached slowly. She wasn't afraid, She had company. It was something else. Miguel was breathing deeply. The girl's head rose and fell on his chest.

Elena was gesturing affirmatively with her eyes. She supported her hand, caressing the pistol with her long fingernails. Violeta drew nearer to take aim. She raised the pistol. Elena adjusted it for her. Her fingers were cold.

Seconds away from pulling the trigger, Violeta tripped over a shoe. The girl's eyes popped open, like a doll. She opened her eyes and raised her head. Now, said Elena, fire, at him, don't look at her.

But Violeta did look at her. Their eyes met and held for a moment. A long moment. The pistol fell on the carpet. Miguel woke up. Violeta took a deep breath and ran out. Still running, she crossed the street and the avenue and the neighborhood. Still running, she arrived at the park. She threw herself on the first bench that crossed her path. The breeze was cool. A soft mist was beginning to fall. She looked around her. Elena was gone.

VIII

For the first time, I felt truly alone.

Translated by Carol Wallace

BIBLIOGRAPHY

I. General Works on Women Writers & Feminist Literary Criticism

Abel, Elizabeth, ed. *Writing and Sexual Difference*. Chicago: University of Chicago Press, 1982.

Anzaldúa, Gloria, ed. *Making Face, Making Soul/Haciendo Caras: Creative & Critical Perspectives by Women of Color.*. San Francisco: Aunt Lute, 1990.

Barrett, Michèle. *Women's Oppression Today: Problems in Marxist Feminist Analysis*. New York: Schocken Books, 1981.

Butler, Judith. *Gender Trouble: Feminism and the Subversion of Identity*. New York: Routledge, 1990.

Chodorow, Nancy. *The Reproduction of Mothering: Psychoanalysis and the Sociology of Gender*. Berkeley: University of California Press, 1978.

Davies, Miranda, ed. *Third World—Second Sex*. London: Zed, 1983.

Davis, Angela. *Women, Race, & Class*. 1981; rpt. New York: Vintage, 1983.

Donovan, Josephine, ed. *Feminist Literary Criticism: Explorations in Theory*. Lexington: University Press of Kentucky, 1975.

Eisenstein, Hester, and Alice Jardine, eds. *The Future of Difference: The Scholar and the Feminist*. Boston: G. K. Hall, 1980.

Ellman, Mary. *Thinking About Women*. New York: Harcourt, Brace & World, 1968.

Enloe, Cynthia. *Bananas, Beaches & Bases: Making Feminist Sense of International Politics*. Berkeley: University of California Press, 1989.

Etienne, Mona & Eleanor Leacock, eds. *Woman and Colonization: Anthropological Perspectives*. New York: Praeger, 1980.

Fetterley, Judith. *The Resisting Reader: A Feminist Approach to American Fiction*. Bloomington: Indiana University Press, 1978.

French Feminist Theory. Special Issue. *Signs* 7 (Fall 1981). Includes essays by Kristeva, Cixous, Irigaray, Faure.

Gallop, Jane. *The Daughter's Seduction: Feminism and Psychoanalysis*. Ithaca, N.Y.: Cornell University Press, 1982.

Heilbrun, Carolyn G. *Toward a Recognition of Androgyny*. New York: Harper & Row, 1973.

Hooks, Bell. *Feminist Theory. From Margin to Center*. Boston: South End Press, 1984.

Hull, Gloria T., Patricia Bell Scott, & Barbara Smith, eds. *But Some of Us Are Brave*. Old Westbury, N.Y.: Feminist Press, 1982.

Jacobus, Mary, ed. *Women Writing and Writing about Women*. New York: Barnes & Noble Imports, 1979.

Kahn, Coppélia, and Gayle Greene, eds. *Making a Difference: Feminist Literary Criticism*. New York and London: Methuen, 1985.

Keohane, Nannerl, Michelle A. Rosaldo and Barbara C. Gelpi, eds. *Feminist Theory: A Critique of Ideology*. Chicago: The University of Chicago Press, 1982.

Koppelman Cornillon, Susan, ed. *Images of Women in Fiction: Feminist Perspectives*. Bowling Green, Ohio: Bowling Green University Popular Press, 1972.

Marks, Elaine, and Isabelle de Courtivron, eds. *New French Feminisms: An Anthology*. Amherst: University of Massachusetts Press, 1980.

Martin, Wendy. "Seduced and Abandoned in the New World: The Images of Women in American Fiction." In *Woman in Sexist Society*, ed. Vivian Gornick and Barbara K. Moran, pp. 329-46. New York: New American Library, 1972.

McConnell-Ginet, Sally, Ruth Borker, and Nelly Furman, eds. *Women and Language in Literature and Society*. New York: Praeger, 1980.

Minh-ha, Trinh T. *Woman, Native, Other: Writing Postcoloniality and Feminism*. Bloomington: Indiana University Press, 1989.

Mora, Gabriela, and Karen S. Van Hooft, eds. *Theory and Practice of Feminist Literary Criticism*. Ypsilanti, Mich.: Bilingual Press/Editorial Bilingüe, 1982.

Morraga, Cherrie & Gloria Anzaldúa, eds. *This Bridge Called My Back: Writings by Radical Women of Color*. Watertown, Mass.: Persephone Press, 1981.

Pratt, Annis. *Archetypal Patterns in Women's Fiction*. Bloomington: Indiana University Press, 1981.

Rich, Adrienne. *Of Woman Born: Motherhood as Experience and Institution*. New York: W.W. Norton, 1976.

Robinson, Lillian S. *Sex, Class, And Culture*. Bloomington: Indiana University Press, 1978.

Showalter, Elaine, ed. *The New Feminist Criticism: Essays on Women, Literature, and Theory*. New York: Pantheon Books, 1985.

Spacks, Patricia Meyer. *The Female Imagination*. New York: Alfred A. Knopf, 1975.

Spivak, Gayatri Chakravorty. *In Other Worlds: Essays in Cultural Politics*. New York and London: Methuen, 1987.

II. Works on Latin American Women

Acosta-Belen, Edna. "Ideology and Images of Women in Contemporary Puerto Rican Literature". In *The Puerto Rican Woman*. Ed. Edna Acosta-Belen. New York: Praeger, 1979, 85-109.

Agosín, Marjorie. *Silencio e imaginación (Metáforas de la escritura femenina)*. México: Katún, 1986.

Boyce Davies, Carole, and Elaine Savory Fido, eds. *Out of the Kumbla: Caribbean Women and Literature*. Trenton, N.J.: Africa World Press, 1990.

Burgos-Debray, Elizabeth, ed. *I, Rigoberta Menchu: An Indian Woman in Guatemala.* Trans. A. Wright. London: Verso, 1984.

De Costa, Miriam, ed. *Blacks in Hispanic Literature: Critical Essays.* Port Washington, N.Y.: Kennikat Press, 1977.

Engling, Ezra S. "The 'Compact' Woman in Ana Lydia Vega's *Pollito Chicken.*" In *La mujer en la literatura caribeña.* ed. Lloyd King. St. Augustine, Trinidad: Dept. of French and Spanish Literature, University of the West Indies, 1984, 94-107.

Fernández-Olmos, Margarita, ed. *Contemporary Women Authors of Latin America: Introductory Essays.* Brooklyn: Brooklyn College Press, 1983.

Fox-Lockert, Lucía. *Women Novelists in Spain and Spanish America.* Metuchen, N.J.: Scarecrow Press, 1979.

Franco, Jean. "Apuntes sobre la crítica feminista y la literatura hispanoamericana." *Hispamérica* 45 (1986): 31-43.

———. *Plotting Women. Gender and Representation in Mexico.* New York: Columbia University Press, 1989.

———. "Self-Destructing Heroines." *Minnesota Review,* ns 22 (1984): 105-15.

García Pinto, Magdalena. *Historias íntimas. Conversaciones con diez escritoras latinoamericanas.* Hanover, NH: Ediciones del Norte, 1988.

Garfield, Evelyn Picón. *Women's Voices from Latin America.* Detroit, MI: Wayne State University, 1985.

Gazarian Gautier, Marie-Lise. *Interviews with Latin American Writers.* Elmwood Park, IL: The Dalkey Archive Press, 1989.

González, Patricia Elena, and Eliana Ortega, eds. *La sartén por el mango: Encuentro de escritoras latinoamericanas.* Río Piedras, Puerto Rico: Huracán, 1984.

Guerra-Cunningham, Lucía. "Algunas reflexiones teóricas sobre la novela femenina." *Hispamérica* 28 (1981): 29-39.

Guerra Cunningham, Lucía, ed. *Splintering Darkness: Latin American Women Writers In Search of Themselves.* Pittsburgh, PA: Latin American Literary Review Press, 1990.

Horno-Delgado, Asunción, et al. *Breaking Boundaries: Latina Writings and Critical Readings.* Amherst: University of Massachusetts, 1989.

Jiménez, Reynaldo L. "Cuban Women Writers and the Revolution: Toward an Assesment of their Literary Contributions." *Folio* 11 (1978): 75-95.

Jordan, Dawn M. "Building a History of Women's Literature in Brazil." *Plaza: Literatura y Crítica* (Cambridge, Mass.) 5-6 (Autumn-Spring 1981-1982): 75-96.

Lavrin, Asunción, ed. *Latin American Women: Historical Perspectives.* London: Greenwood Press, 1978.

Lobo, Luiza. "Women Writers in Brazil Today." *World Literature Today* 61, 1 (Winter 1987): 49-54.

"The Latin American Woman: Image and Reality." *Revista/Review Interamericana,* Special Edition, 4, No. 2 (Summer 1974).

Magnarelli, Sharon. *The Lost Rib: Female Characters in the Spanish American Novel.* Lewisburg, Penn.: Bucknell University Press, 1985.

Meyer, Doris, and Margarite Fernández Olmos, eds. *Contemporary Women Authors of Latin America.* Vol. 1: *Introductory Essays.* Brooklyn, N.Y.: Brooklyn College Press, 1983.

Miller, Yvette, and Charles Tatum, eds. *Latin American Women Writers— Yesterday and Today.* Pittsburgh: Latin American Literary Review Press, 1977.

Miller, Beth, ed. *Women in Hispanic Literature: Icons and Fallen Idols.* Berkeley: University of California Press, 1983.

Myers, Eunice, and Ginette Adamson, eds. *Continental, Latin-American and Francophone Women Writers. Selected papers from the Wichita State University Conference on Foreign Literatures, 1984-85.* Lanham MD: UP of America, 1987.

Pescatello, Ann, ed. *Female and Male in Latin America: Essays.* Pittsburgh: University of Pittsburgh Press, 1974.

Robles, Martha. *La sombra fugitiva: Escritoras en la cultura nacional.* Mexico City: Editorial Diana, 1989. Vol. I-II.

Schipper, Mineke, ed. Fasting, Barbara Potter, Trans. *Unheard Words: Women and Literature in Africa, the Arab World, Asia, the Caribbean and Latin America.* London: Allison & Busby, 1985.

Shea, Maureen. "A Growing Awareness of Sexual Oppression among Contemporary Latin American Women Writers." *Confluencia: Revista Hispánica de Cultura y Literatura* 4, 1 (1988): 53-59.

Solé, Carlos A. and María Isabel Abreu, eds. *Latin American Writers.* 3 vols. New York: Charles Scribner's Sons, 1989.

Steele, Cynthia. "Toward a Socialist Feminist Criticism of Latin American Literature." *Ideologies and Literature* 4, 16 (May-June 1983): 323-29.

Sullivan, Constance A. "Re-Reading the Hispanic Literary Canon: The Question of Gender." *Ideologies and Literature* 4, 2nd cycle, 16 (May-June 1983): 93-101.

Ugalde, Sharon Keefe. "Process, Identity, and Learning to Read: Female Writing and Feminist Criticism in Latin America Today." *Latin American Research Review* 24, 1 (1989): 222-32.

Valis, Noël, and Carol Maier, eds. *In the Feminine Mode: Essays on Hispanic Women Writers.* Lewisburg, Pa.: Bucknell University Press, 1990.

Vidal, Hernán, ed. *Cultural and Historical Grounding for Hispanic and Luso-Brazilian Feminist Literary Criticism.* Series Literature and Human Rights No. 4. Minnesota: Institute for the Study of Ideologies and Literature, 1989.

Virgillo, Carmelo, and Naomi Lindstrom, eds. *Woman as Myth and Metaphor in Latin American Literature.* Columbia, MO: University of Missouri Press, 1985.

Zapata, Celia Correas de. "One Hundred Years of Women Writers in Latin America." *Latin American Literary Review* 3, 6 (Spring-Summer 1975): 7-16.

III. Anthologies of (or including) Latin American Women Writers in English & Spanish

Agosín, Marjorie, ed. *Landscapes of a New Land: Short Fiction by Latin American Women.* Buffalo, N.Y.: White Pine Press, 1989.

Arkin, Marian and Barbara Shollar, eds. *Longman Anthology of World Literature by Women 1875-1975.* New York: Longman Inc., 1989.

Barradas, Efraín, ed. *Apalabramiento: cuentos puertorriqueños de hoy.* Hanover, NH: Ediciones del Norte, 1983.

Bassnett, Susan, ed. *Knives and Angels: Women Writers in Latin America.* London: Zed Books, 1990.

Caistor, Nick, ed. *The Faber Book of Contemporary Latin American Short Stories.* London & Boston: Faber & Faber, 1989.

Erro-Peralta, Nora, & Caridad Silva-Nuñez, eds. *Beyond the Border: A New Age in Latin American Women's Fiction.* Pittsburgh, PA: Cleis Press, 1991.

Gómez, Alma, Cherrie Moraga and Mariana Romo-Cardona, eds. *Cuentos: Stories by Latinas.* New York: Kitchen Table, Women of Color Press, 1983.

Handelsman, Michael H. *Diez escritoras ecuatorianas y sus cuentos.* Quito: Casa de la Cultura Ecuatoriana, 1982.

Lewald, H. Ernest, trans. and ed. *The Web: Stories by Argentine Women.* Washington D.C.: Three Continents Press, 1983.

Luby, Barry J. and Wayne H. Finke, eds. *Anthology of Contemporary Latin American Literature 1960-1984.* London-Toronto: Associated University Press, 1986.

Manguel, Alberto, ed. *Other Fires: Short Fiction by Latin American Women.* Avenal, NJ: Clarkson N. Potter, 1986

Menton, Seymour, ed. *The Spanish American Short Story: A Critical Anthology.* Berkeley: University of California Press, 1980.

Meyer, Doris, and Margarite Fernández Olmos, eds. *Contemporary Women Authors of Latin America: New Translations* (Brooklyn: Brooklyn College, 1983).

Meyer, Doris, ed. *Lives on the Line: The Testimony of Contemporary Latin American Authors.* Berkeley: University of California Press, 1988.

Ortega, Julio, ed. *El muro y la intemperie: el nuevo cuento latinoamericano.* Hanover, NH: Ediciones del Norte, 1989.

Partnoy, Alicia, ed. *You Can't Drown the Fire: Latin American Women Writing in Exile.* Pittsburgh: Cleis Press, 1988.

Picón Garfield, Evelyn, ed. *Women's Fiction from Latin America.* Detroit: Wayne State University Press, 1988.

Rojo, Grinor, and Cynthia Steele, eds. *Ritos de iniciación.* Boston: Houghton Mifflin Co., 1986.

Santos, Rosario, ed. *And We Sold the Rain: Contemporary Fiction from Central America.* New York: Four Walls Eight Windows, 1988.

Sefchovich, Sara, ed. *Mujeres en espejo.* México: Folios Ediciones, 1983. *Mujeres en espejo* 2. México: Folios Ediciones, 1985.

Silva-Velásquez, Caridad L., and Nora Erro-Orthman, eds. *Puerta abierta, la nueva escritora latinoamericana.* México: Joaquín Mortiz, 1986.

Urbano, Victoria. *Five Women Writers of Costa Rica.* Beaumont, Texas: Asociación de Literatura Femenina Hispánica, Lamar University, 1978.

Vélez, Diana. *Reclaiming Medusa: Short Stories by Contemporary Puerto Rican Women.* San Francisco: Spinsters/Aunt Lute Book Co., 1988.

Vigil, Evangelina, ed. *Woman of her Word: Hispanic Women Write.* Houston: Arte Público Press, 1984.

Rodríguez Monegal, Emir. *The Borzoi Anthology of Latin American Literature.* New York: Alfred Knopf, 1977.

Zapata, Celia Correas de, and Lygia Johnson. *Detrás de la reja: Antología crítica de narradoras latinoamericanas del siglo XX,* Caracas: Monte Avila, 1980.

Zapata, Celia Correas de, ed. *Short Stories by Latin American Women: The Magic and the Real.* Houston: Arte Público Press, 1990.

IV. General Bibliographies of (or including) Latin American Women Writers

Alarcón, Norma and Sylvia Kossnar. *Bibliography of Hispanic Women Writers.* Bloomington, IN: Chicano-Riqueño Studies Bibliography Series No. 1, 1980.

Cortina, Lynn Ellen Rice. *Spanish-American Women Writers: A Bibliographical Research Checklist.* New York: Garland Publishing, 1983.

Corvalán, Graciela N. V. *Latin American Women Writers in English Translation: A Bibliography.* Los Angeles: California State University Latin American Studies Center, 1980.

Dolz-Blackburn, Inés. "Recent Critical Bibliography on Women in Hispanic Literature." *Discurso Literario* 3, 2 (1986): 331-34.

Flores, Angel. *Bibliografía de escritores hispanoamericanos. A Bibliography of Spanish-American Writers* 1609-1974. New York: Gordian Press, 1975.

Freudenthal, Juan R. and Patricia M. Freudenthal. *Index to Anthologies of Latin American Literature in English Translation.* Boston: G.K. Hall & Co., 1977.

Knaster, Meri. *Women in Spanish America. An Annotated Bibliography from Pre-Conquest to Contemporary Times.* Boston: G.K. Hall & Co., 1977.

Lindstrom, Naomi. "Feminist Criticism Of Latin American Literature: Bibliographic Notes." *Latin American Research Review* 15, 1 (1980): 151-59.

Marting, Diane E., ed. *Spanish American Women Writers: A Bio-bibliographical Source Book.* New York: Greenwood Press, 1990.

——.*Women Writers of Spanish America. An Annotated Bio-bibliographical Guide.* New York: Greenwood Press, 1987.

Ramos Foster, Virginia. "La crítica literaria de la profesoras norteamericanas ante las letras femeninas hispánicas." *Revista Interamericana de Bibliografía/Interamerican Review of Bibliography.* 30.4 (1980): 406-12.

Resnick, Margery and Isabel de Cortivron, eds. *Women Writers in Translation: An Annotated Bibliography.* New York: Garland Press, 1984.

V. Individual Bibliographies

Margarita Aguirre

1. Works in chronological order (category)

Cuaderno de una muchacha muda. Buenos Aires: Botella al mar, 1951. (novella)
El huésped. Buenos Aires: Emecé, 1958. (novel)
La culpa. Santiago: Zig-Zag, 1962. (novel)
El residente. Buenos Aires: Emecé, 1967. (novel)
La oveja roja. Buenos Aires: Sudamericana, 1974. (short stories)

2. Criticism

Guerra-Cunningham, Lucía. "El concepto de la existencia en *El huésped* de Margarita Aguirre." *Explicaciones de textos literarios.* Vol. 6, No. 11, 1978: 123-127.

Claribel Alegría

1. Works in chronological order (category)

Anillo de silencio. Mexico City: Ediciones Botas, 1948. (poetry)
Vigilias. Mexico City: Ediciones Poesía de América, 1953. (poetry)
Tres cuentos. San Salvador: Ministerio de Cultura, Departamento Editorial, 1958. (short stories)
Huésped de mi tiempo. Buenos Aires: Americalee, 1961. (poetry)
Vía única. Montevideo: Editorial Alfa, 1965. (poetry)
Aprendizaje. San Salvador: Editorial Universitaria de El Salvador, 1970. (poetry)
Pagaré a cobrar y otros poemas. Barcelona: Editorial Llibres de Sinera, 1973. (poetry)
El detén. Barcelona: Editorial Lumen, 1977. (novella)
Sobrevivo. La Habana: Casa de las Américas, 1978. (poetry)
Homenaje a El Salvador. Madrid: Visor, 1981. (poetry)
Suma y sigue. Antología. Madrid: Visor, 1981. (poetry)
"Literatura y liberación nacional en El Salvador." *Casa de las Américas* 21, 126 (May-June 1981): 12-16. (essay)
Flowers from the Volcano/Flores del volcán. Pittsburgh: University of Pittsburgh Press, 1982. (poetry)
Poesía viva. London: Black Roads Press, 1983. (poetry)
Album familiar. 2d ed. San José, Costa Rica: Editorial Universitaria Centroamericana (UCA), 1984. (novel)

Pueblo de Dios y de Mandinga. Mexico City: Ediciones Era, 1985. (novel)
Despierta, mi bien, despierta. San Salvador: UCA (Universidad Centroamericana Editores), 1986. (novel)
Pueblo de Dios y de Mandinga. Barcelona: Editorial Lumen, 1986. (novel)
Luisa en el país de la realidad. Mexico City: Joan Boldó i Climent, Editores, Universidad Autónoma de Zacatecas, 1987. (novel)
Y este poema-río. Managua: Editorial Nueva Nicaragua, 1988. (poetry)

Works Published with Darwin Flakoll

Cenizas de Izalco. Barcelona: Seix Barral, 1966. 2d ed. San José: Editorial Universitaria Centroamericana, 1982. (novel)
La encrucijada salvadoreña. Barcelona. Dossier Cidob, Centre d'Informació i Documentació, 1980. (essay)
Nicaragua: La revolución sandinista. Mexico City: Ediciones Era, 1983. (essay)
No me agarran viva: La mujer salvadoreña en lucha. Mexico City: Ediciones Era, 1983. (testimony)
Para romper el silencio: Resistencia y lucha en las cárceles salvadoreñas. Mexico City: Ediciones Era, 1984. (testimony)

2. Works in translation

Alegría, Claribel, trans. "The Two Cultures of El Salvador." *Massachusetts Review*. Special issue entitled *Latin America* 27, 3-4 (Fall-Winter 1986): 493-502.
Flakoll, Darwin, trans. *Ashes of Izalco*. With Darwin Flakoll. Willimantic, Conn.: Curbstone Press, 1988.
——. *Luisa in Realityland*. Willimantic, Conn.: Curbstone Press, 1987.
——. *Woman of the River*. Pittsburgh: University of Pittsburgh Press, 1988.
——. "Boardinghouse." In *And We Sold the Rain: Contemporary Fiction from Central America*. Santos, Rosario, ed. New York: Four Walls Eight Windows, 1988: 149-156.
Forché, Carolyn, trans. *Flowers from the Volcano*. Pittsburgh: University of Pittsburgh Press, 1982.
Hopkinson, Amanda, trans. *Family Album*. London: Women's Press, 1989.
——. *They won't take me alive*. London: Women's Press, 1987.
"The Politics of Exile." Partnoy, Alicia, ed. *You Can't Drown the Fire: Latin American Women Writing in Exile*. Pittsburgh: Cleis Press, 1988: 171-177.
"The Writer's Commitment." Meyer, Doris, ed. *Lives on the Line: The Testimony of Contemporary Latin American Authors*. Berkeley: University of California Press, 1988: 306-311.

3. Criticism

Arenal, Electa. "Two Poets of the Sandinista Struggle." *Feminist Studies* 7, 1 (Spring 1981): 19-27.

Forché, Carolyn. "Interview with Claribel Alegría." *Index on Censorship* 1984 April. v13(2): 11-13.

Shea, Maureen. "A Growing Awareness of Sexual Oppression in the Novels of Contemporary Latin American Women Writers." *Confluencia: Revista Hispánica de Cultura y Literatura* 1988 Fall v4(1): 53-59.

Yúdice, George. "Letras de Emergencia: Claribel Alegría." *Revista Iberoamericana* 1985 July-Dec. v51(132-133): 953-964.

Isabel Allende

1. Works in chronological order (category)

La casa de los espíritus. Barcelona: Plaza & Janés, 1982. (novel)

De amor y de sombra. Barcelona: Plaza & Janés, 1984. (novel)

Eva Luna. Barcelona: Plaza & Janés, 1987. (novel)

"La magia de las palabras." *Revista Iberoamericana* 132-33 (July-Dec. 1985): 447-52. (essay)

"Los libros tienen sus propios espíritus." *Los libros tienen sus propios espíritus*. Ed. Marcelo Coddou. Mexico: Universidad Veracruzana, 1986. Pp. 15-20. (essay)

Cuentos de Eva Luna. Buenos Aires. Editorial Sudamericana, 1990. (short stories)

2. Works in translation

The House of the Spirits. Trans. Magda Bogin. New York: Knopf, 1985.

Of Love and Shadows. Trans. Margaret Sayers Peden. New York: Bantam Books, 1987.

"The Spirits Were Willing." Trans. Jo Anne Engelbert. *Lives on the Line: The Testimony on Contemporary Latin American Authors*. Ed. Doris Meyer. Berkeley: University of California Press, 1988. 235-42.

Eva Luna. Trans. Margaret Sayers Peden. New York: Bantam Books, 1989.

"An Act of Vengeance." Trans. E.D. Carter Jr. In *Short Stories by Latin American Women: The Magic and the Real*. Zapata, Celia Correas de, ed. Houston: Arte Público Press, 1990: 11-17.

The Stories of Eva Luna. Margaret Sayers Peden. New York: Atheneum, 1991.

"The Judge's Wife." Trans. Nick Caistor. In *The Faber Book of Contemporary Latin American Short Stories*. Caistor, Nick, ed. London & Boston: Faber & Faber, 1989 & In *Beyond the Border: A New Age in Latin American Women's Fiction*. Erro-Peralta, Nora, & Caridad Silva-Nuñez, eds. Pittsburgh, PA: Cleis Press, 1991.

3. Criticism

Agosín, Marjorie. "Entrevista a Isabel Allende/Interview with Isabel Allende." Trans. Cola Franzen. *Imagine* 1 vol. 2 (Winter 1984): 42-56

Antoni, Robert. "Parody or Piracy: The Relationship of The House of the Spirits to One Hundred Years of Solitude." *Latin American Literary Review* 1988 July-Dec. v16(32): 16-28.

Earle, Peter. "Literature as Survival: Allende's The House of the Spirits." *Contemporary Literature* 1987 Winter v28(4): 543-554.

Foster, Douglas. "Isabel Allende Unveiled." *Mother Jones* 1988 Dec. v13(10): 42-46.

Gazarian Gautier, Marie-Lise. "Isabel Allende." *Interviews with Latin American Writers*. Elmwood Park, Ill.: Dalkey Archive Press, 1989, 5-24.

Gordon, Ambrose. "Isabel Allende on Love and Shadow." *Contemporary Literature* 1987 Winter v28(4): 530-542.

Levine, Linda Gould. "A Passage to Androgyny: Isabel Allende's *La casa de los espíritus*." Valis, Noël, and Carol Maier, eds. *In the Feminine Mode: Essays on Hispanic Women Writers*. Lewisburg, Pa.: Bucknell University Press, 1990.

Meyer, Doris. "Exile and the Female Condition in Isabel Allende's *De amor y de sombra*." *International Fiction Review* 1988 Summer v15(2): 151-157.

Moody, Michael. "Isabel Allende and the Testimonial Novel." *Confluencia: Revista Hispánica de Cultura y Literatura* 1986 Fall v2(1): 39-43.

Shields, E. Thomson, Jr. "Ink, Blood, and Kisses: La casa de los Espíritus and the Myth of Disunity." *Hispanófila* 1990 May v33[3(99)]: 79-86.

Albalucía Angel

1. Works in chronological order (category)

Los girasoles en invierno. Bogotá: Bolívar, 1970. (novel)
Dos veces Alicia. Barcelona: Seix-Barral, 1972. (novel)
Estaba la pájara pinta sentada en el verde limón. Bogotá: Instituto Colombiano de Cultura, 1975. (novel)
¡Oh gloria inmarcesible!. Bogotá: Instituto Colombiano de Cultura, 1975. (short stories)
Misiá Señora. Barcelona: Argos Vergara, 1982. (novel)
Las andariegas. Barcelona: Argos Vergara, 1984. (novel)

2. Works in translation

"The Guerillero." Trans. Alberto Manguel. In *Other Fires: Short Fiction by Latin American Women*. Manguel, Alberto, ed. Avenal, NJ: Clarkson N. Potter, 1986.

3. Criticism

Keefe Ugalde, Sharon. "Between 'in longer' and 'not yet': Woman's Space in *Misiá Señora*." *Revista de Estudios Colombianos* 1986 v1: 23-28.

——. "El discurso femenino en *Misía Señora*: ¿un lenguaje nuevo o acceso al lenguaje?" *Discurso Literario* 4.1 (1986): 117-126.

William, Raymond Leslie. "An Interview with Women Writers in Colombia." Miller, Yvette, and Charles Tatum, eds. *Latin American Women Writers—Yesterday and Today*. Pittsburgh: Latin American Literary Review Press, 1977: 155-161.

Pía Barros

1. Works in chronological order (category)

Miedos Transitorios (De a uno, de a dos, de a todos). Santiago: Ergo Sum, 1986. Reedited in Montevideo: YOEA Libros, 1989.
A horcajadas. Santiago: Mosquito Editores, 1990.

2. Works in translation

Transitory Fears. Trans. Isabel Balseiro.
"Muzzle" (Translation of "Mordaza" from *A horcajadas*). Trans. Kathryn Kruger Hickman. Forthcoming in *Latin American Literary Review*.

3. Criticism

Trevizan, Liliana. "La articulación estética entre la variable de clase y la variable de género en un cuento de Pía Barros." *Plaza: Revista de Literatura* 1988 Spring-Fall v14-15: 51-56.

Lydia Cabrera

1. Works in chronological order (category)

Cuentos negros de Cuba. Havana: Imprenta La Verónica, 1940. (short stories)
Por qué... Cuentos negros de Cuba. Havana: Ediciones C.R., 1948. (short stories)
El Monte: Igbo-Finda; Ewe Orisha, Vititi Nfinda. (Notas sobre las religiones, la magia, las supersticiones y el folklore de los negros criollos y el pueblo de Cuba). Havana: Ediciones C.R., 1954. (anthropological study)
Refranes de negros viejos: recogidos por Lydia Cabrera. Havana: Ediciones C.R., 1955. (anthropological study)
Anagó: vocabulario lucumi (El Yoruba que se habla en Cuba). Havana: Ediciones C.R., 1957. (anthropological study)
La sociedad secreta Abakuá: narrada por viejos adeptos. Havana: Ediciones C.R., 1959. (anthropological study)
Otán Iyebiyé: las piedras preciosas. Miami: Ediciones C.R., 1970. (anthropological study)
Ayapá: cuentos de Jicotea. Miami: Ediciones Universal, 1971. (short stories)
La laguna sagrada de San Joaquín. Madrid: Ediciones R, 1973. (anthropological study)

Yemayá y Ochún: Kariocha, Iyalorichas y Olorichas. Madrid: Ediciones C.R., 1974. (anthropological study)

Anaforuana: ritual y símbolos de la iniciación en la sociedad secreta Abakuá. Madrid: Ediciones R, 1975. (anthropological study)

Francisco y Francisca: chascarrillos de negros viejos. Miami: Ediciones C.R., 1976. (short stories)

Itinerarios del Insomnio: Trinidad de Cuba. Miami. Ediciones C.R., 1977. (anthropological study)

La Regla Kimbisa del Santo Cristo del Buen Viaje. Miami. Ediciones C.R., 1977. (anthropological study)

Reglas de Congo. Palo Monte-Mayombe. Miami: Ediciones C.R., 1979. (anthropological study)

Koeko Iyawó. Aprende Novicia: pequeño tratado de Regla Lucumí. Miami: Ediciones C.R., 1980. (anthropological study)

Cuentos para adultos niños y retrasados mentales. Miami: Ediciones C.R., 1983. (short stories)

La medicina popular en Cuba. Médicos de antaño, curanderos, santeros y paleros de hogaño. Miami: Ediciones C.R., 1984. (anthropological study)

Vocabulario Congo: (El Bantú que se habla en Cuba). Miami: Ediciones C.R., 1984. (anthropological study)

Supersticiones y buenos consejos. Miami: Ediciones Universal, 1987. (anthropological study)

La lengua sagrada de los ñáñigos. Miami: Ediciones C.R., 1984. (anthropological study)

Los animales en el folklore y la magia de Cuba. Miami: Ediciones Universal, 1988. (anthropological study)

2. Works in translation

"Turtle's Horse" and "Walo-Wila." In *From the Green Antilles*, edited by Barbara Howes: 275-79. New York, 1966.

"Obbara Lies but Doesn't Lie," translated by Suzanne Jill Levine and Mary Caldwell, and "The Hill Called Mambiala," translated by Elizabeth Millet. In *Contemporary Women Authors of Latin America: New Translations*. Meyer, Doris, and Margarite Fernández Olmos, eds. (Brooklyn: Brooklyn College, 1983).

"How the Monkey Lost the Fruit of his Labor," translated by Mary Caldwell and Suzanne Jill Levine. In *Other Fires: Short Fiction by Latin American Women*. Manguel, Alberto, ed. Avenal, NJ: Clarkson N. Potter, 1986.

"The Mire of Almendares," and "Tatabisako." Trans. Evelyn Picon Garfield. In *Women's Fiction from Latin America*. Picón Garfield, Evelyn, ed. Detroit: Wayne State University Press, 1988.

"The Prize of Freedom." Trans. Lisa Wyant. In *Beyond the Border: A New Age in Latin American Women's Fiction*. Erro-Peralta, Nora, & Caridad Silva-Nuñez, eds. Pittsburgh, PA: Cleis Press, 1991.

3. Criticism

Carpentier, Alejo. "Los cuentos de Lydia Cabrera." *Carteles* (La Habana) 28.41 (1936): 40.

Foster, David William. *Cuban Literature: A Research Guide.* New York: Garland Publishing, Inc., 1985: 122-24.

Gutiérrez, Mariela. *Los cuentos negros de Lydia Cabrera: estudio morfológico esquemático.* Miami: Universal, 1986.

Hiriart, Rosario. "Lydia Cabrera and the World of Cuba's Blacks." *Américas* (Washington) 3 (1980): 40-42.

—— *Lydia Cabrera: Vida hecha arte.* New York: Eliseo Torres & Sons, 1978. Rpt. in Miami: Universal, 1983.

Josephs, Allen. "Lydia and Federico: Towards a Historical Approach to Lorca Studies." *Journal of Spanish Studies: Twentieth Century,* no. 6: 123-130.

Levine, Suzanne Jill. "A Conversation with Lydia Cabrera." *Review: Latin American Literature and Arts.* 1982. Jan.-Apr. v31: 13-15.

Valdés-Cruz, Rosa. "The Short Stories of Lydia Cabrera: Transpositions or Creations?" In *Latin American Women Writers—Yesterday and Today.* Miller, Yvette, and Charles Tatum, eds. Pittsburgh: Latin American Literary Review Press, 1977: 148-154.

Willis, Miriam DeCosta. "Folklore and the Creative Artist: Lydia Cabrera and Zora Neale Hurston." *College Language Association Journal.* 1983. Sept. v27(1): 81-90.

Julieta Campos

1. Works in chronological order (category)

La imagen en el espejo. Mexico City: Universidad Autónoma de Mexico, 1965. (literary criticism)

Muerte por agua. Mexico City: Fondo de Cultura Económica, 1965. (novel)

Celina o los gatos. Mexico City: Siglo XXI Editores, 1968. (short stories)

Oficio de leer. Mexico City: Tezontle, 1971. (literary criticism)

Función de la novela. Mexico City: Joaquín Mortiz, 1973. (literary criticism)

Tiene los cabellos rojizos y se llama Sabina. Mexico City: Joaquín Mortiz, 1973. (novel)

"Historia de un naufragio." *Plural* (May 1976). (short story)

"Literatura y política: ¿relación o incompatibilidad?" *Texto Crítico* 4 (1976): 7-9. (literary criticism)

"¿Tiene sexo la escritura?" *Vuelta* 21 (Aug. 1978): 44-45. (literary criticism)

El miedo de perder a Eurídice. Mexico City. Joaquín Mortiz, 1979. (novel)

La herencia obstinada. Análisis de cuentos nahuas. Mexico City: Fondo de Cultura Económica, 1982. (literary criticism)

"Mi vocación literaria." *Revista Iberoamericana* 51, 132-33 (1985): 467-70. (literary criticism)

"Jardin de invierno." *Vuelta* 10, no. 115 (June 1986): 19-29. (short story)

2. Works in translation

"Story of a Shipwreck," Translated by Beth Miller. *Review, Center for Inter-American Relations* 76, no. 18 (Fall 1976): 66-68.
"A Redhead Named Sabina [Selections from the novel]," and "All the Roses." Trans. Evelyn Picon Garfield. In *Women's Fiction from Latin America.* Picón Garfield, Evelyn, ed. Detroit: Wayne State University Press, 1988.

3. Criticism

Bruce-Novoa, Juan. "Julieta Campo's *Sabina*: In the Labyrinth of Intertextuality." *Third Woman*, 1984 v2(2): 43-63.
Garfield, Evelyn Picon. "Julieta Campos." In *Women's Voices from Latin America.* Detroit, MI: Wayne State University, 1985.
Lagos-Pope, María Inés. "Cat/Logos: The Narrator's Confession in Julieta Campos' *Celina o los gatos* (Celina or the cats)." In *Splintering Darkness: Latin American Women Writers in Search of Themselves.* Guerra-Cunningham, Lucía, ed. Pittsburgh: Latin American Literary Review Press, 1990.

Ana María del Río

1. Works in chronological order (category)

"Cuento para Alsea." In *Los Mejores Cuentos de mí País.* Santiago, Chile: Ed. Nascimento, 1982. (short story)
"Entreojos," "Parece" and "Como los geranios." In *Somos 13.* Santiago, Chile: Ed. Arcilla, 1984. (short stories)
Entre paréntesis. Santiago, Chile: Ed. Arcilla, 1985. (short stories)
"Ojalá se me olvidara." In *Caja de cuentos.* Santiago, Chile: Ed. Ergo Sum, 1985. (short story)
Oxido de Cármen. Santiago, Chile: Andrés Bello, 1986.
"Bus-queda." In *Maleta de cuentos.* Santiago, Chile: Ed. Ergo Sum, 1986. (short story)

2. Criticism

"Algarabía" and "Entreparéntesis." In *Antología del cuento chileno.* By Enrique Lafourcade. Santiago, Chile: Ed. Alfa, 1984.

Lygia Fagundes Telles

1. Works in chronological order (category)

O Cacto Vermelho. Río de Janeiro: Editôra Mérito, 1949. (short stories)
Ciranda de pedra. Lisboa: Editorial Minerva, 1956; 16th ed. Río de Janeiro: José Olympio, 1983. (novel)

Historias do Desencontro. Río de Janeiro: José Olympio, 1958. (short stories)
Historias Escolhidas. São Paulo: Boa Leitura, 1961. (short stories)
Os Mortos. Lisboa: Casa Portuguesa, 1963.
Verâo no Aquário. Sâo Paulo: Martins, 1963; 6th ed. Río de Janeiro: José Olympio, 1980. (novel)
O Jardim Selvagem. Sâo Paulo: Martins, 1965; Río de Janeiro: José Olympio: Civilizaçâo Brasileira Editôra Três, 1974.
Antes do Baile Verde. Río de Janeiro: Edicôes Bloch, 1970; 7th. ed. Río de Janeiro: Livraria J. Olympio Editôra, 1982. (short stories)
Selecta de Lygia Fagundes Telles. Ed. Nelly Novaes Coelho. Río de Janeiro: José Olympio, 1971. 3rd. ed. Río de Janeiro: José Olympio, 1978. (short stories)
As Meninas. Río de Janeiro: José Olympio, 1973; 12th. ed. Río de Janeiro: José Olympio, 1981. (novel)
Seminário dos ratos. Río de Janeiro: Livraria J. Olympio Editôra, 1977. (short stories)
Filhos Pródigos. Sâo Paulo: Livraria Cultura Editôra, 1978. (short stories)
"Depoimento." *Prismal/Cabral.* v3-4, Spr. 1979: 135-39. (short story)
Lygia Fagundes Telles: Selecâo de Textos, Notas, Estudos Biográfico, Histórico e Crítico e Exercício. Montfeiro, Leonardo. Sâo Paulo: Abril Educaçâo, 1980. (short stories and criticism)
A Disciplina do Amor; Fragmentos. 3th. ed. Río de Janeiro: Editôra Nova Fronteira, 1980. (essays)
Mistério ficçôes. Río de Janeiro: Editôra Nova Fronteira, 1981.
Os Melhores Contos de Lydia Fagundes Telles. Ed. Eduardo Portella, Sâo Paulo: Global Editôra, 1984. (short stories)

2. Works in translation

The Girl in the Photograph. Trans. Margaret Neves. New York: Avon Books, 1982.
"The Truth of Invention." Trans. Giovanni Pontiero. In *Lives on the Line: The Testimony of Contemporary Latin American Authors.* Meyer, Doris, ed. Berkeley: University of California Press, 1988: 306-311.
"The Key." Trans. Giovanni Pontiero. In *Landscapes of a New Land: Short Fiction by Latin American Women.* Agosín, Marjorie, ed. Buffalo, N.Y.: White Pine Press, 1989.
"Tigrela." Trans. Eloah F. Giacomelli. In *Other Fires: Short Fiction by Latin American Women.* Manguel, Alberto, ed. Avenal, NJ: Clarkson N. Potter, 1986.
"The Hunt." Trans. Eloah F. Giacomelli. In *Beyond the Border: A New Age in Latin American Women's Fiction.* Erro-Peralta, Nora, & Caridad Silva-Nuñez, eds. Pittsburgh, PA: Cleis Press, 1991.

3. Criticism

"Entrevista a Lygia Fagundes Telles." *Plaza: Revista de Literatura* 1987. Fall v13: 1-11.

Tolman, Jon M.; Neves, Margaret A. "New Fiction: Lygia Fagundes Telles." *Review: Latin American Literature and Arts* 1981. Sept.-Dec. v30: 65-70.

Van Steen, Edla; Matthews, Irene. "The Baroness of Tatui." *Review: Latin American Literature and Arts* 1986. Jan.-June v36: 30-33.

Wasserman, Renata R. Mautner. "The Guerilla in the Bathtub: Telles's *As Meninas* and the Irruption of Politics." *Modern Language Studies* 1989. Winter v19(1): 50-65.

Angélica Gorodischer

1. Works in chronological order (category)

Cuentos con soldados. Santa Fe, Argentina: Club de Orden, 1965. (short stories)

Opus Dos. Buenos Aires: Minotauro, 1967. (novel)

Las Pelucas. Buenos Aires: Editorial Sudamericana, 1968. (short stories)

Bajo las jubeas en flor. Buenos Aires: Ediciones de la Flor, 1973. (short stories)

Casta luna electrónica. Buenos Aires: Andrómeda, 1977. (short stories)

Trafalgar. Buenos Aires: El Cid, 1979; Rosario: Ediciones de Peregrino, 1984. (short stories)

Kalpa Imperial. Buenos Aires: Minotauro, 1983. (short stories)

La casa del poder. Buenos Aires: Minotauro, 1983. (short stories)

Mala noche y parir hembra. Buenos Aires: La Campana, 1983. (short stories)

"Las mujeres y las palabras." *Hispamérica* 13. no. 39 (1984): 45-48. (short story)

"Contra el silencio por la desobediencia." *Revista Iberoamericana* v51. No. 123-24, julio-diciembre (1985): 479-81. (essay)

2. Works in translation

"Man's Dwelling Place." Trans. Alberto Manguel. In *Other Fires: Short Fiction by Latin American Women*. Manguel, Alberto, ed. Avenal, NJ: Clarkson N. Potter, 1986.

"Under the Yubayas in Bloom." Trans. Marguerite Feitlowitz. In *Beyond the Border: A New Age in Latin American Women's Fiction*. Erro-Peralta, Nora, & Caridad Silva-Nuñez, eds. Pittsburgh, PA: Cleis Press, 1991.

3. Criticism

Dellepiane, Angela B. "Contar = mester de fantasia o la narrativa de Angélica Gorodischer." *Revista Iberoamericana* 1985. July-Dec. v51(132-133): 627-640.

Mosier, M. Patricia. "Communicating Transcendence in Angélica Gorodischer's *Trafalgar*." *Chasqui: Revista de Literatura Latinoamericana* 1983. Feb.-May v12(2-3): 63-71.

—— "Women in Power in Gorodischer's *Kalpa Imperial*; Selected Essays from The Sixth International Conference of the Fantastic in Arts. In *Spectrum of the Fantastic*. Donald Palumbo, ed. Westport, CT: Greenwood Press, 1988: 153-161.

Vásquez, María Esther. "Angélica Gorodischer: Una escritora latino-americana de ciencia ficción." *Revista Iberoamericana* 1983. Apr.-Sept. v49(123-24): 571-576.

Matilde Herrera

1. Works in chronological order (category)

Vos también lloraste. Buenos Aires: Tierra Firme, 1986. (stories)
José. Buenos Aires, 1987. (testimonial biography)

Clarice Lispector

1. Works in chronological order (category)

Perto do Coração Selvagem, Rio de Janeiro: José Olympio, 1977. 1st. ed. Rio de Janeiro: A Noite, 1944. (novel)
O Lustre, Rio de Janeiro: Nova Fronteira, 1982. 1st. ed. Rio de Janeiro: Agir, 1946. (novel)
A Cidade Sitiada, Rio de Janeiro: Nova Fronteira, 1982. 1st. ed. Rio de Janeiro: A Noite, 1949. (novel)
Alguns Contos, Rio de Janeiro: Ministério da Educação e Saude, 1952. (short stories)
Laços de Família, Rio de Janeiro: Nova Fronteira, 1983. 1st. ed. Rio de Janeiro: Francisco Alves, 1960. (short stories)
A Maça no Escuro, Rio de Janeiro: Paz e Terra, 1974. 1st. ed. Rio de Janeiro: Francisco Alves, 1961. (novel)
A Legião Estrangeira, São Paulo: Atica, 1977. 1st. ed. Rio de Janeiro: Ed. do Autor, 1964. (short stories and essays)
A Paixão segundo G.H., Rio de Janeiro: José Olympio, 1977. 1st. ed. Rio de Janeiro: Ed. do Autor, 1964. (novel)
Uma Aprendizagem ou o Livro dos Prazeres, Rio de Janeiro: Nova Fronteira, 1982. 1rst. ed. Rio de Janeiro: Sabiá, 1971. (novel)
Felicidade Clandestina, Rio de Janeiro: Nova Fronteira, 1981. 1st. ed. Rio de Janeiro: Sabiá, 1971. (short stories)
A Imitação da Rosa, Rio de Janeiro: Artenova, 1976 (1973). (short stories)
Agua Viva, Rio de Janeiro: Nova Fronteira 1980. 1st. ed. Rio de Janeiro: Artenova, 1973. (short stories)
A Via Crucis do Corpo, Rio de Janeiro: Artenova, 1974. (short stories)
Onde Estivestes de Noite, Rio de Janeiro: Nova Fronteira, 1st edition 1974. (essays and short stories)
De Corpo Inteiro, Rio de Janeiro: Artenova, 1975. (interview)

Visão do Esplendor, Rio de Janeiro: Francisco Alves. 1975. (essays)
A Hora da Estrela, Rio da Janeiro: Jose Olympio. 1st ed. 1977.
Para não Esquecer, São Paulo: Atica, 1st ed. 1978.
Um Sopro de Vida, Rio de Janeiro: Nova Fronteira. 1st ed. 1978.
A Bela e a Fera, Rio de Janeiro: Nova Fronteira. 1st ed. 1979. (short stories)
A Descoberta do Mundo, Rio de Janeiro: Nova Fronteira. 1984.

2. Works in translation

The Apple in the Dark. New York: Knopf. 1st ed. 1967. Trans. Gregory Rabassa.
"The Crime of the Mathematics Professor." *Modern Brazilian Short Stories* (Berkeley, 1967): 146-152. William Grossman.
Family Ties. Austin: University of Texas. 1st ed. 1972. Trans. Giovanni Pontiero.
"The Smallest Woman in the World" and "Marmosets." *The Eye of the Heart* (New York, 1973): 320-328. Barbara Howes.
"The Solution." *Fiction* 3 (Winter 1974): 24. Trans. Elizabeth Lowe.
"Temptation." *Inter-Muse* 1, no. 1 (1976): 91-92. Trans. Elizabeth Lowe.
"The Man Who Appeared" and "Better Than To Burn." *Latin American Literature Today* (NewYork, 1977): 165-171. Trans. Anne Fremantle.
"The Passion According to G.H." *Anthology of Latin American Literature Today* 1 (1977): 779-92. Trans. Jack E. Tomlins.
"Sofia's Disasters." *Review, Center for Inter-American Relations* 24 (June 1979): 37-43. Trans. Elizabeth Lowe.
"The Woman Who Killed the Fish." *Latin American Literary Review* 11, no. 21 (Fall-Winter 1982): 89-101. Trans. Earl E. Fitz.
"A Full Afternoon" and "It's Going To Rain." *Latin American Literary Review* 12, no. 24 (Fall-Winter 1982): 89-101. Trans. Alexis Levitin.
The Hour of the Star. New York: Carcanet Press. 1986. Trans. Giovanni Pontiero.
The Foreign Legion: Stories and Chronicles. New York: Carcanet Press. 1986. Trans. Giovanni Pontiero.
An Apprenticeship or the Book of Delights. Austin: University of Texas. 1986. Trans. Richard A. Mazzara and Lorri A. Parris.

3. Criticism

Anderson, Robert K. "Myth and Existentialism in Clarice Lispector's '*O Crime do Professor de Matematica*'." *Luso-Brazilian Review,* 1985, Summer, v22(1): 1-7.
Clark, Maria. "Facing the Other in Clarice Lispector's Short Story *Amor*", *Letras Femeninas,* 1990, Spring-Fall, v16(1-2): 13-20.
Collins, Michelle. "Translating Feminine Discourse: Mediating the Immediate", *Translation Review,* 1985, v17: 21-24.
Douglas, Ellen H. "Female Quest toward *Agua Pura* in Clarice Lispector's Perto do Coracao Selvagem", Brasil/Brazil: *Revista de Literature Brasileira/A Journel of Brazilian Literature,* 1990, v3(3): 44-64.

——. "Myth and Gender in Clarice Lispector: Quest as a Feminist Statement in '*A Imitacao da Rosa*'," *Luso-Brazilian Review*, 1988, Winter, v25(2): 15-31.

Especjo Beshers, Olga. "Clarice Lispector: A Bibliography", *Revista Interamericana de Bibliografia/Inter-American Review of Bibliography*, 1984, v34: 385-402.

Fitz, Earl E. "The Passion of Logo(centrism), or, the Deconstructionist Universe of Clarice Lispector", *Luso-Brazilian Review*, 1988, Winter v25(2): 33-44.

——. "Discourse of Silence: The Postmodernism of Clarice Lispector", *Contemporary Literature*, 1987, Winter, v28(4): 420-436.

——. "Clarice Lispector's Um Sopro de Vida: The Novel as Confession", *Hispania: A Journal Devoted to the Interests of the Teaching of Spanish and Portuguese*, 1985, May, v68(2): 260-266.

——. "Bibliografia de y sobre Clarice Lispector", *Revista Iberoamericana*, 1984, Jan.-Mar. v50(126): 293-304.

——. "Conflict and Resolution in the Novels of Clarice Lispector: A Structuralist Approach", *Prismal/Cabral: Revista de Literatura Hispanica/Caderno Afro-Brasileiro Asiatico Lusitano*, 1979, Spring, v3-4: 104-119.

Homenaje a Clarice Lispector. *Revista Iberoamericana*, 1984, Jan.-Mar., v50(126): 229-304.

Lindstrom, Naomi. "A Feminist Discourse Analysis of Clarice Lispector's '*Daydreams of a Drunken Housewife*'," *Latin American Literary Review*, 1981, Fall-Winter, v9(19): 7-16.

——. "A Discourse Analysis of *Preciosidade*" by Clarice Lispector, *Luso-Brazilian Review*, 1982, Winter, v19(2): 187-194.

Mazzara, Richard A., Parris, Lorri A. "The Practical Mysticism of Clarice Lispector's *Uma Aprendizagem ou o Libro dos Prazeres*", *Hispania*, 1985, Dec., v68(4): 709-715.

Pallis, Terry L. "The Miracle of the Ordinary: Literary Epiphany in Virginia Woolf and Clarice Lispector", *Luso-Brazilian Review*, 1984, Summer, v21(1): 63-78.

Rosenberg, Judith. "Taking Her Measurements: Clarice Lispector" and *The Smallest Woman in the World*'", *Critique: Studies in Contemporary Fiction*, 1989 Winter v30(2): 71-76.

Sousa, Ronald W. "At the Site of Language: Reading Lispector's G.H.," *Chasqui: Revista de Literatura Latinoamericana*, 1989 Nov. v18(2): 43-48.

Wheeler, A.M. "Animal Imagery as Reflection of Gender Roles in Clarice Lispector's Family Ties", *Critique: Studies in Contemporary Fiction*, 1987, Spring v28(3): 125-134.

Tolentino, Magda Velloso Fernandes de. "Family Bonds and Bondage within the Family: A Study of Family Ties in Clarice Lispector and James Joyce." *Modern Language Studies*, 1988, Spring, v18(2): 73-78.

Vieira, Nelson H. "The Stations of the Body, Clarice Lispector's abertura and Renewal Studies in Short Fiction." 1986, Winter v25(1): 55-69.

Silvia Molina

1. Works in chronological order (category)

La mañana debe seguir gris. Serie Nueva Narrativa Hispánica. Mexico City: Joaquín Mortiz, 1977. (novel)
Ascensión Tun. Serie La Invención. Cuernavaca, Mexico: Martín Casillas, 1981. (novel)
La familia vino del norte, 1987. (novel)
Leyendo en la tortuga, 1984. (short stories)
Dicen que me case yo. Mexico: Cal y Arena, 1987. (short stories)

2. Criticism

Bolívar, María Dolores. "*Ascensión Tun* en la tradición del discurso de la mujer en América Latina." *Nuevo Texto Crítico* 1989 v2(4): 137-143.

Silvia Molloy

1. Works in chronological order (category)

En breve cárcel. Barcelona: Seix Barral, 1981. (novel)
"Parque." In *La Opinión.* Buenos Aires, 1978. (short story)
"Para Luis." In *La Prensa.* Buenos Aires, 1978, pp. 1-2. (short story)
"Rescate." In *La Prensa.* Buenos Aires, March 18, 1979, pp. 1-2. (short story)
"Tan distinta de Mamá." *Maldoror* 15 (1980): 23-25. (short story)
"A veces en Iliria." *Eco* No. 271 (May 1984). Bogotá, Colombia.

2. Works in translation

Certificate of Absence. Trans. Daniel Balderston. Austin, TX: University of Texas Press, 1989.

3. Criticism

García Pinto, Magdalena. "La escritura de la pasión y la pasión de la escritura: *En breve cárcel,* de Sylvia Molloy." *Revista Iberoamericana,* 1985. July-Dec. v51(132-133): 687-696.
Gascón Vera, Elena. "El naufragio del deseo: Esther Tusquets y Silvia Molloy." *Plaza: Revista de Literatura,* 1986. Autumn. v11: 20-24.
Masiello, Francine R. "*En breve cárcel:* La producción del sujeto." *Hispamérica: Revista de Literatura,* 1985. Aug. v14(41): 103-112.
Navajas, Gonzalo. "Erotismo y modernidad en *En breve cárcel* de Sylvia Molloy." *Revista de Estudios Hispánicos,* 1988. May. v22(2): 95-105.

Carmen Naranjo

1. Works in chronological order (category)

América. 1961; not available in the United States. (poetry)

Canción de la ternura. San José: Ediciones Elite de Lilia Ramos, 1964. (poetry)

Hacia tu isla. San José: n.p. 1966. (poetry)

Los perros no ladraron. San José: Editorial Costa Rica, 1966. (novel)

Misa a oscuras. San José: Editorial Costa Rica, 1967. (poetry)

Camino al mediodía. San José: Editorial Costa Rica, 1968. (novel)

Memorias de un hombre palabra. San José: Editorial Costa Rica, 1968. (novel)

Responso por el niño Juan Manuel. San José: Editorial Conciencia Nueva, 1971. (novel)

Idioma de invierno. San José. Editorial Conciencia Nueva, 1972. (poetry)

"Oye," "El aire no trae mensajes en este mirar al río," "No sé tampoco de dónde viniste," "No recuerdo tampoco cuándo empecé a quererte," "La vida era simple para ti," "Siempre fuiste el servido." *Poesía Contemporanea de Costa Rica: Antología.* Ed. Carlos Rafael Duverrán. San José: Editorial Costa Rica, 1973: 231-235. (poetry)

Diario de una multitud. San José: Editorial Universitaria Centroamericana, 1974. (novel)

Hoy es un largo día. San José: Editorial Costa Rica, 1974. (short stories)

Cinco temas en busca de un pensador. San José: Ministerio de Cultura, Juventud y Deportes, 1977. (essays)

"La voz." *Obras breves del teatro costarricense.* Volumen I. San José: Editorial Costa Rica, 1977; not available in the United States. (play)

Cultura. San José: Departamento de Publicaciones del Instituto Centroamericano de Administración Pública, 1978. (essay)

Homenaje a Don Nadie. San José: Editorial Costa Rica, 1981. (poetry)

Ed., *La mujer y el desarrollo: la mujer y la cultura: antología.* Mexico City: Sep Diana, 1981. (essays)

"Manuela Siempre." *Escena* 1984; not available in the United States. (short story)

Mi guerrilla. San José: Editorial Universitaria Centroamericana, 1984. (novel)

Nunca hubo alguna vez. San José: Editorial Universidad Estatal a Distancia, 1984. (novel)

With Gracia Moreno. *Estancia y días.* San José: Editorial Costa Rica, 1985. (short stories)

Ondina. San José: Editorial Universitaria Centroamericana, 1985. Havana: Casa de las Américas, 1988. (short stories)

Sobrepunto. San José: Editorial Universitaria Centroamericana, 1985. (novel)

Otro rumbo para la rumba. San José: Editorial Universitaria Centroamericana, 1990. (stories)

2. Works in translation

"Listen." *Mundus Artium* 7, 1 (1975): 87.

Mathieu, Corina, trans. "The Flowery Trick," "The Journey of Journeys," trans. Marie J. Panico; "Inventory of a Recluse," trans. Marie Sue Listerman. *Five Women Writers of Costa Rica.* Ed. Victoria Urbano. Beaumont, TX: Asociación de Literatura Femenina Hispánica, 1976: 13-18.

"Ondina," and "Why Kill the Countess?" Trans. Evelyn Picon Garfield. In *Women's Fiction from Latin America*. Picón Garfield, Evelyn, ed. Detroit: Wayne State University Press, 1988.

"And We Sold the Rain." In *And We Sold the Rain: Contemporary Fiction from Central America*. Santos, Rosario, ed. New York: Four Walls Eight Windows, 1988: 149-156.

"The Compulsive Couple of the House on the Hill." Trans. Linda Britt. In *Landscapes of a New Land: Short Fiction by Latin American Women*. Agosín, Marjorie, ed. Buffalo, N.Y.: White Pine Press, 1989.

There never was a once upon a time. Pittsburgh, PA: Latin American Literary Review Press, 1989.

"Symbiotic Encounter." Trans. Cedric Busette. In *Short Stories by Latin American Women: The Magic and the Real*. Zapata, Celia Correas de, ed. Houston: Arte Público Press, 1990.

3. Criticism

Arizpe, Lourdes. "Interview with Carmen Naranjo: Women and Latin American Literature." *Signs* 5, 1 (1979): 98-110.

Britt, Linda. "A Transparent Lens? Narrative Technique in Carmen Naranjo's *Nunca hubo alguna vez*." *Monographic Review/Revista Monográfica*, 1988 v4: 127-135.

Garfield, Evelyn Picon. "La luminosa ceguera de sus días: Los cuentos 'humanos' de Carmen Naranjo." *Revista Iberoamericana*, 1987. Jan.-June v53(138-139): 287-301.

Minc, Rose S.; Mendez-Faith, Teresa. "Conversando con Carmen Naranjo." *Revista Iberoamericana*, 1985. July-Dec. v51(132-133): 507-510.

Olga Nolla

1. Works in chronological order (category)

El sombrero de plata (1976). (poetry)
El ojo de la tormenta (1976). (poetry)
Clave de Sol (1977). (poetry)
Porque nos queremos tanto. Buenos Aires: Ediciones de la Flor, 1989. (novel)

Silvina Ocampo

1. Works in chronological order (category)

Viaje olvidado. Buenos Aires: Sur, 1937. (short stories)
With Jorge Luis Borges and Adolfo Bioy Casares. *Antología de la literatura fantástica*. Buenos Aires: Editorial Sudamericana, 1940. (anthology of fiction)

With Jorge Luis Borges and Adolfo Bioy Casares. *Antología poética argentina*. Buenos Aires: Editorial Sudamericana, 1941. (anthology of poetry)

Enumeración de la patria y otros poemas. Buenos Aires: Sur, 1942. (poetry)

Espacios métricos. Buenos Aires: Sur, 1945. (poetry)

With Adolfo Bioy Casares. *Los que aman, odian*. Buenos Aires: Emecé, 1946. (novel)

Autobiografía de Irene. Buenos Aires: Sudamericana, 1948. (short stories)

Sonetos del jardín. Buenos Aires: Colección La Perdiz, 1948. (poetry)

Poemas de amor desesperado. Buenos Aires: Sudamericana, 1949. (poetry)

Los nombres. Buenos Aires: Emecé, 1953. (poetry)

Pequeña antología. Buenos Aires: Ene, 1954. (poetry)

With J. R. Wilcock. *Los traidores*. Buenos Aires: Losada, 1956. (play)

La furia y otros cuentos. Buenos Aires: Sur, 1959. (short stories)

Las invitadas. Buenos Aires: Losada, 1961. (short stories)

Lo amargo por dulce. Buenos Aires: Emecé, 1962. (poetry)

El pecado mortal. Buenos Aires: Universitaria, 1966. (short stories)

Informe del cielo y del infierno. Caracas: Monte Avila, 1970. (short stories)

Los días de la noche. Buenos Aires: Sudamericana, 1970. (short stories)

Amarillo celeste. Buenos Aires: Losada, 1972. (poetry)

El caballo alado. Buenos Aires: Flor, 1972. (short story)

El cofre volante. Buenos Aires: Estrada, 1974. (short story)

El tobogán. Buenos Aires: Estrada, 1975. (short story)

La naranja maravillosa. Buenos Aires: Orión, 1977. (short stories)

Canto escolar. Buenos Aires: Fraterna, 1979. (short stories)

Páginas de Silvina Ocampo, seleccionadas por la autora. Buenos Aires: Editorial Celtia, 1984. (fiction and poetry)

Y así sucesivamente. Barcelona: Tusquets Editores, 1987. (short stories)

Cornelia frente al espejo. Barcelona: Tusquets Editores, 1988. (short stories)

2. Works in translation

Balderston, Daniel, trans. *Leopoldina's Dream*. London and New York: Penguin, 1988. Contains thirty-two short stories chosen from *Autobiografía de Irene, La furia y otros cuentos, Las Invitadas*, and *Los días de la noche*.

Lewald, H. Ernest, trans. and ed. *The Web: Stories by Argentine Women*. Washington D.C.: Three Continents Press, 1983: 27-34. Contains one story ("The Prayer") from *La furia y otros cuentos*.

Manguel, Alberto, ed. and trans. *Black Water: The Book of Fantastic Literature*. New York: Clarkson N. Potter, 1983: 612-618. Contains one story ("The Friends") from *La furia y otros cuentos*.

———.ed. and trans. *Other Fires: Short Fiction by Latin American Women*. Avenal, NJ: Clarkson N. Potter, 1986: 147-150. Contains two stories ("Report on Heaven and Earth" and "The Inextinguishable Race") from *La furia y otros cuentos*.

Meyer, Doris, and Margarite Fernández Olmos, eds. *Contemporary Women Authors of Latin America: New Translations* (Brooklyn: Brooklyn

College, 1983): 46-49/ 215-216. Contains two poems from *Enumeración de la patria y otros poemas* ("San Isidro" and "Buenos Aires", trans. Jason Weiss). Also includes two Ocampo short stories: "The Mastiffs of Hadrian's Temple", trans. Jason Weiss; and a selection from *Los días de la noche* ("Ana Valerga", trans. Frances S. Rivers).

"The Servant's Slaves." Trans. Susan Bassnett. In *Landscapes of a New Land: Short Fiction by Latin American Women*. Agosín, Marjorie, ed. Buffalo, N.Y.: White Pine Press, 1989.

3. Criticism

Aponte, Barbara A. "The Initiation Archetype in Arguedas, Roa Bastos and Ocampo." *Latin American Literary Review*, 1982. Fall-Winter v11(21): 45-55.

Klingenberg, Patricia N. "A Portrait of the Writer as Artist: Silvina Ocampo." *Perspectives on Contemporary Literature*, 1987 v13: 58-64.

——. "The Twisted Mirror: The Fantastic Stories of Silvina Ocampo." *Letras Femeninas*, 1987. Spring-Autumn v13(1-2): 67-78.

——. "The Mad Double in the Stories of Silvina Ocampo." *Latin American Literary Review*, 1988. July-Dec. v16(32): 29-40.

Lockert, Lucía Fox. "Silvina Ocampo's Fantastic Short Stories." *Monographic Review/Revista Monográfica*, 1988 v4: 221-229.

Cristina Peri Rossi

1. Works in chronological order (category)

Viviendo. Montevideo: Alfa, 1963. (short stories)
Los museos abandonados. Montevideo: Arca, 1989. (short stories)
El libro de mis primos. Montevideo: Biblioteca de Marcha, 1969. (novel)
Indicios pánicos. Montevideo: Nuestra América, 1970. (short stories)
Evohé. Montevideo: Editorial Giron, 1971. (poetry)
Descripción de un naufragio. Barcelona: Lumen, 1975. (poetry)
Diáspora. Barcelona: Lumen, 1976.
La tarde del dinosaurio. Barcelona: Planeta, 1976. (short stories)
Lingüística general. Valencia, España: Prometeo, 1979. (poetry)
La rebelión de los niños. Caracas: Monte Avila, 1980. (short stories)
El museo de los esfuerzos inútiles. Barcelona: Seix Barral, 1983. (short stories)
La nave de los locos. Barcelona: Seix Barral, 1984. (novel)
Una pasión prohibida. Barcelona: Seix Barral, 1986. (short stories)
Solitario de amor. Barcelona: Ediciones Grijalbo, 1988. (novel)

2. Works in translation

"The Museum of Futile Endeavors." Trans. Margaret Jull Costa. In *Landscapes of a New Land: Short Fiction by Latin American Women*. Agosín, Marjorie, ed. Buffalo, N.Y.: White Pine Press, 1989. & In *The*

Faber Book of Contemporary Latin American Short Stories. Caistor, Nick, ed. London & Boston: Faber & Faber, 1989.

"Breaking the Speed Record." Trans. Psiche Bertini Hughes. In *Short Stories by Latin American Women: The Magic and the Real.* Zapata, Celia Correas de, ed. Houston: Arte Público Press, 1990.

3. Criticism

Camps, Susana. "La pasión desde la pasión: Entrevista con Cristina Peri Rossi." *Quimera:Revista de Literatura*, 1988. Sept. v81: 40-49.

Castillo, Debra A. "(De)ciphering Reality in 'Los extraños objetos voladores'." *Letras Femeninas*, 1987. Spring-Autumn v13(1-2): 31-41.

Chanady, Amaryll B. "Cristina Peri Rossi and the Other Side of Reality." *The Antigonish Review*, 1983. Summer v54: 44-48.

Guerra Cunningham, Lucía. "La referencialidad como negación del paraiso: Exilio y excentrismo en *La nave de los locos* de Cristina Peri Rossi." *Revista de Estudios Hispánicos*, 1989. May v23(2): 63-74.

Hughes, Psiche. "Interview with Cristina Peri Rossi." in *Unheard Words: Women and Literature in Africa, the Arab World, Asia, the Caribbean and LatinAmerica.* Schipper, Mineke, Ed. Fasting, Barbara Potter, Trans. London: Allison & Busby, 1985: 255-274.

Kaminsky, Amy. "Gender and Exile in Cristina Peri Rossi." In *Continental, Latin American and Francophone Writers.* Eds. Eunice Myers and Ginette Adamson. New York: University Press of America, 1987: 149-159.

Kantaris, Elia. "The Politics of Desire: Alienation and Identity in the Work of Marta Traba and Cristina Peri Rossi." *Forum for Modern Language Studies*, 1989. July v25(3): 248-264.

Lignell, Kathleen. "The Mirror as Metaphor in Peri Rossi's Poem 'Applications of Lewis Carroll's Logic'." *Latin American Literary Review*, 1988. Jan.-June v16(31): 24-33.

Mora, Gabriela. "Peri Rossi: *La nave de los locos* y la búsqueda de la armonía." *Nuevo Texto Crítico*, 1988 v1(2): 343-352.

Moraña, Mabel. "Hacia una crítica de la nueva narrativa hispanoamericana: Alegoría y realismo en Cristina Peri Rossi." *Revista de Estudios Hispánicos*, 1987. Oct. v21(3): 33-48.

San Roman, Gustavo. "Fantastic Political Allegory in the Early Work of Cristina Peri Rossi." *Bulletin of Hispanic Studies*, 1990. Apr. v67(2): 151-164.

Nélida Piñón

1. Works in chronological order (category)

Guia-Mapa de Gabriel Arcanjo. Río de Janeiro, 1961.
Madeira feita cruz. Río de Janeiro, 1963.
Tempo das frutas. Río de Janeiro, 1966.

Fundador. Río de Janeiro, 1969.
A casa do paixão. Río de Janeiro, 1972.
Sala de armas. Río de Janeiro, 1973. (short stories)
Tebas do meu coração. Río de Janeiro, 1974.
A força do destino. Río de Janeiro, 1978.
O calor das coisas. Río de Janeiro, 1980. (short stories)
A república dos sonhos. Río de Janeiro, 1984. (novel)
A doce cançâo de Caetana. Río de Janeiro, 1987.

2. Works in translation

"Brief Flower," trans. Gregory Rabassa. In *The Triquarterly Anthology of Contemporary Latin American Literature*, ed. José Donoso. New York, 1961: 309-316.
"Big-Bellied Cow," trans. Gregory Rabassa. *Mundus Artium* 3, no. 3 (Summer 1970): 89-96. In *Short Stories by Latin American Women: The Magic and the Real.* De Zapata, Celia Correas, ed. Houston: Arte Público Press, 1990.
"Adamastor," trans. Giovanni Pontiero. *Shantih* 3, no. 3 (1976): 20-23.
"Bird of Paradise," trans. Giovanni Pontiero. *Review, Centre for Inter-American Relations* . no. 19 (Winter 1976): 75-78.
Excerpts from *House of Passion*, trans. Gregory Rabassa. In Rodríguez Monegal, Emir. *The Borzoi Anthology of Latin American Literature.* New York: Alfred Knopf, 1977: 793-98.
"Adamastor," trans. Giovanni Pontiero. In Meyer, Doris, and Margarite Fernández Olmos, eds. *Contemporary Women Authors of Latin America: New Translations* (Brooklyn: Brooklyn College, 1983).
The Republic of Dreams. Trans. Helen Lane. New York: Knopf, 1989.
"The Myth of Creation." Trans. Giovanni Pontiero. In *Lives on the Line: The Testimony of Contemporary Latin American Authors.* Meyer, Doris, ed. Berkeley: University of California Press, 1988: 306-311.
"Bird of Paradise," and "The New Kingdom." Trans. Evelyn Picon Garfield. In*Women's Fiction from Latin America.* Picón Garfield, Evelyn, ed. Detroit: Wayne State University Press, 1988.
"I Love My Husband." Trans. Claudia Van Der Heunel. In *Landscapes of a New Land: Short Fiction by Latin American Women.* Agosín, Marjorie, ed. Buffalo, N.Y.: White Pine Press, 1989.

3. Criticism

Issa, Farida. "Entrevista con Nélida Piñón." *Nueva Narrativa Hispanoamericana* 3, no. 1 (January 1973): 133-140.
Pontiero, Giovanni. "Notes on the Fiction of Nélida Piñón." *Review, Center for Inter-American Relations*, no. 19 (Winter 1976): 67-71.
Riera, Carmen. "Entrevista con Nélida Piñón: La vida es la literatura." *Quimera: Revista de Literatura* n.d. v54-55: 44-49.

María Luisa Puga

1. Works in chronological order (category)

Las posibilidades del odio. Mexico: Siglo XXI, 1978. (novel)
Cuando el aire es azul. Mexico: Siglo XXI, 1980. (short stories)
Accidentes. Mexico: Siglo XXI, 1982. (short stories)
Pánico o peligro. Mexico: Siglo XXI, 1983. (novel)
La forma del silencio. Mexico: Siglo XXI, 1987. (novel)
Intentos. Mexico: Grijalbo, 1987. (short stories)
Itinerario de palabras. Folio, 1987.

2. Works in translation

"The Trip." Trans. Nick Caistor. In *The Faber Book of Contemporary Latin American Short Stories*. Caistor, Nick, ed. London & Boston: Faber & Faber, 1989.

3. Criticism

Reckley, Alice. "The Historical Referent as Metaphor." *Hispania*, 1988. Sept. v71(3): 713-716.

Mariella Sala

1. Works in chronological order (category)

Desde el exilio. Lima: Ediciones Muñeca rota, 1984. (short stories)
"Barcelona" *Lima Kurier*, July 1986. Reprinted in *El muro y la intemperie: el nuevo cuento latinoamericano*. Ortega, Julio, ed. Hanover, NH: Ediciones del Norte, 1989.

Luisa Valenzuela

1. Works in chronological order (category)

Hay que sonreír. Buenos Aires: Américalee, 1966. (novel)
Los heréticos. Buenos Aires: Paidós, 1967. (short stories)
El gato eficaz. Mexico: Joaquín Mortiz, 1972. (short stories)
Aquí pasan cosas raras. Buenos Aires: Ediciones de la Flor, 1975. (short stories)
Como en la guerra. Buenos Aires. Sudamericana, 1977. (novel)
Libro que no muerde. Mexico: UNAM, 1980. (short stories)
Cambio de armas. Hanover, N.H.: Ediciones del Norte, 1982. Mexico: Martin Casillas, 1983. (novel)
Cola de lagartija. Buenos Aires: Bruguera, 1983. (short stories)
Donde viven las águilas. Buenos Aires: Celtia, 1983. (short stories)

Novela negra con argentinos. Hanover, N.H.: Ediciones del Norte, 1990. (novel)

Realidad nacional desde la cama. Buenos Aires: Grupo Editor Latino-americano, 1990.

2. Works in translation

Bonner, Deborah, trans. *Other Weapons.* Hanover, N.H.: Ediciones del Norte, 1985.

Carpentier, Hortense, and J. Jorge Castello, trans. *Clara: Thirteen Short Stories and a Novel.* New York: Harcourt Brace Jovanovich, 1976. Translation of *Hay que sonreír* and *Los heréticos.*

Lane, Helen, trans. *He Who Searches.* Elmwood Park, Ill.: Dalkey Archive Pree, n.d. Translation of *Como en la guerra.*

———. *Strange Things Happen Here: Twenty-six Short Stories and a Novel.* New York: Harcourt Brace Jovanovich, 1979. Translation of *Aquí pasan cosas raras* and *Como en la guerra.*

"A Legacy of Poets and Cannibals: Literature Revives in Argentina." In *Lives on the Line: The Testimony of Contemporary Latin American Authors.* Meyer, Doris, ed. Berkeley: University of California Press, 1988: 290-297.

Magnarelli, Sharon, trans. "The Snow White Guard." In *Landscapes of a New Land: Short Fiction by Latin American Women.* Agosín, Marjorie, ed. Buffalo, N.Y.: White Pine Press, 1989.

Rabassa, Gregory, trans. *The Lizard's Tail.* New York: Farrar, Straus and Giroux, 1983.

Sayers Penden, Margaret, trans. "Up Among the Eagles." In *Beyond the Border: A New Age in Latin American Women's Fiction.* Erro-Peralta, Nora, & Caridad Silva-Nuñez, eds. Pittsburgh, PA: Cleis Press, 1991.

3. Criticism

Case, Barbara. "On Writing, Magic, and Eva Perón: An Interview with Argentina's Luisa Valenzuela." *Ms.* 12.4 (1983): 12-20.

Fores, Ana M. "Valenzuela's Cat-O-Nine-Deaths." *The Review of Contemporary Fiction,* 1986. Fall v6(3): 39-47.

Garfield, Evelyn Picon. "Interview with Luisa Valenzuela." *The Review of Contemporary Fiction,* 1986. Fall v6(3): 25-30.

Gazarian Gautier, Marie-Lise. "The Sorcerer and Luisa Valenzuela: Double Narrators of the Novel/Biography, Myth/History." *The Review of Contemporary Fiction,* 1986. Fall v6(3): 105-108.

Glanz, Margo; Perez, Janet. "Luisa Valenzuela's *He Who Searches.*" *The Review of Contemporary Fiction,* 1986. Fall v6(3): 62-66.

Kaminsky, Amy Katz. "Women Writing about Prostitutes: Amalia Jamilis and Luisa Valenzuela." In *The Image of the Prostitute in Modern Literature.* Horn, Pierre & Pringle, Mary Beth, eds. New York: Ungar, 1984: 119-131.

Maci, Guillermo; Perez, Janet. "The Symbolic, the Imaginary and the Real in Luisa Valenzuela's *He Who Searches*." *The Review of Contemporary Fiction*, 1986. Fall v6(3): 67-77.

Magnarelli, Sharon. "*The Lizard's Tail*: Discourse Denatured." *The Review of Contemporary Fiction*, 1986. Fall v6(3): 97-104.

———. "Luisa Valenzuela: From *Hay que sonreír* to *Cambio de armas*." *World Literature Today* (OK) 1984. Winter v58(1): 9-13.

———. "Humor and Games in *El gato eficaz* by Luisa Valenzuela: The Looking-Glass World Revisited." *Modern Language Studies*, 1983. Summer v13(3): 81-89.

———. *Reflections/Refractions: Reading Luisa Valenzuela*. New York: Peter Lang, 1988.

———. "Luisa Valenzuela's *Cambio de armas* : Subversion and Narrative Weaponry." *Romance Quarterly* 34, 1(1987): 85-94.

———. "Women, Language, and Cats in Luisa Valenzuela's *El gato eficaz* : Looking-Glass Games of Fire." In her *The Lost Rib*. Lewisburg, PA.: Bucknell University Press, 1985: (169-185).

Martínez, Zulma Nelly. "Luisa Valenzuela's *Where the Eagles Dwell* : From Fragmentation to Holism." *The Review of Contemporary Fiction*, 1986. Fall v6(3): 109-115.

Marting, Diane. "Female Sexuality in Selected Short Stories by Luisa Valenzuela: Toward an Ontology of Her Work." *The Review of Contemporary Fiction*, 1986. Fall v6(3): 48-54.

Morello-Frosch, Marta. "*Other Weapons*:: When Metaphors Become Real." *The Review of Contemporary Fiction*, 1986. Fall v6(3): 82-87.

Saltz, Joanne. "Luisa Valenzuela's *Cambio de armas:* Rhetoric of Politics." *Confluencia: Revista Hispánica de Cultura y Literatura*, 1987. Fall v3(1): 61-66.

Ana Lydia Vega

1. Works in chronological order (category)

Vírgenes y mártires. Con carmen Lugo Filippi. Río Piedras, P.R.: Antillana, 1983.

Encancaranublado y otros cuentos de naufragio. Río Piedras, P.R.: Antillana, 1983.

Pasión de historia. Buenos Aires: Ediciones de la Flor, 1987.

Editor. *El tramo ancla: Ensayos puertorriqueños de hoy*. P.R.: Editorial de la Universidad, 1988.

2. Works in translation

"Three Love Aerobics." and "ADJ, Inc." Trans. Diana Vélez in *Reclaiming Medusa: Short Stories by Contemporary Puerto Rican Women*. Vélez, Diana, ed. San Francisco: Spinsters/Aunt Lute Book Co., 1988.

"Cloud Cover Caribbean." Trans. Mark McCaffrey. In *Short Stories by Latin American Women: The Magic and the Real*. Zapata, Celia Correas de, ed. Houston: Arte Público Press, 1990.

3. Criticism

Fernández Olmos, Margarite. "From a Woman's Perspective: The Short Stories of Rosario Ferré and Ana Lydia Vega." In *Contemporary Women Authors of Latin America: Introductory Essays*. Fernández-Olmos, Margarita, ed. Brooklyn: Brooklyn College Press, 1983: 78-90.

Vélez, Diana. "Pollito Chicken: Split Subjectivity, National Identity and the Articulation of Female Sexuality in a Narrative by Ana Lydia Vega." *The Americas Review: A Review of Hispanic Literature and Art of the USA*, 1986. Summer v14(2): 68-76.

ANA MENDIETA (cover artist) was a well-known visual artist in New York and Rome at the time of her tragic death in 1985. Born in Havana, Cuba in 1948, she was sent to Iowa in 1961 by her parents in the wake of the Revolution; her sense of exile and orphanhood would remain keen for the rest of her life. Mendieta received degrees from the University of Iowa and began doing performance-photo art there, using her own body, in 1970. During the 1970's she spent several summers coordinating the University's summer program in Multimedia and Video Art in Oaxaca, Mexico. It was outside Oaxaca in 1977 that she executed the work photographed on our cover, which formed part of her "Arbol de la vida" (Tree of Life) series. Ana Mendieta moved to New York City in 1978 and soon joined the A.I.R. Gallery, the first and most prestigious cooperative gallery of feminist artists. In 1980 and 1981 she visited Cuba, the second time with support from the Cuban Ministry of Culture. She received many grants and fellowships between 1978-85 and exhibited her work frequently in group and solo shows. Constantly informing her work is a search for the powers of nature and their relationship to the female body, as she worked with natural materials such as fire, earth, wood and blood. (KR)

Books on Ana Mendieta include the catalogue *Ana Mendieta: A Retrospective* by Petra Barreras del Río and John Perreault (New York: The New Museum of Contemporary Art, 1987), which has been our source for this brief synopsis; and the biography *Naked by the Window: The Fatal Marriage of Carl Andre and Ana Mendieta* by Robert Katz (New York: Atlantic Monthly Press, 1990).